Praise for
Miranda Liasson

"Liasson writes with humor and heart."
—Jill Shalvis, *New York Times* bestselling author

"Emotional, heartwarming romance you can't put down."
—Lori Wilde, *New York Times* bestselling author

SEASHELL HARBOR SERIES

Coming Home to Seashell Harbor

"Picking up a Miranda Liasson novel makes me feel like I'm catching up with old friends!"
—FreshFiction.com

"If you're looking for an engaging, feel-good, contemporary romance for your summer reading, take a trip to the beach with Miranda Liasson's *Coming Home to Seashell Harbor*." —TheRomanceDish.com

ANGEL FALLS SERIES

"Step into the delightful world Miranda Liasson has crafted in her Angel Falls series, a fictional small town bursting with warmth, romance, and nosy neighbors."
—*Entertainment Weekly*

All I Want for Christmas Is You

"A scrumptious holiday treat."   —*Publishers Weekly*

"*All I Want for Christmas Is You* has yummy cookies, Christmas miracles, and a sensational seasonal love story."   —FreshFiction.com

The Way You Love Me

"A sweet, homespun romance that tugs at the heart-strings in all the right ways."   —*Entertainment Weekly*

"Liasson's work here is among the best of its kind."
—*Akron Beacon Journal*

Then There Was You

"Liasson will make you laugh and melt your heart in this can't miss read."
—Marina Adair, international bestselling author

"Ably tugs at the heartstrings with this poignant contemporary."   —*Publishers Weekly*

Also by Miranda Liasson

Coming Home to Seashell Harbor

MIRANDA LIASSON

A Seashell Harbor Novel

FOREVER
New York Boston

Copyright © 2021 by Miranda Liasson
Excerpt from *Sea Glass Summer* copyright © 2022 by Miranda Liasson

Cover design by Daniela Medina
Cover photographs © Shutterstock
Cover copyright © 2021 by Hachette Book Group, Inc.

Bonus novella *Only Home with You* by Jeannie Chin copyright © 2022 by Jeannie Chin

Forever
Hachette Book Group
1290 Avenue of the Americas, New York, NY 10104
read-forever.com
twitter.com/readforeverpub

Originally published in trade paperback and ebook by Grand Central Publishing in May 2021
First Mass Market Edition: April 2022

Forever is an imprint of Grand Central Publishing. The Forever name and logo are trademarks of Hachette Book Group, Inc.

The publisher is not responsible for websites (or their content) that are not owned by the publisher.

Print book interior design by Jeff Stiefel

ISBN: 9781538708521 (mass market), 9781538736234 (ebook)

Printed in the United States of America

OPM

10 9 8 7 6 5 4 3 2 1

For Joellen, Mark, Heather, and Chris,
who rescued the real Bowie

Chapter 1

HADLEY WELLS MANAGED to pee, buy two large chai tea lattes, and grab her luggage from the carousel before racing to her grandmother's usual pickup spot at door number 7 at Philly International Airport. She tugged off her big sunglasses and her floppy hat, blowing out a sigh of relief when no one looked her way. Then she took a seat on her Big Daddy Samsonite and chugged a gulp of her latte. Her phone told her that she was early, with a minute to spare. Good, because Gran had no tolerance for lollygagging.

Hadley couldn't wait to wrap her arms around her grandmother. And she couldn't wait for her grandmother to wrap her arms around *her*, enveloping Hadley in that wonderful lavender-scented squeeze, the cure for all heartaches.

Grandma's hugs might not be a magic bullet for heartbreak like they'd been for her many skinned knees, but they sure would help. Hadley was excited to spend the summer with her family in their quaint Victorian seaside town, where she planned to relax and read escapist fiction on the beach. And eat real food. Maybe then she'd have a chance to recover from the stress, exhaustion, and heartache that had marked the past few months.

Hot tears stung her eyes. She was getting emotional again. Breathing deeply, she reminded herself that she was just thirty-five, even if the tabloids *were* calling her over-the-hill with no prospects. Getting over a breakup was one thing, but her high-profile split with Cooper Hemsley, the beloved A-list actor, hadn't made that any easier, that was for sure. Just more public. She'd watched all her dreams of love and a family of her own disintegrate with millions of people watching.

But in Seashell Harbor, she'd just be *Hadley*, not Cooper Hemsley's jilted ex. She'd get some full-scale pampering from her family, reunite with her two best friends, and help out Gran at Pooch Palace, her dog boarding business, Hadley's favorite place in the world. Because dogs didn't cheat on you, run away with their costars, or publicly embarrass you.

And PR firms that you worked for didn't insist you take an entire summer of paid leave because the damage from your giant, scandalous breakup couldn't be repaired any other way.

Twenty minutes later, she'd unconsciously gulped down her latte and half of Gran's but still no sign of her grandmother.

Gran had a cell phone for emergencies only, but Hadley didn't want to call while Gran was driving. She was just about to text her parents when they pulled up to the curb in their black Lexus.

Her mom got out of the car, a book tumbling from her lap and hitting the pavement with a *thunk*. The big, dusty tome on Victorian something-or-other was no doubt for her research as an English professor at Rutgers. Then her dad also got out, in the no-parking zone no less, which completely freaked her out. As did the too-cheery smiles on their faces.

"Hey, Pumpkin," her dad said, preparing to envelop her in a hug, but her mom got to her first.

"Hey, Mom, hey, Dad," she said, now too nervous to fully appreciate the hugs of her loving but very type A parents. "Where's—"

"Aw, honey!" Her mom gave her a big squeeze, then held her at arm's length to examine her with shrewd eyes. "You're too thin. And you look *exhausted*."

Great. Her mom had seen through the concealer and fresh lipstick, neither of which apparently hid her heartache.

"But you look as beautiful as always," her dad said. As she hugged him, she could feel his phone vibrating in his pocket, which was pretty typical in his role as a high-powered financial advisor. "We're thrilled to have you home for the summer."

"Me too. But where's Gran?" she asked, a creeping sense of dread ruining her chai tea zen. Plus she had to pee again.

"She's fine," her mom said as she inhaled deeply, "but she had a little...accident. We didn't want you to panic, so we decided to tell you in person."

Accident? The loud *no* in her head exploded at full volume. She didn't want to think of Gran getting older. Of bad things happening. Not when she needed her sage counsel, her advice, her love, *and* her killer double-chocolate brownies.

"She's fine," her dad repeated in a reassuring voice, still holding on to her. "Breathe." He waited patiently while she took several breaths. "Atta girl." When he seemed convinced she wasn't going to lose it right there at the pickup entrance, he continued. "She was chasing after Mayor Chaudhry's dog this morning and fell and broke her hip. She's going to be fine and the dog is fine. Except she'll need to go to the rehab hospital for a few weeks because the break is a little complicated but she should do just fine." He glanced at his watch. "Her surgery's at five."

"I could've caught an Uber—"

"She insisted we come and get you," her mom said. "We're going to head right back to the hospital."

Hadley's heart sank. It was an hour-and-forty-minute drive back to Seashell Harbor. And Gran was alone while Hadley and her parents were here.

"Paul's with her, but he has to work at four," her mom said, reading her mind. Paul Farmer was Pooch Palace's next-door neighbor and ran the local ice-cream shop, Scoops. Gran and he were great friends. "She even wrote you a note." Her mom pulled a bright yellow pack of sticky notes out of her purse.

Hadley instantly recoiled, then caught herself. She still despised sticky notes after all these years, ever since her high school boyfriend had broken up with her on one, serving up her first big heartbreak. Silly, she knew. But to this day, her hatred of sticky notes was still fierce, extending to all colors of the rainbow.

Gran's practical, no-nonsense tone rang out loud and clear:

> Hadley, honey, sorry for sticky note but it's all I've got. Listen, I'm going to be fine. Don't worry yourself. All I want is to see you (cont.).

Hadley had to peel that note off to get to the rest of the message:

> And maybe you can bring me a chocolate banana milkshake? We'll split it when I'm out of surgery.
> xo

P.S. You're so much better than that phony scoundrel. Glad you dumped him. Gran

Gran was an optimist if, one, she believed she was going to be hungry for a milkshake post-op, and two, she made it sound as though Hadley had done the dumping when the whole world knew that wasn't true. She'd just pocketed the note when the airport police pulled up and signaled to her dad to move his car *or else*, thank you very much. Her mom hooked her arm through Hadley's elbow and whisked her to the back seat.

For the next hour-plus, Hadley had no choice but to sit back and watch the familiar sights of her home state. The Garden State Parkway ran right along the ocean, displaying the picture-perfect summer day, the sun hitting the water and scattering it into a thousand diamond sparkles. It was the kind of day for heading down to the beach with a book and a folding chair and sticking your toes in the sand, your cares blowing away like the puffy little clouds that sailed by.

She'd envisioned coming home as a vacation: her grandmother spoiling her with all her favorite foods, taking her window-shopping along Petunia Street. Having lunch together at one of the cute outdoor restaurants with an ocean view, lounging at the beach in front of Gran's little oceanfront bungalow, and reading good books, her most strenuous activity of each day being the reapplication of sunblock.

But now all that seemed self-indulgent.

She'd hoped, too, for a chance to reassess her life. When she'd moved to LA five years ago to handle PR for an animal rights agency, she'd dreamed of making a difference. But then she'd gotten an offer for a "better" job in celebrity PR, with so much more pay and a certain amount of... prestige.

The work had been fun, exciting, and glamorous... at first. The parties! The stars! And, of course, that was where she'd met Cooper Hemsley III at a post-award show interview junket. *He'd* approached *her* and she'd almost had a heart attack and swooned on the spot, instantly smitten with his charisma and charm.

And everyone back home had been so proud—her family, the neighbors. *Nearly* everyone, that is, except her grandmother, who'd never cared for Cooper. While Hadley had enjoyed the money and the perks of her new job, handling damage control for celebrities with too much time and money on their hands was a far cry from her passion to make the world a better place.

At last, Seashell Harbor's beloved downtown came into view, as comfortable as a favorite sweater. Hadley took in the seaside park, the quaint Petunia Street shops with their overflowing baskets and pots of flowers, the Pooch Palace sign that said WE TREAT YOUR PET LIKE ROYALTY, the massive white banner flapping indolently in the sea breeze that read WELCOME HOME, CAM!—

Wait, *what*? Better rewind that one. Hadley blinked and confirmed that, yes, the banner was real. Seashell Harbor's famous—or rather infamous—gridiron hero was back? She closed her eyes, but she still saw a billowy white sheet with CAM in bold black letters burning into her brain. At one time, Tony Cammareri had loomed as large as that obnoxious, flapping banner in her life. But that was long ago. She had fresh, adult heartbreak to deal with. And Gran. Gran was all that mattered now.

She tried to enjoy the rest of the sights but it was futile. That awful banner was blocking everything out, including her common sense.

"Tony—I mean, *Cam*—is back?" she found herself asking. Unlike the rest of the world, *she'd* never called him Cam.

But as far as she was concerned, Tony, the boy who'd been her first love, was long gone. So *Cam* he'd be.

Her mom turned in the front seat. "He's been back since his injury, rehabbing his knee. Such a shame, isn't it? Suddenly ending his career like that. I'm sure you two will run into each other." Her voice was just a touch higher than usual, the tone she often used when she was nervous. Well, they were all nervous about Gran.

"I don't want to see him again," Hadley said, a little more adamantly than she'd meant to. She waved her hands dismissively. "He's ancient history." Ancient teenage heartbreak. *That was all.*

Her parents exchanged knowing glances, which made *her* nervous. Then her dad spoke. "Honey, there's something else you need to know."

Hadley white-knuckled her seat as she imagined even worse news. "What is it?"

"Well, your grandmother's thinking of selling the Palace. Actually, she's been considering retirement for some time."

Gran, retire? For a woman who'd once vowed to take her last breath while sitting in Pooch Palace and petting the dogs, Gran's sudden pushing of the panic button to sell her business just seemed *off*. The dogs were her life, her love, her joy.

"I'm sure after the accident she'd have some reservations," Hadley said. "But I'm here all summer. I'm happy to help until she gets back on her feet."

There went another knowing glance. Geez, she felt like she was twelve again, trying to read her parents' private language from the back seat.

"Actually," her mom said, "she's thinking of selling the building…"

"…to Cam," her dad finished.

She could not have heard right. "Come again?"

"He's offered her quite a nice price," her mom said.

"Wait. Gran wants to sell Pooch Palace to…to *him*?" She couldn't say *either* of his names. She kept blinking but the furious scarlet before her eyes would not be erased.

"Business isn't what it used to be." Her dad turned onto the road that led to the hospital. "Even before the accident. Gran's older and it's getting harder for her to chase after all those dogs. Cam's planning to use the building to open a sports bar/restaurant. The money would tide your grandmother off really well for retirement."

Pooch Palace re-created as a sports bar? Gran retiring? It was like Hadley had landed in an alternate universe that looked like home but really wasn't. Because the Gran she knew had vowed to *never* retire. And would never, ever consider selling her building to Tony Cammareri. Before he was Big-White-Flapping-Banner Cam, she'd known him as the One Who'd Crushed Her Tender Teenage Heart and Left It for Roadkill. *On a Sticky Note. That* Cam.

Why would Gran even be friendly with him?

Coercion, that's what this was. Putting pressure on Gran when she was vulnerable. Cam was using his many charms to bamboozle Gran *and* her parents. Because clearly *they* were eating the Cam candy as well.

Her mom and dad exchanged looks *again*. "The business needs restructuring and rebranding. The new pet hotel near the interstate has taken away a lot of business."

"I could help," Hadley piped in. "That's what I do. I could even ask for some unpaid leave if I needed to."

"Honey," her dad said, "your job is way too important for you to come back here and run a *dog boarding* business."

He'd said it like Pooch Palace was an amateur lemonade stand, the kind that she and her best friends Kit and Darla used to set up at the bottom of the driveway as kids. Something that an educated Wells daughter would never stoop to do.

"Hadley," her dad continued, "maybe you can stop by Carol Drake's office tomorrow and tell her we want her involved." His phone buzzed with another call.

Carol Drake, Super Realtor, could sell a falling-down shack as a vintage charmer with potential, and every year she won the top-selling Realtor award. Her office also happened to be two buildings away from Pooch Palace. But Hadley would rather have a dental extraction than ask Carol to handle this deal.

Hadley's mom patted her knee as they pulled into the hospital parking lot. "We'll drop you off so you can run up and say hi. I know you're upset, but now's not the time to get into this with her, okay?"

Hadley restrained herself from a snarky teenage comeback: *I know. Geez, Mom and Dad.* "I get it," she said instead, climbing out of the car and walking through the sliding double doors into the hospital. Somewhere in the floors above, her grandmother was lying in pain, anxious for surgery.

Gran was in the hospital. The villain of her teenage life was back in town, waiting to get his big baller hands on Gran's building. Hadley's beloved Pooch Palace was going under faster than a king tide. This was *not* the welcome home she'd imagined.

* * *

A few minutes later, Hadley burst into Gran's hospital room, out of breath from climbing six flights of stairs because she hadn't wanted to wait for the elevator. But her grandmother was asleep in her bed, looking a little aged and frail. Her hair had gotten whiter, creases lining her face a little more prominently than she'd noticed in their frequent FaceTime sessions.

She sat down on the vinyl chair in the corner next to the window, trying not to tear up. Flower arrangements adorned the sill despite the fact that Gran hadn't even gone into surgery yet. Hadley randomly flipped up the tag on the most beautiful one, a massive bouquet of yellow roses.

Thinking of you. Tony

"Show-off," she mumbled. It would be just like him to send flashy displays of flowers. "But where's the chocolate?" Cam had always been an overachiever.

"Did someone say chocolate?" A weak voice emanated from the bed. Hadley took one look at her grandma and forced back tears again before going in for a hug.

"Oh, sweetheart, I'm so glad you're back." Gran leveled her gaze with Hadley's. "You're thin and wan. But nothing we can't fix."

"Don't worry about me," Hadley said. "Worry about you."

"Tony was here," Gran said instead, a little groggily. "He told me to tell you hi."

Hadley smiled for her grandmother's sake, but secretly thought she'd like to tell *him* a few things too. However, *hi* was not high on the list.

"Hadley, I have to tell you something." Gran took both of Hadley's hands in hers. "I'm sure you've heard that Tony wants to buy my building." Hadley started to speak but Gran shushed her. "You must promise not to judge him too harshly."

Hadley pursed her lips before she said something upsetting, like *How could you?* Instead, she squeezed her grandmother's hands. "Don't worry, Gran. I'm going to be here all summer to help you with the business and to help you recover. You know I love the Palace just as much as you do."

Gran pointed to the little table between her bed and the wall. "He left you something."

Hadley's gaze followed to where Gran pointed. *No. It could not be.* Hanging off the edge of the bedside table, right underneath the flowers her mom must have brought from her garden, was a sticky note, rippling slightly in the current from the air-conditioning.

A *yellow* sticky note.

Bile rose in her throat as she reached forward and snatched it.

Hadley, feel free to call me. I'll be at Pooch Palace tomorrow morning at 10. Talk soon, Tony

Underneath the words, he'd scrawled his phone number. She calmly pocketed the note, but pure unmitigated anger made her crumple it into a little ball inside her pocket.

Just then, her parents walked in, along with Gran's nurse and a tall guy in scrubs with a kind smile. "Hi, Mrs. Edwards," he said. "I'm Nasir. I'll be taking you down to surgery."

"Let's get this over with so I can dance the two-step again," Gran said as the family all kissed her. Her voice was cheery, but Hadley detected a tinge of bravado. Just before she was wheeled out the door, she gave Hadley a wink and whispered, "Don't forget the shake."

As Hadley and her parents prepared to trek down to the surgical waiting room, her mom stifled a yawn. "It's been a long day already," she said. "At some point I've got to run home and grab some overnight things."

"I'd love to stay with her," Hadley said. "I've already got all my stuff with me." She glanced at the ugly beige chair in the corner. Not exactly the bed she'd planned on sleeping in, but it would do.

As she walked out of the room, her fingers brushed against her pants pocket, reminding her of the note. She pulled it out to analyze one last time, struggling to tamp down her anger.

Two things came to mind. One, Cam's handwriting was just as bad as ever. And two, he was not getting Pooch Palace. Not now, not ever. She'd make certain of it.

Chapter 2

CAM'S IN THERE, all right," Hadley's best friend Kit said the next morning. She stood with Hadley and their other best friend Darla across the street from Pooch Palace. "I see his vintage Mustang in the back lot."

"I'm going to go in there and give him a piece of my mind." Hadley tried to unball her fists and calm down. "Except I'm so angry I'm seeing splotches. I may not be responsible for my actions."

"Maybe you should go home and take a nap first," Darla said. Although she was petite with a cute blond pixie cut, she was tough as nails. And she never hesitated to say what she thought.

The WELCOME HOME, CAM banner was draped clear across Petunia Street over their heads, as flashy as the man it paid homage to.

"I'm glad your grandma's surgery went well," Darla said. "But I'm sorry you have to deal with this."

"Me too." Worry squeezed Hadley's abdomen tight. Breathing deeply, she reminded herself that it was sleep deprivation from spending the night curled up in that rock-hard chair beside her grandmother's bed that was making her bad mood a whole lot worse.

"I'm sorry too," Kit said. "But quit looking at the banner. You're just punishing yourself."

"The whole town *is* pretty excited Cam's back," Darla said. "I mean, he's the most famous football player in the world."

Kit shot Darla a look.

"He was *definitely* a jerk to Hadley a long time ago," Darla rushed to amend. Then she added, in true Darla fashion, "But he's still hot."

"*Was* the most famous football player," Kit said, shaking her head sadly. "Before he got his knee crushed."

Darla gave Hadley a squeeze. "I shouldn't have mentioned him."

"It's fine," Hadley said. "This is about my grandmother." Who needed her. "I just wish she would've mentioned something to me if she were really thinking about retiring."

She did not want her grandmother to feel forced to sell the business she'd poured her lifeblood into for the past thirty years, the one that she—and Hadley—loved with all their hearts.

"Maybe she didn't want to trouble you because you've had a lot going on," Kit said. Practical and nurturing, with big brown eyes and a heart-shaped face, Kit had always been most like an understanding mom, even before she became one. Which Hadley desperately appreciated right now.

Kit took a second to roll a hair elastic from her wrist, bending over to gather up her still-damp mass of dark hair into a ponytail, a reminder to Hadley that both her friends were taking time from their busy mornings to support her.

"You're here now." Kit gave her a side hug. "You can make a difference now."

Hadley flashed a grateful almost-smile at Kit, the optimist in their tight-knit group of three, her sisters-of-the-heart. Hadley's dad had jokingly dubbed them the *three musketeers* from the tender age of five, and the moniker had stuck. They *had* stuck together, through thick and thin, ever since.

Hadley thought of the simple joys of their childhood with a longing that nearly made her tear up again. How had her life gotten so complicated? She'd planned to come home to rest, to get herself together—to eat ice cream on the curb faster than it could dribble down her chin. To be surrounded by her tight-knit circle of family and friends. To play with the dogs.

Except now there would be no more dogs to play with.

"Oh, yoo-hoo, there you three are," a voice behind them said. Hadley turned to find Anita Morales, one of her grandmother's good friends and the owner of Ye Olde Yarn, the needlework shop down the street. She was dressed in a vivid floral-print dress with a matching fuchsia purse and shoes. Her poodle, Jesse, wore the same color bows on her ears and had painted toenails.

"How are you, dear?" Anita squeezed Hadley against her ample bosom. "That awful, sneaky, no-good louse. Mr. Big Shot Actor. Don't you give him and his hussy girlfriend a second thought." She patted Hadley on the shoulder. "You're home now."

"Thanks, Anita," Hadley managed. This was exactly what she *didn't* want. To be fussed over. To stand out. Unlike Cam-of-the-Big-Banner, who was probably basking in all the attention. Not that she begrudged him his hard-earned fame, but why couldn't her high school love have been somebody with a low profile, like their classmate with the very prestigious, hush-hush job working for the CIA? *He* certainly wasn't coming home to his name plastered all over the town.

"Why, I can't believe what you've accomplished, what with working in the big city and having all those famous clients," Anita said. "Your grandma tells us all about them. We're all so proud."

"It's great to be home." Hadley tried to deflect the praise. Covering up the outrageous behaviors of entitled stars eighty hours a week was exhausting. Once she'd even gotten roped into figuring out how to deliver warm Krispy Kreme donuts to a movie set two hundred miles away from the nearest Krispy Kreme, only to have her client complain they weren't still warm.

She'd aimed for the stars (not the movie kind), and she'd achieved her goal, but somehow she'd lost something along the way.

She thought it just might be herself.

"You poor thing," Anita continued. "I can't imagine what you must feel like, what with Cooper running off with that gorgeous starlet. And the whole world on their side because of all that humanitarian work they're doing. You must be positively heartbroken."

Before Hadley could even imagine an answer, Anita leaned in, close enough for Hadley to smell her flowery perfume, the same intense scent she remembered from her childhood. Anita dropped her voice and asked, "Did you *really* go on a shopping spree and max out all his credit cards? Or show up at the Chateau Marmont and pour wine on his head?"

"She didn't do that," Kit interjected, jumping to Hadley's defense.

"I didn't do the first thing," Hadley said. But she *had* taken six of Cooper's Armani suits, seven pairs of Louboutin loafers, and five Gucci custom-tailored jackets down to the local homeless shelter, which gave her an immense sense of satisfaction. Maybe she'd done a little bit of good too.

And the other rumor—that happened to be true. Red wine. A vintage pour, $600 a bottle. Right on top of his perfectly-streaked-to-look-natural blond hair.

In reality, Anita's words held some sting. It was difficult to compare the work Hadley did every day to delivering water and vaccines and eliminating food-borne illnesses.

"I'm so glad you're back in Seashell Harbor," Anita continued. "Maybe you'll meet a nice fella and stay."

"We'd sure like her to stay." Kit gave Hadley another side hug. "Even though we've only got her for the summer."

"Maybe you'll *all* meet nice fellas," Anita said with a wink.

"We don't need men to be happy, Anita," Darla said in her usual tell-it-like-it-is fashion. "We can be happy just as we are."

"Oh, goodness, the light's changed!" Kit said loudly, whisking Darla away. "Nice to see you, Anita, but we really have to go." She grabbed Hadley by the elbow and hurried them all across the street.

"We all get it, Darla," Kit said, "but Anita will be matchmaking until the day she dies."

"I love her to pieces," Darla said. "But why, if you're thirty-five and unmarried, does everyone believe it's their mission to marry you off?"

"Chin up, dear," Anita called out cheerily, loud

enough for passersby to turn and stare. "Don't let those cheap dime-store rags destroy you!"

"I know she means well but that's really harsh!" Hadley said once they were across the street. Yes, she'd been heartbroken. Publicly humiliated by Cooper's affair. But not *destroyed*, yeesh.

Never destroyed. She'd come from too long a line of strong women for that to ever happen. And, as her mom liked to say, her great-great-great-grand*father* might have been the very first settler in Seashell Harbor, but that was only because her great-great-great-grand*mother* insisted they put down roots here rather than in Alaska, which was where *he'd* had a hankering to go.

To this day, every street bore her influence. Such as Petunia Street, followed closely by Gardenia, Hyacinth, Daisy, and Tulip Streets. And those were only the main ones.

And then there was the beach. Nothing against Alaska, but the glorious, wonderful, amazing beach was right in their backyard. Hadley had grown up with summer after summer of sun-kissed days playing on the sand in front of the effervescent, ever-changing water. While there was a lot to brag about in Seashell Harbor, the ocean was the giant cherry on top.

"I love it here," Hadley couldn't help saying. "It's quiet and peaceful and everyone's friendly. But it feels like a dream—a place to escape reality." Plus, in spite of her summer plans, she wasn't even sure she remembered what to do with downtime.

"Trust me," Kit said. "If you lived here full-time, you'd see it's not a perfect beach paradise. But it *is* still one of the most beautiful places on earth."

"That's what brought *me* back," Darla said. But

she hadn't just moved back home. Rather, she'd done it spectacularly by buying an enormous modern house right on the beach. "That and being closer to my mom. Even if Nick still lives here."

Kit scrunched up her nose at the mention of Darla's ex-husband. "How's that going, both of you living in the same town again?"

Darla waved a hand dismissively. "When I look out my window onto that gorgeous blue ocean, thoughts of Nick just fade away."

". . . until he jogs by shirtless," Kit said pointedly.

"I wasn't even sure that was him." Darla's fair skin colored.

"He *waved*," Kit said. "*Of course* you were sure."

"Are you blushing?" Hadley asked Darla. Turning to Kit, she asked, "Did I miss something?" And then to Darla, "Are you and Nick a thing again?"

"No!" Darla said vehemently. "Absolutely not."

"You two were so young when you married," Kit said. "Maybe things would be different now."

"Trust me," Darla said. "Once around with him was enough."

Hadley couldn't help but laugh. "I love you both," she said as they arrived at Pooch Palace's front door. "But I've got to go."

Kit glanced at her watch. "I've got to pick up Ollie from day care. I promised him some beach time today. Good luck, Hadley." She gave a little wave. "Call me."

"Bye, Had." Darla gave her a final hug. "Go in there and get it over with. Don't forget we're doing lunch on Saturday; then you're all coming over to help me unpack my bedroom, okay? There will be wine, I promise."

A quick glance at her dear friends reminded Hadley

that she could have it a lot worse. Kit had lost her husband, an air force fighter pilot, a year ago and was raising their sweet little boy on her own. And Darla had just been declared cancer-free after a two-year battle with Hodgkin's lymphoma. Hadley's troubles were nothing compared to what her friends had been through.

"Just remember," Kit called, "you came here to lie low, to let the bad press die down."

"You always overcommit," Darla said. "Look out for you for once."

Hadley nodded gratefully and inhaled a lungful of the fresh sea air from the ocean just blocks away. "Okay, I'm going in."

Chapter 3

AS HADLEY PUSHED open the heavy door of Pooch Palace, it made a familiar scraping sound against the old wooden floor, just as a bell tinkled cheerily above her head. Despite her nerves, an immediate sense of comfort enveloped her as she took in the rose-covered wallpaper that her grandmother had always said reminded her of an English garden. She smiled at the large open area surrounded by colorful plastic gating where the dogs could hang out and play, the comfy carpet squares to nap and hang out, the water bowls along the sides. It was a coffee shop hangout for dogs, sort of.

On closer inspection, the normally bark-filled environment was strangely quiet. The several cordoned-off areas for dog crates were empty. As were the glass-doored rooms that lined the back. Her grandmother called them guest suites, each one lined with wallpaper showing a different dog breed, except for Hadley's favorite, which was covered with cute little painted dog paw prints, a project she'd done herself back in high school.

But where were all the dogs?

A basset hound popped up from a purple velvet dog bed on a window seat, his long velvety ears unfolding from over his eyes as he suddenly perked up, his tags clinking as he shook his head vigorously.

"Bowie!" Hadley almost cried in relief. Bowie was her grandmother's dog, and they were lifelong pals. He turned to her at the sound of his name, blinking the sleep out of his eyes. "How's my boy?" Hadley bent over and tapped her thigh to get him to notice that it was her.

Bowie leaped off his bed and ran over. But just as she went to pet him, he kept going, jetting right *past* her, behind the counter, into the back of the building.

Okay, apparently even unconditional doggie love was going to be denied her today. As she straightened up, she caught sight of an older woman with short gray hair coming out from the back. "Ivy!"

"Hiya, Hadley, sweetie." Ivy gave her a giant hug. "We're so glad you're back."

A woman of about fifty with red hair and a bright yellow flowered dress followed close behind. "Well I'll be!" Mayellen exclaimed in a deep Southern accent. "Look here, Ivy, our baby girl Hadley's back. And she's pretty as a peach."

Hadley hugged her grandmother's longtime employees with affection. "Bowie's okay, isn't he?" Her grandmother hadn't mentioned that he was showing signs of senility. Or failing vision. Or hearing loss.

"He's just as spry as ever." Ivy chuckled. "It's just that Cam—"

Hadley's head jerked up. Before she could react, Mayellen spoke.

"She said *came*. It's just that Bowie *came* late today

and he's starving. Ran right back there to eat his dinner. I'm sure he'll be back out in a sec." Mayellen shot Ivy a look, perfected from her thirty years as a first-grade teacher, her job when she wasn't at Pooch Palace.

Hadley's grandma had said her next-door neighbor was keeping Bowie at night, so she guessed that made sense. Maybe. "I heard about Cam wanting to buy the building. And I saw his car—"

Ivy nervously fingered a newspaper spread out upon the counter, which Hadley recognized as one of those familiar, hateful grocery store tabloids. "Is it true you went to rehab?" She held up a page with Hadley's photo with the headline, HEARTBROKEN HADLEY! JILTED AND JEALOUS!

"Of course not," she said a little defensively. All thoughts of wringing Cam's neck faded as she caught sight of a photo taken at the Academy Awards this past March. She wore a black couture gown and was smiling broadly as she took the arm of a handsome man in a tux whose classic, chiseled features resembled Chris Pine's.

She remembered that night. How swept away she'd been. How thrilled to be there. How blinded by the stars in her eyes for Cooper.

Now she got it, the difference between real and fake. And she wouldn't ever confuse the two again.

"Is that cleft in his chin real?" Ivy held up the paper so they could see.

"It's real," Hadley said. But, as it turned out, many of the most important parts of Cooper were not.

Like his conscience. And his character.

"I still can't believe he left you for that floozy." Mayellen pored over the spread-out pages. "What a shock."

Yes, a shock. She'd been so blindsided by his news that she'd lost her words. She swore she would never let that happen again. Let a man make her voiceless.

However, it was nearly impossible to dislike Maeve Laurent. To most people, she was a kindhearted saint, a goodwill ambassador, and a huge supporter of female entrepreneurs in several countries.

Everyone adored her. When news of the affair blew up, Cooper left the country and traveled with Maeve, plunking down the entire salary from his last movie as a donation to her many causes.

They got adulation. Hadley got... pity.

"Aw, look," Ivy said. "Here's a pic of the two of them playing with kids from an orphanage."

She glanced at Cooper's handsome face, looking adoringly at Maeve as she danced with a little girl from within a circle of children. That was the most selfless thing she'd ever seen him do.

Maeve was the best thing that had happened to him, and that was the plain truth. *That's* what hurt most of all.

Hadley hadn't been enough.

All her life she'd been driven to work hard to achieve the best education, the most challenging job. Her parents were driven and successful, and she'd felt a certain degree of pressure about their expectations. But like them, she was really driven too.

If she were really honest, some deep part of her had been pleased that Cooper was such a catch—but somewhere along the line, she'd confused *high-powered* with *meaningful*.

Yet at one point she'd thought Cooper was *it*. Her someone to love, someone to have babies with. How could her romantic compass have been so... off?

"Oh my goodness." Ivy suddenly clutched a hand to her chest. "This one isn't very flattering." She held up the paper, displaying a grainy photo of Hadley with her head tipped back, guzzling straight from a bottle of Crown Royal. "You sure you didn't go to rehab?"

Hadley winced at the horrible photo that had gone viral. Overwrought and upset, she'd met girlfriends at the very back of a dark, off-the-beaten-path restaurant and had stupidly trusted the owner. Big mistake. The paparazzi had been like flies, buzzing around everywhere. The headlines the next day had her checked in to some chichi rehab facility somewhere in the Mohave desert—that Cooper had paid for, of course.

She reached over and closed the trashy tabloid, only to find there were other similar newspapers open underneath. Time to change the subject. Fortunately, Bowie came bolting out of the back room, followed by the oddest-looking dog she'd ever seen. Tall and lanky and skinny-legged, with a mass of white curly hair, he appeared to be missing an eye. His right ear seemed permanently bent over. Drool dribbled down one side of his slightly crooked mouth.

The dog came right up to her and pushed his snout into her hand, nudging it. She got the hint and petted him, weird little charmer that he was.

"He wandered in off the street and never left," Ivy said with a shrug before Hadley could ask.

"A stray?" A cold feeling iced her insides despite the warm day. No dogs here except Bowie and . . . this?

"He's sort of Labradoodleish," Mayellen said, emphasis definitely on the *ish*. The dog was a gangly-legged, tangly-haired mix of *something*. Hadley thought the dog might be looking at her but couldn't really tell because his hair had grown over his one hopefully functioning eye.

"He had a collar," Ivy said. "Your grandmother thinks someone driving through town dropped him off on purpose."

"I can't imagine why." Hadley pet his ratty-looking head. She couldn't help smiling a little as the dog leaned against her before flopping down to have his belly rubbed.

"His name is Jagger," Mayellen said with a shrug. "He's a lover."

"Jagger?" Hadley said.

"Bowie's friend. Cam thought of it." Ivy immediately clapped her hand over her mouth. Even a hard left in the ribs from Mayellen couldn't take *that* back.

"All right," she said, tackling this head-on. "Where is he?" Why on earth were they protecting him?

Suddenly a voice sounded from the back room. "I don't see any problem with turning the back room into a professional-sized kitchen," someone said. "And wiring for all the big-screen TVs should be pretty routine." A stout, balding man walked out of the back and spread a set of architectural plans on the counter.

A creepy sense of foreboding spread in Hadley's chest. Kitchen? TVs?

"What do you think of the overall size?" asked a second voice.

Hadley closed her eyes. That familiar, low, rumbling voice could only belong to one person.

Hadley stared as the architect—was he an architect?—stepped aside and a tall, imposing figure suddenly filled the doorway behind the counter.

Oh, holy Levi's. It was Tony Cammareri himself.

And lo and behold, he was holding a pack of yellow sticky notes.

He strode out of the back, tall and leanly muscled and with shoulders as broad as a tank, dressed in well-worn jeans that hugged him like a glove. With Bowie hot on his heels, trotting along with the enthusiasm of a puppy.

Hadley wasn't sure what made her more upset—the fact that Bowie was clearly enraptured with him or the fact that he was better looking than that day long ago when she'd first seen him walk out of the boys' locker room and onto the gym floor for badminton class.

Except he wasn't holding a birdie. The cowlick had disappeared, and he had at least fifty pounds of solid muscle on that sweet, skinny sixteen-year-old boy. And he was tall enough to make her crank her head up to look him in the eye.

That added up to about quadruple the good-looking-ness. But, she reminded herself lest she forget, *definitely* not as sweet.

She remembered how he'd left her, the summer after their senior year just before they'd both left for college. She'd been so upset she'd locked herself out of her car in the pouring rain, clutching that sticky note, his awful message running like mascara, and she'd had to call her dad to come get her. Cam's appearance might still give the remnant of her teenage heart a flutter, but as a woman, she was wise enough to know flutters alone didn't count for much.

Her head was whirling as she watched him lean casually against the old Formica counter, shove the sticky notes in his back pocket, cross his arms, and look up.

Their gazes collided at exactly the same time. His

face echoed the same disbelief and shock that were churning her insides. Not to mention a healthy amount of *I-wish-I-was-anywhere-but-here.*

Not that she was still bitter. She'd long gotten over the fact that he'd turned out to be a jerk. It was just that he was in her grandmother's place of business with an architect acting like...

Well, acting like he *owned* the place. She knew his type—after all, she dealt with big personalities every single day. And now Bowie was happily sitting at Cam's feet, beaming up at him.

As she watched, Cam pulled out that sticky note pad, scrawled something on it, and stuck it onto the architectural plans.

She shuddered, but suddenly pulled herself out of her thoughts to realize that he was staring at her. "Hadley." His all-too-familiar-voice reverberated deep and low. Hearing him say her name after all these years, businesslike, without emotion, was strange, even as his gaze swept her up and down in a thorough, assessing fashion.

She sucked in a breath. Because as their eyes met again, his were filled with heat.

She did a double take—but he'd started scrawling on yet another sticky note.

"Hi, Cam." She managed to keep her voice steady.

He used to be just *Tony* to her. She'd never really joined the *Cam* craze.

"Hey, ladies," he said, nodding at Ivy and Mayellen. "Thanks for letting us walk around. I think we're about done." They smiled back, clearly under his spell. Apparently, he was capable of mesmerizing pets and women alike.

But not her. Not anymore.

"No problem, Cam," Ivy said.

Cam looked over Mayellen's shoulder at the spread-out papers, and, to Hadley's horror, started thumbing through them. Hadley's first impulse was to swoop in and gather them all up. Why give him ammo to fuel the fire?

As Cam's eyes roamed over the trashy tidbits, Hadley herself was momentarily thrown by his smile, flashy and white, but still tinged with boyish crookedness, just enough to make him irresistibly human. His Atlantic-blue gaze flicked from her to the papers and back again. She'd loved Seashell Harbor's beautiful aquamarine ocean and she'd loved staring into those eyes, both so similar.

"You look pretty good for being in rehab all these months," he deadpanned. Despite herself, she felt her face grow warm.

Of course, the first thing he would do was crack a joke. Poke fun at her expense.

How tacky.

She recalled that he'd often pulled out that humor when he was nervous, but his cool, level gaze and relaxed posture said otherwise.

He perused the tabloid. "It says right here you were weaving your way through a New York club and had to be escorted out."

"No, it was just— *Wait a minute.*" She pulled back and pulled herself together. She didn't owe him any explanations. "Why are you trying to buy my grandmother's building?"

The alleged architect was off measuring the window-sills, unaware of any drama playing out.

Her nemesis was already working that Cammareri magic, derailing her anger with his humor and that sinful grin. Igniting her hormones and pulling her off course. But this time, she wouldn't fall for it. No siree. She geared up to give him a piece of her mind. More than that. She'd stop him from taking advantage of an older person for his own gain, from tricking her parents and Gran's employees into thinking he was a nice person.

"You don't know?" Cam asked, surprised.

Mayellen's gaze darted nervously between Ivy and Cam.

Ivy stared down at the floor, giving Bowie a little nudge with her foot.

"I heard something about your wanting to open a sports bar," Hadley said. "But I don't understand why you're trying to swindle my grandmother when she's at her weakest."

Cam snorted. *Snorted.* "Your grandmother *wants* to sell this building." Cam crossed his arms and looked down at her from his considerable height, which she swore was a move designed to intimidate. "She *offered it to me.*"

Chapter 4

COME AGAIN?" THE woman in front of Cam stared at him like he'd just crawled out of the gutter covered with goo.

"Your hearing's worse than Bowie's," he mumbled. To which Bowie looked up at him adoringly. "Sorry, buddy." He bent, a little gingerly because of his bum knee, and scratched the animal behind the ears, which gave him a minute to think. *To get a grip*. He hadn't seen Hadley Wells in years. And she was...stunning.

Fresh faced and athletic, her light brown hair pulled back in a ponytail, she looked sort of like the Hadley he'd known so well at eighteen and yet not at all. The same smooth skin but no trace of the familiar freckles. No nose carelessly peeling from sunburn. No T-shirt and shorts and flip-flops, but rather, she wore a black blouse and ankle pants—a sign of her success. As were the expensive sunglasses perched on her head.

And she'd lost that starry-eyed look—the way she used to gaze at him, like he was...well, the most captivating person in the world. Like she was head over heels. No one had ever looked at him quite that way since. Not any of the women who routinely treated him with something akin to adulation.

Hadley had loved him. If you could say that what they'd felt for each other at that age was love.

He wasn't sure, but it was the closest he'd ever come.

As her big brown eyes zeroed in on him like a target, he couldn't help remembering how she'd always been a passionate bundle of energy. Full of fire. How all that passion extended into everything she did—including how she kissed him. And how she used to have the snortiest laugh he'd ever heard.

She definitely wasn't laughing now. "My hearing's excellent," she said in a tone that made him want to snap to attention and salute.

"All right, then." He cleared his throat. "What part didn't you get?"

"The part about my grandmother *offering* this place to you. She would never do that."

She sounded like he'd bound and gagged her poor grandma to seal the deal. So he spoke with exaggerated slowness—and patience. "Your grandmother is looking to get out of the business quick, and I just so happen to need a property quick."

She crossed her arms and glared. "What exactly do you *need* it for, Cam?"

Uh-oh. There she was calling him *Cam* again. She'd *never* called him *Cam*.

She was frowning, standing there stewing. He understood in a visceral way that the conversation they were having now had probably started years ago. When he'd left her a sticky note that said *It's best if we call it quits.*

They'd never really finished that conversation. Not in a way that had resolved anything, anyway.

The way he'd left things gave him a sick feeling. One that he thought he'd let go of long ago but, no, there it was, firing up in his chest like heartburn. Equal parts remorse and regret for being young and stupid. For being careless—with his words, and with her affection.

Well, chalk it up to youth and inexperience. They'd both moved on and from all accounts, she'd done well. He had more important things to worry about than old hurt feelings.

Like this ancient building her grandma was desperate to unload. He *did* need it. Hadley had no idea how badly. The next phase of his life depended upon starting over. After months of dealing with his broken-beyond-repair knee, he understood that his star was sinking. Now was the time to act, when his investors were excited and before anyone had forgotten his name. Or else... or else there would be nothing.

"I'm opening a restaurant," he said. "This will be the flagship, the first of a national chain. Right here, smack in the middle of downtown." No other property around offered what this one did—a central location, a killer ocean view. And he'd been having his people scout the real estate market for months.

"A restaurant." She said it with disdain, as if he were talking about opening a seedy bar with drug dealers, the Mafia, and sex traffickers.

Her agitation discomfited him. There was a time when he would have done everything in his wheelhouse to please her, to get her to smile. But this new Hadley was clearly long over him.

"It's going to be a gathering place with good food, a place to relax and meet your friends and catch a game." Why was he overexplaining, being defensive? He didn't need her to know how important this was to him. How Hadley's grandma had offered him the perfect way to start over again after his injury. And how his restaurant would help his sister, Lucy, who deserved a break to help her realize her dream of becoming a chef.

Hadley had loved this place, long ago. Was she holding on to sentiment? Surely she wouldn't fight her grandmother's wishes?

"Why do we need another restaurant in town?" she asked. "What's the draw?"

"Me." He faced her head-on, pointing a thumb at his chest. "*I'm* the draw. This is my hometown, and people—my fans—would love to see it. Good food and me." He wasn't going to apologize for who he was just because she didn't like him.

The only problem was, he felt bad about that. About her not liking him. Which he couldn't entirely explain.

"This isn't going to be a place with lots of TVs so people can ignore their dates and watch football, is it?" she asked. "A cheesy celebrity chain?"

Uh-oh. That was exactly what it was. Without the cheesy part, he hoped. "You want me to apologize for being a celebrity?"

"I want you to apologize for taking advantage of the fact that my grandma's been through a trauma. She's frightened. Of course she might jump to say she wants to sell."

"I'm not taking advantage of anyone." He surveyed the mostly empty room. "Take a look around. No business. *Nada.*" He swept the room with a flourish. "Your grandma's dealing with a new hip. Maybe she's tired of running after dogs. Maybe she wants to travel. Relax. Do needlework."

Hadley rolled her eyes. "She doesn't do needlework."

"Whatever she wants, Hadley. She's given her life to this business. You can't blame her if she wants to change course."

"She's just been through a major operation." Now it was *her* turn to sound overly patient. "She shouldn't have to think about selling her beloved business."

"She *has* been thinking about it. That's why she asked me."

"My grandma would *not* choose you over me. I'm her blood!" She was more than a little fired up.

"Mayellen and Ivy told me you're only here for the summer. So maybe you're her blood but *I'm* best for her future plans and goals." He tried to sound calm and not let unresolved issues from the past make him overly emotional. But he was failing epically.

He saw his words strike a chord, and it wasn't a good one. "You will *never* be best for my grandmother." She snorted. "That much is obvious. I just can't believe she would sell this place willingly." Then she added, "To *you*. You're...you're just as cocky and arrogant as ever."

Yeah. Ouch. Maybe *she* hadn't resolved those issues either.

Then she whirled on him. "Maybe you intimidated her."

He gave a quiet snort himself. At six four and two twenty-five, he probably *did* look a little intimidating. But he'd never physically threatened anyone off the football field. Except maybe his younger brother, Nick. But that was mostly in fun. "You know I'd never do that."

She was still feisty, that was for sure, and part of him

was relieved to see it. He'd worried that all the negative media attention surrounding her breakup from that ass Cooper Hemsley had squeezed the feistiness right out of her.

On the other hand, that feistiness could be a real problem. Because even as a teenager, she'd fought tooth and nail for passion projects. Like the time she'd picketed a construction zone for a new business that was about to be built over loggerhead turtle nests. And when she took the SAT three times to try to get into NYU. Which she ultimately did. With a *scholarship*.

And him. *He'd* been a passion project. In that she'd loved him wholly and completely. But he'd always questioned whether what she felt for him was real, never allowing himself to believe someone could love him like that. So he'd ruined it. He'd ruined *them*.

"That's just the point, Cam," she said softly. "It's been a long time. I don't know who you are anymore."

Her words punched at him more than he cared to admit. He knew exactly what she thought he was. A first-class jerk. To her, he'd been exactly that, many years ago.

He'd fallen for her in high school, bad. But she'd always been out of his league. So before college, he'd dumped her before she could dump him. And he'd broken her heart. Stupid.

Such was first love. Innocent and sweet and sometimes foolish. He'd grown up and moved on, and he'd left his young self far behind.

But judging by the way his blood was coursing through him right now, maybe not as far behind as he'd like.

"Your grandmother told me to put in an offer," he

said. "She sure was in a hurry to unload this place is all I'm saying." Since he'd come back home, Madeline Edwards had accepted him as a friend and a neighbor despite his history with Hadley. And he helped her out when he could. Like taking Bowie while she was in the hospital.

Hadley frowned, a little V delicately creasing the space between her brows. Which distracted him in a crazy way until she said, "Was she medicated at the time?"

"Oh for the love of—" *Irritating*, that's what she was. He suddenly remembered she'd been *really* good at pushing all his buttons too.

"Okay, you two." Mayellen rolled her eyes. "Enough." Her voice brought Cam back to Pooch Palace, and the fact that there were actually other people in the room. Mayellen's stern look reminded him that she'd had a lifetime of disciplining schoolchildren and he had the feeling she wanted to put both of them in time-out. "You're disturbing the pets."

Neither pet looked very disturbed. Bowie had fallen fast asleep at Cam's feet. And the ratty-haired schoodle or doodle or whatever it was raised his head as if to say *Hey, is anybody paying attention to me?* Then dropped it again and went back to snoozing.

"I want you to know," Hadley said, hands on hips, her parting shot, "that as soon as my grandmother recovers a little, I'm going to tell her that I can help run the business. There's no need to sell."

Cam eyed her with what he hoped was a neutral expression. Maddy had approached him about buying the building long before her accident. And so he spoke as calmly as he could. "You may think you're going to blow in here for a few weeks and make everything right, but I moved back here. I want to be part of the community. Real solutions for this building and for our downtown take time."

"The way I see it," Ivy said, stepping between them like a disgruntled umpire, "there's only one person who can clear this up pronto and she's recuperating from surgery. Which I'm sure you both will take into consideration. Now, we're closing for lunch, so you'll have to continue your argument outside."

Without a word, Cam found himself nudged outside and standing next to Hadley on Petunia Street, the Pooch Palace sign swinging in the breeze above their heads. Pride had him working hard to disguise the slight limp that still plagued him after three knee surgeries.

The last time he'd stood there with her... well. They hadn't been arguing, that was for sure.

She'd been on a ladder painting that sign. The poodle with a crown and the lettering underneath that read WE TREAT YOUR PET LIKE ROYALTY. He could still see his eighteen-year-old self impulsively grabbing her and swinging her around and kissing her. She was so startled she'd dropped her paintbrush and he'd worn his jeans for the rest of the school year with white paint splatters because he couldn't afford new ones.

But it had been worth that kiss.

Part of him wanted to squeeze her shoulder and comfort her, tell her everything was going to be okay. And ask her why didn't they go get a drink and talk about old times?

Maybe if he was a gentleman, he'd let this whole thing go.

But while the building was ancient and in need of

new *everything*, the location was prime, right in the middle of the best block of foot traffic downtown. The main municipal parking lot was right across the street. And best of all, there was a view, from the unused second floor anyway, of Petunia Street dashing down to the spectacular Atlantic, where on any given day you could see white sails dotting the endless blue water.

Hadley wasn't even looking at him anymore. She was focused on something in the distance, at the downhill slant of Petunia Street as it sloped toward the ocean. "I need to find out what my grandma really wants."

He hadn't intended for this to get so complicated. The idea for the sports bar/restaurant had taken hold and had got him excited, the only thing that had even mildly interested him in the past six months of merciless rehab.

It was a way for him to come out swinging. He *had* to.

He hadn't even granted any interviews since his injury, which was driving the press crazy. But when he did speak, he wanted to have another life plan locked in place, or the whole world would look on him as a sad sack. Something he could not tolerate.

In his career as a tight end, he'd learned to trust his instincts. And his gut was telling him that Maddy hadn't been kidding about wanting to get rid of her business, no matter how fired up her granddaughter was. So she might as well sell the building to him. He'd give her a great price. Make sure she'd have lots of extra padding to retire well.

Hadley stared dead at him. "Until I'm convinced that my grandma really wants out of this building, you're not getting it."

He stabbed a finger in the air. "You're just as hard-headed as ever."

She folded her arms. "And you're just as arrogant as every celebrity client I've ever had."

They were standing in the middle of the street arguing like an angry divorced couple. Heads were turning. She was fighting for her grandma, of course. And he couldn't blame her. He couldn't blame her at all.

He struggled not to look directly at her because when he did...when he did, their gazes snagged. Locked and held. And that zippy, crackling electrical current got to buzzing again. The *same* wild, untamed one from—what was it—*seventeen* years ago.

He almost cracked a smile. But softening toward her and remembering a crazy teenage romance were not going to help him focus.

The fact was, he needed this deal. He needed to take this opportunity before people stopped asking him to take opportunities. Before his fame faded.

Plus downtown was sagging, businesses gradually closing up shop. People were feeling the pinch, even with the draw of the beach. Downtown needed a shot of something to invigorate it.

And so did Lucy.

For all these reasons, Pooch Palace would save the day.

And Hadley would have to accept that life had changed, that her grandmother just might want to move on. Once Hadley sat down with her and had a heart-to-heart, this would clear right up, he was certain. And with Hadley here for such a short time...she'd soon be out of the picture anyway.

The door opened, and Ivy came out with Bowie. "We got him ready for you."

"Thanks, Ivy," he said, reaching for the leash.

Uh-oh. Someone was getting their hackles back up,

judging by the way Hadley's face had turned bright red, her hands fisted at her sides. "Wait." She sounded hurt. "You're...you're taking Bowie?"

Oh geez. He wished this old geezer of a dog would remember Hadley better. Actually, he probably did; he just couldn't see more than two feet in front of his nose. And he wouldn't hear the Rolling Stones if they were jamming right in front of him.

Hadley looked stricken. So forlorn that he wavered. "I'm just keeping him while your grandma's in the hospital." He held out the leash. "Here, you can take him."

She looked at the dog and then at Cam, shaking her head. "I'm going to go home and shower and head back to the hospital. It's better if he stays with you."

He nodded. Stress was written all over her face, and he cracked, trying to wave the peace flag one last time. "I'm sure we'll clear this up, Hadley."

She wasn't buying that, as evidenced by the fact that her lips didn't even budge an inch in the *smile* direction.

"The only one who can clear this up is my grandma." She paused and looked dead at him. "Put *that* on your next sticky note."

Chapter 5

HADLEY WALKED INTO her grandmother's hospital room later that afternoon to find her dad carrying an enormous bouquet of roses, lilies, lilacs, and carnations from the bedside table to the windowsill. The ledge was loaded with even more arrangements than yesterday. Her mom sat at her grandmother's bedside with pen and paper, flipping through her grandmother's old floral-covered address book while she munched on what looked like a homemade chocolate chip cookie.

Kit sat there, too, on the remaining space of the windowsill. "Ollie and I made them," she said, holding out a plate with more cookies.

Hadley took one and exhaled in relief. Her grandma was clearly doing better if she was putting her mother to work addressing thank-you notes. She'd drilled the importance of writing them into everyone in the family since birth.

"Who's this one from, Gran?" Hadley pointed to a big floral arrangement full of brilliantly colored, exotic-looking flowers that her dad was currently making room for. She had to peer around another arrangement on her tray to see her grandmother, who had turned a bright shade of scarlet.

"Oh, I have wonderful friends," her grandmother said evasively.

Her mom looked up and mouthed, "Paul."

"Mr. Farmer has great taste," Kit said in a mischievous tone as she inspected the flowers on the windowsill up close. "But why hasn't he asked you out yet?"

"Oh, we're just good friends." Her grandmother waved her hand dismissively, but it didn't escape Hadley's notice that she was still blushing.

Hadley put a Beach Burgers fast-food bag on her grandmother's hospital tray and kissed her on the cheek. "Sorry it's not from Scoops. I thought you might want a whole meal."

"I'll forgive you if it's chocolate banana," Gran said.

"You bet." Hadley had a lot of wonderful memories from Beach Burgers, most of them involving milkshakes and French fries.

"But where's yours?"

Hadley smiled. "I just grabbed something quick." The truth was, she'd been photographed so often in the past year, she'd learned to stop indulging cravings. Which, looking back, had been... pathetically sad. And ever since her breakup, she really hadn't had much of an appetite.

It was clearly on the way back now. She was done denying herself a life in exchange for ideals that didn't make her happy. "This cookie is amazing," she said to Kit.

"Burgers, cookies, milkshakes," Gran said as she pulled out a fry. "I'm going to gain weight in rehab if you all keep bringing me food."

"Is that a bad thing?" Kit chuckled as she polished off her cookie.

Hadley took a seat next to Gran's bed on the opposite side of her mom. She noticed an old copy of *Sonnets from the Portuguese* on the bedcovers. Cracked open, of course, to Sonnet 43, "How Do I Love Thee?"

"You're doing the Elizabeth Barrett Browning class again?" Hadley shouldn't have been surprised that her mom was working. Her dad was already furiously tapping on his phone and answering business calls in the corner.

Gran knew as well as Hadley that overachieving ran in the Wells family—as an only child, Hadley had practically had *Achieve or Die* tattooed onto her forehead.

Her mom smiled. "Just reading it for fun. Such a beautiful poem."

For fun? Hadley skimmed through the well-known poem. "Do you really believe all that lofty Victorian sentiment about love lasting beyond death?"

"And growing stronger with time. Yes, I do." She smiled at Hadley's dad, who looked up from his phone and winked.

Maybe for Elizabeth and Robert Browning. And maybe for her parents. But Hadley was beginning to think it would never happen for her.

"Hadley, did you stop by the realty office by any chance?" her dad asked. "I wanted to get Carol's input on the asking price for your building, Maddy."

"Not yet, Dad," Hadley said levelly. She'd conveniently forgotten her dad's request. But first she had to make certain that this was what Gran wanted. Not her mom and dad. Not even Hadley herself. But her grandmother, free of any well-meaning coercion.

Her dad typed a reminder into his phone. "We need to get on with selling the business."

"Mom's only on post-op day one, Stephen," Hadley's mom said. "Let's give her a little break, okay?"

"Thank you, Liz," her grandmother said. "But I'm fine. And I can speak for myself, thank you very much. The truth is, I'm just not sure what I want."

Hadley's mom touched Gran's arm. "You broke your hip running after a dog. It just wouldn't be safe to go back to work."

"I'm just thinking that it might be nice not to have to chase after crazy little dogs anymore," her dad said. "Maybe it's time for a new phase in life, you know?"

Her grandmother fretted with the cardboard hospital menu in front of her, a sure sign of nerves. And she'd barely touched her food. "I'm not certain what I'm going to do. I'm just exploring options."

Her grandmother was sharp as a tack, and usually just as feisty. But this surgery had sucked the wind out of her sails. Hadley was determined to help her get it back. And the burning question remained in Hadley's mind, *Why* Cam? *Why, why, why?*

"We just want you to be aware of all your choices, Mom. No stress." Her mom exchanged a worried glance with her dad, who then checked his watch.

"I've got to run to a meeting." He kissed Gran on the cheek before taking her hand. "I don't want you to worry about a thing."

"That's kind of you, Stephen," Gran said.

Her mom stood and gave Hadley's grandmother a kiss too. "I've got a conference call with a student about her dissertation. I'll be back later with my iPad so we can watch Netflix."

Her grandmother smiled. "Well, okay. But only if you go home to sleep in your own bed afterward."

Once Hadley's parents had left, Kit jumped off the windowsill. "I've got to get back to work. I'm glad you're doing okay, Mrs. Edwards. Next time I'll bring Ollie, if that's okay. He's asked if he can make you some cupcakes."

"Thank you, Kit." Gran winked. "Be sure to tell him I like chocolate."

"Will do." Kit gave a little salute.

Kit hugged Hadley quickly. "Darla and I were thinking maybe lunch at Mussels on Saturday, then head over to her place. Still sound good?"

Hadley gave a quick thumbs-up as Kit disappeared out the door.

Then she walked over and sat down on the vinyl chair, aka her bed from last night. Her grandmother was now sucking down her shake and playing *Words with Friends* on her iPad, both of which reassured Hadley that she was on the mend.

"Does it hurt?" Hadley asked. "Your hip?"

Her grandmother set down the shake with a satisfied sigh. "Honestly, this is the best thing that's happened to me all day. Besides seeing you." She squeezed Hadley's hand. "And the answer to your question is yes, it hurts a little. But nothing compared to how it was before surgery. Honestly, I'm ready to do whatever it takes to mend. I promised Paul I'd be ready for salsa dancing lessons before his daughter's wedding in the fall."

Hadley blew out a breath she didn't realize she was holding. "Hearing you say that just made *my* day." For some reason, she found herself blinking back tears.

"Oh, Hadley. You always were the sentimental one. I'm just fine!"

Hadley swiped at her eyes. Yes, sentimental. One of her worst traits. She wished she could be more practical and logical. Maybe then she wouldn't have gotten swept away by Cooper. She shook her head, not wanting emotion to overtake her.

"I don't want you worrying about me." Gran patted Hadley's knee. "Taking care of me isn't how you'd planned to spend your summer." She tilted the shake cup toward Hadley, who took a sip.

The drink slid down her throat, ice cold and chocolatey and tasting like home. It almost made her forget what was on her mind. "I need to discuss something with you."

Her grandmother set down the shake. "Okay. Shoot."

"I don't want to stress you by talking about this but—"

Her grandmother slid the shake in her direction again. "Have some more. And don't treat me like I'm fragile. You sound like your parents. You know how I hate to be babied. I'm not *that* old yet."

She politely refused. Then she took a big breath and spoke. "I ran into Tony—*Cam*—at the Palace this morning."

Silence descended, thick and dark as the shake. Her grandmother suddenly got very busy poking the shake with her straw. As the wall clock let out a lurching tick, Hadley realized she had absolutely no clue what her grandmother was going to say next. But she was nearly certain she was not going to like the answer.

"Well," Gran said, "I admit, I told him that his buying the building might be a good idea. That was before I fell. We'd been talking about it as he's been making his own plans."

So they were buds? As in, people who talked about things? Like, friends? Hadley's head swirled with questions. "Why him, Gran?"

"Oh, Hadley." Her grandmother looked her over with kind eyes. "Try not to judge him too harshly by what he did when he was eighteen. People change and grow. And right now, he's in great need of a fresh start, whether he shows it or not."

Only, Hadley could not be rational about Cam. Maybe she could forgive, but forget? *No way.* "Do you *want* to sell the business?" Hadley asked instead. "I'm here all summer. I can keep things going until you're healed. You know I love Pooch Palace almost as much as I love you. You can take as much time as you need to think about things."

Gran grasped Hadley's hand, squeezing hard, and looked straight into her eyes. "You've always been such a sweet child. You're so big-hearted and you feel so deeply. But you have your own life. And maybe it's time for me to do what your parents have been trying to get me to do for quite a while."

"Take a cruise?" Hadley smiled. Her grandmother was about as anti-cruise as you could get. All cruise ships reminded her of the *Titanic*, she said, and that was enough for her.

She rolled her eyes. "No. *Retire.*"

"Do you *want* to retire?" Hadley wasn't sure how to sort out if her grandmother was frightened by her health scare, if she felt pressured by Hadley's parents to quit working, or if she really did want to.

Her grandmother sighed and looked down. She fidgeted again with the menu card. "You know what happened. I lost Louie."

Louie was the mayor's pampered Yorkie. "You *temporarily* lost Louie," Hadley reminded her.

"He was bound and determined to go after that greyhound Joy Steele walks right by our yard every single day. Why she does that I have no idea, because it works all the dogs up. And Louie decided to bolt after him, even if he is ten times his size. Somehow the gate got open and Louie just launched himself at that dog." Hadley knew what happened next. When her grandmother went to grab Louie, she'd fallen. Her grandmother crossed her arms. "Stupid old bones."

Hadley put her hand over her grandmother's, trying to think what she could say to make a joke or to change the subject.

"Louie is fine," Hadley said. "It was an accident. Have you spoken to Mayor Chaudhry?"

"Yes, and Nira was very nice about the whole thing, even if she was the tiniest bit upset. But that new boarding place near the highway has been stealing away my business for a few months now. They started calling themselves a fancy-schmancy dog hotel and advertising like crazy and *poof!* There went my business." She gave a heavy sigh. "Televisions and soothing classical music in dog rooms! Dog massages! *Ridiculous.*"

"Gran, I can fix this," Hadley said. "Besides, you're the town's top citizen. You chair a hundred committees and volunteer for everything. We can get your business back."

Hadley flicked her hand in a no-big-deal gesture, but in reality she was worried.

"I'm so embarrassed," her grandmother said. "I've never lost a dog before. Maybe your parents are right. It's time to give it up. I'm too old."

Before Hadley could respond, someone called out from the hallway. "Hey there, Maddy. Where can I put these?"

The man standing in the doorway held a *huge* bouquet of flowers—giant fluffy white hydrangeas, daisies, black-eyed Susans. Judging by the muscular, jean-clad thighs beneath the floral arrangement, it was Tony. Or rather *Cam*. She was *not* going to call him Tony.

Was that weird, Hadley wondered, that she knew him by his powerful *thighs*?

"I picked these from your garden," he said.

Oh my. She pushed aside a sudden image of a big burly man full of muscle picking posies and had to admit it was a little…charming. But then she came to her senses, instead wondering, Why was Cam visiting again? Bringing flowers and sending arrangements. *How* had he insinuated himself so thoroughly into her good graces?

He handed her grandma a box of chocolates—the good kind, from the gourmet chocolate shop downtown.

"Oh, Cam, you're such a dear," her grandmother said. "Flowers and chocolates. And my favorite magazine!"

Hadley didn't have to look hard to see it was *WE* magazine. Yet another scandal sheet. "Gran, don't read that. That one always says terrible things about me."

"I need to keep up with the gossip," her grandmother said, already flipping through the pages. "So I know how to defend you."

"You don't need to defend me," Hadley said, a little irritated. "I don't care what people say."

"At least the photos are flattering this time," Cam said.

"Go ahead and joke," Hadley said. The Crown

Royal thing had been an accident. She was normally in complete control of her image.

"Oh, dear," her grandmother said. "This one's got Cam in it."

"Me?"

Hadley was secretly pleased to see his sudden look of alarm. Color crept up his neck, visible despite his tan. "What are they saying about me?"

"It says you'll never play football again, and so you're drowning your sorrows with expensive vacations and lots of young women in teeny bikinis."

Hadley tapped her finger against her lips. "Hmm. So they *do* tell the truth sometimes."

"Actually . . ." Cam cleared his throat, his gaze darting over to Hadley. "I've been here working for my dad. No Caribbean vacations for me."

"You aren't going steady with anyone now, Anthony, are you?" Gran asked, wearing her matchmaking face.

He had the decency to turn redder. "No, ma'am. But I'm not looking for a girlfriend," he added hurriedly.

"Hmm," Gran said. "That's so interesting, because Hadley happens to be free as well. What a coincidence."

"I'm *definitely* not looking for a boyfriend." She couldn't say the words fast enough.

Her grandmother went on as though she hadn't heard. "Now, isn't it wonderful that you're both back home for the *whole summer*? And in need of a fresh start. What a marvelous opportunity to get reacquainted. Rediscover that chemistry."

"*No chemistry*," they both said adamantly at the same time.

"Well, now that you both are here, I have something

to say." Ignoring their protests, her grandmother spoke in a surprisingly authoritative tone, much different from how weak she'd appeared when Hadley's parents were in the room. She closed the magazine and folded her hands on top of it.

"Just tell him we can handle our business, Gran," Hadley said, casting a nervous glance at Cam. "That there's no need to sell." Gran's demeanor was giving her a sense of foreboding that sent her stomach churning.

"I'm still terribly upset about what happened," Gran said, looking them both over. "And I've got to go to the rehab hospital, so I'm out of commission the rest of the summer. Maybe permanently."

"I'm happy to take that old building off your hands, Maddy," Cam said.

"I can take care of everything," Hadley said at the same time. "There's no need to—"

Gran crossed her arms, looking rather like a queen on her throne of a hospital bed. "Hush, both of you." She cleared her throat and stuck out her chin at a defiant angle. "Cam, I know I told you to look the place over and see if it would be good for your restaurant, but the truth is, I haven't quite decided yet exactly what I'm going to do."

Yes! Hadley mentally fist-pumped. *Atta girl, Gran.*

Cam eyeballed Hadley. "She said *she hasn't decided*," he said slowly, as if she hadn't heard right. "I wouldn't get overly excited just yet."

"And I wouldn't put pressure on my grandmother." Hadley crossed her own arms. "It's her decision."

"No pressure here." Cam threw his hands up.

"Cam's not pressuring me." Her grandmother cast a glance over at Hadley. "Hadley, I'm not ruling out selling Pooch Palace. The thing is, I've been running it for the past thirty years. God's given me this opportunity to slow down for once and decide what I want to do for the rest of my life. Sort of making lemonade from the lemons, you know? I need time to see what's possible with my new hip. You're both smart, creative people. And we all know the business can't function like it used to. Why don't you both see where you can take your ideas and then I'll decide."

Hadley had a million questions. Gran wanted them *both* to move forward on their ideas for saving the Palace? What a disaster. But she bit her lip to keep from stressing her grandma out.

"You mean, like, come up with a business plan?" Cam raised a thick brow as he leaned against the windowsill. "Because I can totally do that. In fact, Mayor Chaudhry was really excited about opening a vibrant business in the heart of downtown. Said it would be just what Seashell Harbor needs to get that extra shot in the arm."

Hadley opened her mouth to protest, but what *was* her plan? Her grandmother's dog boarding business had evaporated. She'd have to think about crisis communication. Winning back customers. Or going in an entirely different direction. Before she could say something, a young nurse entered the room.

"Mrs. Edwards, it's time for your medicine— Oh!" Judging by the way she blushed and stared at Cam, she was one of the many females who regularly fell under his spell. "Oh dear. I wasn't expecting to see the most famous tight end on the planet here." She batted her pretty eyelashes and held out a hand. "I'm Amanda."

"Nice to meet you, Amanda," Cam said, flashing his high-beam smile. "May I call you Mandy?"

"You can call me anything you want, Mr. Cam-mareri," she said with a little chuckle.

"Mrs. Edwards is a very special friend of mine," he said. "She deserves the best care."

"You bet," Amanda said. Cam still hadn't let go of her hand. Clearly, the young woman was going bone-less. Hadley wondered if she should step forward and catch her before she melted into a puddle of butter at his feet.

"Don't let us stop you from what you have to do," Cam said, looking over at Hadley. "We can get out of your way if you need us to."

"That'd be great," Amanda said. "I'll only need a few minutes." She handed Hadley's grandmother a pill, plumped her pillow, and tossed a few more adoring glances at Cam.

"Gran, we'll be back in a minute, okay?" Hadley said.

Cam, who had already walked over to the door, swept his arm wide. "After you."

She tried not to glare at him as she walked past him out of the room. She felt his gaze following her, quietly assessing, predatory. It made the hair on her neck stand up. Because Tony Cammareri didn't just look at you. He *engulfed* you with the intensity of his gaze.

But then, everything he'd ever done was intense. From being the offensive rookie player of the year, to going to the Pro Bowl nine times, to breaking the single season touchdown record for a tight end, to the sudden and ter-rifying way his career had come to a screeching halt.

She tried not to remember other things, equally as intense. The way he kissed her, as if they both had minutes to live. The way he'd whispered, soft and breathless, that she was the only one he'd ever love.

Ha. She'd believed every word he'd ever said. How could she have been so naïve?

She walked out into the brightly lit hallway, which was filled with colorful framed paintings from local grade schoolers. Down the hall, staff at the nursing station bustled about. Occasional beeps and buzzes peppered the background.

Someone walked past, calling out to Cam and asking to shake his hand, which he did with a smile.

Hadley couldn't help but remember the days before the fame. When he was just a humble boy with killer blue eyes and a bad haircut who'd had the audacity to dream an outsized dream.

What had happened to *that* boy?

He leaned up against the wall and crossed his feet and his arms, kicking the sexy up another notch. "Can I say something?"

He was big as in *legendary*, but up close, he was physically big—tall and broad-shouldered and muscley. You could probably bounce a quarter off his chest.

Ugh. Whatever chemicals had attracted her to him years ago were apparently buzzing around in spades.

"Your grandmother is appeasing you by telling you to try and save the business," Cam said. "My gut tells me that she wants to give it up."

Hadley's mouth dropped open in disbelief. The *gall*. "Maybe listening to your gut might've worked for football games, but real life is a different story."

"She's seventy-two, Hadley. Things have changed since you've been here last. Maybe she wants to retire. She *deserves* to retire."

"Or maybe she's just frightened. Maybe she panicked and got embarrassed by the negative attention. But I'm here now. You can…find another location for your restaurant. Or flirt with other young nurses." She waved her hand in the air. "Whatever." She shouldn't have made this personal. But the dig just slipped out.

He ignored her. "I'm serious about opening up a restaurant at that location."

"I'm sure you can do whatever you set your mind to. I just don't want you doing it in my grandmother's space."

He didn't say anything, just looked thoughtful, like he was musing over something. "It never would have worked out with us. Even if I hadn't been an idiot."

She jerked her head up, stunned. Idiot? He'd just admitted that he'd been one? Maybe she hadn't heard right. "Why not?" she managed, swallowing hard.

"Because you fight tooth and nail."

"For what I believe is right? Yes, that's true. I have conviction."

"You always did," he said. "I always knew you'd go places. Even when I was an average Joe riding a scholarship to college."

"You were never average." She sucked in a breath. Why did she just say that? She felt a flush rise up her face.

"Neither were you," he said with the slightest shrug. His gaze trailed to hers, and for a moment, they collided. Adrenaline took over, making her heart pound, freezing her in place, making it impossible to look away. She got lost in the blue of his eyes, lost in the honesty of the moment. But then she shook her head, certain it was just old remembered feelings from too long ago.

The door to her grandmother's room opened, and Amanda popped her head out, saying they could go in now.

"Play nice," Hadley whispered. "We're causing her stress." That was the last thing Hadley intended.

Cam gave her an *Of course I'll play nice* gesture back.

After they filed back in, her grandmother said, "I need some time to think. In the meantime, Cam, you spell out all the plans for your restaurant. Hadley, you figure out some way to reinvigorate the business. After my mind is in a better place, I'll consider the idea that does the most good for our town."

Hadley glanced at Cam when he wasn't looking. He seemed as unhappy about this as she did.

"Now, then." Gran gestured at them like a mom trying to get two siblings to kiss and make up. "I want you two to shake on it."

Hadley could tell from the admiring look her grandmother was giving Cam that there would be no bucking her decision. He clearly had her wrapped around his little finger, and everything about that was positively revolting.

"But, Gran—"

"Hadley, I know you want things to go back to what they were. And, Cam, I know you're chomping at the bit with your new idea. But I need to decide what's best for me. And hopefully that will also be the best for Seashell Harbor."

"That sounds fair," Cam said in a level voice.

It didn't sound fair to Hadley. But her grandmother looked tired, and this was way too much stress. So she sucked it up for her grandmother's benefit and held out her hand. "Okay. Let's shake."

"Rules are," her grandmother said, "you both play fair with one another."

As far as Hadley was concerned, they could easily

steer clear of each other. Because she didn't want any-thing to do with him. And she'd tell him so, too, just as soon as they were out of her grandmother's hearing.

"I'm waiting." Gran folded her arms. *How* could she look so formidable when she was in a pink dressing gown and a hospital bed? "You don't have to like each other. You just have to shake."

Hadley told herself she had to do this. Until she could really get a handle on how her grandmother truly felt. Over the next two months, she vowed to get the business into such tip-top shape, her grandmother would feel fan-tastic about it. Plus, *her* gut was telling her not to give up Pooch Palace. Not to anyone. Especially not to Cam.

Maybe he would soon move on to a more exciting challenge. *Just as he'd left her.*

People changed their minds all the time. Like Cooper, who'd said he'd love her forever. Turned out forever had only lasted as long as his next movie.

"May the best idea win," Cam said.

"You bet," she said in her most businesslike voice.

Hadley met his gaze, now impassive and unreadable compared to a few minutes ago, and stuck out her hand to get this whole thing over with.

Cam caught her hand in his big grip, his long fingers curling around her palm, warm and encompassing. His deep blue eyes met hers, confident and certain.

It must've been the muscle memory of holding that hand so many times, of strolling hand in hand through the sidewalks of their town, of that hand touching her cheek, of that hand being *tender*.

Against her will, something in her cracked. Maybe it was the sentimental girl in her, the remembrance of a first all-encompassing love.

They'd both moved away and become people with lives that were so different from how they'd grown up here, in this place, where everyone knew everyone else, for better or for worse. They'd experienced success, wealth, and celebrity. Big-city life.

Yet the way he held her hand was exactly the same. So was the tender, hungry way he looked at her. Just like when she was a girl, she seemed helpless under the power of his gaze.

She shook her head, forcing herself to break the connection. It was okay, she thought, talking herself down from the ledge—she'd grown past it, past *him*. Like everyone else who'd ever had a broken teenage heart, she'd moved on.

"It's a deal," he said softly, his voice sounding a little muffled and strangely soft.

"A deal," she said back before snapping out of the haze. Yes, a deal. That was *all* it was. A competition. That she would win. Regardless of how much her hand was tingling.

Chapter 6

HEY, WANT TO go to lunch?" Cam asked a few days later, sticking his head around the gray fabric partition dividing the customer part of his family's renovation business office from the desks.

His sister, Lucy, jumped in her seat, where she was loading numbers into a spreadsheet on the computer. A hand flew to her chest as she gave Cam the stink eye. "Tony! Geez. Give a woman a heart attack!" Her black-and-white Border collie, Molly, who was lying in her bed next to Lucy's desk, startled.

Cam chuckled in the way that only an older brother could, then shrugged innocently.

"Sorry about that."

"You don't sound sorry," Lucy said. Molly stepped out of her bed and ambled over to greet Cam.

"Hey there, Mol." He stooped to pet her, catching himself before he bent too far on his bad knee. "You want to go to lunch too?"

A desk chair rolled back into view from the next cubby. Not just any desk chair. A leather model with padded head- and armrests and wait—was that a *cup holder*? "I can be ready in five minutes," his younger brother, Nick, said. He grabbed a pen from behind his ear and tossed it onto his desk.

"What are you doing here?" Cam asked. Usually his brother and dad were out and about in the town, renovating one of the many Victorian-era homes that were their specialty. Seeing him in an office chair—even if it was the Cadillac of office chairs—was a little strange, since Nick loved nothing better than drilling, pounding, sawing, and stomping around a construction site.

"Hey, I have brains as well as brawn, you know," Nick said.

"Well," Lucy said, a devilish look in her eyes, "why don't you use your brains to get moving on that job on Gardenia Street? I need the paperwork by one if you want that special reproduction tile by next week."

Cam laughed. "Guess you're getting a doggie bag today, Nicky."

Nick shot him a look. "Where are you two going?"

Cam looked to Lucy for the answer. "Let's go sit outside at Mussels," she said. "Sound good?"

"Perfect," Cam said. Dining at the oldest seafood restaurant in town would be a treat.

Nick now wore that middle-child expression over missing his favorite restaurant. "Bring me back some shrimp scampi, okay?"

"If you're good," Cam said, raising a brow, "we might even throw in a piece of cheesecake. And a coffee for your cupholder."

As Nick made a face, his sister entered one last number into her spreadsheet, then closed her file. "Shall we go?" she asked as she grabbed her purse.

Lucy did a great job as the front person for Cammareri Vintage Home Remodeling Inc., and she did it with a smile. She worked some weekends for a local caterer too. But Cam understood, maybe more than Nick or his dad, how much Lucy had given up to do this job, and that made his heart ache.

She'd studied accounting in college, but that Cammareri thirst for risk and adventure had made her apply to the Culinary Institute of America in New York to pursue her dream of becoming a chef. But right after she'd found out she was accepted, she'd also found out she was pregnant, and things hadn't worked out with her ex.

Cam had offered a million times to finance her tuition. To get her an apartment and a nanny, a car, and whatever else she needed, but she'd always refused. She'd taken the job crunching numbers at the company because it was safe and close to family, but Cam knew she loved spreadsheets about as much as he loved not playing football.

She was a big reason why he'd come back home. Now that he was back, he had a plan to help her fulfill her dream. And he couldn't wait to tell her about it.

It made him more determined than ever to prove to Maddy that *he* should be the one to take over her building.

Before they could leave, their dad came in, probably to grab the sack lunch that he ate every single day at his desk.

"Hey, Dad." Cam slapped him on the back. "Want to come out to lunch?"

"No thanks," Angelo Cammareri said. With his leonine features and full head of silver hair, he was an imposing presence. Looking up at Cam, he said stoically, "And have my accountant back in twenty minutes."

"I'll be back in an hour." Lucy kissed him on the cheek. "But we'll bring you back a piece of cheesecake too."

"Well, fine." He cracked a little smile at Lucy, the only girl in the family and his clear favorite. Second only to Baby Bernadette, who was an adorable eight-month-old and already showing the discerning Cammareri taste for good pasta. "All right, then. Make it plain. With cherries on top. None of those fancy flavors." To Cam, he said, "I ran into Mayellen and she told me you're thinking of buying Maddy Edwards's property and turning it into a restaurant."

"Maddy approached me about it," Cam said.

"But Hadley's not having it," Nick butted in.

Cam gave his brother a look. "How do you know that?"

Nick sat back and propped his feet up on his desk. "You can't argue with your old flame in the middle of the street and not expect people to notice."

Small towns. He kept forgetting how quickly everyone figured out his business.

"I've always liked Hadley," was all his dad had to say about *that*. "She back in town?"

"Just for the summer," Cam said.

"And how does she feel about you being around?" his dad asked.

Cam shifted his weight a little nervously. Something he probably hadn't done since the age of twelve. "It's complicated, Dad."

His dad didn't say anything for a long moment. "Okay, well, as far as the food, I can give you all the old family recipes."

"Even Grandpa's pizza dough?" Lucy asked. His dad kept that sacred recipe on top of his dresser, in a polished wooden box that *his* grandfather had brought over from Italy.

His dad smiled at him. "If Anthony wants it, yes."

Whoa. No one saw the famous dough recipe. *No one.* It was no secret that his dad had been worried about Cam these past few months as he'd struggled through rehab and the fact that he could no longer play the sport he loved. Even though Cam always did his best to show that he was doing just fine.

But then his dad had worried about all of them. He'd raised them as a single father since their mom jumped ship when Cam was eight and Lucy was just a toddler. From what Cam could gather from his dad, she'd followed another guy out West somewhere and had never looked back. As the oldest, he'd driven all this from his mind as best he could and focused on helping his dad keep the family together.

He attributed the fact that he and his siblings were so close to his dad, who had taught them to value family above all else. Angelo was practical, no-nonsense, and loved them all down to the bone.

But his dad must *really* be concerned if he was offering *the recipe*.

And that touched Cam greatly. He liked—no, *loved*—the idea of using their family's recipes from Italy in his restaurant one day. Of course, his investors had pitched his new restaurant as a sports bar, trying to take full advantage of his career. They hadn't been interested in a mom-and-pop type of place with homemade recipes...so far.

"I'm speechless." His dad hated it when they made

a big deal of things, so he didn't rush to hug him. "Thanks, Dad," he said, a little flummoxed.

"Wow," Lucy said, incredulous. "And I thought *I* was the favorite."

"Hey, what about me?" Nick said, lowering his boot-clad feet to the floor with a clunk.

"No one's my favorite unless the work gets done." His dad shook a warning finger.

"I'm staying to get *my* work done, Pop," Nick said, always the charmer.

"Good boy, Nicholas." His father patted his brother on the shoulder. Then he turned to the other two. "So, get going on the fancy-schmancy lunch so you can get back to work."

"You mean it about the dough recipe?" Cam asked, still a little stunned at the offer.

"Only if it's an Italian restaurant," his dad said. "By the way, I'm making ribs on Sunday with my famous sauce," his dad added. "Come for dinner."

"Wouldn't miss it," Cam said.

"*Definitely* wouldn't miss it." Nick rubbed his rock-hard belly.

"Maybe you could bring Hadley," Cam thought he heard his dad say as he headed for the back.

* * *

"So," Cam said, once he and Lucy were seated on the oceanfront deck at Mussels with some Cokes. His knee was a little stiff and creaky today, but with the warm breeze, hot sun, and miles of sparkling blue ocean spanning in front of them, Cam realized how lucky he was to call this place home. "You know I'm trying to figure out my next steps."

He'd spared his family as much of his problems as possible over the past six months. It was what came naturally to him as the oldest and the one who'd needed to step up for Nick and Lucy after their mom left.

He was supposed to be tough and strong, not weak and floundering. But that was exactly how he'd felt these past months, mourning the sport he loved and would never play again. Struggling to find a way to carry on.

"Everything you've done so far has been football," Lucy said, sipping on her Diet. She looked happy to be out of the office. It reminded him of when they were teenagers and he used to take her out for burgers, mostly to get her to talk and keep tabs on her. "But this restaurant thing…it makes sense to me. You love food, you love being around people. I think it might be a good fit."

He nodded his agreement, even though just talking about leaving football behind forever made him break out in a cold sweat. But Lucy seemed like she was in a good mood today and he didn't want to spoil that with his own troubles. He hoped she'd be open to his idea for her. "You love good food too…"

Cam waited for his opening.

"You bet." She took a warm roll from a basket and passed it to him. "And I'll be happy to eat there all the time." Lucy looked young and pretty, her dark hair piled on her head in a messy bun. It was hard to believe she was all grown up and a mom.

He wanted Lucy to be happy. To have a chance to live her dream. To do anything she wanted, to again become the adventurous soul he'd known her to be. To do anything but sit in the corner of that office entering charges all day, watching others pass by the big plate-glass window, living their lives. "I was sort of thinking of something more than that," he said.

"What are you talking about?" She put down her butter knife.

"You always wanted to go to cooking school. So go, then come back and be my chef."

Her mouth dropped open, and she looked genuinely startled for the second time that day. "You're insane."

He took her hand from the table. "Now's your chance, Luce. Go. You'll have a job waiting for you right here when you get back."

Cam looked hopefully at his sister. But Lucy wasn't meeting his eyes. And she wasn't smiling.

"You're angry," he finally said. He'd thought this would be it. The magic bullet that would get her excited enough to jump back into her life. That was the *other* thing about Cammareris, besides pretending they were fine. They were as stubborn as they come.

"Bernie is just a baby," he said, trying to make his case one more time. "By the time you're done with school, she'll be ready for school. It's perfect timing."

Her eyes flicked up. They looked a little watery. "Look, Cam, I love you. You're the best big brother anyone could have. But you don't have to take care of me anymore. In fact, the idea that you feel you have to is sort of insulting."

Ouch. All right, then. How could he make her see? "Look, I'm reinventing myself. What's wrong with including you in my plans? I want you with me at the helm. It's win-win for both of us."

"I know what you're trying to do. Whenever there's a crisis, you always jump in one hundred percent and start swimming. And handing out the lifeboats. But I'm different. I'm not you. And I'm not ready to go to cooking school. Bernie needs a mom around and I need family, for her sake. I can't just go off to upstate New York by myself and start over."

"I just want you to be happy," Cam said. "It's not the money, is it? You know I've got enough to send everyone in Seashell Harbor to cooking school." *In Paris*, he added to himself.

Lucy pulled her hand away. "You can't swoop in just like that and solve people's problems." She was killing him. Because he *was* a man of action. Every success he'd ever had was because he'd done anything and everything in his capability to make it happen. Her resistance to his help was endlessly frustrating.

"I love you," Cam said. "You know that, right?"

She nodded, clamping her lips together to keep from crying. "I know that. But this is something I have to figure out for myself. Okay?"

Cam wondered if this was what being a parent was like, this kind of awful helplessness. The thing was, he knew his sister too well. She used to laugh out loud—a lot. And crack jokes. And be bawdy and rambunctious. She wasn't just suffering from heartbreak over the idiot she'd dated for four years, who'd then left her when she was pregnant. Nor could he attribute her seriousness to the maturity that came with being a parent— at least, he didn't think that was the case. She'd lost her confidence, her joie de vivre, her *sparkle*. *Sparkle* was a word he'd never admit to using but that was how he saw the problem. And he had no idea how to help her.

"Okay." He acquiesced for her benefit. *For now.*

He was about to say more, but out of the corner of his eye, he saw a petite woman with short hair approaching, her stride fast and purposeful. As she came closer, he recognized her as his former sister-in-law, Darla Manning, Nick's ex-wife. She was also a very successful thriller writer and one of Hadley's posse. Of Hadley's two best friends, Darla was the feral one. Always passionate and protective. And clearly she was on a mission.

Cam was always a little relieved over Nick and Darla's breakup, for the simple reason that Darla never hesitated to give her opinions on any injustice. Like his breakup with Hadley, which she regarded to this day as an unforgivable offense.

And right now, he had a feeling she was about to let him have it.

"Hi, Darla." He tried for an upbeat tone as she approached, hoping friendliness might preempt her anger.

No such luck.

"Hi, Lucy," she said, ignoring his greeting. "Pardon me for talking to your brother for a sec." Then she turned to Cam. "Hadley's in the bathroom," she said without saying hello, "so I'll get right to the point." But he'd almost stopped listening. Hadley was here? He scanned the deck until he saw Hadley's other best friend, Kit, sitting with her little son, Oliver.

They were right near the table he and Hadley always occupied when they'd come here long ago. The two of them would hang out and view the water and share the restaurant's signature steamed mussel dish. Or sometimes just split dessert. Except what he remembered most about those times was staring not at the ocean but at *her*. Usually as she enjoyed the mussels, butter sauce dripping down her chin.

That thought made him smile a little. Until he realized Darla was lecturing him.

" . . . She came home to escape the media attention," Darla was saying. "She doesn't need more headaches on top of all that."

Cam opened his mouth to respond but Darla kept talking. Lucy was taking it all in from across the table and, of course, learning all his business. "You have money, fame, and anything else you could ever want," Darla continued. "Why on earth you've got your sights set on a run-down building in the middle of downtown, I have no idea. Build your restaurant *anywhere* else." Darla waved her hand at the surrounding beachfront. "And leave her be, okay?"

"Darla?" Hadley came up and stood next to his chair, right in the crossfire between Darla and him. Cam was both surprised and a little relieved to see her, and not just because he was hoping she'd call off her friend. "There you are," Hadley said. "Our food just came." She pointed to their table where Kit was feeding Ollie a bread stick.

Hadley looked like a breath of fresh air, standing there in a yellow sundress with strappy sandals. The breeze off the ocean blew her hair into little wisps and molded her dress against her soft curves. And she had red lipstick on. And, if he wasn't mistaken, she smelled good, something summery and fruity and lemony that made him want to sniff her neck.

What? *Sniff her neck?*

Cam forgot everything—his restaurant, the angry woman at his table, the trouble about the building, and most of all his injury, which always monopolized every other thought. Hadley had somehow pushed everything else out of his brain.

She didn't seem to notice his confusion. In fact, she barely noticed him at all. "Lucy!" Hadley said. Next thing he knew, Hadley and Lucy were hugging and talking animatedly with their hands, Lucy laughing loudly.

As Hadley and Lucy chatted, Darla dropped her voice and bent close to Cam. "We're watching every move you make, and we're not going to let you hurt her this time. And in case you happen to forget, just know that every day, I google hundreds of different ways for people to get away with murder."

Cam put his hands up. "I'll be sure to keep that in mind, Darla," he said as innocuously as possible. "But I'm not thinking about pursuing a relationship with Hadley." He lowered his voice. "I'd be the last person she'd want one with."

"Darla, let's go." Hadley grabbed her friend's elbow. "Our lunch is getting cold."

He felt a sense of relief as Darla left. But also guilt. Darla had been through hell for the past two years with her cancer treatment, and he understood she was defending her friend. He respected that.

And he'd meant what he'd said. A relationship with anyone, *especially* Hadley, was the last thing on his mind.

"Stop by and see me at Pooch Palace," Hadley said to Lucy, giving a little wave. But she barely glanced back at Cam.

"I really like Hadley," Lucy said once their food came. "I always have. Now that she's back, I was hoping we could get together. You wouldn't care if I did that, would you?"

"Of course not. There's nothing between Hadley and me."

"Oh, okay. Because you've been staring at her ever since she came over to our table."

"I have not."

Lucy grinned. "Have too."

Just then, Hadley looked up and caught him looking at her. All his muscles froze, and, dumbfounded, he could not look away. Until Lucy poked him gently in the arm and he felt himself blushing. Blushing! That's what it took for him to break his gaze—and the weird spell Hadley seemed to cast upon him.

Cam tried to nonchalantly take a drink of water and turn back to Lucy but she was totally on to him. She'd always had a knack for reading his mind. "I know you might think it's too late to apologize, but it's never too late."

"Trust me, it's too late." He'd screwed up his relationship with Hadley so badly, there was no making it better. He wouldn't even know where to begin. And he wasn't touching that hot potato with a six-foot poker.

"You might think it's impossible but it's not." She smiled at him. "It's just hard. But you're really good at doing hard things."

"It runs in the family." Cam turned her words around on her. Their father had raised them all to understand that any worthwhile venture took hard work and effort. "But some things are better left alone."

Lucy took a sip of her drink and let out a big sigh. "I'm really glad you're back home." She reached over and gripped his hand. "Even if you *are* extremely hardheaded."

What lay unspoken between them, steady as the sea breeze, was that they'd both have to figure out their own best ways forward. "I'm glad I'm back home too," he said.

Lucy shot him a mischievous grin. "Now, can I have some cheesecake?"

Chapter 7

AFTER LUNCH, IT was Hadley's job to get the wine. That made her the last one of her friends to arrive at Darla's brand-new beach house. She'd also brought a friend—Jagger, the long-legged Labra-something who needed a change of scenery. Or at least, he'd given Hadley such a forlorn look when she'd stopped by the Palace that she busted him out for the afternoon.

As they climbed one side of a giant double staircase leading to a second-story front door, a seabird made a cross between a screech and a caw. It sounded like a warning. *What are you getting yourself into? Go back to your old life now!*

Her handshake deal with Cam would mean fighting to the death for her grandmother's business, against what her parents wanted and possibly against what her grandmother wanted too.

Yet she felt more conviction than ever to save Pooch Palace. She loved that place and everything it stood for—a safe refuge for animals while their owners were away. *We treat your pet like royalty* was not only the slogan on the sign, but also her grandmother's mission statement. If only she could figure out a way to bring that mission into the present and make Pooch Palace more necessary for the community than ever.

She rang the bell next to the aqua-blue double door. A few seconds later, it opened wide, revealing a panoramic view of the Atlantic and a mile-high ceiling.

Just as she looked down to see who had opened the door, small arms wrapped around her legs. "Aunt Hadley, Aunt Hadley!" Except her name came out sounding like *Hadwey*, which was sweet as pie.

"Oliver Wendell Holmes Blakemore," she said, kissing a mop of unruly hair before she swept Kit's four-year-old son into her arms. "Hello!" She grinned at her godson, a little boy full of sunshine and life.

"You got a doggy." He bent at the waist to examine Jagger, who said hi by licking his nose. Which made Ollie giggle and wipe his face. As Hadley walked inside, he patted her cheeks with his hands. "Mommy's been talking about you."

"She has been?" Nothing like a sweet, innocent child to help infiltrate the web of what her best friends chatted about when she wasn't there.

"Yep," he said, nodding solemnly. "With Aunt Darla."

"What did they say?"

"That you've been sad about your boyfriend." Ollie frowned. "But he's not nice."

"Oh." Well, what could she say to that? Before she could say anything, Oliver replied for her. "He's a poopyhead." Then he giggled as if that was the funniest joke in the world.

Hadley privately found the word choice to be spot-on. Cooper *was* a poopyhead. But she was Ollie's godmother, which she took *very* seriously, so she tried not to agree.

"But don't worry," Ollie continued. "You can be *my* girlfriend."

"Thanks, Ollie." He'd been that way since birth. Sweet dispositioned and generally one to roll with the punches. And for a four-year-old, he'd had a lot of punches to roll with, from his daddy being gone to Kit doing the best she could while being clearly over-whelmed. She kissed his head again and let him down. "I'll *always* be your girlfriend."

"I know," he said, taking her by the hand. "And then we'll get married." Except with his little lisp, it came out *mawried*, which made her want to melt.

"Sounds like a plan." See? Oliver wanted to marry her. And he was a really nice guy. All she had to do was wait twenty or so more years.

She walked into the most giant great room she'd ever seen. Beyond the floor-to-ceiling windows and several sets of sliding glass doors, the day was bright and sunny, but the ocean had become riled up since lunchtime, the waves tumultuous and crashing, indicating a storm was likely on the way.

Jagger bolted straight for some open boxes next to the couch, filled with neatly packed books. One glance confirmed that they were brand-new copies of Darla's latest and most highly anticipated thriller, ready to hit the shelves after her two-year hiatus. Darla had been through so much, first with her divorce and then her cancer diagnosis right on the heels of that, and Hadley couldn't be happier that she was healthy and gaining her strength back and writing again.

As Jagger sniffed the books, Hadley petted him and said, "I *knew* you had good taste in reading material." Quite pleased by the compliment, he leaned in and allowed Hadley the privilege of petting him more.

Hadley found her friends in the master bedroom,

where, here too, there was no shortage of breathtaking views. A set of French doors, topped with a huge palladium window, led to a private deck. Open boxes were scattered around the room. Kit was making trips to a walk-in closet with handfuls of clothes already on hangers. Darla was sifting through a box of packed clothing with her usual attacking-the-task enthusiasm. Hadley still felt strange no longer seeing the waist-long hair Darla had worn since she was a girl. It was now cropped very short, making Darla's brown eyes look even more huge. And her hair was bouncy and curly. It hadn't been before the cancer.

"Mommy." Ollie ran to Kit. "Aunt Hadley and I are getting married," he said matter-of-factly. "And she got a dog!"

"Hmmm," Kit said, looking Jagger over. "Interesting . . . dog." Kit handed Hadley a glass of wine and kissed her son.

"Is it a dog?" Darla looked over Kit's shoulder. "Never mind, don't answer that."

"Shhhh." Hadley covered Jagger's good ear, making him duck and dodge. "He'll hear you. Is it okay I brought him? He's a real sweetheart."

"Uh-oh," Kit said. "That means you're keeping him."

"Just getting him out for some fresh air," Hadley said.

"I have to go build my LEGOs now," Ollie announced. "Can Jagger play too?"

Jagger, not waiting for permission, bolted after Ollie into the next room.

"I'll call you when it's time for a nap. Okay, buddy?" Kit called after him.

"'Kay!" he said over his shoulder.

"He's so sweet, Kit," Hadley said. "He's like a teddy bear. I just want to squeeze him all day."

"I know." Ollie was clearly Kit's pride and joy. "Except his hair is getting *really* long, and he refuses to get a haircut. A few months ago I took him to my mom's stylist and he got a little spooked."

"What happened?" Hadley was horrified someone would frighten Ollie enough to make him hate haircuts.

"Oh, he was being a little difficult, but she didn't have the patience or the sense of humor for a wiggly kid."

"I'm cringing for Ollie's sake," Darla said, taking a sip of her wine. "And yours."

Kit sighed. "I stopped the haircut, apologized because she's my mom's friend, then got Ollie out of there as fast as I could and bought him ice cream. He was just... being a kid. But now he can't see and he's starting to look like he's in an eighties hair band."

"He's adorable," Darla said. "And even with the long locks, he looks a lot like Carson." Darla was never one to skirt the truth, which Hadley admired. Hadley often found herself fumbling with words, unsure of how mentioning Carson would affect Kit in her grief.

Kit shrugged and smiled wistfully. At least she didn't cry, like last year when the mention of her husband's name would often cause tears to form. "Well, Carson would be proud. He *is* a sweet boy."

"I'm happy to try cutting Ollie's hair," Hadley said. "If you don't mind an amateur cut from someone who's had no practice since college."

"Oh, would you?" Kit said. "Just to get him over the fear. Then when he's a little older I can reason with him better." She took a sip of wine. "I think."

"You know, there's nothing wrong with wanting it long," Darla said.

"I get it, but it's just easier," Kit said. "You

know...my dad. Enough said." Kit had moved back in with her parents after Carson's death, and her dad was a retired admiral. He was pretty easygoing but Hadley could see how Kit hadn't wanted this to become an issue. Kit chuckled a little. "Dad tries to pretend he doesn't care but I can see his gaze wandering to all that hair multiple times a day."

"Well, regardless of what length his hair is, he's a great kid. Whip-smart too," Hadley said, searching for something to make Kit laugh. "Except he called Cooper a poopyhead." She looked from one friend to the other. "Wonder where he got that from?"

"That was supposed to be a secret." Kit barely held back a grin.

"Hey," Darla said. "At least we controlled ourselves and didn't teach him anything worse."

Hadley took a sip of wine. She felt better already, being among her dearest friends. They always had her back. And always would.

"So we want to hear more about your run-in the other day at the hospital." Darla dumped a pile of sweaters on the bed. "With Cam."

"Ancient history." Hadley waved her hand. "Wait a minute..." She looked at Darla. "How did you know I had a run-in with him at the hospital?"

"Because I was getting some bloodwork drawn and I ran into Jenny Falkes. It was huge news that Cam showed up on the ward."

"Who knew your high school ex would become so famous?" Kit said.

"Do you even call high school boyfriends *exes*?" Darla asked. "More like *first loves. Sweethearts.*"

"I'm definitely sticking to *ex*," Hadley said. "Nice

and unemotional." Yes. She didn't want to complicate her current dealings with Cam with any words that would bring back memories of being head over heels for him. Or remind her how he was still capable of raising her body temperature a hundred degrees, two hundred if he happened to smile.

"Agreed." Darla clinked glasses with Hadley.

"At least Nick is a nice guy for an ex," Kit said.

"Being nice doesn't guarantee you can make it work," Darla said. She and Cam's brother had married young, right out of college, and had divorced a couple of years later. As far as Hadley could tell, they did their best to avoid each other.

"Do you two ever talk?" Kit asked.

"Not really," Darla said. "I mean, he called me every week during my chemo and always offered to drive me but we really don't have much to say. I originally wasn't going to buy this place because he's nearby but then I thought, life's too short, you know? I didn't want anything to stop me from moving back home, close to my mom and the place that I love most in the world."

It was also no accident that Darla had bought the most modern house on the beach. Cammareri Vintage Home Remodeling didn't have a chance of ever stepping foot in this home.

They got to work unpacking boxes and helping Darla load up her closet. But when Hadley sliced open her next box, she found, atop a pile of clothes, an old cigar box, like the kind she used to store her crayons in as a kid. "Where do you want this?" she asked, holding it up.

"I have no idea what's in there." Darla walked over to examine it. "Oh, I remember. My mom gave me this.

It's some old stuff from when her great-aunt died. She said something about vintage scarves—thought I might be able to use them. But my hair was pretty grown in by then so I never got around to opening it."

Inside the box was a bundle of letters tied with a rubber band, a few old silk scarves, and...an old sock.

Hadley held up the sock. It was long, handmade, and woolen, with darning over the toes and heel. "Keep or pitch?" Hadley asked, making a face. Because it definitely did not look like the kind of sock anyone would keep.

"Just pitch it," Darla said.

Hadley tossed it onto the pitch pile, but a weight in the toe pulled the sock down, falling on the wood floor with a *thud*. Jagger tore back in from the other room in a heartbeat, picking up the sock and trotting back to Hadley with it.

Hadley took the sock from his mouth, praising him for the save. "There's something in the toe." She felt the sock over with her fingers as she walked over to Darla. "It feels like a stone."

Darla worked the object up the length of the sock. They all waited in suspense as she pulled out something shiny. It caught the light and sparkled so much that Hadley had to blink a few times. It was a vintage ring with a silver filigree band.

Darla's breath caught. "Wow."

"That's beautiful," Kit said. "And old, with that filigree work around the stone."

"Is it a diamond?" Hadley looked at the sizable rectangular-cut stone.

"I'd say it's a Seashell Harbor diamond." Darla was wide-eyed. "I think you might have found my great-great-grandmother's ring."

"Whoa," Hadley said. "A family heirloom?"

Darla looked completely thrown, which was unusual for her. "I grew up hearing stories about the ring but no one knew what became of it."

They all knew what Seashell Harbor diamonds were—bits of quartz that had made their way down streams and tributaries in the Catskills, getting polished and hewn as they bumped their way down to the ocean and washed up along the beaches. Local shops had been selling them for as long as Seashell Harbor had been a tourist attraction.

"Is it her *wedding* ring?" Kit asked.

Darla sat down on the bed, staring at the ring. "It's not a wedding ring." She turned it over in her hand. "But there's a family legend. My great-great-grandmother bought this ring herself—it was pretty cheap then—and pretended to be married so she could buy property at a time when only men could. She became the very first businesswoman in town."

"What was her business?" Hadley asked. Darla's mom was a nurse who lived on a quaint little farm just outside of town. This was the first she'd heard of a feisty great-great-anything.

"She bought the Kepler House," Darla said.

Kit examined the ring. "No way. I've always loved that place. It's got great bones."

Only Kit would say that. To everyone else, the place was an old, run-down, turreted mansion on the outskirts of town. But then, Kit had inherited an old house that had been in Carson's family for years that she'd placed on the market because she couldn't afford to rehab it.

"She escaped a bad marriage but pretended to be a widow and bought the house and turned it into a home for unwed mothers." The ring caught the sunlight from the windows and cast prisms on the walls as Darla spoke. "She ran classes about childcare and personal finances and helped the young women get jobs and an education. She was a real trailblazer for her time."

"This gets even more amazing," Hadley said. "I'm so glad you found it."

"It's not that surprising," Kit said. "You have a lot of her traits, Darla. Courage, going against the grain, speaking out when something's not right."

"You make me sound heroic." Darla gave a little shrug. "All I did was survive cancer treatments."

"Which is *extremely* heroic," Hadley said.

A little while later, when the last box was finally unpacked, Hadley realized Jagger had snuck out of the room. And it was awfully quiet. "Uh-oh," she said, looking around. "Where'd my furry friend go?" She envisioned the kitchen torn apart, food scavenged from the counter, Ollie huddled somewhere, frightened.

"Come see this," Kit whispered, beckoning with her hand from the doorway.

Hadley walked over to Kit, Darla right behind her. There, on what had to be a designer couch in the great room, was Ollie, fast asleep, curled up against Jagger.

"What a sweetheart," Darla said. "He's not shy about making himself at home."

"I'd love to give him a home," Hadley said, "but he's bigger than half my apartment in LA." Knowing that Darla had never owned a dog, she turned to Kit first. "How about some company for Rex?" Rex, a black Lab, had been Carson's dog.

"No thanks," Kit said adamantly. "I can barely take care of Ollie and me."

"Don't look at me," Darla said. "I sit in a chair and write all day. I'd be a terrible dog parent."

Eventually they went back into Darla's bedroom and poured one more glass of wine before sitting on the floor talking.

"You both are the best, you know that?" Darla said, a little bit teary-eyed.

"Darla, is something wrong?" Hadley's stomach dropped like a bag of bricks. Between the sudden teariness and the mention of bloodwork, she couldn't help thinking what if Darla's cancer was back and she'd waited till they were all together...

Darla sat back against the bed frame. "Nothing bad." She looked at Hadley. "It's just...when was the last time we were all together? I don't even remember. I mean, I've seen you both separately when you came to see me during chemo, but when was the last time all three of us were in the same place for a while?"

"Last Christmas?" Kit asked.

"No," Darla said. "Hadley was skiing in Aspen."

Cooper's idea. How had she let him talk her into not coming home for the holidays?

"Well, we're all together now and I just want to say...I've missed you all." Darla raised her glass to her friends. "Thank you for coming to help me. And for all you've done for me over these past two years. I'm so happy to have you as my friends."

"Hear, hear." Kit raised her glass next.

They all toasted to the panoramic view of the Atlantic just outside the window. Hadley was thrilled for Darla's good health and good fortune and for being together with her friends.

"And now I want some gossip," Darla said.

Kit sighed. "The only juicy gossip I have these days involves who stole a kiss in the play kitchen at day care."

"Was it the teacher?" Darla asked.

"No. It was two four-year-olds."

"Then you're right," Darla said. "That *is* pathetic. Aren't any of us getting laid?"

"Don't look at me." Kit shook her head. "I'm a frazzled mom. I'm barely keeping it together."

"Any potential with the guys at work?" Darla asked. Kit's job of processing claims and scheduling at the auto body shop was stressful, mainly because of her awful boss. She was biding her time there, saving money with the goal of finishing her psychology degree.

Kit snorted. "Well, one of the auto body specialists *did* tell me last week that I didn't need any body work myself."

"Wow," Darla said. "*That's* a pickup line?"

"Don't be too hard on him," Kit said. "He's only twenty-one."

Darla blinked and smiled slowly.

"Don't even go there. Why would I have any interest in a twenty-one-year-old?" Kit rolled her eyes, even as she blushed. "Hadley! Your turn. *Please.*"

"Hold on a sec," Darla said. "Why not go for a twenty-one-year-old? Could be fun."

"No thanks," Kit said. "I have a four-year-old, re-member? I don't want to date anyone who even remotely makes me feel like their mother."

"Hadley, how about you?" Darla asked. "Any prospects?"

"Oh, no." She held her hands up in defense as they both turned to look at her. "I'm definitely not interested in dating. Besides, considering I'm in every grocery store tabloid right now, no guy would dare to come near me unless he wants his face blasted all around the country."

"It will die down," Darla said. "It may take until Cooper gets himself in trouble all over again, but it will die down."

Kit showed her agreement by clinking glasses with Darla. Her friends had never liked Cooper. Neither had Gran, whom he'd constantly called "Granny," much to her chagrin. Hadley definitely should've paid more attention to that.

"What was it like," Kit asked, "seeing Cam again after all this time?"

Hadley's heart skipped a beat at the mention of his name, making her far more uncomfortable than she wanted to be. "No big deal," she said a little too quickly. "I mean, all that was a long time ago, you know?" For some reason, she'd rather talk about Cooper's bad behavior than Cam.

"That was always so weird," Darla said, "how he dumped you just like that"—she snapped her fingers— "right before you both left for college."

"No, it wasn't," Hadley interjected. "He was destined to be a phenomenon even back then. He didn't want his hometown honey getting in the way." That was the truth, no matter what Cam said now about being an idiot. He'd wanted his freedom, and when he'd started getting all kinds of notoriety for playing football, he'd wanted to play the field. So he'd dumped her.

It still stung. It was also wildly similar to what she'd just been through with Cooper. How had she missed the signs...a *second* time?

"Cam's definitely enjoyed the perks of celebrity life," Darla said. "A different girlfriend every few months."

"I saw him out to dinner with his sister last week at Stargazer's," Kit said. The popular restaurant was just outside of town. "After dinner, he took photos with a family. Signed autographs too. All with a smile on his face."

"What's not to smile about?" Darla asked. "I'd love to be a multimillionaire and retire at thirty-five."

"Not to excuse him," Kit said, "but it was probably a terrible blow to have to stop playing when he was at the top of his game."

Darla frowned. "That doesn't give him the right to steamroll all over Hadley's grandma."

"I'm not going to let that happen," Hadley said. Despite her resolve to save Pooch Palace, she couldn't help thinking about what it must be like for Cam. Even as a young man, he was determined to succeed. To go places. He worked harder than anyone she'd ever known, and she could only imagine what a blow it must be to never be able to play football again. "I mean, I wish him well." She paused. "As long as he stays away from my grandma."

"Well, he's certainly not bad to look at," Kit said.

"And he seems to have charmed your grandmother," Darla said. "Just make sure he doesn't work his old magic on you."

"Ha!" said Kit. "He might have that effect on *all* the women in your family."

Hadley tipped her glass to take another sip. "I am completely immune." As if to taunt her, an image flashed unbidden in her head. Cam, sitting at the restaurant today, glancing up at her when she'd come over to drag

Darla away. He'd done a double take. And for a second, she'd forgotten to breathe.

"Hadley?" Kit asked. "Earth to Hadley."

Hadley shook her head free of her musings. "Cam said something when we were in the midst of arguing about the business. He sort of acknowledged that he'd been an idiot all those years ago."

"Did he apologize?" Darla asked. "Because a half-apology doesn't count."

"Geez, Darla," Kit said. "Let her explain."

"He said it never would've worked out between us." Hadley gestured to Darla to pass her the wine and poured herself a little more. "Even if he hadn't been an idiot."

"That's it?" Kit asked.

"Well, we were in the hospital hallway arguing. And he was trying to make the point that I can be hard-headed. We weren't exactly having a heart-to-heart."

"So, what do you think of that?" Kit poured another glass too. "It sounds like he's trying to make amends."

"I guess I was glad he'd said something after all this time. But I'd like to know the whole story. To set my mind at ease once and for all."

"Or to see if there's a possibility for more?" Darla chimed in. "Especially if he actually apologizes."

"No." Hadley hoped she'd spoken firmly enough to shut that topic down forever. "He and I are old news. It's just that there's this…this current of something that I wish…I wish wasn't there. Just something left over from before, I guess. I don't understand it, but I can accept it and ignore it."

"Maybe you shouldn't ignore it," Kit said. "Maybe it's a sign that you two can actually get on the same page."

Hadley snorted. "Doubtful. We fight about everything."

"So what are you going to do?" Darla asked.

"Focus on my grandma. You know, I was remembering that when I was a teenager, I used to tell Gran that I was going to come home after college and run Pooch Palace with her."

"You used to talk about that all the time," Kit said.

"You spent every spare minute with those dogs," Darla said.

Hadley shrugged. "I feel somehow that I've let her down. Or maybe I've let myself down."

"It's normal to have these kinds of feelings after a breakup," Kit said.

Hadley took a sip of wine and shook her head. "Don't let me off the hook so easily, Kit. I changed when that teenage dream didn't feel big enough. Seashell Harbor didn't feel big enough. I got stars in my eyes for someone who *seemed* to have it all. But the reality is, I looked for all the wrong things. Just like I fell for Cam—the same kind of guy. All flash and no substance."

Why hadn't her dreams felt big enough? Was it because she'd felt pressure to become like her parents, high-achieving, hardworking people? She couldn't fault them for pushing her to succeed. And she *was* hardworking. And ambitious. But maybe they'd inadvertently pushed her toward something that wasn't...true success? Or that looked like success to everyone else...

"You aren't shallow." Kit set her wineglass down on a box. "You made a mistake with Cooper. Live and learn."

Hadley had spent the past eight years aiming for bigger and better, building her career. And she'd fallen for a guy who had looks, fame, and influence. But she'd somehow mistaken those traits for kindness, humility, and trust.

"You were always finding strays and bringing them to your grandma to find homes for. Remember that?" Kit asked.

"It's just now that I'm grown up, I have to come up with something to try and turn the business around. All I've done so far is offer to walk people's dogs while they're at work."

"Every time we talk with you, you say how spoiled your PR clients are," Darla said. "You wish you could be making a real difference. Maybe there's a way to do that here." She would know.

"I'm just going to do the best I can and use my gut instincts," Hadley said.

"That sounds just like you, Hadley," Kit said. "Trust yourself."

"I'm not sure if it's possible to turn a whole business around by the time I have to go back to LA."

"Right. Impossible," Kit said. "Even with your superb organizational skills."

"And your PR skills," Darla said. "And your smart brain."

"I also don't know what my grandmother really wants," Hadley said.

"What do *you* want?" Darla asked.

What *did* she want? "I want to help my grandmother get her business back together. And her confidence. If she does want to sell, I want her to leave the business from a position of strength. And I want to walk dogs and pet dogs and be out of the spotlight until I figure out what *I* want."

Whoa. Where had all that come from? Clarity from good friends, no doubt.

"Sounds like you made a decision." Darla got up and walked over to Hadley.

"Here. Take this." She held out her palm, which held the fabulous ring. The facets of the stone sparkled, catching the bright light from the windows. The dainty silver filigreed base looked both vintage and feminine. It was a beautiful ring.

Hadley pushed Darla's hand back. "You're silly. I can't take your heirloom ring!"

Darla gripped her wrist. "Had, listen to me. Take it to remind you to make authentic decisions. To be bold. To act from your strengths, not to do what you think you should do because of what other people want."

"Darla's right," Kit said. "You should wear it. It might help you sort out your life."

Hadley looked from one friend to the other before giving a resigned sigh. "Okay, fine." If it worked, Hadley would thank her friends, the would-be psychologist and the passionate, independent free thinker.

Darla dropped the ring into her palm and closed her fingers over it. "Have an amazing summer."

"To summer!" Kit held up her glass.

"May we all have an amazing summer," Hadley echoed, reluctantly slipping on the ring. *And whatever it may bring.*

Chapter 8

CAM, COME OVER here." Cam's longtime agent, Ian Felding, walked over to him that evening, crossing the deck of the little bungalow Cam was renting. "Let me introduce you to some people."

Cam bent to grab a few beers from an ice chest. His bad knee caught him off guard, but he reclaimed his balance and held back a wince before smiling and handing Ian a beer.

"We'll make the lady an offer she can't refuse," Ian said. "It will be a win-win for everybody. The restaurant team is thrilled."

"Wait—you told the team I had the building?" Cam asked. It was far from a done deal.

"Relax." Ian held up the beer. "We've got this. Everything is going to come together."

A server wearing black and white held up a tray of hors d'oeuvres as about twelve people milled around in small groups. A small bar was set up in the corner of the patio so people could enjoy the unobstructed ocean view, with the sun just setting and stars already dotting the sky. Cam didn't mind the setup, but poor Bowie had been booted out of his usual resting place near the patio furniture and seemed beside himself with all the commotion.

Ian put an arm around his shoulder. "The guys I'm about to introduce you to are the owners of Dudley and Dolittle. They've come all the way from LA. I think we need to emphasize that we've all but locked in the location."

Cam suddenly saw Hadley's determined face, plotting to stop him any way she could. Waves of guilt shot straight through him.

But thinking of her also reminded him of the insecure kid he'd been. Of not being good enough. Of feeling like a *failure*. Except, once again, he simply could not afford to fail now. He had to rebuild his life, and he had to succeed, or he'd have...nothing.

Ian pulled him back and spoke in a low voice. "We have to tell Dudley and Dolittle that we're committed and ready. Dudley's assistant alluded that if you're not a sure thing, they're going to try for Tom Brady."

"Tom Brady?" *Geez.* These people didn't mess around.

"This is *the* power team, as far as these deals go. Once they choose to invest, they go all the way. We have to be decisive and quick, or we'll lose the deal."

"Got it." Ian did his job, and his at times unapologetic pushiness had served Cam well over the years.

He soon found himself shaking hands with Mr. Dudley. Or had Ian just introduced him as Dolittle? They even looked similar, both with expensive haircuts and slim-line suits. And they both kowtowed to him, which was phony to the max.

For the hundredth time, he glanced over at Maddy's

bungalow next door. He was almost certain Hadley would be staying there and kept waiting for a door to click, a light to turn on. But so far, nothing.

Ian introduced him to an expensively tailored suit named Rocco. "We love that the flagship restaurant will be smack dab in the center of your hometown, Cam. It will really liven things up amid all those kitschy little mom-and-pop businesses. We crunched the numbers and we think with all the tourist traffic, we could do very well here. And if this one takes off"—he gestured upward with his hands—"New York. LA. Chicago. The sky's the limit."

"That's terrific," Cam said, but inside he just felt...off. Anyone who wore sunglasses once the sun had already set couldn't be trusted.

"Our job is to expedite and get things rolling," Rocco said, "which we can do in a number of ways. I brought some plans based on what our architect drew up."

Whoa. The architect he'd taken to Pooch Palace the other day had already drawn up plans?

"Yes," Mr. Dudley (or Dolittle?) said. "I hope you don't mind, but we're in a time crunch. We're very good at what we do, Mr. Cammareri, and we know very well that it's urgent to seize our window of opportunity."

"What kinds of plans are we talking about here?"

"All the restaurant chains we own are fairly similar in scope and design," Rocco said, "so it wasn't too diffi-cult." He must've seen the uncertainty in Cam's eyes, because he patted him on the shoulder. "No worries. Trust us. We've been down this road before."

"Gentlemen, can we get you a drink?" Ian tele-graphed Cam a look that said *Let me take care of this*. "Our staff just invented something fun called the Camminator to celebrate."

Our staff? Did he mean the two guys tending bar who looked no older than twenty?

"You okay?" Ian pulled Cam aside on the way to the bar. "Think of all the reasons you want this. Financial security for life. Revitalization for your town. A comfortable life for Mrs. Edwards, who can sail into retirement with a fortune. I don't see a downside here."

Financial security for life. The town, reinvigorated. Maddy, happily retired. Lucy potentially working as his chef—if he could change her mind.

Hadley would eventually accept her grandmother's retirement. She would go back to LA. He'd be the one to stay on here. So he needed to start building his future now.

It would all work out in the end, in the best way for everybody.

He shouldn't be worrying about Hadley with so much else on the line.

Yet he *was* worrying.

Cam walked over to the edge of the small patio. The old bungalow was small but immaculate, the little patio tiny but tidy, with a bajillion-dollar view. An image appeared in his mind, of him sitting out here with Hadley, just the two of them, on a warm summer night. With a glass of wine and a warm breeze blowing, just enough to keep them cool from the hot day. With a sky so dark you could see a million stars, and maybe silver ribbons of moonlight glistening on the water in front of them. Him holding her in his arms, soft and warm.

What was wrong with him? He'd been fine until that handshake in Maddy's hospital room. That simple touch had caused him to…remember things. *Feel* things. Like how much he'd loved holding her. How perfectly her hand fit in his.

It made him feel *protective*, which was exactly what he did not want to feel.

She would kill him if she got wind of that. She didn't need or want his protection.

And he needed to stop with the sentimentality.

He could not restart his life unless he took this opportunity.

Servers suddenly appeared with trays of green and blue fluorescent bubbling drinks. Reluctantly, he accepted one, but it looked more like something to remove grass stains from his uniform than a classy summer drink.

"So what will it be, Cam?" one of the investors asked.

He forced a smile, telling himself again that it was the right thing to do. "I'm in." He raised his glass for a toast. "Let's do it, gentlemen."

* * *

The party was winding down when Cam made his way onto the beach with Bowie. As Bowie sniffed around, Cam took in a big breath of air. He should feel relieved now that he was forging ahead with the restaurant plans, which were clear, logical, and well thought out. All he had to do was let his people handle their end and relax a little. And steer clear of Hadley and hope that in time she'd see this was best for everyone. In the meantime, he'd avoid her as much as possible until she returned to LA.

Suddenly Bowie tore through the brush and headed straight for the water. Cam emerged from the path to see the dog running straight for the person approaching them—Hadley.

Seeing her in that yellow dress, carrying her sandals and walking along the shallow water with Jagger at her heels, stopped him in his tracks and flooded him with raw longing. He didn't know if it was the warm summer night or the moonlight washing over everything, or the unexpected sight of her, but he just . . . stopped, right in his tracks.

Bowie was smarter. He trotted up and began running circles around Hadley, excitedly jumping up and down. She bent down to receive a sloppy kiss on the side of her face amid the sniffing, pawing, and tail wagging. Jagger, not to be outdone, showered Hadley with as much enthusiastic love as his buddy.

How the old dog could recognize her now in the dark and not the other day in broad daylight was beyond Cam.

"Well, finally I get a hello!" She stroked Bowie's ears and his silky-smooth back, giving him a good rubdown. Then she put her cheek against his head. "I missed you. I missed my special boy. Yes, I did."

Bowie nuzzled her like old times, and she was clearly loving it.

"He just had to get close enough to figure out who you were," Cam said as Bowie licked Hadley's face and made her break out in a laugh. With the sea breeze ruffling her dress, she looked good enough to eat, as Bowie continued to demonstrate. Lucky dog.

It had taken Cam all of ten seconds to lose his objectivity. *Nice.*

"What are you doing up this way?" she asked. "Aren't you renting on the South Shore?" This was the older end of the beach. The *way* older end. More like the tiny-old-house area, not the giant McMansion section where she'd probably imagined he would stay.

"I'm renting a bungalow," he said. "To sort of lie low." He shifted his weight and put his hands in his pockets, deciding there was no point in hiding the truth. "It's...um...it's next door to your grandma's."

Even Bowie's fur couldn't hide her gasp. "Somehow she didn't mention that." She dropped her voice to a barely audible level. "Like some other things."

Cam rushed to explain. "I know you're not exactly thrilled, but I was thinking this could be a good thing."

She stared at him.

"I'm a very good neighbor," he said. "I like fixing things. When she gets back, her place will be in great shape."

"Fixing things?" Hadley said.

"Yeah, you know." Cam nodded. "It's an old house. I've already replaced a bunch of bad light switches and the ceiling fan in her bedroom."

"Why are you...why are you being *nice*?"

He tossed back his head and laughed. Mainly because he was supposed to be aiming for cool and detached and completely failing. He surprised himself by saying, "I *am* nice."

"So *this* is how you did it." Hadley crossed her arms. "*This* is how you worked your way into my grandma's good graces."

He frowned. "What are you talking about?"

"Charm." She made an animated gesture with her hands. "It oozes out of all your pores. You can't even help it."

He shrugged that off. "I really like your grandmother." Sincerity filled his voice. "I would never take advantage of her." It was the truth, and he wanted Hadley to know that. The conversation came to a lull, both of them glancing out over the water at the lights from distant boats bobbing on the horizon.

"So you think I'm charming?" he said after a minute.

A frown creased her brow. "Maybe, but that doesn't give you a pass for bad behavior."

He laughed again. "You've *never* given me a pass."

She narrowed her eyes at him. "What do you mean?"

"It's a good thing. You treat me like . . . like a normal person. Like I'm just . . . Tony."

"You're not just Tony," she said.

"I am, and I'll prove it. See?" He pointed up at the sky.

"No." She shook her head. "Not that." When they were kids in high school, they'd often stargazed on this same beach. He'd tried hard to impress her by acquiring a knowledge of the night skies that sounded far more vast than it was. But judging by the kisses and making out that the stargazing led to, he'd done all right. More than all right.

He stood beside her and pointed above their heads. When his shoulder grazed hers by accident, he became very aware of her, the softness of her skin, her sweet scent. "The summer triangle." He tried to sound like a scientist but inside his brain was a bowl of oatmeal. "Altair, Deneb, and Vega."

She rolled her eyes. "I only remember the Big Dipper, and I don't even see it."

"Sure you do." He looked down at her and smiled. "There's the dipper."

"Still don't see it."

He moved behind her, resting his arm lightly on her

shoulder, and pointed high above their heads. Big mistake, touching her. It reminded him of sweet old times, and set his every nerve on edge. "It's right there. See?" Her brief glance at him looked troubled. Like she was feeling the same conflict he was. And maybe all the same desires too—but neither of them wanted them.

"When you get lost, you just look for the North Star," he said quietly. "You follow the two stars on the handle of the Dipper and that leads you right to it. Never fails."

"You make it sound easy." She stopped studying the sky and met his gaze. She was so close that he could reach out and touch her cheek. Or curl his hand lightly around her neck and pull her to him. Kiss her on those full lips. Take her into his arms.

"Maybe it's not so complicated," he said with a shrug.

He was pretty sure he wasn't talking about stars.

And he was also pretty sure he was making a big mistake. Especially when Hadley suddenly stepped back and crossed her arms, bringing him back to reality.

What was he doing, reminding her of the past? Wanting her to like him. Wanting her *period*. All things he'd have to stop doing if he wanted his life back.

* * *

Running into Bowie on the beach and getting such an enthusiastic welcome was awesome. But running into Cam was what really threw Hadley. With his swagger and his easygoing humor, he reduced her immediately into . . . well, into her teenage self.

And even if he was trying to remind her of the sweet times, drawing her to him like a magnet, looking like the boy she once loved, she couldn't let the lethal combination of moonlight and ocean get to her. Even if seeing him like this again really did shake her. And even if he *did* know how to fix her grandmother's light switches.

She needed to move, to break the spell of the moonlight, but her legs refused to take her away.

Her hand fell, and the cool, smooth surface of Darla's ring skimmed her leg, reminding her of her friends. Of her commitment to being honest. And of being her real self. "Explain the idiot comment," she blurted.

"Idiot comment?" Before he could properly answer, Bowie and Jagger, who were running in and out of the water chasing the waves, had caught his attention. A young couple holding hands walked by, and both dogs trotted up to say hi. Cam stepped forward to call them back, but the woman laughed and told them how sweet they were.

Hadley took advantage of the time to try not to hyperventilate. "You said you were an idiot for breaking up with me. What did you mean by that?"

Cam pointed to a small dune nearby that was clear of grass. "You have a minute to sit?"

They sat side by side on the sand, which was still radiating warmth from the sunny day, watching the dogs sniff and frolic until Cam finally spoke. "The differences between us suddenly seemed so huge. I ... couldn't handle it."

"What differences?" she asked. "We barely fought."

"You were so bright—you scored the highest in every subject. And you were dying to bust out of here and experience the world. I knew you were headed for greatness."

She shook her head vehemently. "*You* were the

shining star of the school. You broke every record and stole every girl's heart."

He turned his sea-blue gaze on her. "The only heart I wanted was yours."

Hadley turned to the sea with its familiar rhythms, sure and steady. Funny how the water looked like it was going to come and bowl you over, only to turn back at the last minute, every single time. She could use a little of that reassurance, because this conversation was threatening to do the same thing.

She pushed down the wild fluttering of her heart and made herself face him. "Then why? Why did you break it off? We were in love. At least, *I* loved you. I would've done anything for you, given you anything."

I gave you everything. My heart, my body, my soul.

High school relationships rarely lasted. It was naïve to think that they'd been headed for forever. Nevertheless, what he said mattered. Really mattered, more than she'd realized.

Part of what had attracted her to Cooper was how beloved he was—by everyone. Yet his popularity hadn't guaranteed him to be a good-hearted person.

Cam had a big personality too—but when she'd fallen in love with him, he hadn't had fame or money. She'd just loved…him. But he'd left her too. And she needed to understand why so it didn't happen again.

He heaved a sigh. "I figured it was just a matter of time before you broke it off with me." He paused. "I wasn't from an old town family. I didn't belong to a country club. You were into leaving for NYU and I…I felt like a country bumpkin. I didn't get my scholarship because of my smarts. I butted and tackled and pushed my way through the dirt to get a ride to college."

None of that had mattered to her. It hadn't mattered to her parents either, who'd loved Cam from the start because he'd been bright and ambitious and driven. Their concerns had been more about how fame and stardom would impact their relationship.

"I never cared about how much money you had." Looking at him was a huge mistake. Those beautiful eyes of his were full of something she'd rather not see. The truth.

"I was a scared kid who had no idea how far I could go. I had to prove myself." He shrugged. "I'm not making excuses for being a dumb kid."

"I loved you, Cam." She still couldn't tear her gaze away from his face. "A lot."

"I loved you too." He took her hand. "And I'm sorry I hurt you." She was caught up in the warmth of his hand holding hers, in the tender look in his eyes telling her that he meant it.

"Thank you—for saying that." Her voice came out low and strange, choked up. She went to pull her hand away, sensing that something between them had shifted. Something that had nothing to do with high school love or teenage insecurities or resolving their long-ago past.

How could she tell him that hearing his explanation had closed a very old wound—one from years of wondering, maybe. But if she were completely honest, it had done something else. Opened the crack in her heart she was trying very hard to keep closed. The one that kept her from letting him in.

For a moment, she was mesmerized, lost in the heat of his gaze, in the feel of his strong hand over hers. She hadn't felt this—this *force*—whatever it was between them that she'd always been helpless to resist—in all these years. Not like this.

She swiped her eyes on her arm so he wouldn't see her getting emotional and stood up fast, looking down the beach. "Oh, Bowie's wandering off. I better go grab him."

The old dog hadn't budged more than a few feet from where he'd been frolicking in the surf. And Jagger sat on the shore, chewing on a big chunk of driftwood. But she needed to step away, to break the strange connection still sparking between them.

Suddenly a man in salmon-colored shorts and a collared shirt patterned with rows of tiny whales approached. "Hey, Cam." He handed him a bright green drink. "We've been looking all over for you. I brought you a Camminator."

A *Camminator*? What the . . .

Cam touched her lightly on the elbow, sending an unwelcome shiver through her. "Hadley, this is my agent, Ian Felding. Ian, my friend Hadley. We . . . grew up together."

"A pleasure," Ian said, barely acknowledging her. "Cam, our investors are finally talking money. This is going to be huge. They're really excited to work with us on this. Oh, and they brainstormed a name. They came up with *Cammareri 1.0* for the flagship, and then each restaurant afterward would count upward from there. Isn't that cool?" He hiked his thumb in the direction of the bungalows. "I think you should get back up there as soon as you can." He turned to Hadley. "Nice to meet you, Hailey."

"I'll be right there." As Ian headed back up the beach path, Cam turned to her. "I've got a little group of businesspeople up there. Everyone's discussing the restaurant. Guess I'd better go."

Cammareri 1.0 ran through Hadley's mind as they walked back up the path in silence. It was the most impersonal name for a restaurant she'd ever heard, but it wasn't her business to tell him so. While she'd been caught up in reminiscing, he'd been furthering his plan to take over the Palace without missing a beat.

As they approached the space between the two bungalows, she heard laughter. A crowd of people with drinks in their hands had gathered on his patio. He surprised her by walking her all the way to her door. "Look," he said. "I...Do you mind keeping Bowie tonight? He really hates the noise and the crowd."

"Of course I will," she said, unable to keep the emotion out of her voice. He was giving her Bowie? Just when she tried hating him, he did something that made it impossible.

As if Bowie understood, he brushed by her legs and trotted into the house, Jagger right behind. But Bowie circled back and sat down on Hadley's foot, an old habit of his. Her Bowie was back. And right now that gave her a great deal of satisfaction.

Dogs were easier to read than men, that was for sure.

Hadley flicked on all the lights within reach. As if illumination would somehow bring her some desperately needed sense.

Cam hadn't changed since high school. He was still the life of the party, the extrovert, the guy who attracted anyone within fifty feet like a magnet. A force at getting what he wanted.

"Well, thanks for the talk." She started to close the door.

"No problem. I— Look, about that." He nodded toward the voices on his porch. "Those people. My agent—"

"Don't, Cam." She put up a hand. "It's okay. We are who we are." She tried not to look at him, because she knew she'd read a good deal of remorse in his face. But that wasn't enough. Feeling bad about something didn't count when you were still doing it.

"Thanks for Bowie," she said quickly, and then closed the door.

Chapter 9

CAM WALKED INTO the Cammareri Vintage Home Remodeling office on Monday morning to find his sister in a panic. Lucy sat at her computer, trying to talk on the phone while Bernie wailed loudly in a sling around her mom's neck. In the middle of the floor lay a large, brindle lump. On closer inspection, Cam saw that it was a bulldog, grunting and wheezing, its tongue lolling to the side.

Molly the Border collie ran over to Cam and nudged his hand, as if to say, *Have you seen this intruder? Have you? Get him away from my people!*

"Can I help?" Cam mouthed, reaching out for the baby. Lucy nodded gratefully, still on the phone, and passed over Baby Bernie, who now resembled an angry little plum.

One sniff and Cam regretted the handoff.

"She's poopy." He tried to hand her back.

"No takebacks," Lucy whispered, her hand over the receiver. Sending him a smile that might've meant *Good luck, buddy*, she mouthed her thanks and then went back to her phone call, silently chuckling.

"Okay, Bernadette," he said to the wailing baby, "I may not be able to catch or block anymore but I'm pretty sure I can figure this out." He walked to the back room, where a changing table was set up, and fumbled through the diaper change. He was more than a little proud of his accomplishment when he brought Bernie back. He cradled the snug little bundle like a football as she displayed her usual sunshine smile, smelling like baby wipes.

"You love your uncle Tony, don't you?" Cam said to the baby. "I haven't lost my ability to charm, have I, sweetheart?" *Too bad Hadley didn't think so.* The thought popped unwillingly into his head.

Last night, he'd felt a connection between them, strong and powerful, that Ian had quickly ruined with his talk about the restaurant. Which highlighted the impossible conundrum between them.

"Okay, Uncle Tony." Finally off the phone, his sister rolled her eyes. "I'm glad you two are in love with each other. Because I have a couple of problems here."

Cam nodded toward the lump on the floor with the lolling tongue. The dog stared at Cam and snorted. "Is he one of them?"

"My sitter called off and...ask *him*." He followed her chin dip over to Nick, who had just walked in, happily humming.

"Nick!" Lucy said. "This dog cannot stay here. *Not today.*"

Cam put a hand on Lucy's shoulder. "Okay, what's going on here?"

"We finally finished that awful job over on the east harbor," Nick said. "A divorced couple who insisted on renovating a cottage together but fought about everything." Nick nodded at the dog. "He got caught in the crossfire."

"I don't get it," Cam said. But he did. Nick had always been a softie, often following his heart and not his head. It was what had led to him getting married at twenty-one. And now it surely had led to his saving this dog.

"They were having a yelling match in front of him." Nick waved his arms as he discussed the dog's plight. "He just laid down in the middle of the floor with his head on his paws. It was almost like if he could've covered his ears, he would have."

Cam suppressed an eye roll. "And?"

"They were going to take him up to Evanston, to the pound up there."

"They'd put him down for sure." Lucy clutched her chest. In Cam's arms, Bernie drooled on his hand.

"Look at him," Cam said. "He's a medical bill on steroids."

"Exactly," Nick said. "I couldn't stand watching them fight over the poor animal. And picturing him in a pound...He'd be first in line to get... *you know*." The sappy look on Nick's face told the whole story. He'd never been able to say no to anything in distress—stray kittens, elderly people who couldn't afford their house repair bills, and the kind of women who didn't feel bad about taking advantage of that trait.

"So how about *you* keep him?" Lucy suggested.

Nick shook his head adamantly. "The dog park would be a great place to meet women, but my landlord has serious issues with slobber on the floor."

Lucy's expression softened. "You did the right thing. But...what do we do? He can't stay here in the office all day." She bent down and stroked the dog behind the ears. Molly sidled in, wanting some affection too. She got some chuffs and wheezes from the interloper in response. Bernie pitched forward in Cam's arms, holding out her arms and making noises at the dogs, clearly wanting in on the action too. "I can't take another dog now," Lucy said. "How about you, Cam?"

"I'm watching Bowie," he said, holding up his hands. *Thank goodness.* "One dog is all I can handle." Not to mention he already had something he couldn't handle— a pretty woman determined to have her way with his potential restaurant location.

"I was thinking we could ask Hadley," Nick said.

Cam's head jerked up. "Ask Hadley?"

"I think there's a chance she might take him," Nick said. "I heard she's started walking people's dogs. And people keep asking her about taking in strays. I sort of think she might cave because the Palace has been empty." Nick glanced at his phone. "I'd walk him over there, but I've got to meet Dad at a job."

Taking in strays? Like, using Pooch Palace as a *rescue*?

It was a great idea. People would sympathize with it. Her grandmother would too. And his restaurant plans would go up in smoke, just like that.

"I tell you what. Let me hang out with Bernie today." Cam nodded toward the dog. "And I'll take...him too."

"You'd do that?" Lucy's features lightened. "All day?"

"Piece of cake," Cam said while Lucy jotted down some notes, handed him a giant diaper bag, and kissed Bernie on the head.

He was happy to spend time with his favorite niece, although he had no idea what to do with a baby other than talking nonsense and carrying her around like a football. But he needed to see exactly what Hadley was up to.

* * *

Hadley was sitting in the back room of the Palace at her grandmother's desk, an ancient oak monstrosity littered with photos tucked under its glass top—of dogs and family, many of herself from way back when. She'd spent the morning walking a bunch of dogs for busy downtown shop owners and a neighbor of Gran's who'd recently broken a leg, and that had been really fun. Not only from a spending-time-with-dogs standpoint but also because it had reconnected her to people she hadn't seen in years.

But now she was brainstorming a plan to sustain Pooch Palace. Dog walking was okay, but it certainly didn't utilize the space. She'd said no to having boarders again because the new place by the highway was indeed booming, and attracting customers back would be no small feat. A doggie day care? A possibility. Several people had asked her about taking in strays, including Lucy, who had called her this morning with another sad story.

A shelter was of course the worst option money-wise. But it made her heart feel good. She found herself telling Lucy to bring the dog over, unable to say no.

She wished Mayellen and Ivy would return soon with the doubly caffeinated something or other they'd promised to bring back because she needed something to help her think more clearly before she caved and invited in even more homeless dogs. Plus she was dead on her feet.

She'd tossed and turned last night worse than the rolling ocean waves outside her windows. Thinking about what Cam had said about their breakup. About how it had felt to hold his hand and stand next to him on the beach gazing up at the stars as they had so many times before.

Being with him had felt like a *triple* espresso shot. But that was just her broken heart remembering better times, right?

She was relieved when a knock on the door pulled her from her thoughts. Paul Farmer stood there with a big grin on his face...and her grandmother's wheelchair in front of him.

"Surprise!" Her grandmother extended one arm for a hug, grinning from ear to ear. Her other arm held a cardboard drink holder with three milkshake cups.

On hearing his owner's voice, Bowie shot from his bed straight to the door. Hadley had to gently hold him back so he wouldn't jump on her grandmother, but he only settled for putting his head on her leg and wagging his tail so hard his entire body seemed to be wagging too.

"My sweet boy!" Gran kissed Bowie on the head over and over. "I missed you so much!"

Jagger, never the wallflower, decided to run circles around the wheelchair. Hadley made a lunge to stop him but Gran beckoned him into the fold. "Come here, Jagger." Gran wiped tears from her eyes. "There are plenty of kisses for you too."

Hadley felt a little teary. That was her grandma. She loved everyone.

Even Cam, she thought wryly.

Paul intercepted the milkshakes while Hadley gave her grandma a big squeeze. She looked a little tan and was smiling, and she had on a bright pink blouse and matching flip-flops. All a far cry from how she'd looked in the hospital.

"You look amazing!" Hadley said. "Bowie and I have missed you so much." Bowie had not budged an inch from Gran's side. "Hey, Paul." Hadley gave him a hug too.

"So nice to see you, Hadley," he said softly. His tidy gray beard, spectacles, and bow tie made him look like the distinguished gentleman he was. As he bent to pet Jagger, he asked, "And who's this character?"

"Poor little guy," Gran said. "Doesn't look like he's had much love, does he?"

Paul smiled as Jagger looked up at him sweetly. "Did you say *little*?"

Jagger was too busy getting love to take offense. "What are you two doing here?" Hadley asked.

"I'm officially a week out from surgery," Gran said proudly, "and I got the okay to go to the park."

Paul gave a laid-back laugh. "But she conned me into taking her a little farther."

"So you're AWOL." Hadley wasn't surprised. "But what's in the cups?"

Paul handed them to Hadley as he wheeled Gran to a more open space. "Breakfast ice cream," he said.

Gran laughed and gave him a look that Hadley could only describe as...smitten. And Paul was giving her the same exact look back.

Awww. She loved what passed between them, even as she wondered if someone would ever look at her like that. If she would trust anyone again after all her hurt. And more importantly, if she would trust *herself*.

"Okay." She pulled herself away from the edge. "*What* is breakfast ice cream?"

Paul chuckled. "Well, you won't know until you taste it, will you?"

Hadley laughed. "I'm always up for a challenge." Then she held up her milkshake in a toast. "To busting out."

Her grandma laughed again as everyone raised their cups. "To busting out!"

Inside the cup was cold, smooth, caffeinated deliciousness. A coffee milkshake? Frappuccino? Something? "Wow."

A close second to holding hands with Cam—no, no, she didn't mean that.

"You like?" Paul looked a little pleased with himself.

"I love it. Can I marry it? What's in here?"

"Lots of caffeine, like your grandma requested. And my secret blend of coffee and ice cream."

"Breakfast ice cream," Hadley mused.

"I have another way to make it with low-fat yogurt and skim milk but my philosophy has always been don't wait to enjoy the good stuff."

A few months ago, Hadley wouldn't have even touched it, too afraid of being plastered on seven different magazine covers looking like she actually ate food. But she had to admit, he had something there. When life gave you ice cream, you said *thank you* and enjoyed it, regardless of the time of day.

"Will you give us a few minutes, Paul?" Gran smiled. "Then I promise I'll be a good patient and go straight back."

Paul checked his watch. "Only fifteen, because your nurse is going to skin my behind if I don't have you back under that tree by ten-thirty."

"I promise." As they watched him leave, Gran said,

"He's a good friend." She lowered her voice. "And a drill sergeant. He means what he says about having me back exactly on time."

"It looks to me like he might be more than a friend." Hadley waggled her brows.

"Oh, stop, Hadley." She waved her arms so adamantly that Bowie startled.

"He's wonderful to you," Hadley said, "and I can see that he cares a lot. So what's the problem?"

"Look at me." Gran said. "I'm...old." She was blushing again. "Anyway, I'm not here to talk about my love life."

This was new, seeing an area where Gran might be the one to need advice. "You have a brand-new hip. You'll be dancing again in no time."

"Listen," she said, effectively closing off *that* discussion, "I want to know how you're doing here." Gran took a sweeping glance around. "Still no business, I see."

Hadley set down her shake. "I didn't open for business yet. I wanted to wait and talk with you. What I am doing is walking dogs. I've got a handful three times a day. It's bringing in some income and keeping us busy. So far, I've said no to boarders and to people wanting doggie day care. But there's another issue."

As if on cue, there was an urgent rap on the window. Outside, Anita Morales stood not with Jesse, her poodle, but with a little brown squatty-looking dog, who was scratching urgently behind his ear.

"I was walking my Jesse when this little guy followed us home," Anita said through the screen door, a little out of breath. The dog, a miniature pinscher the color of a Hershey bar, scratched again, the poor little guy.

"He's full of fleas, Hadley, and I don't dare come in."
Anita held the leash away from her as if the fleas were
about to jump on her too. "I dropped Jesse off at home
so he wouldn't get them. And I need to take this one
straight to the vet, but my elderly mom is coming for
a visit later today. I was wondering if maybe you might
take him? Maybe someone will claim him? I've already
called the police and the pound in Evanston."

Hadley walked outside and looked the dog over. "He
has fleas, all right. If you're willing to take him to the
vet, I can take him in." She bent down to the dog's
level. "You're kinda cute." But the poor miserable dog
only batted his ear in response.

"I've got to go." Anita glanced at her watch. "The
new vet said he could squeeze me in right now. He's
very young and handsome. Have you met him?" Anita
peered through the screen again and did a double take.
"Maddy, is that you?"

Anita was saying a quick hi to Gran when Hadley's
phone rang. "I'm giving you a heads-up," Lucy said on
the other end of the line.

"The bulldog's not coming after all?" Hadley guessed.

"Um, no. It's coming all right, and Cam's bringing
it. Like, as fast as he can walk it down to you. I think
he wants to suss out his competition. Oh, and he's
got Bernie too. *By himself.* I trust him…kind of. But
will you please keep an eye out for my daughter just
in case?"

Cam…with a wheezy bulldog and a *baby*? This she
had to see. "Thanks for the heads-up, Lucy. I promise
to look out for Bernie."

Hadley ended her call, walked back inside, and
pulled up a wooden chair next to her grandmother's

wheelchair. "Lucy Cammareri called me a little while ago," she confessed. "Nick brought in a wheezy bull-dog, a casualty of a divorce."

Her grandmother narrowed her eyes.

"I couldn't say no, Gran." She felt a little like she was a teenager again. "Not when we have room. I'll front the upkeep costs. I just couldn't turn him away. Or the little fleabag." She cracked a half-smile. That was a little funny, wasn't it?

Her grandmother gave her a knowing look. "You haven't changed in the slightest."

Oh dear. Maybe she was angry. And keeping strays when there already wasn't much income coming in was probably a terrible idea.

"They're going to start coming like an *avalanche*," Gran said.

Oh no. "I'll control it, I swear. I'm sorry, I—"

Gran interrupted her apology. "Hadley, dear, I'm not scolding you. I'm just pointing something out. You've always wanted to rescue dogs, you know."

"I can't help myself," she confessed. "It's just that they're all so sweet and innocent. They don't deserve to have to deal with hardship." Especially hardship brought on by negligent owners. "I'll rein in the compulsion. I'll focus on the direction you want to take your business in. I was just waiting for you to tell me—"

"Hadley. All I'm saying is you've got a fresh slate here. And a couple of dogs who need homes. And your skill set includes everything it takes to rescue animals"—she paused—"as a business."

"Wait," she said. "You're telling me to . . . rescue more dogs?" The thought was scary. But a little thrill ran through her.

"And make it work." Gran was on a roll now. "Donations, fundraising, networking...unless you're fed up with that stuff and you just want to walk dogs all summer. That's okay too."

"No, I...What are you saying?" Was Gran saying that she do exactly what her impractical, silly teenage self would have done? But she was *serious.*

"Why not take this opportunity to explore what you might want to do?" Gran opened her arms wide to indicate the possibility. "There's no pressure because we've got Cam working on his ideas too. And I know you have a job to potentially return to. But maybe now's a good time to...reassess."

"My life?"

"Yes." She nodded emphatically. "Your *life*. As I'm reassessing mine. I...I might enjoy retirement. I think I'm done with the boarding business. So now's your chance to take that info and run with it wherever you might want." She eyed Hadley carefully. "And I do love Cam but you're my granddaughter, so I'm telling you first." She paused. "We don't get many opportunities to reimagine ourselves, but this might be one of them. So think about what you truly want."

"I..." She couldn't even spit out an *I don't know*. Her head was whirling. No. This was too ridiculous. She wasn't sixteen and dreaming of working at Pooch Palace for the rest of her life. Begging Gran to help poor homeless animals.

She'd gone on to do other things. Serious things. She'd moved away to climb the ladder of success.

Except the view from the top hadn't been all that great.

"Oh, look at the time," Gran said, eyeing the old

clock on the wall with different dog breeds marking each hour. It was cocker spaniel o'clock, apparently. Otherwise known as 10:20. "My drill sergeant will be here in no time. Before I go, how are things going with Cam?"

Hadley sighed. "He's just as hardheaded as ever."

"And...?"

There was no use lying. Her grandmother made it just as impossible now as she had when Hadley was eight and stole cookies from the pan fresh out of the oven. She'd confessed as soon as Gran walked into the kitchen. "And as handsome." Hadley sighed. "I met him on the beach last night walking home from Darla's. We had a little...talk. He told me he was sorry for breaking up with me all those years ago."

"Is that right?"

"Don't get your hopes up," Hadley warned. "I really don't like him any better."

"But?" Gran couldn't disguise her hopeful look.

"Well, I appreciated the apology," Hadley said. "He told me he felt I was out of his league and it was just a matter of time before I moved on. Do you believe that? Someone like him, who's always been so confident and successful?"

Gran tapped her lips thoughtfully. "There are few of us who are as confident on the inside as on the outside. I guess the question is, do you believe him?"

"I...I almost did," she said. "But then his agent or his manager or someone came up and started talking about all these things that are going on about naming his restaurant and...it's clear he's going full speed ahead."

"Did you ask him why?"

"Why he wants this building so badly?" She peeked out the window for a frazzled man with a baby and a wheezy bulldog. Nope, no one in sight.

"That, but also why he wants the *restaurant* so badly. Why he's in such a hurry."

Hadley shook her head. "I guess he's always been focused. I just assumed he's going at this like he did everything else." She frowned. "I can't help but feel that you like him a little too much." This time she checked her watch. How many minutes did it take to wheel a baby and a dog four blocks? She'd better get Gran out of here quick or she'd be drooling all over Cam.

"I've always believed people's behavior is driven by certain things. Maybe it's important to understand each other." She cleared her throat. "As part of your reassessment plan."

Hadley was onto the blatant matchmaking attempt. She looked up to see Paul on the sidewalk, ready to walk in. "Okay, Gran, but this goes two ways."

"All right, ladies," Paul said through the screen door. "Time's up."

Hadley lifted her brows and tilted her head toward Paul. "*Your* reassessment plan has arrived."

Gran's face instantly turned scarlet. As she kissed Gran goodbye and watched Paul wheel her out, she realized that being able to give Gran some advice—and receive it—felt really good.

Chapter 10

CAM COULD HANDLE strolling Bernie the four blocks to Pooch Palace—but add a wheezing, snorting, drooling dog whose leash kept getting tangled in the stroller wheels every two feet into the equation and what you got was a sweaty mess. And he wasn't talking about the dog.

When he finally arrived at Pooch Palace, Ivy took the bulldog off his hands right away, and everyone gathered to check him out. But then Bernie, who'd loved the stroll through town because of her many admirers along the way, started to fuss. "Hey, it's okay, sweetheart." He lifted her out of the stroller and walked with her a little. It appeared that he wasn't the only sweaty one after all.

"Look how handsome he is," Hadley said as she knelt in front of the dog. With the dog's wrinkly face, hanging jowls, and lolling tongue, that definitely wouldn't be his first descriptor. She was way too softhearted, that's what she was. That was no way to run a business.

Suddenly she was next to him, slipping off the fussy baby's sun hat, which had somehow flopped over Bernie's eyes. "Can I help?" she asked with a smile.

She was a drink of cool water in jean shorts and white tennis shoes. And she'd just said the magic word. "Her sling's down there," he said over Bernie's cries, pointing to a compartment underneath the stroller. "But last time I tried to use it, it took me a half hour to put it on."

Hadley pulled the sling out and somehow rotated, smoothed, and placed it over his head before helping him ease the baby in. He caught a whiff of her shampoo, which he could only identify as...delicious.

"Thanks." He moved his shoulders to adjust the sling, his gaze snagging on hers again. Something he seemed powerless to prevent. "I...um...appreciate it." Now he felt guilty for coming down here to find out what she was up to.

"No problem." She shifted her gaze to Bernie, who had calmed down in the sling. "There." She rubbed her back. "All better now?"

The baby flashed them a big gummy smile. Being in Hadley's presence made him feel better too. And worse. After last night, he wished for things to be different. He wasn't a money-grabbing party person like she thought.

Well, he did love a good party—sometimes. But the Camminator had been too much.

Those few minutes when he and Hadley had talked, where they'd actually discussed something other than the building, had been unexpected—in a nice way. But Cam understood that their differences put them at an unresolvable impasse. If only he could stop his brain from dwelling on her.

Hadley walked into the back and Ivy came up to talk with him. "Hey, Cam," Ivy said. "You here for the meeting?"

He glanced at his watch. "I have a few minutes." He had no idea what she was talking about, but if it helped him find out Hadley's plans, he was game.

Ivy looked out the window. "It *is* a beautiful day out there."

Mayellen, who had walked over to a table behind the counter where they usually held their meetings, shook her head. "It might be beautiful now, but a gullywasher's coming."

"A gully-what?" Ivy asked.

"It means a big storm with a lot of rain. Predicted for tonight."

"Are we ready for the meeting?" He hadn't heard Hadley use that businesslike tone before as she set down a giant box of donuts from Mimi's Bakery.

Everyone had corralled around the donut box. Ivy was petting the bulldog, whom she'd named Bubba, and saying how he could use a tune-up at the vet. Even Jagger and Bowie were present and accounted for.

Perfect. He'd arrived just in time to get some intel. Plus there were donuts. Win-win.

Cam was just about to take a seat himself when Hadley gave him the stink eye.

"I don't mind your staying but you can't be part of our meeting." That CEO tone was back. He halted with a jelly donut almost to his mouth.

Ivy stifled a chuckle by taking a sip of coffee.

"I mean it, Cam," Hadley said. "You can have all the donuts you want but you'll have to go somewhere else." She shoved the donut box toward him.

"Okay, so the dog walking is actually getting more popular," he heard Hadley say once he'd moved as far across the main room as he could and still eavesdrop.

Fortunately Bernie was nodding off, so he did a slow turn near the windows, walking and rocking her gently as he listened in. He could even see a little if he craned his head around a few of the dog crates. "It's bringing in a little bit of revenue. How are you all feeling about it?"

"I've lost two pounds," Mayellen said.

"And I'm getting some weekend dogsitting jobs," Ivy said, "because people are really pleased with the dog walking."

"I've liked it too," Hadley said. "But as you know, Gran wants me to come up with another business plan. I've decided I'm going to put out some feelers about starting a nonprofit."

"You mean like a rescue?" Ivy asked.

"I think I need another donut," Mayellen said. "Honey, that sounds like a ton of work. Aren't you leaving soon?"

"Taking in strays...that's a big expense," Ivy said. "They need a lot of medical care and food and stuff."

"And Hadley can't say no to anybody." Mayellen patted Hadley's hand.

Cam stifled a chortle. Because she'd never had any trouble saying no to *him*.

"I'm just putting out feelers and also giving Gran time to recover," Hadley continued, scribbling something on a legal pad as she talked. "I plan to talk to the local vet group and to a bunch of shelter owners to learn what it takes to become a nonprofit. I have a whole list of things I need to research."

"We can help," Mayellen said.

"Great," she said. "So no matter what happens, we could work on building up our social media platforms," Hadley said. "It's never too early for that."

"That sounds fun," Mayellen said. "I love Pinterest. So colorful. And the recipes!"

Unable to stay silent, Cam popped his head around the counter. "Pinterest works well for restaurants, Mayellen. In fact, I'm looking for someone to help me with that for my place. But for a pet rescue, I think you'd have to use Facebook."

"I create different accounts for my clients all the time," Hadley said. "I color-coordinate Instagram accounts based on theme. And run ads. And specials and incentives."

"Nice." Yet another reason Hadley should be his friend, not his enemy. Because the woman could clearly kick butt.

"I'm not sure how I feel about this," Ivy said. "We never had to use the Internet before to advertise our business."

"Well, for starters, do we even *have* a social media presence?" Hadley asked.

"We sure do," Mayellen answered cheerily. "Our Facebook page has got twenty-five likes."

"That many?" Ivy asked with astonishment.

"Do we have an Instagram account?" Hadley asked.

"No," Ivy said, "but I take photos of nearly all the dogs I groom. The owners love it. Maybe we could use those for something?"

"That's a great idea," Hadley said, writing that down.

"Don't forget Groupon," Cam added, popping in again. "Just trying to be helpful."

"Haven't you left yet?" she called.

"As soon as I finish my donut."

Ivy chuckled. "That Cam. He's so funny."

"The other thing is, you should sign up for a booth

at the Blueberry Festival," Cam said. "This is the last week to register."

"That's a great idea," Mayellen said. "We can try to get these sweethearts adopted." The bulldog huffed. Jagger twitched an ear in his sleep.

The phone rang, and at the same time, the bell above the door tinkled. Mayellen and Ivy both got up to tend to business.

"I got a festival booth for myself," Cam told Hadley. "But you better hurry—they're going fast."

"Why are you telling me this? Because you're trying to be nice instead of a cold-blooded opportunist?" She smiled sweetly.

It was his turn to frown. "That's not fair."

"Let's be honest," she said. "Neither of us is stopping at anything to get this place. I saw your . . . your cronies last night. You're in this to win it."

Cronies? Okay, so Ian and his Camminator had been over the top. He wanted to tell her that wasn't who he was. But what would be the point? "Look, Hadley. I *am* in it to win it. But only because I think it's the best thing for everybody."

"Whatever." She waved her hand dismissively in the air.

"Don't be angry with me." A giant red warning light should have turned on in his head because *what was he doing saying that*?

Just then, Lucy walked through the door, a slightly panicked expression on her face. "Is Bernie . . . okay?"

Cam rotated slowly, showcasing Bernie fast asleep in the sling.

"Oh, thank heavens." She gripped her chest. "She's not crying."

"I take deep offense at that." Cam flourished his arms proudly, demonstrating the sweetly sleeping baby. "Because this big tight end is tough on the field but gentle where it counts."

Hadley rolled her eyes, but Lucy still looked a little frantic. "I came down because I have to breastfeed her before I go back to work." She approached Cam and held out her hands.

He turned his mouth up in a smile and lifted his arms. "Get me out of this straitjacket and she's all yours." Lucy proceeded to work some kind of unhooking/untangling magic and placed Bernie effortlessly back into the stroller.

"I think I'm going to stop at the courthouse to get a booth for the festival," Hadley said to Lucy. "I'll walk with you." She turned to Mayellen and Ivy. "I'll be back in a few." She tossed Cam the slightest wave as she left with Lucy, leaving him staring after her.

What was he doing? This attraction would be the death of him.

He needed to separate what he wanted—no, *needed*—from his desire for her. He had to get his life back on track, and she would be a formidable foe unless he stayed on his toes.

And following his feelings could only lead to disaster.

* * *

Hadley was more than happy to get out of Pooch Palace and away from the effects of the Camminator, which was how she was beginning to think of Cam. Away from not only his disruptive presence, unwanted advice, and competitive nature, but also his hot, hot body.

Ugh.

It was good to get out, because her mind was spinning. Gran had given her a heads-up on wanting to retire. And she had to admit, excitement fluttered in her stomach at the idea of a rescue. She hadn't felt this sort of thrill about anything for a really long time.

Well, except for when she was near Cam. But that didn't count. She chalked that up to pure, raw chemistry. She might not be able to control her physical reaction to him, but she was determined to control her mental one.

A block away from the Palace, Lucy put a hand on Hadley's arm. "Do you have a minute to sit?" She pointed to a bench along a big grassy knoll in the park.

"Sure. Of course." Hadley hoped that talking to Lucy for a while might distract her from her troubles.

As they crossed the expanse of green lawn, the sun was warm on Hadley's skin, and a gentle, salt-tinged breeze blew in from the ocean. They picked a bench in a shady area for Bernie and sat for a few moments enjoying the perfect day. When the baby stirred, Lucy picked her up from the stroller and placed her back in the sling, slipping her little brimmed sun hat on her head.

Past the park, Hadley could see the walking path that led to the beach. Kids ran about laughing and playing tag, moms strolled babies, and a couple sat on a blanket under a tree. Summer in Seashell Harbor was hands down Hadley's favorite time of year, and just sitting here listening to the kids giggle and the gentle sound of the surf made her feel calmer.

"So, about my brother," Lucy said, sending Hadley's

one minute of summer serenity right out the window. On the horizon, clouds were gathering…a reminder of Mayellen's looming gullywasher.

"Your brother," Hadley echoed. She hoped this wasn't about to get awkward. "Lucy, you know I've always thought of you like a little sister. But Cam—"

"He's got a good heart," Lucy interrupted.

Hadley cracked a smile. "If you say so."

"He might be a little misguided." Lucy squinted against the sun to watch two girls tossing a softball in the distance. "But there's a reason."

Hadley sat up straighter and faced Lucy. She knew how much Lucy looked up to Cam, and she would never ruin that. "Lucy, I know you want to defend him. And you should, because he's your brother. But I'm not sure we're going to agree about this."

"Cam's always plowed full force ahead whatever the obstacles, you know that. Even when our mother left, he never cried. I mean, he probably should have, but he took the opposite tack. He would ask us to toss the football with him over and over. He'd do push-ups and pull-ups until he was exhausted. He drove himself hard. I'm not saying that was necessarily healthy, but I think that's what he might be doing now."

Hadley knew exactly the kind of drive Cam had. And Lucy was right—Hadley had never known him not to be in motion. "You mean rehabbing from his injury?"

"This restaurant scheme. He's more determined than ever to make it work." Lucy blew out a sigh. "And there's something else, but it's a little personal."

"Lucy, it's okay." Hadley held out her hands. "You don't have to say anything else. I get that Cam is driven and focused and throws his whole self into anything until he succeeds and that failure isn't an option." All that made him a formidable opponent. Except none of that scared her. She was capable of giving him a run for his money.

"I have to," Lucy insisted. "I have to tell you for *his sake*."

"For his sake?" Was Cam in trouble?

"Cam's pushing to open that restaurant because of *me*."

Opening the restaurant because he was a star and it fit with his big personality, yes, she could see that. Because he loved crowds and joking and entertaining people—yes, that too. But because of *Lucy*?

"I used to talk about going to cooking school." Lucy glanced down at Bernie, now snoozing again. "I actually got into the Culinary Institute of America when I applied last year. But life had…other plans." She kissed Bernie lovingly on the head. "Cam's trying to make it easier for me to get my life going again."

Cooking school. A memory pierced Hadley's consciousness. Lucy at thirteen baking endless creations, always looking for taste testers. She and Cam had gotten a lot of free—and tasty—cookies that way.

"Is that what *you* want?" she asked.

Lucy's watery eyes gave Hadley the answer. "Sometimes I get so angry at him for interfering." Lucy swiped away her tears. "He makes it sound like it's easy to pick up and start a new life with an eight-month-old." She shook her head in an exasperated way. "Imagine! I mean, I'm not complaining—I love being a mom. But cooking school would take my life to a whole new level. It would require me to cash in every single favor. It would mean leaning on my family, on Cam—and on myself—in ways that would be really scary."

Lucy looked up, and in that flash of her eyes, Hadley saw...a lot. A fiercely independent woman, for one. And a giant unrealized dream, for another.

"You agree, don't you? It would be crazy."

That was a loaded question. "Maybe not so crazy," Hadley finally said. "I'm sort of up to my ears in what to do about my grandmother's business. And the whole world knows about my giant romantic failure. So, I might not be the best person to ask."

"My brother's a real pain in the rear," Lucy said, wiping her eyes.

"We can definitely agree on that." Hadley couldn't help smiling just a little. One thing she *could* say about Cam was that he certainly hadn't left his family behind as his fame had skyrocketed.

Lucy stood up then, straightening her baby sling and gathering her diaper bag. "Well, anyway, I...I just thought you should know. It might make you dislike him a little less."

"Lucy, I don't hate him," Hadley said. "I've just accepted that he's not going to back down. We're going to have to duke it out until one of us wins."

That sounded awful. She didn't want to do that. But what choice did she have but to fight for what she believed was right?

"My brother can be difficult, but don't give up on him." Lucy smiled at her. "You two were kind of wonderful together. Maybe it's not too late."

Kind of wonderful. What did that even mean? Lucy had been just a kid when Hadley and Cam had dated, and she'd looked up to both of them. But her words made Hadley admit that what she'd had with Cam...it was the best first love anyone could have ever dreamed of. It *had* been wonderful. Until it wasn't.

She wished she hadn't known about Lucy. The fact that this whole restaurant scheme involved helping his sister was one more reason to like Cam. And she could not afford to like him. Too much was at stake.

Chapter 11

CAM AWAKENED AROUND midnight to Bowie climbing into his bed. A flash of lightning and a clap of thunder sent the dog burrowing under his covers.

"It's okay, Bowsers." Cam got up to close some windows just as the rain began to pour down in buckets. When he returned to his bed, the dog was in the middle, cozied right in with his head on Cam's pillow, staring up at him with big, moony eyes. Cam climbed in, heaving a sigh. "You can stay, as long as you scoot to your own side, okay?"

An hour later, he woke up again, this time to a loud crash from outside that sounded like raccoons in the trash cans. Bowie's long body was draped across his chest, his ears flopping beneath Cam's chin.

"You might consider brushing your teeth before bed next time, bud." He gently slid the dog off. He seemed to weigh a hundred pounds limp and asleep.

When he flipped on the outdoor floodlights and peeked through the kitchen curtains, he found Hadley rummaging around in her grandmother's garage, loading buckets and flowerpots into her grandma's Prius.

"What's going on?" he asked, walking outside.

As soon as she looked at him, he knew something was wrong. And not because he'd forgotten a shirt and his hair was in a jumble from sleeping. "What is it?" He raked his fingers hastily through his hair to get presentable. "What happened?"

"Jared Chen called me. The ceiling is leaking over at the building."

Before he could ask how the police chief had noticed, Hadley continued. "He was on his way home after a late-night call when he happened to see water gushing into the main room."

"Gushing?"

"I have to get over there," she said, slamming down the lid of the hatchback.

"Are there any dogs there?" he asked.

She shook her head. "Mayellen and Ivy took the two strays we're caring for." And of course Bowie and Jagger were safe with Hadley and him.

"I'll be right back," he said, turning back to the house. "Don't leave," he called over his shoulder.

"Where are you going?" she asked.

He stopped at the doorway. "I'm grabbing a shirt and keys. I'm going with you, and we're taking my truck." He preempted the protest he was certain she was about to express, probably loudly. "You don't have to like me, just my muscles, okay? And yes, I don't just own a vintage car. Be right back."

Cam called Nick to put him on standby for help with the roof. Then he and Hadley drove over together in the rain, because there was no way he was going to let her go alone. But first they grabbed some recycling bins, old storage containers, and whatever else they could find that would hold water.

He was protecting his would-be investment, he told himself. But honestly, he knew that for the lie it was.

A short while later, the rain still dumping down in buckets, he pulled his truck up to the back of the Palace and dragged in the empty trash cans that stood against the building. He had a feeling they were going to need all the help they could get.

That was confirmed a minute later when they stood in the middle of the main room, staring up at a gaping hole in the ceiling, watching a waterfall spill onto the old tile floor.

"I don't even know where to begin." Hadley shook her head incredulously.

Cam cursed, a sound mostly obliterated by the loud splatting of water. "It's okay," he said, although it definitely wasn't. "We'll clean it up. It'll be all right."

"How did this happen?" The dread lacing her voice made his stomach sink.

He followed her gaze to the ugly white-tile drop ceiling. An enormous water ring encircled a considerable area. In the center, the cheap foam-like tiles had fallen to the floor and broken into multiple pieces, leaving a gaping black hole.

"The water leaked into the space above the drop ceiling," Cam said, "and it just couldn't hold the weight."

He should be glad on some level for this disaster. It might make Maddy want to give up the building for good. And it would surely make Hadley see what a money pit it was.

He should be feeling positive. Only he just felt bad. They were both entitled to make their case for the building, but this curveball might make the playing field uneven, because he could afford a thousand roofs. And he didn't want to win that way.

But also, he hated to see her distressed and upset.

"You know, you don't have to be here," she said. "This isn't your problem."

He almost said that no matter how complicated things were between them, she could always count on him to be there. But instead he chose a safer response. "Well, I do have a vested interest, you know."

"Guess we may as well start bailing." Hurt flashed in her eyes as she picked up a saucepan and positioned it under one of the drips, the water pinging sharply as it hit the metal.

"You should probably use something bigger," he said matter-of-factly.

She stared at him as if he had two heads. "You're kidding, right?" They were getting wetter and wetter as the ceiling kept springing leaks. Water spouted from different holes, dripping on their heads and splashing up from where it fell on the floor.

"Kidding about what?" he asked. She ran behind the desk and brought back a wastebasket, which she placed under a leak. And she looked *angry*.

"Tell me you didn't just give me advice about bailing water."

"I was just *suggesting* that you use the smaller containers on the smaller drips and the larger ones on the big ones."

She grabbed a lobster pot from the pile and held it toward him. "Would you like to tell me where to put *this*?" She gave him a deadpan look and waited a beat before frowning sharply. "Because I might have a few ideas."

"Ha-ha." As he took the pot, he said, "You never took my advice anyway."

"Probably because you dispense it like an Italian grandmother."

"Italian grandmothers are wise." He tried not to get her goat but it was so much fun he couldn't help himself. "Besides, I can't help it if I'm always seeing more efficient ways of doing things."

She rolled her eyes. "There's nothing worse than a guy who thinks he's right all the time."

Only he hadn't been right about her. After all, he'd thought he could forget her. Holding up his hands, he kept his tone light. "Hey, I'm just trying to be helpful. You must admit bringing the trash cans inside was a great idea."

She cracked a wry smile. "You've always been a man of action. Resourceful. I'll give you that."

Her small concession pleased him more than he wanted to admit. Their sparring reminded him of the old days. In a good way. She was *fun* to argue with. And for some reason he loved teasing her. "I don't think I'm right *all* the time."

She pointed up at the ceiling. Waiting for a concession.

"Okay. I'm sorry for trying to tell you what to do." He held out an empty bucket as a peace offering. She stared at it. "I'm trying to be nice, okay?"

"If you were nice, you'd give this up and go find yourself another place to open 1.0 and all your other points."

"Now you're making fun."

She sighed and looked as if she was carefully weighing what to say next. "It's just that every time I say that name, I can't help thinking it sounds like Thing One and Thing Two. Or like a giant restaurant chain. Impersonal."

"Thanks for your opinion." They were back to square one. Where they would always be as long as they were on opposite sides.

He'd busied himself with setting out a few more containers when she said, "I'm not saying that to be mean. I guess I've always given you my honest opinion. I have more thoughts, too, if you want to hear."

He stopped hauling water for a moment and turned to her. She stood there, in the middle of all that dripping, her gaze direct and quiet. "Sure. Tell me." When had she ever *not* had an opinion?

"I can see you opening up a restaurant," she said, animatedly gesturing with her hands like she was imagining it herself. "Greeting people, because you know everybody. Shaking their hands. Asking about their families. Planning the menus, putting little twinkle lights all around outside. It would be called something simple and welcoming like Cam's Place, not Cammareri 1.0, which sounds like a robot droid or something."

He snorted. "A *robot droid*?"

"Impersonal. Cold. Unoriginal."

He laughed. Not because she'd said something critical. But because her eyes still got that dreamy look in them when she was seeing another place, another world.

"That sounds like me. Except I think *you'd* have to be the one to add the twinkle lights."

How had she settled for covering up the mistakes of spoiled celebs? She should be running her own show, taking over the world. Because she had the insight to do it. To lead, not to follow.

Suddenly he could see himself walking around an outdoor area strung with lights, hearing the murmurs and laughter of people having a great time. Smelling the savory Italian dishes cooking in the kitchen. Taking the time to talk to people.

She was dead-on. He loved doing that—schmoozing. He'd greet every single person who walked in. Ask after their families. Walk over to each table and make sure their meals were a great experience. As for the food—it would be all homemade Italian cuisine. Pasta made by hand. Fresh bread from the local bakery. And of course the Cammareri secret pizza dough recipe. With wines he would select himself.

"Cam?"

He shook his head to clear it, only to find her handing him a giant paint bucket overflowing with water. "What made you want to open a restaurant?" she asked.

He shrugged, trying to think of a neutral answer. One that would keep her at a distance, where she needed to be. But instead, the truth spilled out. "My dad. He raised us by himself and worked all day, but we had the best family dinners—spaghetti with homemade sauce, lasagna, gnocchi, braised ribs. He'd stay up at night prepping things for the next day so we could sit and eat together, and that's how he kept tabs on us. By feeding us well. By making sure we showed up for dinner no matter what. I think that's the reason we've all stayed close."

"My stomach is rumbling and it's four in the morning," she said, emptying a flowerpot into a bucket. "So it was something you'd always planned on doing?"

He shook his head. "Not really. The restaurant executives came calling at just the right time. I felt it was important to capitalize on my popularity before it fades." Okay, he definitely had to shut up now. He was giving away the truth to the competition.

"Your popularity will never fade," she said with absolute sincerity. "You're really famous. I mean, people call you a young Tom Brady."

He tried to smile, like hearing those words wasn't hard. "Thanks, but I'm a few Super Bowl rings shy of him. And that's where the comparison will end." He'd never get the chance to stand up to Brady's record. Fate had dealt him a different hand.

There was an awkward silence. She was looking at him with what looked an awful lot like pity. Cam was kicking himself for admitting weakness when she said, "That's *not* where it ends. Because you've always been more than a football player."

He snorted. "I just don't want to be the kind of person to sit on my laurels my entire life." That's why the restaurant appealed—it was something completely different. A fresh start. Far removed from the constant reminder football would always be of his shattered dreams.

She moved a giant garbage can under another avalanche of water. He helped her position it, accidentally placing his hand on top of hers.

He forgot about the waterfall as they locked gazes, very aware of her touch. "I know for a fact you would get very bored of laurel-sitting. Besides, I know what your secret weapon is," she said. "Do you?"

He laughed. "I could use a secret weapon about now."

"You have a natural ease with people." She eyed him closely. There wasn't any pity in her voice, which, for better or for worse, made him believe her. "You may not want to go near a football field right now, but you'd be an amazing example, say, for high school boys. And girls, for that matter. Everyone respects and likes you. You can do a lot of good with a personality like that."

"Do *you* like me?" he asked, his pulse beating strong and heavy. He suddenly realized he hadn't moved his hand.

A moment passed between them, charged with electricity. Every hair on his body felt like it was on end, as if he was touching one of those energy balls in a science museum.

Hadley finally moved her hand, breaking the spell. "Your cell phone's ringing," she said.

Cam wrenched his gaze away, reaching into his pocket. "Nick. Hi," he said, putting the phone to his ear. "Bring the big one. I'll meet you in a minute."

"Where are you going?" Hadley asked as he headed to the back room. "It's still pouring out."

"Nick and I are going to toss a tarp over the weak spot on the roof. It'll save a lot more headaches if we do it now."

"You're going up on the roof with a ladder *now*?" Concern laced her voice.

Maybe she didn't hate him *that* much. "It won't take long," he said.

"But it's dark. And really wet. Isn't that dangerous?"

"Yeah, it's pretty dangerous." He bit down on his lip to keep from grinning. "I might not even come back." He had to admit, knowing she was worried pleased him in a weird way. "I'm kidding," he said when she'd failed to crack a smile. "We do it all the time. Trust me. It will prevent a lot more damage." He grabbed his phone from the counter and headed for the back room.

"Tony." He turned around at her summons. And at the fact that she'd called him by his given name. "Be careful, okay?"

He flashed her a grin. "Aw, so you *do* care."

Hadley rolled her eyes as she reached for a mop and bucket. "That was an accident. I just don't want any broken bones on my conscience."

As she ran from one drip to another, shifting various containers, an unwelcome thought struck him. She looked...hot. Drenched but definitely hot.

The truth was, she'd be sexy any hour of the day.

Her weird combination of earnestness and total obliviousness about her appearance made her sort of...adorable.

"Don't slip on that floor," he called as he tore his gaze away and got to work.

It took all of ten minutes for Cam and his brother to set the tarp, and when Cam came back in, he was soaked to the skin. Hadley was mopping and tossing huge chunks of tile into a garbage can. He made sure not to let his gaze linger—especially on how her wet sweatshirt clung to her curves or on her shapely behind as she bent to work.

Nope. No more rain porn for him.

She handed him two full buckets. "Would you mind dumping these?" she asked. "I've made about a hundred trips outside."

"No problem." Their fingers grazed during the hand-off, and hers were ice-cold. "You should get out of those wet clothes."

She stared at him.

Oh, geez. "I mean, when you get *home*. Because you don't want to get *sick*." He emphasized his intention, then turned to go dump the bucket before he said something else equally stupid.

Suddenly, another enormous chunk of the cheap,

soaked ceiling cracked open. Instinctively, Cam dropped the buckets and grabbed Hadley by the arm, pushing her—and himself—out of the way. But he overshot, driving a little too hard to get them clear and lost his footing on the slippery tile.

He managed to cushion her fall as they went down, so Hadley landed on top of him. His arms were suddenly full of warm, soft woman, and the pure pleasure of being next to her—touching her, their limbs intertwined—took away all his sense. He started to untangle himself, but then he made the terrible mistake of looking up.

One glance at Hadley, soaked to the bone, a little dazed and stunned, made something turn over in his chest.

Maybe it was the primal memory of being like this with her a long, long time ago. Or the shock of being thrown together suddenly, against their will.

He meant to let go, but in her pretty, expressive eyes he saw . . . something. A flash of feeling. A spark of heat. *A challenge.* He couldn't move his hands or look away. And he knew, sure as the electricity coursing hot and quick between them, that she felt it too.

He *wanted* her, as loud and demanding as his pulse throbbing at his temples, as certain as the fire coursing through his veins.

"Hadley, I—" He stopped, unable to put into words all that he was feeling. Finally, he forced himself to look up at the terrible mess of a ceiling.

"Please don't tell me there's another leak," she whispered.

"No, I . . . I mean, I don't know. It's a wreck." *He* was a wreck. A wreck of desire for her. Yet he was paralyzed in place, holding on to her soft arms, one heartbeat away from dragging her lips to his.

Another waterfall suddenly burst down from a new hole, close enough to splatter them thoroughly.

And then she laughed. A slow giggle at first—and then the unladylike one he remembered so well.

It was just as ridiculous and incongruous and—okay, snorty—as before. And then he laughed too.

"Had, that laugh," he said softly, shaking his head. His voice sounded too quiet, too tense. Unnatural. "It's... exactly the same."

"Hey, I owned my laugh a long time ago," she said, starting to roll off of him.

"No, I—" He held on to her arms, preventing her from leaving. "I wasn't being critical," he hurried to say. Her eyes, bright and assessing, were wary. But was her heart beating as his was, fast and steady in his chest, like his entire body was on alert? "I missed it," he blurted out.

"Oh." She looked puzzled. Surprised.

A slow, aching heat rose up inside him, and suddenly he knew the truth. He'd missed more than her laugh. He'd missed... her.

His gaze dropped to her lips, full and lush and open in surprise. And then he bent his head and kissed her.

* * *

Oh, holy moly.

She hadn't expected *this*.

One minute they were arguing and then... and then in a flash, everything had changed.

Yeah, clearly no arguing going on now.

His lips met hers, purposefully, smoothly, and they were warm and soft, and she was... lost. Completely lost, wrapped up in the familiar, clean scent of him.

He wrapped his big arms around her and pulled her closer. She clung to his hard, wet body like he was a life raft in a stormy sea.

The cold, wet floor was forgotten with the heat flashing through her, igniting her into flames.

Then his mouth shifted, and his tongue met hers.

Behind her closed eyelids, stars and fireworks exploded, and whatever other sparkly things you were supposed to see when you were kissing someone who could *really* kiss. That's when she realized that in all the years since Tony Cammareri, in all the kisses and the other loves, in all of the very full life she'd led, no one had kissed her like this.

No one.

He broke away, drawing back and leaving her to steady her erratic pulse.

"Um, okay." His voice was a little shaky.

His expression was dazed, confused. *Affected.* But his arms still cinched hers, firm and sure.

His voice was never shaky. *He* was the confident one, the sure one. Goal-directed and purposeful.

But not now. Right now he looked...flummoxed. Uncertain. And a little flushed. And she would have taken great pleasure in all those things except for the fact that she was completely discombobulated too.

"Hadley," he said. "Look, I—"

Suddenly Nick walked in, swinging two bright orange paint buckets. "I brought some five-gallon..." His voice trailed off when he saw them tangled up together, completely soaked. "Oh, hey, sorry," he said, starting to back away.

"Come in, Nick," Cam called as he released her, and they both scrambled to their feet. She felt relieved and sad all at once, more proof of how upside down he made her feel. Still staring at her, he spoke to his brother. "I was just telling Hadley . . . telling Hadley that I think we sprung another leak."

"Oh yes, definitely." She smoothed down her wet hair and grabbed one of the buckets from Nick. "I'll get right on it."

"Okay," Nick said, "I see . . . things are a little out of control here. I'm going back out to my truck to bring in more cleaning supplies."

Out of control was an understatement. Hadley wanted to curl up in a dog crate and disappear. But she couldn't. So she started picking the ceiling pieces off the floor. When Nick left, she turned to Cam, who seemed to be making a concerted effort to stay as far away from her as possible. "What . . . what were you about to tell me?" she managed.

"Oh. Um, just that . . . you'd better watch out. I think we're in for more trouble." He pointed up at the ceiling, where more huge chunks looked about to give way.

She had no idea what he'd been about to say, but it wasn't *that*.

And yet . . . trouble. Yes. That was very, very true.

How had they gotten from sloshing around buckets of water to . . . this?

All she knew was that things between them had just gotten a whole lot more complicated.

Chapter 12

TWO DAYS LATER, thanks to his talk with Hadley, Cam found himself on the bleachers at the high school football field watching the football team finish their laps around the track. From his vantage point high up in the stands, they looked like a tiny colony of ants following their leader. The rain from the past few days had finally stopped and the sun was out, a brilliant yellow ball in a perfectly blue sky.

Being here always made him emotional, but today, doubly so. This was where it had all begun—the moment he'd been picked out of a crowd and set on a fantastical path he could never have dreamed of. The idea that he could make a living doing what he loved the most was something that had never seemed possible before then.

It was also the place where he'd first talked with Hadley—*really* talked with her. He'd thought she'd basically written him off as a dumb jock until one evening she'd sprained her ankle running, and he'd carried her to his car and driven her home.

Back then he'd thought that a girl like her would never look twice at a guy like him. He'd been the first person in his family to go to college. Belonging to a swim club, being gifted with a car, even if it was an old one, assuming access to a college education was a gift— those were all part of a foreign world.

And yet...deep down where it counted, he and Hadley had been very much the same. Hardworking, determined, both wanting to make the world a better place.

So here he was. Trying to set aside his own dilemmas and do something to help somebody else, thanks to Hadley's voice in his head. He knew he had some serious work to do to get himself together. And he was ready to start.

But just seeing a field again in the summer heat, sitting in the empty bleachers, and hearing the roar of the crowds in his head bombarded him with memories of other fields and accolades and triumphs, and even the crushing defeats. The memories brought on a desperate yearning he feared might crush him.

But still, he stayed. Like everything else he'd ever done, he understood that he was never going to be able to truly move on unless he faced up to his fears.

Hadley had been right about that.

It was weird to agree on something instead of butting heads or poising to fight to the death over the Palace.

Yet their kiss two days ago had proved that they still had the same unholy chemistry as ever.

Times *ten*.

A slap on his back pulled him from his thoughts. "Hey, you showed."

Cam stood and clasped hands with his old high school friend Drew McDowell, then hugged him, returning the back slap Drew gave him. "I couldn't let the youth of this community be brainwashed solely by you, could I?"

"Hey, I'm respectable now." Drew ran a thoughtful hand over his short beard and assessed Cam in that way he both loved and hated. Loved because Drew always saw him for who he was. Hated because, true to his being a counselor as well as the football coach, Drew sometimes saw too much. "But my guys can use a talk from a hometown boy who became a big star."

"Still the same hometown boy."

"Noted. I'm glad you're here. The boys will be too." Drew paused then added, "Hey, I heard the Palace got deluged. What's the damage?"

"Extensive."

"Sorry to hear it. How's Hadley taking that?"

Cam shrugged. "She thinks her grandma wants to keep the place going. But I'm not so sure."

"I hate to see you two on opposite sides." Drew must have taken Cam's silence as a license to give some advice. "She's still a catch, man. You two were crazy about each other. Good opportunity to rekindle those old feelings, right?"

Cam frowned. "Why does anyone who's happily married want everyone else to be too?"

"Because it's great. Also, Christine wants you to come over for dinner."

"I'd love to." Drew and Christine had dated since high school and were expecting their third child. Cam knew that, in a different world, that could've been him and Hadley.

Where had that thought come from? Because they were talking high school here. How many people actually ended up with their first loves?

The boys were running up the bleachers, pounding big feet against the aluminum stands and making a racket. "So, how's your team?" Cam asked, eager to talk about something safe like football.

"It's a little different here than when we were young. The economy's not as good. Some of the families have fallen on tough times. These kids don't have enough role models to push them to dream big dreams. That's why I took you up on your offer to come today."

"I get it." Cam certainly didn't grow up in an easy time—money was tight and his dad was a struggling single parent who worked hard to provide. Yet Cam had grown up believing that any goal was possible with hard work and discipline.

"I meant what I said about you joining us once a week," Drew said. "I know you've been going through a lot, so if you're not up for it—"

"I'm doing great," Cam said quickly. He was fine in every way that mattered—he'd had every fortune and a big dose of luck on top of his talent. The fact that he was expected to be a role model when he couldn't even play football anymore was a little dicier. And made him feel like a bit of a fraud. "Let me think on it. And I meant what I said about funding the uniforms."

As they walked down the bleachers, the boys gathered around, many of them stealing glances at him, some staring outright.

"Hey, Cam," one said. "Will you autograph our jerseys?"

He stood and walked down the remaining concrete steps, being careful not to catch his bad knee, to the front of the stands so he could face the team. Smiling at the boy who spoke, he said, "Sure, but for the next few minutes, I want you to think of me not as someone famous but as someone just like you—from our town, born and raised here.

"My story is all about dreaming big and working hard to achieve your dreams. And working hard on the field teaches you how to work hard in life. So today, I'm going to start by talking about training techniques. Then we're all going to jog a few laps and hit the gym."

Suddenly it seemed no one was paying any attention. *Great.* He'd had a platform to make a difference and he'd blown it by being preachy and long-winded. Cam turned to see what everyone was looking at. Two people were crossing the field with a handful of dogs, Alaskan mush team style, the animals straining at their leashes.

Hadley.

Drew reached into the first row of seats and pulled out a big wire basket of tennis balls. He turned to Cam. "I might've forgotten to mention that Hadley's bringing a few rescue dogs that need some exercise."

Cam raised a brow, as in, *you've got to be kidding me.*

"I thought having the guys play with the dogs would be good for physical conditioning. And fun too." He rushed to add, "Of course, you can do whatever you want with them afterward."

Cam crossed his arms and stared hard at his friend, who for some reason seemed to think that was hilarious. "Hey, it's for the team," Drew said. "Plus, it's good for them to learn service."

"Service?"

"Yeah. Dog walking. Good for the community." Drew punched him in the arm, leaving Cam to stand there, grappling with his suddenly rampant emotions. Bowie and Jagger led Hadley's pack, along with three dogs he'd never seen before. A motley crew, bolting down the field, towing Hadley behind them. Mayellen walked behind Hadley with another bunch of dogs.

The boys clamored out of the stands and rushed the field, his inspirational talk all but forgotten. Soon everyone was laughing and chasing dogs around.

Hadley had begun talking to Drew and a few of the team members, only to catch Cam's gaze and look quickly away, back to laughing and talking with the boys. But Jagger noticed him and broke away, bolting toward him.

Cam leaned down and scratched behind the dog's ears. "Hey, buddy, how'd you get a pile of friends, huh?" The dog leaped up and licked his face, wiggling his skinny butt.

Cam straightened to find Hadley directly in front of him. *Oh no*, was his first thought as a barrage of feelings hit him like a Mack truck. That four a.m. kiss had stirred everything up, taken away his peace of mind. What had he been thinking? Because he couldn't *stop* thinking about her. How she'd felt tangled up with him on that wet floor. How her lips had felt on his.

She was wearing jean shorts and a T-shirt that read WALK A DOG, MAKE A FRIEND. Her hair was up in a ponytail and she looked not much older than the kids on the football team. Several of the boys were openly checking her out, making Cam instinctively step sideways to block their line of vision.

It struck him that being with her now felt just like before, all those years ago. The same excitement. The same thrill. The same *ease*. It was as if they'd been together yesterday, not twelve years ago.

Cam grabbed a ball from the bucket. Jagger

immediately perked up, jumping and anticipating Cam's throw. Cam gave it a good toss, and the dog bolted after it, his long legs flying.

"Maybe he thinks he's a greyhound," Hadley said.

"Well, a dog can dream," Cam said, laughing a little nervously. "So, how's the roof?" She seemed nervous, too, not looking directly at him, keeping her focus on the dog.

She shrugged. "We're getting estimates to fix it. I think my grandma's insurance will cover it, though."

He nodded and lifted a brow at the dogs. He saw some new recruits among the pack. "More?"

She shrugged. "Word of mouth, I guess. Anita Morales brought in a stray that followed her home while she was walking her own dog. Some kids found that little pit bull mix hiding under a woodpile, and that cute little black one wasn't getting along with their family's cat." She flicked her gaze up at him. "Are you avoiding me?"

A direct, unexpected shot. That's how she was, no BS'ing. Plus, she still saw through him clearer than a plate-glass window. "Of course not."

Her eye roll showed him that she wasn't buying that. "Oh my gosh, you *are* avoiding me."

He crossed his arms, hoping to appear calm and case-closed. "I'm not avoiding you."

"It's been two days since…that kiss. And you've gone radio silent. And you're acting funny now."

"I'm talking to the boys about hard work and persistence. And overseeing their workout. If we can ever get them into the gym."

"Cardio's important too." She smiled, gesturing to the boys running around with the dogs. Suddenly their gazes locked and held in a way he absolutely did not want. His pulse kicked up and that same undeniable feeling hit him like always, regardless of how he tried to steel himself against it.

"Seriously," she said after a bit, "that's terrific you're sharing your expertise. And being an inspiration."

"Right." His answer came out less than enthused. Jagger dropped the ball at his feet and Cam picked it up and tossed it far out into the field. The dog loped after it, full speed ahead. For such an odd-looking dog, he ran like a gazelle.

"So, what's the worry?" she asked.

He shouldn't have looked at her again. Because one look at her concerned expression and he was spilling the thoughts heavy on his mind. "Truth is, I feel a little like an imposter. Someone who can't practice what I preach." He immediately winced. He wasn't one to talk about weaknesses—*ever. Fake it till you make it* was basically the mantra he'd lived by his entire life.

"It's not like that," she said, her eyes filling with compassion. Or pity. He wasn't sure which, but he hated both. "You're the most famous tight end in the country."

"*Was* the most famous tight end."

She frowned in protest. "You have tons of experience and expertise. Plus, you're inspiring to anybody who dreams of getting out and making something of him- or herself."

"I appreciate the pep talk but I'm the one who's supposed to be giving it." The boys were horsing around, the dogs getting all riled up and loving it. He wished he were out there, too, carefree and young, his whole future ahead of him.

Hadley was looking him over, assessing him. He understood she was trying to help and didn't deserve his sarcasm. "Sorry." He rubbed his neck. "I didn't mean to sound snarky."

"I'm not offended," she said. "Maybe show them with actions, not words. I mean, kids respond better to showing not telling, you know?"

He nodded. "I get it." But really, he didn't. If only he *could* show. But his knee wouldn't allow it. Ever again. Yet she seemed to actually believe he could be inspiring. But how, when he could barely stand here on this field that he loved without breaking into hives?

Despite his confusion, there was one thing he needed to set straight for her sake. "Listen, Hadley. The truth is, I *have* been avoiding you. I'm sorry about the other morning."

"You're *sorry*?" She narrowed her eyes. "Maybe you better clarify what exactly you're sorry about—the ceiling disaster or kissing me."

That kiss was the best thing that had happened to him in a long time. But how could he allow himself to get involved with her when he didn't know who he was anymore? He needed that restaurant. It was the only thing now that would make him feel that he hadn't failed. And he couldn't let Hadley stand in the way of that.

He would never take the chance of hurting her again like he had back when he was young and stupid. She had enough on her hands with that snake Cooper, and she deserved better. And *better* just wasn't him.

"Oh." The deadpan quality of her voice showed him she was disappointed in him. And he deserved it. He'd acted no better than the dumb kid who'd broken up with her all those years ago.

"I mean," he said, "we clearly have the same attraction between us but we're older and wiser now. We don't need to act on it." His words sounded shallow. Like he was making excuses and being an idiot, which he was. But he had no choice. Acting on his desire for her would be a big mistake.

"Right," she said quietly, frowning.

"It was a weak moment," he said. "I never should've let it happen."

"Well, I let it happen too. It doesn't have to mean anything. I mean, neither of us are in the right place for...for that."

"For *that*?"

"For...kissing. For more than kissing. For a relationship."

"Right. No. *Definitely* not that."

She smiled at him. "Don't worry. It was only a kiss. No biggie."

Only a kiss? That kiss was smoking hot. It had incinerated his insides. But maybe it was only a glass of lukewarm water to her.

She tossed a ball back into the bucket. "Well, I better be going. See you around." She bent and patted her thigh. "C'mon, Jagger babe, time to roll."

Then she walked away, the dog trotting happily at her side.

Chapter 13

I THOUGHT WE were meeting at Scoops," Kit said as Hadley slid into a corner booth with her friends that evening at the back of the Sand Bar, a quaint little hole-in-the-wall right on the beach where you could grab an ice-cold beer and the best wings in town.

"This was my vote," Darla said. "Not that I don't like ice cream. But judging from your tone of voice, I was thinking maybe we need the hard stuff."

"Actually," Kit said as a big plate of wings was delivered to their table, "I like anyplace where I can sit down for more than five minutes at a time. I might actually be able to taste my food for once." She clapped her hands a little and reached for a Thai chili wing.

"Why the emergency summons?" Hadley asked. "Not that we need an emergency to have a drink." She was glad the focus would be on Kit, who'd asked them to meet. After her talk with Cam at the football field earlier, she'd decided the issue with Cam—not that it was actually an *issue*—wasn't worth talking about. He was her past, and that kiss, while off the Richter scale in hotness, was nothing but an accident, brought on by familiarity and the close proximity that resulted when he pushed her out of harm's way.

Under the rustic wooden beams, big, colorful sea life done in papier-mâché hung from the ceiling. A giant squid hung over the bar, along with an octopus, a crab, and a swordfish. A big red lobster, claws waving in the breeze, floated directly above their heads.

As the lobster's claws swayed, Hadley decided Cam was like that lobster. Colorful and appealing but with claws that she had to stay away from. Because despite that open-the-floodgates kiss, he'd made it clear he didn't want anything else. *Windex* clear.

What she needed was protection against the charms of Tony Cammareri. An anti-Cammareri vaccination. Something to build her immunity that would last forever.

Maybe she *did* need the help of her friends more than she thought.

Hadley suddenly became aware that Kit was talking. "…and a few days ago, I got *this*." Kit pushed an airmail envelope covered with a lot of foreign stamps across the table.

"From Alex de la Cruz?" Darla read the envelope. "I haven't seen him since we were all in your wedding party together. Except when I was in the middle of my chemo, he sent me a card from the air force base in Baghdad. So he's probably still somewhere flying top-secret missions and looking super hot."

Kit looked distressed. They all knew Alex, who had been Carson's best friend since high school. Hadley knew him as a quiet, upstanding guy, if somewhat of a loner. "He's done with his tour of duty and now he's headed home to Seashell Harbor," Kit said. "And he's asking *my* permission to fix up the old McKinnon place."

Darla choked a little on her mojito. "What?"

Before he'd died, Kit's husband, Carson, had inherited his grandparents' falling-down ancestral home. The Queen Anne Victorian, half obscured by weeds, looked more like Boo Radley's house than a civilized place to actually inhabit. Which was why no one in Carson's family had wanted it. And why Kit, overwhelmed as she was with expenses, had promptly placed it on the market.

Of course it was still sitting there, because it was essentially a tear-down. Unless someone came along with deep pockets and a very optimistic attitude.

"Apparently he found out that I put it up for sale," Kit said. "He says it will bring in a lot more money if someone fixes it up."

"And *he* wants to be the one to do that?" Darla shook her head incredulously.

Kit sighed heavily. "He says he'll finance the renovation himself and just take the cost of materials from the sale. Honestly, I'm going to tell him there's no need to feel this misguided loyalty to Carson."

"Maybe he's doing it for you," Hadley said. "And Ollie," she made sure to add, because any suggestion that the daredevil fighter pilot might have a thing for Kit would be very unwelcome. "Regardless of why, if he wants to have a go at it, why not let him?"

"Sit down with him when he gets here and discuss the possibilities," Darla said.

Kit snorted and rolled her eyes. "Alex barely speaks to me. He prefers grunting or flat-out ignoring me. Honestly, having to actually speak with him would be...unsettling. He didn't even leave a phone number." She picked up the envelope and waved it in the air. "And look how he communicates. Via *letter*. It's like he's trying not to discuss this at all. So I got his email and told him thanks but no thanks."

"You told him no?" Hadley leaned forward.

"I can't bear dealing with him through an entire house renovation. And I don't want him paying out of pocket for anything. Plus, I don't need his help. Ollie and I are doing just fine." She held up a different finger for each excuse, one-two-three.

She'd certainly given this some thought.

"Do you think he still wears black all the time?" Darla mused as she grabbed a blue-cheese-crusted wing. "He's so dark and broody and sexy. There's a story there, Kit. Waiting to be unlocked."

Hadley would've teased, too, but she could tell Kit was growing even more uncomfortable.

"I'm changing the subject," Kit said. "I've already said no. It was just a little bit of a shock hearing from him after all this time." She folded the letter back into the envelope and flicked her gaze to Hadley. "How's everything going after the roof disaster?"

"The roof's getting fixed," she said. She did not want to discuss the roof. Or the kiss.

"It hasn't discouraged Cam from pursuing the building?" Darla asked. "I was sort of hoping that would happen."

"Of course not," Hadley said. "Cam is like a missile locked on a target. Nothing stops him from getting what he wants." It had been like that with football and everything else he'd set his sights on. Once, it had been that way with *her* too.

Kit took a sip of her chocolate martini. "But surely this competition, or whatever it is, is giving you two opportunities to work together and reconnect?"

"The only thing we've done together is mop up water from the floor. And that ended in disaster."

Oh no. It had taken less than thirty seconds to spill to her friends.

"Disaster?" Kit asked.

"It's nothing," Hadley rushed to say. "Just that the gross drop-down ceiling was caving in from all the water and he pushed me out of the way. I literally fell into his arms and..."

"Oh no." Darla tried to disguise her smile with her hand. "Not on the floor of Pooch Palace."

"Nothing happened," Hadley said hurriedly. "It was just a kiss." She shrugged. "Okay, quite a kiss. Like, a ten out of ten. Old hormones just took over."

Both of her friends stopped eating and stared at her. "It was an *accident*." Hadley wished she hadn't brought it up. "We both regret it. He told me so today. It was just the weird situation and the fact that I landed on top of him..."

"Of course," Darla said. "I mean, when I accidentally fall on top of men, I always kiss them. That would be a natural reaction."

Kit giggled. "Darla's right. That kind of thing doesn't happen by accident. Especially with you two."

"He's not happy it happened. And...and I'm not either. It's just that I've had moments where I've seen this other side of him and those are...confusing me." There. She'd said it and felt an immediate sense of relief at telling her friends. Who wouldn't judge her. Too much.

Darla raised an elegant brow. "Moments?"

"He brought my grandmother a bouquet of flowers when she was in the hospital that he took the time to pick from her garden. And he gave this cute—well, it was a little boring, but still—inspirational spiel to the boys on the football team. And he talks this silly nonsense to Jagger, sort of treats him like he's an AKC breed instead of a gangly one-eyed mutt. And part of the reason he wants to do a restaurant is to help his sister out. Not that any of that excuses him but—"

"Whatever happened to 'Cam's a jerk'?" Darla asked.

"Well, he did sort of apologize for that," Hadley said.

Of course, Darla jumped right on that. "Sort of?"

"He said he ended things before I could break up with him. He felt certain I would once I left for New York. He said he was sorry."

"For breaking up with you?" Darla said.

"Uh-oh." Kit shared a look with Darla.

"What?" Hadley said. "What's the *uh-oh* for?"

Kit licked the wing sauce off her fingers, then wiped them on her napkin. "He's sorry. He's single. You two *kissed*." She threw up her hands. "Do I have to spell out the possibilities?"

Hadley watched her friends chuckle. She shouldn't have gone so easy on Kit for sure.

"There's something else," Hadley said. "He let something slip at the football field. He said he felt like an imposter talking to the boys. Someone who can't practice what he preaches. Weird, huh? When he's one of the most famous football players in the world."

"Wait a minute," Kit said. "He told you he feels like an imposter?"

"I don't think he meant to say it. It just kind of came out."

"That's...that's really telling, Hadley," Kit said.

Darla nodded in agreement. "Cam has always had a big personality—confident, fun. To say something like that...well, that sounds serious. Especially after what happened to him."

"Maybe he's struggling," Kit said. "For a man who's had such a huge amount of success, it's probably terrifying to be sort of free-falling like he is."

"But he's a bajillionaire," Hadley said. "He can do anything he wants. Or nothing."

Darla shook her head. "I can't imagine Cam ever doing nothing."

"And yet his main goal seems to be going after a crumbly old building in the middle of his hometown. That happens to belong to your grandma." Kit leaned forward. "Why do you think that is?"

Hadley lifted her shoulders and hands in a demonstrative shrug. "Because he lives to torture me?"

Kit tapped her lips, something she always did when she was in deep thought. "Maybe he's latching on to this so tightly because he's...afraid."

Hadley snorted. "He's six four and built like a tank. Cam's not afraid of anything."

"I mean, like, of failure," Kit said. "If he fails at this, what has he got? He's not one to rely on his past achievements like some people would do, especially if he's thinking he's an imposter. Maybe he's looking for something else to replace his football career—in a desperate sort of way."

Darla put down her glass. "A career-ending injury might be like cancer. I'm sure it changes your life in ways you can't even imagine."

Kit nodded solemnly. "Maybe he's sort of subconsciously

reaching out to you—the kiss, the little confession—at a time when he feels a little…confused. I mean, that's probably a foreign feeling for him."

"I don't know if you're right," Hadley said, "but that's a lot to think about." Cam at a crossroads and confused—yes, it did make sense. And it might also explain why he was reaching out but then pushing her away.

"Sorry if I'm a little too enthusiastic," Kit said. "I've already made it through the entire online general psych curriculum from Princeton."

"You mean you've been following a syllabus?" Darla asked.

"A bunch of them," Kit admitted. "I get the used textbooks cheap online."

"This is what you do for fun?" Darla shook her head sadly. "You *definitely* need to get laid."

Kit shrugged. "I want a better way to support Ollie. Something I'm interested in."

Hadley put down her spoon and leaned over the table. "Kit, let Alex fix that awful old place up. Then you'd have college money for Ollie. And yourself."

"She's got a point," Darla said. "Plus, if he's grouchy and doesn't talk, that might be a positive. If he wants to work silently and get stuff done, let him."

"This has been great, but I still feel anxious." Kit placed a hand over her heart.

Hadley didn't mention the uncomfortable, steady pounding of her own heart. She knew Cam well enough that she totally understood his unilateral focus on a goal. But what her friends had just said took Cam's dilemmas to a whole new level. One she wasn't sure she really wanted to understand.

Chapter 14

THE DAY OF the Blueberry Festival dawned clear and hot, a perfect summer day. Hadley was up early setting up her booth on the green, along with what seemed like every other business in town, artists and artisans alike. She loved being part of this yearly ritual, loved being around all these talented people taking pride in their town.

Food trucks were stationed in the lot of the oceanside park, filling the air with wonderful aromas from all kinds of delicacies. Like her favorite, Italian sausage with peppers. And fresh-squeezed lemonade that quenched a thirst like nothing else.

She turned to the doggie playpen she'd assembled earlier, which was now filled with a motley assortment of dogs.

"Okay, all of you." She approached the pen and clapped lightly. "Listen up. It's a big day, and I want you all on your best behavior." Jagger, who was heads and tails taller than all the other dogs, immediately pranced up and began aggressively nudging her hand, as if he were saying, *Bust me out of here! Take me home!*

Hadley laughed and smothered him with kisses and

hugs. "You are a lover, aren't you?" Of course then she had to take a turn with all the other dogs too. She had to admit, Jagger had stolen her heart with his silliness and the way he seemed to intuit her moods. But how could she bring him into her tiny apartment? How could she leave him alone all day with the gruesome hours she kept? It wasn't a good life for a dog. And so she straightened his spiffy green bow and smoothed down his nicely groomed hair and went back to the business of trying to get these fellas and ladies adopted.

She was straightening pamphlets when she saw a couple approaching, hand in hand.

"Mom and Dad?" she exclaimed. "What are you two doing here?" Every Saturday morning, her dad jumped on a conference call with his partners. And her mom usually left her weekly work behind to focus on writing her next book.

Her mom laughed and gave Hadley a hug. "We decided to take a morning off and enjoy the festival."

"We don't work *all* the time," her dad said, a little defensively, as he hugged her too.

"Plus we wanted to see what you have going on here," her mom said. "Your grandmother is so excited that her doctor gave her the okay to sit with you today."

"I brought that nice cushioned outdoor chair for her to sit in," her dad said. "It's in my car."

Her parents walked over to the dog play area and examined the crew.

"Where did all these dogs come from?" her mom asked. "Oh, look at the darling little bulldog, Stephen." She'd noticed Bubba, the brindle bulldog that Nick had rescued, who was snorting and wheezing a little but not too bad. "He's so cute!"

Her dad moved to her mom's side, sliding his hand sweetly around her back as they bent to pet Bubba, who sat stoically with his wise old expression and proud jaw. "He's a cute little guy, isn't he?" Before Hadley could even put in a pitch, her mom said, "Maybe we should adopt one."

Who were these people, and what had someone done with her workaholic parents who'd said a million times they were too busy for a pet?

"You're not giving Bowie away, are you?" her mom asked as he nudged his way to the side.

"Nah." Hadley waved her hand. "He's just hanging out with his buds."

Next they inspected Hadley's table. Her dad looked over the pamphlets. "Nice job on these."

"My goodness, you've done a lot in a short time here." Her mom's words struck Hadley. Her parents understood the value of hard work. Maybe they could come to see that running Pooch Palace required a lot of it.

Her dad patted his pockets. "I keep forgetting, I left my phone at home."

"You left your *phone* at home?" Hadley asked incredulously.

Her mom nodded. "We've started something called phoneless mornings." *Phoneless mornings?* "Let's go get one of those giant elephant ears with sugar on top." She turned to Hadley. "Can we bring you one?"

"I'm holding out for the sausage hoagie myself. Have fun, you two kids."

As she watched them wander off hand in hand, stopping at various booths on the way, she felt like she was in an alternate reality, where her parents actually took time off to do normal things.

A deep voice from behind her interrupted her thoughts. "You must be Hadley."

She turned to see a good-looking, tall, blond guy in dark blue scrubs that perfectly matched his eyes.

"I'm Fuller Mason." He glanced down apologetically at his scrubs. "I'm afraid I'm not dressed for the festival but I just finished my office hours and I wanted to meet you." He pointed down Main Street in the direction of the vet practice.

"Are you the new vet?" Hadley asked, offering a hand. "I'm Hadley Wells."

"Great to meet you." Fuller took her hand with a strong, firm grip. His eyes really did match his scrubs. Very nice.

Out of the corner of her eye, she saw movement. A quick glance showed Cam walking by. More like *stalking* by, full-out staring at her and Fuller with a big, growly frown. She ignored him. She was not going to allow him to ruin the first time she'd spoken to a cute guy since...since her breakup disaster.

"I heard you were taking in strays." Fuller crossed his arms and looked over the dogs. "Seashell Harbor could really use a dog rescue."

"I'm just helping my grandmother for the summer while she recovers from surgery," Hadley said hurriedly. She didn't want him to think she was full speed ahead on the dog rescue. "But to be honest, I'm wondering about the possibilities."

"I'd love to talk to you about the possibilities," he said, flashing her a smile that made her wonder if he was flirting with her. "I think you may have inadvertently started something important for the community, and there might be ways to find you veterinary help."

"Vet help?"

He nodded eagerly. "I'm a part-time clinical professor at the vet school at Rutgers. Our residents need the experience doing spays and neuters, and if they came down here to do them, it would be part of their training. Basically, a free service. Or very cheap. Maybe even covered by grant money."

"Is that right?" That got her head spinning. So did Cam, who was making yet another pass. This time he waved. And she ignored him *again*.

"Anyway, I'd love to drop back later and talk some more."

"Oh, that would be great." She was excited to *hear* more. *Vet help*, *grants*, *important service for the community*. All affirming words. "Thanks."

"Maybe you can even take a break." He held out his hand again. Which she took—but he didn't let it go. "I hear the taco truck is completely rocking it."

Now Cam was *charging* back. But this time he was stopped by a bunch of teenage fans.

"It's great to meet a fellow dog lover who's also a humanitarian." His hand lingered even longer in hers as he broke into a nice smile. "And who's very attractive too."

"Oh, thanks." She smiled back and dropped her hand. "You do know I've just had a massively public breakup, right?"

He shrugged. "I don't pay much attention to Hollywood rags." He looked her over with concern. "You doing okay?"

Just have some lingering trust issues with men. And by the way, my old high school boyfriend who kissed the bejesus out of me but then blew me off now seems to be stalking me. "It's great to be home, thanks."

"Well, seeing as I'm new to Seashell Harbor, I could sure use a tour guide to show me important things, like where to get a real burger sometime."

"I'd be happy to help you with that." She would have felt a tingle, she just knew it, if only Cam didn't look like he was about to bust through his line of admirers and block his way downfield to tackle Fuller.

Fuller left and Hadley turned back to setting up pamphlets. Flirting with someone had been...fun. Someone she had no baggage with. Someone who hadn't kissed her like the world was ending and then snuck away. Someone who was *not* Cam.

Chapter 15

OKAY, WHO WAS that guy holding Hadley's hand for a half hour? Cam had just set up his booth and had been walking over to see for himself when he'd gotten waylaid by autograph seekers.

When he'd finally signed every slip of paper, jersey, and cup lid in sight, the guy was gone. So he walked straight over to the freshly squeezed lemonade truck and bought two giant-sized drinks. He knew he shouldn't, but he couldn't help himself.

He found Hadley stacking pamphlets and talking to a handful of motley dogs all hanging out together in a plastic doggie playpen. "Well hello," Hadley said as she stroked Jagger's neck. "You are one dapper dog." In response, Jagger's tail twirled in delight. "Actually, you *all* look amazing. Today might be the day!"

"Hey," Cam interrupted. She looked fresh and pretty in a flowered sundress, and she smelled incredible. He held out the lemonade.

"Oh, hi," she said, a little warily, but didn't take the drink.

"Here, I—" He nudged it toward her again. "Please take it."

Nothing he could say would make up for lying about that kiss or blowing her off. Or make the strong ache in his chest go away.

It didn't seem right to say *Good luck today* or *May the best person win*. After all, that's why they were here today—to gather allies.

Instead he found himself fisting his hands, trying his best to keep from touching her. Even as he wondered if she even cared that he'd blown her off.

"Thanks," she said, finally deciding to take his paltry peace offering.

"Hey, Jagger. What's up, buddy?" He knew talking to the dog instead of facing her was a cowardly move. "You look…terrific." He scratched the dog behind the ears. "He cleans up well," he said, straightening out. "And he's filled out some too. So today's the day, huh?"

"Maybe some of them will get forever homes." She tipped her head toward the gated enclosure.

He couldn't help but grin. "Just make sure you don't accidentally adopt Bowie out too."

"That would be horrible." She did her little snort-laugh thing. "Can you imagine?"

"The repercussions of selling off your grandma's best buddy?" He laughed. "Um, *no*."

Taking a sip of lemonade, she said, "You've spent a lot of time with Jagger too. Anything I should pass along to a potential family?"

Cam's stomach turned. He'd always had difficulty letting go of things. And he had to admit he was getting accustomed to hanging out with Jagger.

"Well, he's a great dog," he said as he bent to wrestle

with him. "He's very eager to please. He loves to watch TV. Especially ESPN. And he's pretty good about not hogging the bed."

"ESPN, huh? With me it's HGTV," she mused. "He's a complete bed hog with me. And not that I'd ever admit to feeding him people food, but he does have a passion for Havarti cheese."

Cam straightened up, a grin spreading over his face. "Cheetos."

She made a face. "Ew, you eat Cheetos?"

"When I'm not training." He'd slipped for a second back into his old life. "I mean, when I *wasn't* training."

He thought he saw a flash of concern in Hadley's eyes, but then the same guy from before approached the booth, gave him a friendly nod, and started talking to Hadley. He was definitely checking Hadley out. In all fairness, who wouldn't be?

The hair on Cam's neck bristled a little. The guy had stepped right in without so much as an *excuse me*, and essentially pushed Cam right out of the conversation, something he was definitely not used to.

"I grabbed some business cards," the stranger said, handing her a few. "I think the vet students at Rutgers would welcome the opportunity to perform spays and neuters for you. Under a vet's supervision, of course. But it could be a win-win for you and the dogs and the students—and cost-effective too."

"Thanks, Fuller. I'm really excited about this." Hadley turned to Cam and gestured. "You know my old friend Tony Cammareri, don't you? Cam, this is Fuller Mason. He's the new vet in town, and he's on the faculty at Rutgers's vet school."

Old friends? Ugh. That chest ache was starting to feel like a downright heart attack.

The guy vigorously shook Cam's hand. "Great to meet you. An honor. I was just telling Hadley I think we can collaborate to help the pets who are up for adoption." He turned back to Hadley and grinned. "I'll stop by later and we'll talk more."

"Great. Thanks, Fuller." She flashed him a wide smile right back, a move that raised Cam's hackles even more.

"In fact," Fuller said, "maybe we should discuss it over dinner. What do you say?"

Smooth. Had he no shame? Because he was trying to pick Hadley up right in front of Cam. Did this man not fear for his life? Because he should, the way the adrenaline was pounding through Cam's veins. He practice-flexed his pecs just in case he had to crush someone.

"Sure, that sounds like fun," Hadley said.

It sounds like a toothache, Cam thought.

"How'd you meet him?" Cam asked after the guy had finally walked away.

"He just moved here and we struck up a conversation over the dogs."

Of course. Not very creative as a pickup vehicle either. "He's single," Cam said.

"He'd better be." She smiled sweetly. "He just asked me to dinner."

Cam frowned so strongly he felt a headache coming on. "I'm not so sure that's a good idea. He was...on the prowl."

"On the prowl?" She laughed. *Laughed.* "That sounds like something my *grandma* would say."

"*You know* what I mean." Did he really need to explain? "He was doing this thing with his eyes, like nodding his head and pretending to be interested, then sneaking a peek." He moved his brows up and down to demonstrate.

"A peek at what?" she asked.

Cam dropped his gaze to her breasts. And oh, wow, she did have lovely curves. His inner self groaned.

"Quit staring at my boobs!"

He shook his head. "I wasn't. I...I mean, I was demonstrating." Geez. How had this taken a turn?

"Well, your mind is in the gutter." She smoothed down the front of her dress. "And anyway, my dress isn't revealing at all. I could wear this to church and Gran would be pleased."

"Yeah, but you look...you look..." Apparently, lust had made him dumb.

She crossed her arms. "I look *what*?"

He was sweating. What was *wrong* with him?

She smiled. "What's gotten into you?"

"Look. I...I just want to say I never meant for us to be on opposite sides like this. And what you're doing with these dogs...it's a great idea." What else could he say? That Fuller-the-vet was too smooth and he didn't like it one bit? He had no right. "And one more thing. I hope...I hope that however this turns out, we can be friends."

Friends. What a load of baloney. He could *never* be friends with her when all he wanted to do was wrap his arms around her, pull her close, and get lost in the sweet softness of her. He swallowed hard, trying to get a grip.

"For what it's worth," she said, "I'm sorry we're

fighting. That we're enemies in this." Her gaze snagged and caught his. She looked honest and sincere, her usual MO, but there was a guardedness about her.

He'd told her that kiss hadn't mattered.

It *had* mattered. He'd felt it down to his marrow. Yet he'd pretended it hadn't meant anything. That *she* didn't mean anything.

"I could never be your enemy," he said quietly.

Their gazes locked again, and something passed between them. Something he could not define. Sadness, longing, chemistry...parts of all three.

"Listen, Hadley—"

Before he could speak, a family with two young children walked up. "Excuse me, can we ask you about this white one?" the mom asked.

Cam's stomach churned in an ominous way—he didn't know why—because Jagger could use a good family to love and cherish him. When he watched the kids petting him, he felt his heart twist. He'd grown fond of the mutt. Saying goodbye would be...awful.

"What kind of dog is that?" the mom asked.

Hadley smiled and waved to the kids, including a little guy, maybe one year old, in the dad's arms. "We believe Jagger is mostly Labradoodle," she explained. "We found him underweight and missing an eye. He's precious."

"He's awfully tall," the dad said. "He almost looks like a deer with those skinny legs."

Cam bit his lip to stop from saying something to discourage them from the dog. Jagger deserved better. "He's a great dog," he managed, suddenly needing to clear his throat.

Someone called his name from the main thoroughfare

next to the booths. A dad with two young sons. "Cam? Hey, would you do us the honor of your autograph?" At his side, the boys looked at him with that starry-eyed excitement that he'd always loved but that now ripped out his heart a little.

How long would it last? A couple more years maybe?

"Of course," Cam said, pulling out the permanent marker he kept in his pocket, ready to go.

* * *

"Cam sure looks adorable standing across the way in that red checkered apron," Gran said later that day as she sat next to Hadley, helping pass out information and giving families doggie advice.

Hadley checked her watch. "Did you say Paul is coming to get you after he finishes his shift at his booth? Because I'd say it was definitely time."

"Don't get smart with me," Gran warned. "I'm allowed to think Cam is cute no matter what you think."

Sadly, she was right. Across the way, Cam was standing in front of his booth wearing that ridiculous apron, still somehow managing to look super hot.

"What on earth is he passing out?" Gran asked, following her gaze. There was a large crowd gathered, a line snaking down the grassy main aisle of the festival clear down to where the food trucks were parked. All the volunteers in the pie booth next door, mostly senior citizens, were watching in fascination. People were holding up their phones, shooting pics of Cam, who was smiling and glad-handing and passing out something on a tray. Lucy came around the back of the booth with

more trays and handed them to Nick, who was also
helping. Even Mr. Cammareri, in his own black apron,
was passing out craft beer samples.

"We're doomed," Hadley said. "He's got his entire
family and half the town over there. And the answer to
your question is, homemade pretzel balls. Lucy baked
them and created the cheese sauce recipe. Everyone's
raving about them."

"Well, what are you waiting for?" Gran's lips turned
up in a bemused smile. "Go over there and get us
some."

"I can't. It would be like I'm selling out for pretzel
balls." Her stomach suddenly chose to rumble audibly.

Gran narrowed her eyes down over her glasses. "Are
you saying your pride won't allow you to ask Cam for a
pretzel ball?"

Hadley made a face. "Well, if you put it in those
terms, yes." She tried not to look but Cam's low, rumbly
laugh drifted across the way as he posed for photos,
shook hands, and gave away endless samples.

"Hi, Mrs. Edwards." Kit approached with Ollie in
her arms, who was busy getting blue cotton candy all
over his face and in his hair. And on Kit's shirt. "Hey,"
she said to Hadley as Ollie reached over to give her
a big blue kiss. "Why are you fanning yourself?" Her
gaze drifted across the aisle. "Oh my goodness. Never
mind, I get it."

"Kit," Hadley said, "I promise to babysit next Friday
if you go and get us a couple of Cam's pretzel balls."

"Babysitting for pretzel balls?" She took about a second to think. "Deal. I'll make Ollie ask." They headed
off in the direction of Cam's booth.

"She's a true friend," Gran said. After watching

Hadley stroke a little chihuahua mix who somehow ended up in her lap, Gran added, "I'm amazed at how many you've taken in over the past two weeks."

Hadley looked up and smiled. Because how could she not when the little dog had just fallen fast asleep.

"Mimi's daughter and her husband are taking this one," Hadley said.

"Mimi as in Mimi's Bakery?" Gran was sitting in a sturdy chair that Hadley's dad had brought for her, positioned between Hadley's booth and the dogs, her right leg stretched out on a footstool. The dogs were in reach for her to pet, and her cane was propped up nearby. She wore a wildly flowered dress and bright pink sneakers, both definite signs that she was getting back on her game.

"Yep," Hadley said proudly. "That's two dogs so far today."

"Hadley, that's wonderful." Gran patted her on the arm.

Jagger put his chin on top of the pet playpen near Hadley, just to check in. "There's a young family who might be interested in him too." She stroked his now-silky fur. "I've never met such a sweet dog. He's really chill and he gets along with everyone. Whoever gets him is going to be lucky."

Gran raised a pointed brow. "Sounds like somebody's going back to LA with you."

Hadley shook her head. "Can you imagine? He's big as a pony. Kind of looks like one too. He needs more room than I have."

Her grandmother just shrugged and looked at her with her signature *stop BS'ing* look she'd known all her life.

"Seriously, Gran. That dog? In the city?" The look

didn't soften. "Just go ahead and say whatever it is you want to say, since I know you're going to anyway."

Gran crossed her arms, another sign she was in for it. "It's obvious to me Darla's ring has given you no pause to think out of the box *in the slightest*."

Okay, she was going to look up Paul's cell and text him STAT.

"Just because I can't take Jagger back to LA doesn't mean I haven't been thinking out of the box," Hadley protested. "I have plenty of ideas about a rescue. Being downtown brings in a ton of people off the streets who stop in from shopping. And did you know some pet rescues in communities like ours offer beachgoers the opportunity to take dogs to the beach for a few hours? Isn't that cool? It gives people a chance to get to know the animals. So many creative ideas out there."

"Well, you're a very creative person." Gran patted her knee. After a considerable pause, she asked, "Have you given more thought to pursuing these ideas?"

Hadley shifted the dog on her lap. "The problem is, there's a difference between doing something that brings you joy and earning a living."

"You sound like your father," Gran said. "I love the man but he's always been a tad too practical for my tastes. No one declared you had to be miserable in your job."

"I mean, I have an important job, Gran. It pays a lot of money. It's very stressful."

"Do you enjoy it?"

"Yes?"

"Yes with a question mark?" Gran made a noise that sounded a lot like a raspberry. "What on earth does *that* mean?"

"I mean, it's work, Grandma." Hadley almost never called Gran that, except when she was irritated. "Work is about financial stability and achieving something and hopefully making the world a better place. Happiness in work is a luxury few people really achieve."

"You're absolutely right. However, I prefer to believe work is the way we lovingly contribute to the world. And what we do joyfully, we do well. But I certainly would never put pressure on you to change your life. It's yours to decide how to spend." Her grandmother wasn't going to make this easy. "You sound like you've decided what you want."

"Not really. I've sort of been waiting for you to tell me what it is *you* really want when you're feeling well and not pressured about doing what other people think you should."

Her grandma beamed. "I know you want the best for me." Her eyes were actually misting over. "Because you're not rushing me to decide."

"Gran, are you crying?"

She dabbed at her eyes with a tissue. "When you get older, people want to take responsibility away from you because they think that's what's best. I can't tell you how wonderful it feels to have someone treat me like an adult."

"I just know how much you love the dogs."

"You love them, too, don't you?"

"Yes," Hadley said. "Of course."

"Well, I hope you understand when I tell you that as much as I love them, I'm ready to start a new chapter in my life that's about more than just working."

Wait. What? "Gran, are you...have you decided to retire?"

Her grandmother sighed. "This little fall of mine was a bit of a wake-up call. It made me think about the things I want to do that I've never done. Like travel. Sleep in. Binge-watch TV shows. Sit out in my garden at noon and watch the sun sparkle on the water. Spend time with my great-grandchildren."

"You don't have great-grandchildren."

"Well, I might one day. You never know." She reached over for Hadley's hand. "I want you to know I appreciate everything you've done to help me. But now you've got to decide where *your* heart is. Because *I've* got to decide what to do with my business."

Now *Hadley's* vision was blurring. "I understand." At least, she was trying to. She couldn't quite wrap her head around her grandmother not being inside Pooch Palace, with the dogs. With *her*.

"I want you to think on what you've started here and about what your next steps would be. I just hate the thought of you and Cam fighting. I was sort of hoping you two would find one another again."

"Well, we're *trying* to be friendly. But Cam's not interested in a relationship. I mean, I'm not interested either," she rushed to add. "It's probably not a good idea to try and relive the past. Especially after our history."

"You both needed to grow up and see the world. So you did. And miraculously, you've both ended up in the same place again. Now you have an opportunity to get to know each other again. That's not reliving the past. It's getting to know each other as adults." She seemed to think carefully before adding, "I just want you to be happy, whether you decide to go back to California or stay. I want you to live without regrets, whatever that means for you."

Hadley had never been more confused. She'd worked

so hard to achieve success. She'd made so many sacrifices—of time, of hard work, of pouring her entire self into achieving success.

That's what it had taken to rise to the top of her field.

To slow down her life and relocate to start a nonprofit from scratch seemed incredibly risky, even foolhardy.

That's what her brain said. But her heart…

Her grandmother rose slowly and carefully and stretched. "I think I'll go try some ice cream." She glanced across the grassy aisle to where Paul was passing out treats. "While you sit here and stare at Tony."

"Gran!"

"Yes?"

"That's unfair. I'm not staring at him. I'm just…hungry. For…um…pretzel balls." *Right.*

"Oh, okay. But just to let you know, he's been staring at you, too, when you're not looking."

Kit returned, Ollie in one arm, a plate of pretzel balls in the other. "Here you go, everybody." She held the plate out so everyone could take one. "I'm going to have such a great night out next week. This was totally worth it."

"Ha-ha," Hadley said.

"This is excellent," Gran said.

"Mommy, I want one." Ollie reached out his hand.

"I think you've had enough junk food for today, Oliver Wendell."

"Please." He clapped his little hands together. "Just a teeny one. Okay, Mommy?"

"Just *one*," Kit said.

They all ate while silently watching Cam commandeer the crowd. He shook hands. He autographed old programs, baseball caps, and even a football.

"If he signs that woman's boobs, I'm leaving," Mayellen said as she joined them.

Kit's eyes went wide. "Do women ask him to do that?"

"I'm sure they do." Hadley tried to look away. She recognized the woman in question as someone from high school, Mabel Martin, who'd always had a crush on Cam. Hadley hadn't seen her since shortly after Hadley's breakup with Cam. Mabel had wasted no time telling her that she and Cam had slept together. The memory still made Hadley wince.

Just then, Cam looked over and waved. They all waved back. Except Hadley, who was still a little stunned.

"I knew he was too classy to sign those boobs," Mayellen said. "He's still our Cam."

"He's drawing a crowd and they all love him," Gran said.

"But didn't you say you found homes for two dogs?" Kit asked. "You're doing well too."

"It's not enough," Hadley said. "Can't we give something away for free?"

"Like a dog?" Kit asked. "You're already doing that."

"I want a dog." Ollie put his hands on Kit's cheeks to get her attention, getting blue cotton candy all over her face. "Please, Mommy! Get us a doggie."

"Rex is our doggie. We don't need two." She grabbed the plate from Hadley. "Have another pretzel ball."

"Nice," Hadley said, catching Kit's eye.

Cam's dad walked up with a ginormous platter of pretzel balls. "Hello, ladies," he said, handing the platter to Mayellen. "Compliments of our chef, Lucy."

"More pretzel balls *and* a babysitter," Kit said, scoring one. "Thanks, Mr. C."

"Maddy, you're looking amazing," Mr. Cammareri

said. He smiled at Hadley. "How are you doing, sweetheart? I heard you're finding homes for those dogs."

"Two so far today," she said. She used to be a fixture around the Cammareri house, and she'd always thought the world of Cam's dad.

"I just wanted to say hi. And to tell you that my son is strong-willed because of our Italian heritage. But underneath that he's soft as a baby's bottom."

Hadley laughed. Mostly at what Cam would have thought if he'd heard that.

"You should have one, May." He flashed a smile that looked almost as charming as his son's.

"It's not good for my figure." She waved her hand dismissively. "I'm always trying to lose five pounds."

"Oh," he deadpanned. "I was just going to say I thought you needed to gain five pounds."

Mayellen laughed and waved him off. "Bless your heart."

"I better get back. Nice to see you, honey," he said to Hadley. He gave a nod in Mayellen's direction. "May, wonderful to see you too."

"Thanks for the pretzel balls, Mr. C," Hadley said as he waved and made his way back across the aisle. Hmm. Interesting. "Mayellen, is there anything going on between you and—"

"Hush, not a thing," she said hurriedly, suddenly very interested in selecting a pretzel ball.

"You're blushing," Gran said pointedly.

"I am *not*," she said adamantly. "It's just the heat." Suddenly she pointed across the way. "Will you take a look at that."

Sure enough, there was Cam, chatting up Mayor Chaudhry, surrounded by all six members of the town council, all of whom were eating pretzel balls and drinking craft beer.

Frustration rolled through Hadley. They'd agreed to play fair. But this…

The mayor would campaign hard for something like a restaurant that brought a lot of business downtown, hands down. Plus Gran had said the mayor, while polite, might still be a little miffed about Gran almost losing her dog.

She had to do something.

"That does it," Hadley said. "I'm going over there."

Chapter 16

CAM WAS HANDING out craft beer samples and postcards to what seemed like half the town. A line of people snaked before him far down the grassy main aisle of the festival, almost to the big fountain in the park. And he couldn't pour fast enough. "It's a local IPA," he said as he lined sample cups up on the table in front of him. "It's got a hint of citrus, so it's really refreshing, and it's light and crisp. What do you think?" He kept working the crowd, saying hi to everyone he knew and posing for about a thousand selfies.

He had to admit, it was kind of fun. The low profile he'd kept since his injury had kept him away from what he loved best...talking with people. *His* people, neighbors and friends, all of whom had the same town pride that he did.

"My restaurant is going to serve great beer *and* great food," he said to the council members. "It's going to bring a ton of people downtown."

"I'm excited for the possibilities," the mayor said. "Now we just have to get Maddy on board."

"Why do I have the feeling that getting Maddy on

board means getting *Hadley* on board?" Nick, who'd been helping him out, asked in a low voice.

"Right." Cam hoped his tone didn't indicate how impossible that seemed. He'd stepped back to try to let Hadley and her grandma work this out. He wasn't one to pressure, even if he *had* just signed a contract with the restaurant executives for the branding and naming of the restaurant chain. Now his butt was really on the line.

His phone vibrated in his pocket. It was Ian. "Hey, Cam. I'm just calling to give you a heads-up. The LA execs wanted to send some reporters over to your local festival today to drum up some interest in the new venture. It would just involve taking some photos at your booth, maybe giving a general statement about the restaurant. Sound okay?"

"Sure, thanks, Ian. I'll look out for them."

"Uh-oh." Nick gestured with his head just as Cam hung up. "Here comes Hadley. And she looks like she's definitely *not* on board."

Cam looked up suddenly to see Hadley standing there. "Want one?" Cam waved his hand over the carefully lined-up beer samples, wishing she wasn't looking at him like he'd just robbed the bank. He wanted to tell her how excited everyone was about the beer and pretzels. And about his restaurant. But of course he couldn't.

It took less than a second to see that she was, indeed, royally angry. She stood there, fidgeting a little, doing this nervous thing with her hands she always did when she was mad, and frowning deeply. Yep, he was in deep trouble.

"No thanks." Her voice was whisper-low but sharp.

"I'm here to ask you to please stop glad-handing influencers."

"Influencers?" He looked around, half expecting to see young fashion icons with huge Instagram followings modeling expensive clothing. But, no, it was just everyone they knew eating and drinking and having fun. She pointed toward the mayor, who was across the aisle visiting with the pie ladies, a few members of the town council by her side. "Oh, you mean the mayor? I just handed her a beer."

"*Exactly.*" She crossed her arms. "You're schmoozing the town council."

Cam leaned in. Unfortunately, doing so gave him a whiff of her scent, summery, fresh, ocean-breezy, and it threw him. "You're forgetting your grandma holds the keys to the front door." He tried to sound firm, but inside his emotions were everywhere. He loved seeing her. He hated that they were fighting, hated more that he'd started driving along this road and couldn't find a way to exit.

And even worse, it was getting harder and harder to fight his crazy impulses. Like the one he was having right now to reach out and kiss her frown away. He used to have the power to do just that. Crack a dumb joke, say something to make her blush, and nine times out of ten she'd abandon her bad mood and laugh.

Wait. *What was he doing?* He was supposed to stay safely on the other side of this chalk line they'd drawn between them. But he kept dangling his toes over into her territory.

"Look, Hadley," he said, giving a smile and a wave to the people gathering in line behind her. "I intend to give every single person who passes by here a sip of beer and one of my sister's outstanding pretzel balls and tell them about my restaurant because my strategy is winning. You're welcome to employ your own strategy."

She planted her feet in a stance that clearly signaled he should back down *or else*. "My strategy doesn't involve political bribery."

His anger flared. Instead of backing down, he went ahead and threw gas on the fire. "Yeah, well, you were apparently entertaining the vet school over there."

She tossed him a *you idiot* look. Which he deserved. But he still couldn't help egging her on.

"That was strictly business," she snapped back. "Fuller was giving me suggestions."

"And he was holding your hand for, like, three minutes."

She gestured in frustration. "What has that got to do with anything?"

"Right. Single and holding hands and checking out your butt." He was really burying himself. "I saw him."

"I thought you said he was checking out my boobs."

"Those too."

"You couldn't possibly be upset because I was talking to a vet about spaying and neutering animals?"

"See?" He jabbed a finger into the air. "You were talking about sex."

Hadley was fired up and in his face. "At least I wasn't handing out beer samples to women who were asking you to autograph their boobs." She poked his chest. "Or to certain women that *you slept with* after we broke up."

"What are you talking about?" Had she gone mad?

"You mean *who*. Mabel Martin."

"Mabel? I never slept with her." He waved his hands in exasperation.

Hadley snorted. "She *told* me you did."

"You'll believe anybody, won't you?" he said. "You'd take any dog, and you'd take anyone at their word. Except me, apparently."

"People have to *earn* my trust," she snapped.

"Hey, you two." Nick walked over. "Take the lovers' quarrel into the bedroom." He chuckled and dropped his voice, hanging his arms over each of their shoulders. "And you might want to be careful. You never know when someone's going to press the record button on their phone, if you know what I mean."

Cam lowered his voice. "Let's face it, a nonprofit versus a restaurant...it's not the same." He held up an imaginary ball in each hand and pretended to balance them.

He was being an ass. He knew it. But he had to find a way to win his case. Now that he'd signed that contract, his reputation depended on it.

"As far as income maybe," she said firmly, crossing her arms. "But not for value." She leveled her gaze on him. "*Pets have value.* Besides, there *is* no restaurant. Not yet."

"But there will be." They were head-to-head now, the decibels increasing. A few heads were turning. But he couldn't seem to stop.

"This is about more than just profits," she said.

"Is it really?" he said with a sigh. "A restaurant would bring people downtown and then they'd stay there, fill their stomachs with some great food and then shop around. It's hard for me to see that a nonprofit would do the same things for our town."

"Success is measured by more than profit margin, Cam. We *need* an animal rescue. It fosters community.

Your restaurant will bring noise, congestion, and car traffic, not to mention parking nightmares to the middle of town, a place where everyone *walks*. I can't imagine why *any* of that would be a good thing."

"That can all be worked out." But secretly, he wondered if it could. He knew how much he needed this restaurant. He knew how much his good name depended on following through with the contract he'd signed. And he wished she would back down but it seemed she'd only gotten more conviction.

One thing he knew was certain—whoever won, it was going to make them enemies forever. Could he really stomach that? The sick feeling that simmered in the pit of his own stomach seemed to answer that question.

"I've got to get back to my booth." She sounded as miserable as he felt.

A familiar bark had them turning their heads. Across the aisle at the Pooch Palace booth, Jagger had jumped up on the plastic fencing and was staring at them from across the aisle. He was excitedly barking and pawing at the fence.

"While we're . . . discussing things"—Cam ignored the fact that a crowd had gathered from the commotion they'd created—"I want you to know that I think Jagger is a great dog. I've decided I want to give him a home." Across the way, Jagger was now jumping and barking himself into a frenzy while Hadley's grandmother and Kit tried to calm him.

"Jagger is *my* dog," Hadley said. "It's obvious that he's attached to me. *I'm* his person."

Well, that didn't go well either.

"I love him too." Cam planted his feet solidly on the ground, staring her down. Somewhere in the back of his mind, he wondered—no, he knew—that they had some-how chosen to argue over buildings and dogs instead of address more important things between them. Yet blind frustration pushed that thought away.

She threw up her hands. "Now you're arguing just to argue with me."

A panicked scream broke through their heated words and made them both turn. The pie booth next door was in an uproar, the volunteers standing up, exclaiming, chairs tipping, people scattering.

They stopped squabbling and rushed over together to help, coming to a halt in front of the booth, only to find Jagger on his hind legs inhaling a pie.

"Jagger, no!" Hadley commanded as she fought through the crowd, which had devolved into laughter. "Down, boy!" she said as they approached the booth. Jagger stood across from them, the pie table between them.

The dog, hearing his name, made eye contact and tilted his head to the side, as if considering whether or not to behave.

"There. He's going to listen," Hadley said.

But Jagger, apparently choosing to follow the advice of the little devil on his shoulder instead of the angel, promptly returned to sucking down the pie, plunging his entire face into it with gusto.

"I think he likes the coconut cream," Cam said.

"And the strawberry," Hadley said in dismay. "*And* the blackberry."

Hadley somehow managed to pull the culprit away from the crime, but not until after he'd dug into at least three pies. There was whipped cream and pie filling everywhere—on the table, the grass, *the dog*. A crowd had gathered and everyone was laughing and pointing and taking snapshots of Jagger, who had whipped cream along his snout and blueberries in his fur.

"Anthony Cammareri." A commanding older woman was shouldering her way through the crowd. "And Hadley Wells. Do you mean to tell me you two are still together?"

"Is that...?" Cam whispered.

"Mrs. Doyle." Hadley nodded. "English Lit, junior year."

"Mrs. Doyle, great to see you again," Cam said. "We'll reimburse your booth for the damage right away."

"We're so sorry," Hadley added, elbowing Cam in the ribs, which he took to mean stand up straighter and behave himself.

The elderly woman shook a finger at them. "It doesn't surprise me that you two are still causing trouble."

"Oh no," Hadley said, "I—"

Cam gently touched her elbow in a move that said, *Save your breath.* He dropped his voice and whispered in her ear, "All she probably remembers are the notes we passed in her class."

"And how we didn't pay much attention," she whispered back. "To this day I can't tell you the difference between Melville and Hawthorne."

"They're both dead." A wide smile overtook Cam's face. "Don't worry about it." He plucked a blob of whipped cream out of Hadley's hair. "All I paid attention to in that class was you."

Cam was pleased to see her blush a little at that. "We really are sorry, Mrs. Doyle," he said. "I'd love to make a donation to"—he looked around for some kind of sign that said where the pie profits were slated for—"any charity you choose."

She folded her arms. "The proceeds go toward the Christmas festival. But that won't make up for all this disruption."

"I'll double the donation," Cam said. "Triple it."

"In fact," Hadley added, "Cam was just telling me he'd like to volunteer to help put up all the decorations next winter."

"And of course, Hadley would like to help too," Cam added. Then he realized she wasn't going to be here by Christmastime. And even after all this—the arguing, the chunks of pie everywhere—he really wanted her to be.

The retired teacher's expression finally softened. "Well, all right. In that case—"

More flying whipped cream made Cam quickly turn to Jagger, who had suddenly decided to shake out his fur. "*Your* dog is a mess," Cam said, unable to stifle a grin. Jagger was kissing Hadley, getting whipped cream on her cheeks and her dress. Then he stood and shook himself again, whipped cream launching far enough to get all over Cam too.

Ben Gazera, the owner of the hardware store, walked over with a leash from the Pooch Palace booth for Hadley, who thanked him and clipped it on Jagger's collar. Then she cast Cam a look that was actually— Wait, was she holding back a smile? "You got him too excited."

"Sorry. I tend to have that effect on people." He pointedly raised a brow.

"You mean *dogs*." Hadley rolled her eyes. Then she laughed. Her snorty, ridiculous, wonderful laugh.

The joy of hearing that made him throw back his own head and laugh.

He'd just caught her eye when something flashed—a camera light.

"Hey, are you two a couple?" someone asked over the whirring of more cameras.

"Hey, Cam, how do you two know each other?" another voice shouted. "Were you high school sweethearts?"

Cam squinted and shielded his eyes. They'd somehow become surrounded by a sea of paparazzi.

Suddenly a video camera appeared, inches from Hadley's face. "Hey, Hadley. Who's sexier, Cam or Cooper?"

"Me, of course," Cam interjected. He tried to guide Hadley away but they were pretty much enveloped, the cameras zooming in.

"C'mon, you two, give us a big smile."

Cam managed to take a firm hold of Hadley's elbow. "Okay, ladies and gents, you got some pics. Now let us go, okay?"

"Are you two dating?"

"Just friends," Hadley answered, putting her head down as they struggled to move through the sea of reporters.

"Hadley. What's your reaction to the news about Cooper and Maeve?"

Hadley's head jerked up. "What news?"

"They're baiting you," Cam whispered as he steered her and Jagger through the crowd.

Hadley gripped him tightly and tipped her head in the direction of Pooch Palace, which was just across the park from where they stood. Cam gave a nod, signaling they should go for it. As Cam pressed onward for the last hundred feet, he wondered how much the

photographers had captured. He knew the answer—
enough for the scoop of him and Hadley as a couple
to spread all over the world just as fast as the footage
could be downloaded.

The sanctuary of the Palace was fifty feet away
when a photographer elbowed forward to volley a final
question. "Hey, Hadley," the reporter persisted, "how
do you feel about Maeve being pregnant?"

Hadley stopped dead in her tracks, her body stiffening.
Cam turned to see shock spread over her face. He tightened his grip on her but nothing seemed to register.

He saw everything in that one expression.

The devastation. The *hurt*.

It hit him like a gut punch. Because for her to look
like that, she had to have *loved* the bastard.

"Enough questions." He tugged on her arm. Finally
she was moving again. If only he could throw a few
blocks to open a hole, he could get them safe.

Hadley surprised him by turning to face the cameras.
"I'm thrilled for them," she said with a wave and a
smile. No one would notice, but he could tell her voice
was stiff and unnatural. "I wish them the best."

"Are you sad it's not you?"

"Aren't you still heartbroken?"

"How does it feel to know that the woman he left
you for is pregnant with his child?"

As fury raged inside him, Cam stepped between
Hadley and the cameras. She might just kill him later
but he didn't care. "Hey, folks." He waited for silence
to descend as everyone focused their attention on him.
"We're happy for Cooper and Maeve. But that's old
news." He stopped talking until everyone quieted down.
"I have another scoop."

The commotion suddenly dialed down to complete silence as Cam faced more cameras than he had since his injury.

"I'm getting a new dog," he deadpanned.

The crowd of reporters chuckled because Cam was...being Cam.

"Or, I should say...*we* are. Meet our dog, Jagger." He took Hadley's hand and smiled. She was frowning a little, but also looked a little confused. Later she'd probably have his hide for using words like *us* and *our dog*. But for now, he was desperate to distract the wolves from preying on her. "That's way more interesting, in my opinion," he continued. To help him out, Jagger sat down at his feet and began licking blueberry filling off his paws, which drew a few chuckles. He just hoped that Jagger's licking would stay socially acceptable while he was in front of the cameras. "Plus, no one's asked me how I like being home. Or the secret recipes for my new restaurant. Geez, you folks are really losing your touch."

"How *are* you doing, Cam?" someone asked.

"Great, thanks." He snuck a sideways glance at Hadley, who looked a little less thrown. If he could just keep the attention off her until they could reach the Palace, his job would be done. "There've been a lot of changes in my life since football ended."

"Is Hadley one of them?"

He gave a little laugh for the benefit of the cameras. But the irony wasn't lost on him. Hadley had crashed into his life like a giant ocean wave, throwing him sideways. But now *she* needed *him*. And he was going to do everything he could to help her.

So he kept steering them toward Pooch Palace.

"How about an exclusive interview?" someone said. He looked over to see a couple of reporters he recognized from a national network—probably the ones Ian had told him would be here. "We've been waiting months to sit down with you."

"Call me later," he said, forcing a smile. Oh no. Why had he said that? How could he not? It was the ultimate distraction from Hadley.

"Wait," said a local reporter who'd pushed his way forward to stand next to the big guns. Cam had to admire his chutzpah. "If you're going to do an interview, how about letting us do it, Cam?"

They'd finally reached the Palace, and Hadley had pulled out a key. He turned to the swarm of photographers around him. "Yes, I'll do an interview," he said, even as a chilly sense of dread crept into his veins. He hadn't wanted to talk to the press yet. He didn't want to leave any room for people to pity him. To call him *poor Cam*. Yet he'd just steered himself right into that hole.

"That's it for today, folks." He waved cheerily at the crowd. "This guy needs a bath. Don't forget to grab some homemade elephant ears and enjoy the festival."

Once they and the dog were inside, Cam locked the door and drew the shades. The faint and very familiar smell of new construction materials reminded him that Pooch Palace's ceiling was now intact after the leaky roof that seemed so long ago. Leaning against the locked door, he took a second to process what had just happened.

"Are you okay?" Hadley asked.

He turned in surprise. "After all that, you're asking *me*?"

He walked over and took hold of her arms. Which might have been a mistake because her skin was smooth and soft under his calloused hands. But he focused on the fact that she was shaking. "How could you be worried about me at a time like this?" Jagger, not worried in the least, walked over to his bed and plopped down, getting blueberry filling all over.

"You did everything to get their attention off of me," Hadley said. "Including promise them an interview. You put yourself on the line for me."

He would've promised the reporters a trip to the moon on the rocket ship of their choice if he'd had to. *Anything* for her.

That thought startled him. Because he knew in his heart it was a hundred percent true.

"Those reporters were here because of me. I had no idea they would use me to come after you."

"No," she said firmly. "They capitalized on the moment. The scoop about...the baby. It's all right." *Was* it all right? He tried to read her face for a sign.

"You...implied we were together."

He rubbed his neck. "Yeah, about that. I...hope that was okay. I was trying to give them other info besides your reaction to...to—"

"To the *baby*. It's okay to say it." Her arms were wrapped tightly around herself, but her gaze was level and clear, her wide brown eyes melting him on the inside.

"Let me get you some water," he said, dropping his hands because they were starting to shake too.

"I'm not helpless," she said. "Just a little thrown. I can get the water."

He held her back gently. "Just sit down for a minute. I'll be right back."

"Okay, fine." He was already halfway to the back when she called out, "Will you please bring Jagger some too?"

In the back room, Cam grabbed a few ice-cold drinks from an old fridge, including a bowl of water for the dog, who surely must be thirsty after consuming all that pie. He found himself pressing his forehead against the closed refrigerator door and taking a couple of deep breaths.

Anger flowed through him but he inhaled again, trying to get it together for her sake.

But one question kept ringing through his mind, nagging at him. *Did she still love Cooper?*

No, no, he told himself. *Wrong question. That didn't matter. Just stay calm and be a friend to her.*

But it *did* matter. That skunk Cooper. How much more could he hurt her? He wanted to hang him up by the balls. And that was the censored version. But there was something he wanted even more.

To know what she was thinking. He wanted her to say something. Something like, *I don't care what Cooper does. I don't love him anymore.*

That's what he wanted. For Cooper not to matter.

There was no denying it.

Then it suddenly dawned on him that what he was feeling wasn't anger at all. It was identical to what he'd felt when the new vet—Fuller-What's-His-Name—had gone over to Hadley's booth and flirted with her, which now seemed about a hundred years ago.

No, Cam wasn't angry at all. He was *jealous*. And that was a whole lot worse.

Chapter 17

IT WAS THE baby that got her. Not the images Hadley couldn't stop from passing through her mind of Cooper with Maeve, holding their future sweet infant. Not the way she imagined Cooper would look at Maeve and beam, a look of pure love.

Nope. It was *the baby*. *That's* what punched her in the gut. Her longing for a loving partner and the chaotic, wonderful mess of children and dogs filling up a household and making it a home. Something she feared she would never have.

She was fine, really she was. As she sat and drank the ice-cold Diet Coke Cam had scrounged up from the back of the fridge, she watched him prepare to give Jagger a bath, which strangely helped her get her mind off of everything else.

Cam, who'd stepped up to protect her—even though she could handle herself. Who hadn't hesitated to insert himself between her and the paparazzi. Who'd promised them the interview she knew he didn't want to give. She'd seen his face—it had been full of dread.

"Sorry for the bath, buddy," Cam said as he started to

spray Jagger down. His strong arms scrubbed, bubbles flying, the scent of dog shampoo filling the air. Except Jagger hated every minute and used every opportunity to shake himself out—which meant Cam was full of blueberry stains, whipped cream, and dog suds. Then the dog wriggled out of Cam's grasp and began to run furiously around the room in circles, his tail tucked between his legs.

She couldn't help laughing. It almost made her forget how mad she was at Cam for glad-handing the entire town, including the mayor.

"Okay, Ms. Wise Guy," he said, big arms folded and dripping with suds. "See if you can do any better."

"Come here, Jaggy," she said. As the dog whizzed by, she grabbed him by the collar and half led, half dragged him back to the dog bath.

Cam followed her over. "You're going to need help." He stood next to her as she kicked off her flip-flops and grabbed the handheld faucet. "I'll be right here if you need me."

"I got this." She eyed him. "Are you forgetting I'm an expert? All those summers I worked here, remember?"

Cam swept his arm in deference. "Please. Be my guest."

"Now, Jaggy," Hadley crooned, "I'm just going to rub you down with soap and warm water. Who wouldn't like that?"

Cam mumbled something. She thought it was, "Yeah, who wouldn't like that?" but she wasn't completely sure.

The dog reached out and licked her.

"There," she said, laughing a little. "See? He's calming down." She hosed the dog down with warm water, talking to him in a reassuring voice the whole time.

Then she poured another round of shampoo on him and scrubbed.

"You're essentially giving him a massage," Cam said from behind her. She turned and caught his gaze, which contained that spark of heat she recognized all too well.

"Almost finished." Hadley focused on rubbing behind Jagger's ears. She grabbed the faucet head and rinsed through his fur. "Well, look at that. You're not blue anymore. Isn't that great? You'll be white and fluffy again in no time."

"I wouldn't exactly call him fluffy," Cam said. He was leaning against the wall, watching her work.

"Shhh," she said as she continued to rinse Jagger's fur. "You'll make him feel bad; then he'll shake himself all over."

"Okay, Jag, you're very handsome," Cam said. "And...clean."

Hadley laughed. "As soon as I turn the water off, you throw the towel over him."

"Yes, ma'am," Cam said, catching the clean towel that Hadley tossed, then sneaking up on Jagger with it. "Hope you still love me." Cam toweled the dog off before finally giving him his freedom. Which Jagger took, but not after he shook all the extra water in his fur out on Cam. Then he did more laps around the room, excited and a little flummoxed after his big day of adventure. He finished the show by guzzling from his bowl in what seemed like an endless draught.

"All that sugar," she said, shaking her head, "makes a naughty dog very thirsty." Jagger looked up at her, water dribbling from his chin, looking like a guilty toddler, too cute to be angry with.

"We can work together when we want to," Cam said as he used the towel to wipe up the floor around the dog bath.

She nodded. He was so close, she could smell his soap. Dial, if she wasn't mistaken. And shaving cream. He smelled ridiculously good. From this close up, she could see the coarse, heavy grain of his beard. She had to stop herself from reaching out and running her hand along its rough surface.

He was a handsome man. A *good* man. One who'd offered himself to the paparazzi on her account.

She smiled. "Yes." Her mind was whirling.

"I mean, we handled everyone out there," he said. The way he was looking at her was unnerving. "We stood together."

She swallowed. He had such nice lips. She tore her gaze from them.

He'd done something unselfish for her. He'd thrown himself into the line of fire. That didn't change the fact that they were on opposite sides of...of everything. Although at that moment, she was having difficulty remembering what *everything* was.

"Thank you for what you did," she blurted. "It was unselfish. And...and kind."

He reached out and put his hands on her arms again, a move maybe meant to calm her but instead made her pulse shoot through the roof. "I'd do anything for you, Had."

He'd called her *Had*, something that had always gotten to her.

"I know how much you hate giving interviews," she said.

"It's no big deal," he said, shrugging.

"No, it *is* a big deal." Could her friends have been right? That Cam was struggling with feeling like a failure and looking for a replacement for football? That would certainly explain why he hadn't wanted to talk to the press. And why he was fighting so hard for his restaurant.

"Don't worry about it."

"You're the most successful, driven person I know," she said, trying to put everything she was feeling into words. "And... I appreciate the sacrifice."

He leveled his gaze on her, his eyes deep blue and full of a concern that was melting through the ice around her heart. The ice that protected her from *him*. "I meant what I said. Building or no building, I'd do anything for you. And I want you to know you can trust me to listen," he added. "You can tell me anything."

"As a friend?" She bit her lip. *Why* did that fall out of her mouth? Stupid, stupid her, setting herself up for more pain.

"I'll always be your friend," he said. "I'll always want to protect you from harm. I hate that you have to go through this in public. I'm angry *for* you."

Yes, a friend, but... did he want more? Because she did. She couldn't deny it any longer.

She was way too aware of him, his strong, lean body, the grip on her arms sure and comforting. In that moment, she realized she *did* trust him. And that scared her more than anything. She glanced from his hands to his eyes.

He was still holding on to her, still staring at her. "Listen," he said. "I'm sorry about what I said at the festival about a rescue somehow being less beneficial for the town than a restaurant. Your idea about a pet rescue…it's a good one. A brilliant one, in fact. I keep trying to put distance between us but I…I just can't. I'm sorry I resorted to that. It was a cheap shot."

"I'm sorry too. I hate that we're fighting."

"And just to clear this up once and for all, I never slept with Mabel."

"I believe you," Hadley said. "But back then, I believed *her*. It was awful to think you did that right after we broke up."

"I would never do that to you." He paused. "But then, you couldn't have known that. Because I left. That was just another way I hurt you."

"You couldn't have known. I'm just…I'm just glad I know the truth now." She grinned suddenly. "It's just one more reason why I can't think of you as a jerk."

"I'm not a jerk, Hadley."

She looked at his full lips and every part of her wanted to kiss him, and not just because he'd taken a bullet for her.

But this stupid building was everything between them. It made anything else between them impossible.

She realized she was holding on to him, too, her hands gripping his upper arms.

Cam glanced over at the shaded windows. "There's probably still a huge crowd out there. I'm afraid we're stuck here for a while."

Except the place where he was holding her arms was tingly and warm, and that sensation was spreading rampantly through her, like bunches of fireworks exploding in little bursts, one at a time.

Right. Not good. Cam's gaze dropped to their hands. As if he suddenly realized he was still holding her, he pulled back.

Oh. He was just being comforting. Trying to help. He wasn't really holding her in *that* way.

"Cam, listen," she said. "There's something I need to tell you. My grandmother told me she wants to retire, and I think she means it. She told me to think about what I really wanted as far as starting a rescue. I've been spending a lot of time thinking about how it could work, how I could transform this place."

He nodded carefully. "I've signed a contract with the restaurant people. My name's on the line as far as seeing this through. They believe this is the ideal location. I have to admit I do too. There's no other like this on the market."

Yearning, sadness, confusion all flooded her. But sadness won. "Then we're still on opposite sides."

The only sound was Jagger's steady breathing as he slept off his sugar coma. Her heart felt strangely heavy and achy. She wondered if things would be different if they didn't have this massive barrier—in the form of a century-old building—between them.

"You told them Jagger was our dog," she said as they sat side by side on a bench under the windows.

"Well, for now he is," Cam said, maintaining a healthy distance. "That okay?"

She nodded. "Sure. Okay."

"Friends can share a dog," he said.

"Friends," she said, nodding a little. Lying. Because her pulse was pounding and her body was telling her they would *never* be *just friends*.

He was simply being nice because of what had happened. A *nice friend*.

She felt a stab in her chest. A warning to not let his kindness melt her heart. To keep on disliking him and being angry with him and...

Hadley's phone buzzed with a text from Darla:

WAVING RED FLAG! GRANDMA ON HER WAY!

There was a rap on the door. Cam, still in warrior mode, quickly walked over to see who it was.

"The press again?" she asked hopefully. She must be panicked if she'd take those salivating vultures over her determined grandmother any day. She and Cam had made a scene, and Gran wouldn't be happy about that. And now the reporters thought they were a *couple*. Hadley could only imagine what people were saying about that.

"It's Paul," he said. "And your grandma." He turned and grinned, making her heart free-fall again despite herself. "And she looks like she's on a mission."

* * *

As Cam opened the door, he was brimming over with frustration.

Had he really just told Hadley that baloney about being *friends*?

He'd panicked because…because of Cooper. Because of the heartbroken look on her face when she found out Maeve was pregnant.

And then the building, always the building. Standing between them, preventing them from talking about other things.

Important things.

In the doorway, Paul was standing behind Maddy's wheelchair, an apologetic expression on his face.

"Thanks, Paul," Maddy called cheerfully over her

shoulder as she muscled her way over the threshold, surprisingly adept. "I can take it from here."

Cam caught Paul's eye. The older man shrugged and lowered his voice, patting Cam on the back in sympathy. "I couldn't stop her. She's on a mission. And she wanted to walk all the way over here but I insisted on taking the chair."

Cam walked over to where Hadley now sat on Bowie's favorite window seat and dropped down beside her. Whatever Maddy was about to say, Cam couldn't work up much worry over it. He had something else on his mind entirely. And it wasn't *friendship*.

"I'm so glad you two are getting along," she said, looking them both over. "I heard the reporters saying you two are a couple."

"We're not a couple," they both said in unison.

"Okay. But you also created quite a scene at the festival. Mrs. Doyle hasn't stopped talking about it. Neither has anyone else. They're all taking sides."

"Taking sides?" Hadley asked.

"Yes. Some are saying a restaurant is just what Seashell Harbor needs. And others are wanting a pet rescue. You've created quite a stir." They'd been so into their argument, he hadn't really noticed much of anything else.

"We can explain," Hadley rushed to say.

Cam chimed in. "Things got a little out of hand but..."

"But *nothing*," Gran said adamantly. "The trouble is, you were both working to prove your point to the other instead of working *at* your point. Do you get what I'm saying? Now the pie ladies are angry and everyone is all worked up. I'm afraid you've made your story more about each other than the good of our town."

"I can have my team issue a statement," Cam offered.

Gran shot him a look, but Hadley sent him a little smile, like she knew exactly what he was thinking. Her grandmother was not someone to be messed with. Or brushed aside by his *team*.

The last time he'd seen Maddy so fired up was long ago. He and Hadley had gone out one night when she was spending the weekend with her grandma. They'd fallen asleep on the beach and returned to the house at 4:00 a.m. to find her grandmother was waiting up, frantically pacing, the police chief sitting in her easy chair. She'd hugged and kissed Hadley when she'd finally walked in safe but she'd made her mop the Palace floors for the next month. And made Cam scoop poop. And she'd given both of them lectures on responsibility and being in love and using birth control and he'd almost died of embarrassment.

"You can't wave a magic wand over this and make it go away, Cam," Maddy said. "There was misbehavior. Bickering. *Runaway dogs*." She tossed a glare over at Jagger, whose good ear drooped as he became aware that he, too, was on her Z list. Finally, she threw up her hands. "You two became the story, not your dog rescue, Hadley. Or your restaurant, Cam."

That made him feel awful. Leave it to Grandma to bring him, a six-foot-four former tight end, to his knees.

"I think you may both want to do some damage control after the little stir you caused."

"We'll tone it down," Hadley said, looking at him. Her expression was somber but she had a little glint in her eyes. Not mischievous, exactly, but something that showed him she saw a little bit of humor in this. He couldn't help smiling a little, despite everything.

Cam cleared his throat and sat up. "Maddy, we'll do what we can to show everyone we're serious about helping."

"Yes. Good," Gran said. "And I have just the thing to help you do that. I have a responsibility I need to hand over because I'm laid up, and I've decided that I'm giving it to you two." She put on her bifocals and pulled out a letter from a little red crocheted pouch hanging on the side of her wheelchair. "*Both* of you. *Together.* And it means forgetting about repurposing this building for right now."

Gran didn't wait for protests as she read the heading on the paper. "The Annual Seashell Harbor Medical Services Benefit. Margie Goldman took my place as chair after my accident but her daughter had her twins early and she's already flown to San Francisco to help her. So, I'm putting you two in charge."

Cam stifled a groan.

"Wait a minute," Hadley said. "That's just two weeks away." The big themed outdoor party took place the third weekend in July and was the town's largest fundraiser.

"Correct," Gran said. "And if a world-class PR expert and a world-famous ex-football player can't pull this off, no one can. The goal is to bring in gobs of money to build the new regional pediatric outpatient center, so kids don't have to drive an hour and a half with their frazzled parents to see specialists at the children's hospital. Most everything's been done, thanks to Margie. You just have to make sure it goes off without a hitch. This will show everyone you both truly have the best interests of Seashell Harbor in mind. And then the town can decide which idea they're most inclined toward."

One glance at Hadley showed that she looked about as happy as he did.

He did *not* want to spend more time with her. Work with her. Be in the same room with her. Just when he needed to focus on sealing the deal. He couldn't allow his unruly feelings to ruin his opportunity to build a future here.

Chapter 18

WHERE THE HECK are those keys?" Nick asked a few days later as he groped around the dashboard of the Cammareri van, patted his pants pockets, and felt above the visor, all to no avail.

Cam reached into the cup holder, grabbed the keys his brother had clearly overlooked, and dangled them in front of his face.

"I knew that," Nick said, snatching the keys and starting the truck. But finding the keys didn't lift his mood. He kept smoothing down his hair and tapping his fingers on the wheel. Cam understood his normally laid-back brother was definitely *not* laid-back about the thought of fixing his ex's rotted screened porch ceiling.

"So why are we doing this again?" Cam asked. "I thought your goal was to avoid Darla at all costs."

Nick sighed and fidgeted his fingers on the wheel. "She only acts like she's tough. I mean, she *is* really strong, because she got through the cancer and everything, but all that toughness is a front."

Cam held up his hands. "I was just wondering how we happened to be doing a job on her beach house when you two are barely speaking, that's all."

"I hate to break this to you, but this is what I do for a living," Nick said.

"I get that, *bruh*," Cam said. "But when was the last time you touched a house under a hundred years old?"

Busted. Nick's glance was wrought with conflict. "I ran into her at the festival and told her we were the best ones to do the job, and she agreed. That was all."

"Oh, okay," Cam said, unable to resist baiting his brother. "This has nothing to do with being curious about where she lives?"

"Of course not," Nick said. "I'm an old house person. I hate those clunky-looking contemporaries. You know that."

Yeah, Cam knew all right. Knew his brother was nervous. More nervous, in fact, than he'd seen him since his divorce. Except maybe for when Darla was going through chemo and Nick had been frantic to help in any way he could. "So you don't want to get back together with her?"

His brother stared at him like he was deranged. "No, of course not. *Never.*"

"Okay," Cam said, ready to let it rest.

But Nick, apparently, wasn't. "I'm dating someone, remember? Lauren's really nice."

Lauren *was* really nice. And smart. And cute too. Nick usually went for women who didn't have potential for real, lasting connection. But then, Nick had made it a point not to do relationships at all in the eight years he'd been divorced. "How did you ever meet a librarian?"

"I'm getting my MBA, remember?" His tone was a little edgy. "She helped me with some of the online stuff I was having trouble with."

"That's great," Cam said. "I'm glad you're dating again. Does Dad like her?"

"I haven't brought her home yet."

Cam let the subject die, but Nick had been dating this woman for four months and never brought her home to meet their father? That was...unusual.

Nick parked in Darla's driveway and they got out of the van, Nick lugging a ladder and Cam bringing a reciprocating saw to cut through any rotted wood. "She said to just walk around," Nick said, gesturing to a small path.

As they circled the sprawling contemporary, they caught sight of Darla lying out on a lounge chair on her expansive ocean-front deck. Apparently asleep, with earbuds in her ears and a book lying on the ground next to her chair.

Nick halted so fast Cam nearly ran into him with the saw. Before Cam could say *Hey, watch it*, Nick was making a beeline straight to Darla. He walked up to her chair and picked up her fallen book from the ground.

"Hey," he said quietly. Her eyes flew open and she scrambled to sit up. "Nick!" she said, rubbing her eyes.

"You always did fall asleep reading," he said, offering her the book. If Cam hadn't already realized his brother was in trouble, Nick's dopey half-smile immediately gave it away. "Hope you put sunscreen on." She was wearing a bikini top and jean shorts, and to Cam's amusement, his brother appeared to be checking-her-out-but-not-really-checking-her-out.

She laughed and cranked her sunglasses up to the top of her head. "I'm not an idiot like I used to be. I try to take care of myself now." She turned and saw Cam. "Hey, Cam."

He nodded and said hi, eyeballing her amazing panoramic view. It was a heck of a home. Good for Darla.

"You've got quite a front yard," Nick said, gesturing at the royal-blue ocean glittering before them in the sun. "You living here by yourself?"

She smiled. "Yes. Just me."

"Do you have an alarm? Maybe you should get a dog. Like a German shepherd. Or a Doberman. Or maybe an Akita." Nick's brain seemed to be on power saver mode as he turned to Cam. "Maybe Hadley can set her up with one."

"I'm good, Nick," she said softly.

Cam tried to stanch the bleeding. "We're . . . um . . . here to take care of your roof." He pointed to the adjoining screened porch. "Okay to go in?" He made his way over there, not failing to give his brother a *get it together* look.

"Oh, yes, for sure. Let me show you the problem." Darla got up and led them into the porch, where she pointed to a stained circle of water damage involving two corners of the ceiling. The damp smell of decaying wood confirmed the problem.

"The roofing company fixed the main issue," Darla said. "Are you guys sure you want to look at it?" She directed her question mostly to Nick, who couldn't seem to take his eyes off of her. "I know newer houses aren't your specialty."

"We're the best," he said, pride in his voice, "and we'll do it right without charging you an arm and a leg."

"Okay. Well, I've got a conference call with my editor in a bit." She started walking down the hall and gestured with her thumb. "I'll be in my office if you two need anything."

"Sounds good," Cam said.

He must've given his brother an incredulous look without meaning to because Nick said, "What? I had to at least offer to fix it. She was going to call Cunningham's." He appeared to shudder at the mention of their biggest competitor. "What else could I do?"

Cam was about to say, *Maybe just let her call them,* but he figured it was better to shut up.

Nick didn't say much as they got busy, but Cam figured he was just concentrating. They'd been working for about an hour when Darla brought in a tall cold pitcher of lemonade and some cookies.

Not just any cookies. Oatmeal with chocolate chip—Nick's favorite. Cam was starting to wish he'd made up some excuse not to come.

"I've got that call now," she said, smiling. "You guys okay?"

Nick barely gave a nod, so Cam made sure to smile and wave from the top of his ladder. "Thanks, Darla," he said. When the coast was clear, he assessed his brother, who was using a crowbar to scrape rotten wood from the ceiling. "You okay?" Cam asked.

Nick halted whatever he was doing with the crowbar. "Fine," he said, before starting up again.

"Okay," Cam said, but he kept standing there. Because he knew his brother enough to know something was off.

"Will you get back to work?" Nick said, exasperated. "We're burning daylight."

"It's just that you seemed excited to be here but you barely thanked her." Cam crossed his arms. "And also, it wouldn't kill you to tell me what's bugging you."

Nick rolled his eyes. "Don't tell me you're going to stand there until I say something."

"Yeah," Cam said, chuckling. "That's what I was thinking. So maybe you'd better spill."

Nick shook his head. Cam was ready to give up and get back to work when Nick said, "This could've been my life."

Cam squinted out at the hundred eighty degrees of sun and sea in front of them. "Oceanfront? Panoramic views?"

"I don't care about any of that." Nick paused a long time, leaning his body against the ladder. "I mean working on a project around the house like this. Eating cookies. Reading on the deck. It just...it makes me think about what could've been."

Working on projects? Eating cookies? Nick being sentimental? Cam walked down from his ladder and took a cookie, holding the plate up to Nick. As far as he could tell, his brother was talking about being with Darla. Doing everyday-life things...together.

He was also certain Nick was going to hate what he had to say. But he said it anyway.

"Maybe it could be again."

Nick snorted.

Cam threw out his hands. "You're both still single is all I'm saying."

"I wasn't ready to be a grown-up," Nick said in a voice almost too low to hear. "I...caused a lot of pain."

That made Cam's thoughts swing back to Hadley, who was never far from his mind. While he and Nick had been working, he'd found himself doing double takes, thinking that a woman with her brown hair pulled back in a ponytail was Hadley as she ran through the waves or that she was one of a trio of women on the beach laughing. Every part of Seashell Harbor seemed to remind him of her.

And the fact that he'd blown it too.

"Maybe you *should* have another go at it," Cam said, realizing he was probably the worst person in the world to give advice.

His brother wouldn't meet his eyes, choosing instead to look out on the horizon, where a few tiny white specks of boats made frothy trails and puffy white clouds sailed by, oblivious to any human angst.

Nick gave an uneasy laugh. "You've always been an optimist. Ever since we were kids. Remember Boomer?"

Now it was Cam's turn to shake his head. "Please don't bring that up." Boomer was their longtime golden retriever. One day when Cam was twelve, he'd come home from school to find Boomer gone. His dad had sat him down and explained it had been his time, and he'd had to cross the rainbow bridge.

His dad had done his best, but there'd been no good-bye. No ceremony. No burial. Boomer was just...gone. Sort of like his mom.

"You asked for weeks if he was coming back, remember?" Nick said. "Like you just couldn't accept that he was gone. Like you could wish him back to life."

Cam had loved that dog. It still hurt to think about it.

"Maybe what's wrong with us goes back to Mom," Nick said.

Out of the three of them, Nick was always the one who brought up their mother. Lucy was too young to remember her and Cam...well, he'd always put his energy into forgetting about her as best he could. "I don't want to talk about her," Cam said, trying to harden his heart like usual. But it seemed as though Hadley had changed the consistency of his heart to melted ice cream.

"A mom's supposed to love her kids no matter what," Nick said. "If she doesn't, how do they ever feel anyone else can?"

Cam winced a little, but he was going to punt on this one, so he kept his reply light. "Maybe you should be getting your psych degree instead of an MBA, Dr. Phil."

"We don't talk about this," Nick said. "But maybe we should is all I'm saying."

"Nick, I don't disagree that Mom leaving maybe messed us up," Cam said. "But you and Darla were really young. Maybe you both made mistakes. But…she's here now."

"Too much water under that bridge. And it's too late. We've both moved on." Then he went back to prying wood slats.

Cam walked to the other corner of the porch and kept ripping out his area, planning to meet his brother in the middle.

He was a little jolted by what Nick had said about their mom's effect on them.

Except he couldn't help but see the irony. He was telling his brother to examine his heart, to take a leap of faith, to salvage a relationship that at one time meant everything to him.

Hadley had meant everything to him too. He kept telling himself that his head wasn't right, he wasn't settled, he still had a lot to prove. That she might still be hung up on that ass Cooper. That she wouldn't remain in Seashell Harbor for much longer.

But she was here now, and so was he. And his heart wanted what it wanted.

Chapter 19

LET ME GET this straight," Kit said as she walked with Hadley down Petunia Street on her way to work at Seaside Auto Body, where she ran the front desk. They'd just dropped Ollie off at day care on the kind of summer day that made you want to skip work and lie on the beach all day loading up on sunshine and salt breezes, reading a book, playing paddle ball, and collecting shells. All of which Hadley hadn't done in... When was the last time she'd had a beach day? Did nothing? She couldn't even remember.

Cooper had hated the beach, at least in the U.S., because he was constantly mobbed by people. He even had a rule about not giving autographs when people sought him out, which Hadley found embarrassing.

"You're meeting Cam at the courthouse to work on arrangements for the benefit? Really?" Kit was positively apoplectic at the prospect of Hadley and Cam working together. Nothing Hadley said could calm her down.

"Gran felt it would be an opportunity for both of us to refocus on how we're trying to help out the town," she admitted.

"I heard customers in the shop buzzing about Cam's restaurant versus your dog rescue. It's quite the heated debate. And that doesn't even count the fact that there are photos of you two getting into it all over the Internet. They're speculating that you and Cam are an item."

Hadley groaned.

"One of them is even calling you a gold digger— '*From Cooper to Cam*' I believe is what they said. I might have that one on my phone—"

Hadley held out a hand. "No thanks. I can't bear to look." Kit shoved her phone in front of her. On it was a photo of her and Cam at the festival. She was gesturing passionately and he was standing there looking very angry and...looming over her. Not in an intimidating way...in a Sandra-Bullock-with-Ryan-Reynolds kind of way.

"This is actually sort of cute," Kit said, "in an enemies-to-lovers sort of way."

"I'm not looking," Hadley said, pushing Kit's arm aside and blinking to erase the image from her retinas.

Cam's fault. The root of all evil thoughts and acts. At least she kept telling herself that to prevent herself from thinking about the incredible sacrifice he'd made for her by taking the press heat. And to keep herself from thinking that he'd also friend-zoned her.

"I'm no psychologist, but this photo is...interesting," Kit said, dropping her phone into her purse, which was next to her work bag, which was next to her knitting satchel, which had a bright orange ball of yarn sticking out.

"You bring your knitting to work?"

She shrugged. "You know I stress-knit. I'm part of the Scarves for Santa project. We knit all year long."

Kit turned. "Don't change the subject. That photo is interesting because it looks like the movie poster for a rom-com."

"Kit, what are you talking about?" Her friend was reading too much into a few pictures.

"Stop and take another look," she insisted.

"Kit, I'm trying to survive here until the end of summer. Cam is in my grill and it's impossible for me to think objectively about him, but I'm trying, okay? I'm really trying."

"There's nothing objective about this shot. Sorry, Hadley."

Kit was determined to force the photo in her face, so she stopped and looked again.

"Here's another one. Look at the body language," Kit said.

Two people at odds with each other. Her hands balled into fists. Cam frowning, his muscular arms crossed against his broad chest.

Kit used two fingers to blow the photo up. "You're in each other's faces. Close together. Your gazes are literally locked on each other. And you both look more amused than angry. There's a psychological term for this...*repressed sexual tension.*"

Hadley batted the phone away and kept walking.

"All I'm saying, babe, is you're going to have to face your feelings, one way or another. Because they're *there.*"

"He's not interested."

Kit stopped walking and put a hand on Hadley's arm to stop her. "Did you ask him?"

"I did, actually. He said he cared for me and hated to see me hurt and I sort of said, as friends?"

Kit halted on the sidewalk. "And then what happened?"

"He said he'd always be my friend."

Kit sighed, the kind she gave Ollie when she was struggling with her patience. "Do you really believe that?"

"I don't know. But, Kit, he...he did something amazing for me. He agreed to an interview to get the press away from me. And I think I get why he hasn't done an interview."

"Why is that?" Kit asked, steering her off the sidewalk and onto the green in front of the courthouse.

"I think you and Darla were right about Cam. He hasn't wanted to talk to the press because he can't stand to admit he doesn't have a solid life plan. I think...I think it's a real struggle for him. How he sees himself without football."

"Maybe he's right about not being in the right headspace for a relationship. He left you once before because of his own insecurities."

"I know! But he's not the power-hungry success machine I thought he was. But if I soften toward him...I just don't know what I'll do."

Kit, sensing that Hadley was getting emotional, laid a hand on her arm. "You still have feelings for him. And so there's only one thing to do." In response to Hadley's confused look, she tapped the ring on Hadley's finger. "Be bold like Darla's great-grandma. Do something. Get things off your chest."

"I guess I'm...afraid. What if Cam is just like Cooper?" Another in-the-spotlight, charismatic man who could break her heart—*again*.

"Oh, Hadley," Kit said. "What if he's *not*?"

Kit's words struck home.

"You were so happy once with him," she continued. "Maybe you should let yourself try again. I mean, while you're working together on the benefit. It might be a chance you'll never have again."

Hadley took a deep breath, a hand to her chest, where she felt a sudden pain. One last chance, dangling right in front of her, if only she'd be courageous enough to take it. "You're making me emotional." Hadley swiped at her eyes. "I love you for knowing me so well. Thanks for…"

"Being your friend? You're welcome." Kit rummaged through her knitting bag, bright skeins of yarn threatening to tumble onto the sidewalk. "What's your favorite color?"

"I don't need a scarf!" she called as she turned to walk up the big concrete staircase under the town hall bell tower.

She pushed open the heavy wood door and entered the dim interior, her footsteps echoing on the smooth white marble flooring as her eyes adjusted to the light.

She found Cam standing in front of the ancient elevator, leaning against the wall as he glanced at his phone, looking delicious.

Delicious? How was she going to work with him when she couldn't even control her *thoughts?*

"Hi," he said, looking her over with that hungry-alligator look again. Maybe Kit was right. Maybe he wasn't as neutral toward her as he pretended to be.

Or maybe she was just seeing what she wanted.

If that was what she wanted.

"Hi," she said, managing to push the voices from her head. "That elevator is over a hundred years old. Maybe we should take the stairs?"

"I'd like to but my doc said no more than two flights at a time. But you can take them if you're nervous." He flashed a wide smile as the elevator shuddered open and they got in. "That way when I don't show, you can send the fire department for me."

"Remember when we got stuck in an elevator at Macy's in Trenton?" The words spilled out before Hadley could censor herself. What was it about being with him that took away her filter?

Cam gave a little cough. "I...ah...I was the one who stopped it, remember?"

Hadley felt a flush start at her neck and work its way north. "Oh! I forgot." She tried to sound neutral and businesslike, like she was in a business meeting, but the truth was, she would never forget. As the elevator squeaked and creaked its way up to the fourth floor, she tried not to suppress the visions of that *other* elevator ride. His body pressed up against hers, her back against the wall, his lips devouring hers, his hands...

"Whew! It's hot in here," she said, flapping the collar of her blouse. His eyes dropped to her chest, where her hand clutched her shirt. Which was also awkward.

He met her gaze, then looked away, toward the control panel. "I'm not sure the fourth floor is air-conditioned."

Oh no. Her thoughts alone were generating enough heat to warm this whole building in the middle of January.

"Here we are," Cam said pleasantly as the elevator squeaked open, rattly and rumbly, like the creaky joints of an old arthritic person. He held his big hand over the door opening and gestured her out. "After you, ma'am."

"Thank you, sir." As she passed him, she couldn't help but notice his scent—subtle and clean, like fresh air. Cooper always smelled like the newest and most expensive designer fragrance. It often clung to his clothes so it was overpowering and inescapable. But Cam's scent was...wonderful. Just right.

The top floor was small, dark, and hot as an attic on a summer day, which was pretty much exactly what it was.

Cam dug in his pocket for a key and went over to unlock a battered door, circa 1888. It opened onto a musty, dormered office with a dark wooden table and two chairs. A large white box labeled BENEFIT in big letters sat in the middle of the table. Two dirty windows overlooked the park and town square. The first thing he did was try and open them, but he had to dust his hands of the cobwebs.

Hadley watched him struggle, thinking that this small, stuffy office with a slanty ceiling might just be a safe space. It was so hot that you had to concentrate to just breathe. Which meant you couldn't think other thoughts. Plus, they each would take their own side of the table, and never the twain would cross. She'd make sure of it.

"Well, look at that." Cam gave a low whistle. "What a view."

As she walked over to the small paned windows, he stepped aside for her to see.

"Wow," slipped out of her mouth before she could think of something more sophisticated. The streets of downtown with their square brick buildings gave way to lines of houses and tree-lined streets, which rolled down to the brush of the coastline. And to the right the wide strip of beach and endless blue water sparkled in the sun on this fine June day. A few umbrellas were already dotting the shore even though it was only nine in the morning.

She suddenly wanted to be out there, free, her toes wiggling in the sand, soaking up warmth and light.

He looked down at her. "That view is pretty spectacular, isn't it?"

Oh, yes, he is. She accidentally grazed his shoulder, then compensated by taking a step backward, which made her bump into the table.

For a beat, his gaze burned into her. It dropped to her lips, and once again she felt the pull between them, strong and steady as the tide.

"I remembered something else you should know." He spoke slowly and quietly, with a serious tone that made her pulse jump in anticipation. "When I came home from college over Thanksgiving that year we broke up, I came looking for you."

"Wait." She ticked off the memories in her mind. "After we broke up? But you didn't come home for Thanksgiving that year."

He nodded. "I found a ride all the way from Penn State. I was miserable. I knew I'd screwed up, and I wanted to beg your forgiveness."

"Wh-what are you saying?" Her limbs felt heavy, like she was treading water. "I never saw you over break that year."

"I got in on Wednesday night and walked straight to your house, but your car wasn't there. So I went to the Crab Shack. I saw you sitting at a table with the girls. I remember there were Christmas lights up already, strung around the windows. You were all sitting together in a booth with dates. Laughing. You were sitting next to a guy with light brown hair. He kissed you."

Suddenly her knees grew weak. She had to lean against the rickety table for support. "My friends made me go out that night. Darla fixed me up with one of her friends from college...I don't even remember his name. Only that he kissed me without permission and I nearly clubbed him right there at the table." She rubbed her temples. "Why didn't you tell me? Why didn't you try to see me?" But she already knew.

He lifted his shoulders in a shrug. "After that, I knew we were over for good. Seeing you with a guy confirmed my worst fears, that it wouldn't take you long to move on from me."

There was a lump in her throat. And she had to cross her arms since she was shaking so badly.

He stepped over to her and steadied her with his hands.

"I'm telling you now that I would never hurt you like that again. I hurt both of us by what I did. And the only way I know how to make up for that is to be honest now."

She swallowed hard and managed a nod. Longing overcame her. For lost years, yes. But more importantly, what about now? What about having a chance with each other *now*?

Perhaps more in frustration than anything else, Cam cracked open the box and picked up a note that was sitting on top of the inside contents.

"Your grandma wants us to mail out everyone's tickets," he said, reading the note as if nothing had happened. "We have two hundred envelopes to address. By hand."

"You're kidding," Hadley said, fanning herself with a bundle of them. "We may die first." His gaze slid over her, slow and steady, which made the heat problem even worse. Despite being a wreck inside, she grabbed a batch of tickets and envelopes and split them, half for him and half for her. "The sooner we start, the sooner we'll be done, right?" She took a seat and tried to focus, writing out an address, tucking in the tickets and a letter giving details about the event, and then licking it.

He'd been addressing his own envelope but she found him staring at her. That strange unearthly zing passed between them, and she swore she knew what he was thinking, and it wasn't about licking envelopes.

She was overwhelmed by everything. By being shown again and again that he wasn't who she thought he was. By wanting him so badly she could barely breathe. Tossing her envelope into the box, she drummed her fingers on the table. "I can't do this now."

He tossed his into the box and scraped his chair back. "I have an idea. It involves going someplace cooler." He placed the lid back on the box. "Let's do what your grandma said."

She gave him a wry smile. "Forgo all sleep, food, and fun until the job is done?"

He chuckled. "How about putting the building behind us for now and see what we're like without it between us?"

"I'd like that," she said quietly.

He leaned forward and took her hand. His thumb absently stroked her palm, something that made her forget . . . well, everything else. "I have to leave tonight for New York. I've got some business meetings for a couple of days and an offer to do some commentary for Sunday Night Football. So this might be our only chance to bust out of here."

He sounded like he was eighteen again, when they really did do crazy things like what he was suggesting. "You mean...play hooky?" she asked.

He grinned widely. "Yes. Hooky." She went to pull her hand away but he held on to it and looked right at her with those eyes the same exact color as the ocean outside the window, full of sincerity and...mischief. "Trust me to plan an afternoon for us."

Again, a memory hit her. A big, intimate one. The first time they'd made love. They'd played hooky all right, leaving their high school graduation celebration early, bringing blankets to the beach. They were ecstatic about graduating but all they wanted was each other. The surf was sounding its gentle roll and the moon was a big bright crescent above them and his face...his face above her...his sweet, precious face. And he'd whispered to her, *Are you sure, Had?*

And she'd said, *I'll never be more sure.*

And he'd said *I love you.* And then—

She was suddenly choked up and badly in need of air. Worse, she realized that he'd stepped out into the hallway to make a call.

She rotated the ring on her finger. She was falling for him all over again. Yes, she was afraid. To trust herself after being hurt. To start something when they had so much unresolved between them about the future of her grandmother's building. Not to mention all the uncertainties about her own future.

Maybe she didn't have all the answers. But maybe she could let herself...take a chance. Take a trip down memory lane with him to a time when she was really happy.

It was only an afternoon, right?

"We're all set," he said, pocketing his phone as he walked back in. "I'm going to drop us off at home and then I'll pick you up in a half hour. Dress for the beach."

"Okay, let's do it," she said, sweeping scattered papers into the box. She realized that for the first time in a long time she was...excited. To go to the beach. And to be with him. She looked up at his handsome face and smiled. "Let's get out of here."

Chapter 20

CAM SAT BEHIND the wheel of his '65 Mustang convertible, watching Hadley toss a beach bag into the back seat and climb in. She looked pretty as a picture wearing a white swimsuit cover-up, a floppy sun hat, and a big smile.

One afternoon. He had that much time to show her that they were the same people they used to be when they weren't standing on opposite sides of a fence.

He *needed* to do it, for reasons that he didn't fully understand. But it had something to do with Nick and lost opportunities and not letting the best relationship of his life go.

Plus other things Nick had said were worrying him. Cam had made success his all-time goal.... He needed to be the best at everything he did. Was he still really struggling to prove his worth, even though their mother was long gone? Who exactly was he trying to prove himself to?

Hadley was shaking her head.

"What? What is it?" He hadn't even had a chance to put his foot in his mouth yet.

"Of course you'd buy a red sports car," she said, the corner of her mouth tipping up in a smile.

"Well, it beats that red Chevy Astro I had back in high school, right?" Before he could stop himself, he reached over and rubbed a little blob of sunscreen off her nose. He was pleased her breath hitched at his touch. If she was feeling the same things he was feeling, he intended to find out. Today.

"I wouldn't call that old Astro red exactly," she said. "Unless you're defining rust as red?"

"Ha!" he said. "Those were the days."

The soft expression in her eyes melted him. "We had fun times," she said.

He dropped a hand from the wheel and it accidentally grazed hers. He met her gaze again. "Especially the times we played hooky."

"We only did that a few times," she said.

"Because you wouldn't skip class."

"You talked me into it," she said, "and we both got detention."

"It was worth it." He suppressed a grin. "Buying T-shirts on the boardwalk was fun."

She punched him in the arm. "I don't remember anything else we did." But she was smiling.

He wanted her to remember. And from what he was going to show her today, she'd remember even more.

"So where are we going in this flashy car?" she asked.

"Somewhere you'll like." In answer to her puzzled expression, he impulsively reached down and squeezed her hand. He couldn't stop himself. And…it just seemed right. To him. But to her?

She glanced down at their hands, then up at him. "Okay," she said softly. "You're in charge of the afternoon."

"Is the car too flashy for you?" Most women fawned

more over his car than over him. But not Hadley. She was about to give him grief about it, he could tell.

"Well, it does attract attention," she said.

"You're going to forget all about that when you feel that sea breeze flying through your hair." And then he started the car with a little jolt. "Hold on to your sunbonnet, sugar."

"Call me sugar again and you're going to be wearing it yourself." She gripped the brim of her hat against the breeze.

He grinned. "Noted."

He drove out past the marina, following the shoreline until he pulled onto an out-of-the way road he hadn't driven for a long time.

Her eyes grew wide. "You're taking me to the Crab Shack?" They pulled into the familiar parking lot, memories from their favorite teenage hangout flooding him. He didn't miss the excitement in her voice, and he hoped what he was about to do would make her happy.

"It's empty," she said, noting that the squat, square little building was vacant, the blinds drawn, and the parking lot abandoned, weeds growing through the cracks in the pavement. "Where is everyone?"

"The Millers are moving to Florida."

"Oh no!" she said. "I've been so busy since I've been back, I haven't thought of this place. But I can't imagine it not being here."

"Best crab burgers on the East Coast."

"And best jalapeño poppers. Not to mention the crazy Christmas lights they used to put up, remember?" He gave a smile at that. "Bob and Marilyn. Are they okay?"

"They're fine." He pulled out of the parking lot and

continued a short way up the winding road. "Just ready to move south to be closer to their grandchildren."

At a bend in the road, Cam turned into the driveway of a picturesque Tudor-style cottage.

Hadley gasped. "I'd forgotten all about this place. But why are we at Bob and Marilyn's house?"

"You'll see." The property sloped down to a little bluff overlooking the ocean, complete with a winding stone path and wild roses blooming everywhere. When he ran to open the door for Hadley, she hesitated, her expression wary. But he held out his hand, lifting a brow as if to say, *Why not?*

Finally, she took it. A small victory. As they walked together to the house, the door opened and a gray-haired couple greeted them.

"Order's ready," Bob said, carrying a basket. "Can I put it in your car?"

"I can get that." Cam took it from him. "It's enough you got it ready for us."

"For you, we have curbside pickup." Marilyn came right up and hugged Cam. "We're so glad you're back, Anthony. Makes us sad about leaving." Then she engulfed Hadley in a hug too. "Hadley! I'm so glad you've come home too."

"Mrs. Miller," she said. "Great to see you."

"My good friend Gladys just fostered an older dog for Ivy, and it's a match made in heaven. Oh, and I see you and Cam have found each other again." She clapped her hands together. "That's so wonderful!"

Bob put a hand on his wife's arm. "We should let them get to their picnic."

"I really appreciate you doing this for us," Cam said, surveying the house. "Find a buyer yet?"

Bob and Marilyn exchanged glances. "We were lucky to find one," Bob finally said.

"Then that's a good thing?" Cam asked.

"The buyer we found is going to tear down the Shack *and* level the house," Marilyn said. "They're going to build some modern monstrosity for the view."

"Level this house?" Hadley asked, looking around at the quaint stone exterior, the window boxes brimming with flowers, and the petunias growing in riots, spilling all over the walkway.

"I don't mind them leveling the Shack," Marilyn said, "but the house...it's over a hundred years old."

"It's a piece of history," Cam agreed. It made him sad to think of such a beautiful old property getting torn down on a whim.

Bob couldn't suppress a heavy sigh. "We're not very happy about it, but we're ready to retire and it's a good offer."

"I'm so sorry," Hadley said.

"We're excited about the next phase of our life." Bob placed an arm around his wife. "We want to have some sunshine in the winter. And play with our grandkids. So don't feel too badly for us."

Marilyn smiled at her husband and turned to Cam. "Anthony, we can't thank you enough for calling us. It was a pleasure to make up a picnic lunch for you."

"I don't know what Seashell Harbor will be without your crab burgers," Cam said as they headed to the car. "Would you mind if we parked in the Crab Shack lot for a while? I thought we might follow the old trail down to the beach."

He tried to gauge Hadley's reaction. Having a special Crab Shack lunch was one thing, but mentioning that quiet, out-of-the way trek was another.

"Sure," Bob said as they climbed back into the car. "But you might find it's a little different than it used to be."

A minute later, they were back at the Crab Shack. "Want to have a look?" Cam asked, pulling his keys out from the ignition.

She nodded. "Sure thing, *Anthony*."

"Hey. No making fun of my name."

"I'm not making fun," she said quietly. "I just think it's funny that some folks around here still call you that."

"*You* used to call me that," he said. "Well, *Tony* anyway." He wished she would again.

She gave a quick nod and made a sudden point of exclaiming about all the wildflowers along the road.

Cam opened the trunk and slung a bag containing a beach umbrella over his shoulder. The elevated slice of coastline the Shack sat on had a million-dollar view.

"You brought us an umbrella?" Hadley said.

He decided not to remind her how easily she sunburned. "Mind grabbing the towels?"

She held up her bag. "I brought you one too," she said.

"Because I always used to forget mine."

As they gathered up their lunch and headed in the direction of the beach, Cam halted and turned to her. "I wanted to bring you here like old times. This place meant a lot to me. And...I'm sticking to what your grandmother said about not discussing business today, if that's okay with you."

"Okay, deal."

"And...and I want you to remember what it was like to be eighteen and sneaking away for a picnic, on a day too beautiful to spend with anyone but who you want to share it with the most."

"Okay," she said, clearly uncomfortable.

"I want to share it with you." He held his breath, half afraid she'd cut and run.

But instead she smiled. "I want to share it with you too."

Okay. Now they were getting somewhere.

"Cam, look what they did to the beach paths." Hadley pointed to a marked trailhead that pointed with an arrow to the beach. Another arrow sign read MARINA TRAIL 2.1 MILES.

"Well, what do you know," Cam said, looking at the well-manicured path. "They turned them into walking trails."

A trailhead. Marked trails. Cleared, not wild.

"It was more fun when it was wild and dangerous," Cam said. "And led to private places." He shot her a pointed look.

Hadley rolled her eyes, but her lips twitched a little. "The police chief is probably relieved. So many teenagers sneaking off and getting into trouble."

"Which brings me to part two." He took her hand. "Come on."

"I changed my mind," she said, resisting his pull. She probably saw the glint in his eye that he was having trouble disguising. "Maybe we should go to the beach near Gran's place," Hadley offered, "where there are a lot more people."

"I don't want a crowd," he said without thinking.

She stopped suddenly. Looking a little flustered, she said, "I know where you're taking us. And...I think maybe more people is a good idea."

He set down the basket and took her other hand. "Come back there with me." The passion in his voice shocked him a little. But he wasn't sorry for it.

Her eyes widened. "So you *are* taking us there."

"*There* has a name," he said. "Pritchard's Cove." Except they'd never called it that. As teenagers they'd had a different name for it.

She shook her head. "*Passion Cove* was a long time ago."

"Not that long ago, Had." He tipped his head toward the bulging picnic basket. "No worries. It's just lunch."

Every bone in his body told him it wasn't.

She still resisted. "Dessert's included," he said. "Chocolate," he added, attempting some lightness. But the gravity of wanting to be honest weighed on him. "Look, Hadley. I wanted us to have lunch together somewhere special. Somewhere that not only reminds us of you and me but...a place that *is* you and me, you know? At our best. I'm not going to lie. I want us to stop being enemies."

He was tired of fighting about the building. And he was tired of fighting himself.

You're beautiful, and please don't love that ass Cooper anymore, ran through his mind. But that kind of talk would have to wait.

"I don't want to be enemies either," she said.

"Besides, we have to work together on this benefit. We have to be friendly. And...the burgers are getting cold."

She laughed. "Okay, fine, you win," she said, tossing up her arms. "Let's go have lunch at the biggest make-out place on this side of the harbor." She picked up her bundles. "But there'd better be chocolate."

* * *

Hadley was getting lost. She knew exactly where her feet were taking her as she followed Cam through the dunes and the cleared marsh grass, but it was her heart she was worried about.

Take away that silly building and you got...Cam and Hadley, just as they once were. And that was...terrifying. And electrifying. And the fact that he'd taken pains to bring her back to *their place* from so long ago...well. Her heart felt full and heavy with possibility. And for once she was going to listen to him and just go with it.

They walked in the sand, through the dunes and the beach grass until they came to a part where the path narrowed. Cam had insisted on carrying Hadley's beach bag on top of everything else, even though at times he seemed to favor his bad knee.

"Be careful," she said as the path wove around an out-cropping of rocks. "Can I please carry something?"

He stopped again and faced her. His sheer hand-someness bowled her over, even though he was just wearing a gray T-shirt over swim trunks. He pulled down his sunglasses and gave her a look. She wished he would stop doing that because everything he was doing today was reminding her of how they used to be. Fun, flirty, intimate. He wasn't acting like the *just friends* he'd said he wanted. And every time he looked at her, her stomach plunged and she had the distinct feeling he was thinking most *un*friendly thoughts. She knew *she* certainly was.

"I'm big and strong and I love to carry stuff," he said. "So as long as you've got the towels, I'm fine."

"All right, then, keep being a show-off. Just don't hurt yourself."

The next time he stopped, she realized they were there—at a very out-of-the-way, private strip of beach, sheltered by a tall outcropping of rock. And right now it was empty. No sign of humans anywhere.

Cam dropped all their stuff onto the sand. Without a word, she reached into the beach bag and handed him the little plastic drill, as they'd done countless times before. She spread out their towels, but she was really watching his biceps bulge as he rotated the drill into the sand.

She didn't miss the fact that it would've taken her seventeen times longer to accomplish that task. "Did you bring the umbrella for me?" she asked, secretly pleased that he remembered how easily her fair skin burned.

He gave a little chuckle. "Let's just say I didn't want you turning into a lobster by dinnertime."

"I brought plenty of protection." She held up two bottles, SPF 30 and 90-plus. Realizing how that sounded, she backpedaled. "*Sun* protection. Sunblock. Protection for skin cancer. *Really* important."

His gaze swept her up and down in a way that made her light-headed. Or maybe it was just the heat. He pointed to the sunblock. "Maybe you can help me with that later," he said.

He said it like a challenge. Like she was actually going to rub sunscreen on those hills of muscle that rippled under his shirt. Not going to happen.

Once the shade was secured, she moved to set out the lunch, but Cam gently placed his hand over hers. "Oh no," he said. "This is a surprise."

Her heart skittered and jumped at his touch. For a second, she stared at their hands, hers small and pale, his large and tanned. He'd always had elegantly shaped hands, with long fingers. Seeing their two hands together struck her as if she were looking at a beloved old photograph, distant but so familiar.

"No peeking," he said.

"Okay," she said, closing her eyes, "you're in charge."

"I love it when you say that." She heard the squeak of the basket hinge, the clinking of plates, the flapping of a cloth as he began setting out their lunch.

"Don't get too used to it."

"You know I'm teasing. We've always treated each other as equals." He paused. "Except you were always the better half. Now open your eyes."

She felt her insides tumble as he unveiled the famous crab burgers, along with a fruit salad and an ice-cold bottle of chardonnay, complete with stemmed glasses. Dessert, as promised, was homemade chocolate chip cookies, the heat making the chips melt a little in the best way.

He'd gone through all this trouble for her. To take her back to a beautiful place and to a time when she was happy. When she'd been able to relax and just be herself.

If that was his plan, it was definitely working.

They didn't say much as they devoured the delicious lunch. Afterward, happy and full, she lay back on her towel. Cam sat nearby, finishing his wine, looking out over the sandy hill to the water.

"It's a little weird being here," she said. "But a nice weird." She glanced over at him. "What do you think?"

He tossed his head back and laughed. "Yeah, a nice weird."

"I mean, never in my wildest dreams could I have imagined we'd come back after all these years and eat lunch here."

"Well, one thing is, we never came here in broad daylight. There's no full moon shining on the water. No cool evening breeze."

"No sand in our shorts." She sat up and took a sip of wine.

"No old Astro that sometimes ran and sometimes didn't."

"Maybe no privacy either." She lifted her head and looked around. "I thought I heard some hikers earlier."

He chuckled a little. "This place has gotten far too civilized." He paused before adding, "But some things haven't changed."

"Oh, what hasn't?" He was looking at her with an intensity that made her feel as though a swarm of sea-birds were flapping about in her stomach.

Cam stretched out on his side on the blanket next to her. She froze in place and swallowed hard, her pulse throbbing in her throat, at her temples, *everywhere*.

"Well, you're more beautiful than you were before," he said. "I marvel at it all the time. How you've changed from a girl into a woman."

"Well, it happens," she said, but her mouth seemed unable to form words. Or only able to form them into stupid jokes.

"More importantly," he said, taking up her hand, forcing her to meet his gaze, "you haven't changed on the *inside*."

"Cam, *everyone* changes on the inside. We were just kids."

"You're still honest and kind and loving."

So was he. Her heart knew it, no matter what. "I'd do anything for my grandma. Don't make it seem like I'm something special."

"I'm not just talking about your grandma," he said, "but about everybody you come into contact with." He grinned suddenly. "Not to mention all animals."

"You're kind too. What you did for me with those journalists—"

He cut her off quickly. "I already told you, I'd do anything for you."

He was very near. How did he get so close? She was falling into the blue of his eyes. Maybe it was just the magic of this crazy place, this Passion Cove that brought back so many memories.

"Cam, I...I know you would." She *did* know it, despite all her wariness about men in general. A thousand feelings threatened to bowl her over—hope, yearning, *need*. And despite their vow not to discuss it, the impossibility of reconciling their plans about her grandmother's building.

More confused than ever, she searched his eyes. In response, he smiled, tucking a wisp of hair behind her ear. "Great memories here. But those are part of our past, and the past is done. The future is ahead of us. If we want it to be."

"I thought you wanted to be friends," she said.

"I said that because I saw how crushed you looked when you found out about Cooper and Maeve's baby. I...I was afraid you still loved him." He hesitated. "Do you?"

She shook her head. "Hearing about their baby devastated me because that was the life *I* wanted—babies, love, a family. But not with Cooper."

He blew out a big breath. "I can't even tell you how happy I am to hear that."

Desire flooded her. Every part of her wanted him, wanted his lips on hers, wanted to feel his arms wrap tight around her. She tried to speak, but emotion clogged her throat.

"I'm not sure this is a good idea," she managed. Trusting him to take her on a picnic and trusting him with her heart were two different things entirely.

She reached out and touched his cheek. It was warm, holding the heat of the sun, the sandpaper edge of his five o'clock shadow getting a hefty head start. He leaned into her hand, which was now shaky.

"I know you've been hurt," he said. "But I'm not Cooper. I'm just...me. Just Tony."

Tears welled up. Was he the boy, now the man, that she'd always known? She believed that he was. Her heart *felt* that he was.

She reached up and tugged him down to her, her lips finding his. His lips were soft and warm as they slid over hers, and he angled his head to take her mouth more freely. He tasted wonderful, like the sweet wine and...himself. In the warmth of the sun and the saltwater-tinged air, a feeling overtook her that was akin to relief. A rightness that she hadn't felt for years.

Suddenly they were lying on the towel, and the feel of him over her, strong and sun-kissed and warm, was both familiar and new as the soft sand shifted subtly beneath them and their kisses turned from tentative to deeper and more urgent.

She slid her hand around his neck, under the curling length of his hair, feeling the powerful muscles of his back as she pulled him closer.

His kisses were... perfect. Just right. Insistent, skilled, yet... gentle. She kissed him back like this was their last day on earth. Like it was their last day on this beach. Like *he* was what had been missing all these years.

He broke from her lips to kiss her neck, nuzzling the soft, sensitive hollow between her neck and shoulder. Heat built in her lower abdomen, spreading everywhere, her body arching toward him, achy and wanting.

"You taste... amazing," he said, his hair brushing against her cheek as he continued leaving a trail of kisses on her hot skin.

"You too," she managed, her fingers tangled in the silky, close-cropped waves of his hair.

He kissed the swell of her breast above her swimsuit top. A whimper escaped her throat, and she was unable to stop the warm, languid sensations flowing like liquid gold all through her. He smiled up at her, then returned to his task, the rough scrape of stubble pleasantly rough against her sensitive skin.

Suddenly from above they heard scuffling and laughter. "There's some old people over there having a picnic and making out," a male voice said.

Cam rested his forehead against her chest as they both froze. He seemed in no hurry to move but she scooted out from under him and sat up on the picnic blanket. A couple of teenagers were at the top of the path, peeking out from over the boulders. "Ew, gross," the girl said, giggling. "Where else can we go?"

Hadley put her head in her hands. Cam finally sat up, clearly not in a rush, and gave her a wry half-smile, lifting her hand and kissing the palm. "Come on, *Grandma*, I think our picnic's over."

"Grandma?" she exclaimed, mock-incensed. She busied herself by gathering their towels, trying to slow her rampant pulse.

He ambled to his feet and slid into his flip-flops. As they gathered the remnants of their picnic, his words echoed in her head. *Just me. Just Tony.* Someone still capable all these years later of stealing her heart and running with it. And that was exactly what she was most afraid of.

* * *

The timing couldn't have been worse for Cam's business meetings in New York. Was that interruption on the beach karma or what? He should've taken Hadley somewhere private, somewhere far away from giggling teenagers, where they might've had the chance to finish what they started.

Now, three days later, he was back and waiting for her at the beachside park downtown to decide on the final layout for the gala.

Maybe the universe had stopped him in his tracks for a reason. It had only been a few months since her breakup. She was wary. His life was unsettled, and he still had to get through that television interview.

All of which was making him very cranky. Because he really didn't care about any of that anymore. All he could think of was her. Her beautiful smile, her snorty laugh, her sense of humor that always kept him on his toes.

"Hi," she said as she met him at a picnic table in the

late afternoon. She was wearing glasses and carrying a clipboard. "Did you mail your half of the envelopes?" was her first question.

"Yes, ma'am." When had she gotten glasses? He felt like he was talking to a hot librarian. Or a schoolteacher. "Did you mail *yours*?"

"Three days ago." They'd tag-teamed all the chores for the benefit and gotten the tickets mailed out ASAP.

"I've done everything on my list," Cam said. "I've talked with the tent people, the table and chair people, the portable restroom people, the park staff, and checked with the city about parking regulations."

Not to be outdone, she said, "Well, I've done the flowers, the programs, the music, and made sure the speakers know what to do. And I've confirmed all of our business sponsorships and done media outreach on radio and TV. And, by the way, I booked you to do a TV spot with some pediatric specialists at the hospital to talk about why it's important to have a regional center for kids to have their health needs met. While you're there, you're also going to get to talk to some kids about football. Would that be okay?"

"Only if you bring some dogs."

She did her snorty laugh thing. "Why on earth would you want me to bring dogs?"

At least he'd gotten a smile out of her. "I don't know. Don't people bring dogs to visit sick kids?"

"Can you imagine Jagger with a bunch of kids? First of all, he's taller than most of them."

"And he might lick a few to death."

She shook her head at that, but she was still smiling. "After the photo op, you're going to meet with the CEO of the hospital and—"

"Nice PR work," he interrupted. "I'm game for whatever you set up. Did you miss me?"

"Look, we have a lot to do to get all this work done on time," she said. "I'm not going to mix business with pleasure until we're through here. Because look what happened the other day."

He stabbed a finger in the air. "Aha! So you were thinking of pleasure."

Her cheeks colored at that. "No, I'm thinking that we have to tell all our vendors exactly how we're going to set up this gala. We've got a food tent, tables, portable bathrooms, and a dance floor. There's parking and a band. And it all has to flow."

"So what are you thinking?" he asked, crossing his arms.

"Well, the lot by the beach isn't big enough for all the cars. So there will be overflow parking on the grass. Except the problem with that is people should enter the event on the end of the lot farthest from the beach. So it doesn't flow right. Also, I had this idea that we could turn the boardwalk into a dance floor. String it with lights. But we can't have people parking right near the dancing."

"Look," he said, "you need to think of this like a football field."

"A football field?" She crossed her arms too. "Are you mansplaining?"

"No, I'm demonstrating." He gestured with his hands. "Just hear me out, okay?"

"I'm a little afraid of how you can possibly conceive of this event to be centered around a football field analogy, but go ahead."

He grinned. Because going back and forth with her, not

really arguing but, well, whatever they were doing, was fun. He waved his arms around and demonstrated, like a coach at the SMART Board before a game. "See, the ocean is one end zone and the start of the Petunia Street buildings is the other. Parking goes on that end, the tables go on the field, the podium is on the fifty-yard line, and the band and the food tent are on the sidelines. And the beach lot is not a problem because we won't use it. See? Simple."

She shook her head. "You're... impossible. But... I get it. Sort of."

He smiled. "See, I'm a good brainstormer. That's why you like me. You do like me, don't you?"

"Absolutely not. Although I was thinking that maybe there was a reason those kids stopped us. Like, now that we hit pause, we can have more sense."

"I lost all my sense the moment I set eyes on you that first day in Pooch Palace."

He could tell by the way her eyes softened that he'd thrown her. "I'm having my friends over tonight for ice cream," she said so matter-of-factly he thought at first she was still talking about the benefit. She checked off something on her clipboard and glanced up. "Why don't you come over?"

Come over? She was inviting him over? "Well, it depends," he said. "What kind of ice cream do you have? And if I come, are you going to make me do more work on the benefit?"

Her mouth twitched. "Not if you let me set it up the way I want."

"What did you think of the beach the other day?"

"It was beautiful."

"No, I mean... what did you think of *us* on the beach?"

She shook her head and smiled. "Well, I've been thinking about it." She pulled off her glasses. "Yes, I loved the kisses. Yes, I loved being with you. And, yes, you're the most annoying man in the world."

"Two out of three isn't bad." He leaned over and kissed her quickly on the cheek. "I'll stop by tonight. But I'm *not* coming for the ice cream."

Chapter 21

IS IT TIME for ice cream now?" Ollie asked that evening as he used Gran's low stone garden wall as a racetrack for his Hot Wheels. Every time a car crashed to the ground, Jagger jumped and Bowie ran to sniff it, something Ollie obviously found fascinating, as he did it over and over again. Hadley stood by with Kit and Darla, enjoying the dogs' antics and the beautiful evening on the patio as the sun began to set.

Hadley felt like she was in a different world. Maybe she'd dreamed everything about the other day—the reckless feeling of freedom, the picnic lunch, Cam's kisses.

Cam's kisses. Oh, those kisses that made her head reel and her heart squeeze and made her feel light-headed, as if she were eighteen again. Those kisses put Cooper to shame and made her heartache over him fade into the background just like the setting sun in front of them that was currently preparing to plunge into the sea.

Yet she had to be smarter than to get swept away like when she was a girl. She knew it was too soon after Cooper to jump into another relationship, especially with a man who was grappling with his own issues. A man who'd left her before as a result of his own struggles.

Plus, she was in the middle of creating a dog rescue that would soon need a solid commitment if it was to continue. And what about her *job*?

"Right, Hadley?" Kit asked.

"Oh, I'm sorry." She was suddenly aware of her friends staring at her on the small patio. "What did you say?"

"Ollie's haircut. Do you still have time to do it? Please?"

"No, Mommy," Ollie said, shaking his head vigorously, which showcased his riot of curls. "No haircut."

Hadley ruffled his mop of hair. "Is Ollie under all these curls? Hmmm. Let me check." She pushed back the hair covering his eyes and planted a kiss on his cheek. "Oh my gosh, *there* you are."

Ollie pushed his hair out of his eyes. "Aunt Hadley, I don't want a haircut. I like my hair *long*."

Kit said quietly to Hadley, "Look. I really believe that if he was older I would say he doesn't have to follow the crowd and he could just be himself because that's the way I feel. But I'd also like him to *see* what he's doing and also show him there's nothing to be afraid of."

Too bad Hadley hadn't taken that lesson to heart herself. If she had, maybe she'd be heading up a whole bunch of dog rescues instead of enabling the bad behavior of celebrities.

Darla sat on the wall next to Ollie and said, "We're going to make delicious sundaes and you can put anything you want on yours. After your haircut."

Ollie stuck out his lower lip.

"I have chocolate ice cream," Hadley said. "And hot fudge sauce."

"I want *vanilla*," he said, hugging Hadley and then giggling.

"...and a puppy," Ollie qualified, still giggling. "One of *your* puppies," he said, pointing at Hadley.

"Oh, one of my puppies, huh?" She glanced over at Kit, who had a stern look on her face. "Tell you what. Let's do the haircut first and then the ice cream. The puppy you'll have to take up with your mom."

"She said no puppy," he said, sticking out his lower lip again.

"Kit, this kid is so stinking cute." Hadley kissed his head. "How do you ever discipline him?"

Kit rolled her eyes and laughed. "With everything that's happened, thank goodness I got a kid who's easygoing and lighthearted. For the most part." She blew him an air kiss. "I love you, Oliver Wendell, but it's time for a haircut."

"No, Mommy," her easygoing kid said.

Just then the sun decided to set, flaming down in a spectacular show of orange, purple, and salmon that made Hadley's breath catch.

"You never forget about the spectacular sunsets when you leave here," Darla said as she sipped some wine. "It makes it even better when you come back."

"You're right," Hadley said. "I missed them too." She stole one last furtive glance next door. No lights on. Where was Cam? Had he forgotten her invitation?

Meanwhile the sun plunged below the horizon in one last brilliant ball of light, mesmerizing all of them, even Ollie.

Except Darla, who whispered in her ear, "Why do you keep looking next door? Did I miss something?"

"Oh, no," she said, downplaying all the rampant emotions that were threatening to burst out of her at any moment. "It's nothing. Cam might stop over is all."

"'Cam might stop over, is all'?" Darla echoed, lifting her brows.

"I'd love to discuss this with you but I have a haircut to prepare for." Hadley chuckled as she walked into the house and came back with a tall chair with a sturdy back.

When she returned, Ollie was watering her grandmother's geraniums, and judging by the looks her friends were giving her, they were talking about her behind her back—*again*.

"I'm scared, Aunt Hadwey," Ollie said as he eyed the dreaded high-backed chair and the makeshift cape in Hadley's other hand, which was actually one of her grandmother's small tablecloths that she'd commandeered.

"Time to put on the Avenger cape," Hadley said. It was a print tablecloth with a wild floral pattern all over it, but oh well. "And no worries, Ollie. I promise it won't hurt."

Ollie crossed his arms and sat down on the wall. "Don't want it!" he said.

"Ollie, *please* just let Aunt Hadley cut your hair!" Kit said, her frustration seeping out around the edges.

"We're going to get the ice cream sundae stuff ready to celebrate when your haircut's done, okay, Ollie?" Darla steered Kit toward the kitchen. "Call us if you need anything," she said to Hadley over her shoulder.

Hadley gave Darla a grateful look, but at the same time it occurred to her that she was now on her own to deal with Ollie's fear.

Hadley wanted this to be the least of Kit's worries, so she walked around Ollie's chair and faced him, leaning against the patio table.

Maybe she didn't know that much about young children, but she did know dogs, and they could be a great emergency distraction if all else failed. She reached into her shorts pocket and pulled out two bone-shaped dog biscuits.

"Will you hold these for Jagger and Bowie?" she asked.

He nodded and held out his hand while she broke them into little pieces as the dogs immediately crowded around, much to Ollie's delight.

"I have an idea," she said, pulling out her phone and hitting the search bar. She showed him a photo. "How about something like that?"

His little face lit up.

Oh *hurray*. "If we start now, the ice cream will be ready when we're done."

"Do you promise it won't hurt?" His eyes, so like Kit's, were huge and round.

"Promise," she said, holding out her pinkie to lock with his.

She found her hands shaking a little. Not because Ollie was scared but because *she* was. And his hair was gorgeous—silky and golden blond—and she felt like she was cutting something precious, like Delilah hacking Samson's locks. Also, if Ollie or Kit wasn't pleased with the outcome . . . well, she wasn't going to go there.

She wasn't sure who was more nervous, her or Ollie. Amid a constant stream of chatter aimed to distract and amuse, and the tossing of more dog biscuits than either dog needed, finally it was done.

"Ollie," she said, putting her hands on his little shoulders. "You look so handsome. Want to see?"

He nodded, his expression wary. *Please, God*, Hadley prayed. *Please let him like it.*

She handed Ollie a mirror as Darla held Kit at bay in the doorway.

"What do you think?" Hadley held the mirror so he could see.

He examined himself carefully, scrutinizing from several angles. "I like it." He gave a wide grin. "I'm handsome. Look, Mommy!"

Thank goodness. As Hadley placed the scissors out of reach of little hands, she realized she'd broken out in a total-body sweat from worry. "*Very* handsome," Hadley said.

"Mommy," Ollie called. "Come see me. I look like Daddy!"

Kit walked over, her eyes tearing up a little. "Yes, you do, my handsome boy!" she said, giving him a kiss.

"I didn't realize that was the style I was going for, Kit," Hadley said in a low voice. The last thing she wanted to do was give Kit a reminder of Carson, who probably wouldn't have cared one way or another about his son's long tresses.

Kit gave her a hug. "It's wonderful. How can I thank you?"

"Super cute," Darla said, taking her turn. "Hadley, you're really talented."

"I know," she said a little smugly. "It was actually fun."

"Nice fade, buddy," came a deep voice from behind her.

Cam. The simple sight of him walking over from

his back patio started her heart knocking crazily in her chest. He stopped next to her, his arm lightly grazing hers, flashing her a quick and knowing smile that made her knees threaten to buckle, before fist-bumping Ollie. "My man," he said, to which Ollie grinned even more.

"It's short like yours," he said to Cam. "And long, too, on top."

"Hidden talent?" Cam asked, giving Hadley a head-to-toe look that made her toes curl.

She shrugged and flashed him a smile. "One of many."

Had she just blatantly flirted with him? One look at her friends showed they were both staring. Well, she couldn't help the giddy way he made her feel.

Cam, nonplussed, grinned and gave her a long, appreciative look before turning to Ollie. Hadley could barely hear him talking to Ollie and her friends over the sudden swooshing of blood in her ears. She felt dizzy and breathless. Putting a hand to her chest to try to calm her heart did nothing to stop this whole-body meltdown. She was *doomed*.

"Is it time for ice cream now?" Ollie asked, trying to pull the knotted tablecloth from his neck.

She freed him from the makeshift cape. "Yes, my sweet. Time for ice cream."

Then just like that, he scooted down from the chair. Kit picked him up and twirled him around. From across the patio, she mouthed, "Thank you."

Darla turned to Hadley. "I'll go start dishing out the ice cream. Can I make you a sundae?"

"After all that, I'd rather have wine," she said. "I'll be there in a sec. I just want to sweep up."

When she returned with a broom and dustpan, she found Cam lingering outside. "You're amazing," he said quietly as he leaned against the outdoor table, watching her. She pretended to shrug off the compliment, but the heat that rose to her cheeks revealed that she was pleased.

"It turned out all right," she said as she leaned the broom against the house and they headed inside to join the others. It didn't seem like he'd been talking solely about her haircutting skills. His look was too intense. Too *hungry*.

"I'm glad you came over," she said. "Can you...stay awhile?"

"Sure," he said. "We can...talk." He was staring at her in a way that made her forget to breathe.

"Hey, you two, ice cream's melting!" Darla called.

"You heard her." Hadley struggled for sense. "Ice cream's melting."

So were her insides. Her brain was having a meltdown too.

Ice cream was Hadley's favorite food, but it could've well been a bowl of sand she was eating because her appetite was shot. After the sundaes, Kit went on a hunt to round up all of Ollie's various little cars and dinosaurs, one of which mysteriously ended up in Jagger's bed, and she discovered a few more sticking up in the dirt around the potted plants. Cam surprised Ollie by hoisting him up on his shoulders and walking him around the patio, prowling around and growling and pretending they were *T. rexes*.

"It's getting late," Kit said to Hadley. "See you tomorrow, okay?" Ollie was clawing leaves on a tree and he and Cam were making chomping noises. She lifted a poignant brow at Hadley that might've meant *What a great guy* but didn't say anything. As Cam headed over, Ollie handed Kit a bloom from a bright pink *Mandevilla* vine that was climbing a trellis on the side of the patio. "Here, Mommy. Put it in your hair."

Kit stuck it behind her ear and held out her arms for her son. "Time to go, bud. What do you say to Cam and Aunt Hadley?"

"Thank you for the haircut, Aunt Hadwey," Ollie said, bending to give her a kiss. "Bye, Cam," he added a little shyly, then kissed him on the cheek too.

"Anytime, buddy," Cam said, looking a little taken aback. "Next time bring a ball, okay?"

He rubbed his eyes and held out his fist for Cam to bump.

"You just said the magic word," Kit said. Then she turned to Darla. "I've got to go before somebody falls asleep in the car."

"I'm coming," Darla said, who had caught a ride with Kit. To Hadley, she said, "Thanks for a fun evening." Then she dropped her voice and winked. "Hope your fun is just getting started."

As they left, Hadley could hear Ollie saying, "I'm not going to fall asleep in the car," as he rested his head drowsily on his mom's shoulder.

Cam didn't appear to be in a rush to go anywhere. "She's so good with him," Hadley said, desperate to fill a sudden void. Because now they were *alone*. "It's hard though. She worries about him not having a male role model. So I'm sure your offer to play ball is much appreciated."

"Well, I happen to love to play ball," he said, grinning.

Hadley cleared her throat. "Well." She grabbed the broom again and did another sweep. She must've swept the hair out from under that chair seventeen times. Her obsessive cleaning skills would make Gran proud.

As the sky faded to indigo over the sea and the summer surf churned softly in the distance, she was filled with that familiar longing again, rolling through her stomach and making her heart beat with anticipation—but for *what* exactly? Sex? Admittedly, yes, sure. For connection, love, the start of a real relationship?

It had only been four months since Cooper. How could she know what she wanted in that short amount of time?

And she was leaving.

And what if *he* left *her*? He'd done it once before. She understood all his angst over his injury, his need to restart his life... and how all that uncertainty could lead to another heartbreak.

And that's not even mentioning the *building*.

All great reasons to go running in the opposite direction. Yet her heart whispered, *Stay*. And the very air felt electric with possibility after those incredible kisses on the beach. Try as she might, she simply couldn't muster up any regrets.

As if sensing her turmoil, Cam walked over to the chair vacated by Ollie. Hadley thought he was going to pick it up and carry it back into the house, but he sat down instead. "Actually...," he said, raking his hands through his hair and shooting her a sheepish half-smile. "Would you mind?"

"Mind?" Mind *what*?

He smiled at her confusion. "I'm sort of desperate for a haircut. They want me to take photos tomorrow with the team."

"You're kidding, right?" Of course he was, because he could afford a two-hundred-dollar haircut. And getting one for a picture with a high school team? Hardly a hair emergency.

Plus...if he was serious, which she very much doubted he was, in order to cut his hair, she'd have to *touch* him. And that would remind her again of their time at the beach and...well, she was shaking a little just thinking about it. "I literally haven't done a guy in years," she said.

Oh no. Did she actually just say that? "I mean, *cut a guy's hair.* I haven't done an *adult male haircut* in a long time."

Okaaay. Maybe that would scare him enough to redirect this conversation.

He sat there unfazed, his full lips quirked up in a smile. "I'm sure cutting hair is like riding a bike."

"You never forget how to do it?"

"You might fall off and get hurt, but you get back on and discover it's not so scary as you thought—with the right person."

She frowned, pretty sure they weren't talking about haircuts anymore.

Hadley crossed her arms and tried to rein this discussion in. "Maybe I used to cut your hair back in the day when you were saving every penny." She held up her hands defensively. "But I really don't want to be known as the one who ruined Tony Cammareri's hair."

"You used to do a really nice job, remember?"

Oh no. No, no, no. She did *not* want to remember. Yes, she used to give him haircuts, but...but there were certain other things that went along with those haircuts. Like talking and laughing and kissing. Sometimes *lots* of kissing. And other things. Haircuts that devolved into full blown make-out sessions that ended up...well, where they would've ended up if those kids hadn't shown up.

Yeah. She was suddenly having another hot flash, twenty years too soon.

When she'd hated him, she didn't think about the possibility of him walking into her house and her life and her bed. She didn't have... fantasies. She didn't... imagine. When you didn't indulge in pretending, you didn't set yourself up for another heartbreak.

And he just might be a heartbreak waiting to happen.

And she was a smart woman. She'd let him break her heart once. But twice? *Never.*

"You're not afraid, are you?" he asked.

"Afraid?" She swallowed hard. "Of ruining your hair?" She was as afraid of touching him, yet the pull toward him was a magnet she was completely helpless against. "You can afford to have someone fly in from New York straight to your doorstep and cut your hair. You don't need an amateur who learned her trade from YouTube videos."

"Please?" He rubbed his neck in a self-conscious gesture she found endearing. "It's getting really long." Then he pointed to the top of the brick garden wall. "Look, all your stuff is right there."

He was prodding her. Egging her on in his usual amiable, irresistible way.

She was kidding if she told herself this was just a haircut. Touching him would be, in this case... intimate. *Sensual.* And it would have consequences she wasn't sure she was ready for.

Chapter 22

SO," CAM SAID a little while later, in the middle of his haircut, "how's it going?" Hadley had dropped the scissors twice, startling the dogs as they slept on the patio. But she wore this look of intense concentration where she sank her teeth into her lower lip as she worked that was the cutest thing he'd ever seen.

"You still have beautiful hair," she said as she lifted each layer and carefully measured as she cut. "Super thick and wavy." The sensation of her fingers sliding through his hair was familiar and felt way too good.

"I might lose it one day," he said, but even that thought didn't alarm him enough to stop thinking of how much he wanted to kiss her, to pick up where they'd left off the other day at the beach. But he knew that she was thinking...a lot.

She laughed. "Somehow, I can't imagine that. But I'd still think you were cute."

He flicked his gaze up, and it got snared in hers, caught and trapped in the pull of her warm brown eyes. "Why would you still think I was cute if I was bald?"

"Because you have a nicely shaped head." She ran

her hand along his scalp, assessing. "Your face is nice and oval, and you have a strong jawline." Her hand grazed over his cheek. "And as far as I can tell, your head is perfectly egg shaped."

"Hmmm. Egg shaped. Now that sounds *really* sexy."

She laughed. "The point I was trying to make is that I would like you regardless of whether or not you had hair. I always liked you for what was on the inside."

He wasn't really sure how many people in his life he could say that about. Especially in the past few years.

"What is it?" she asked, putting down the scissors. "You look so serious."

"Just thinking that when you get famous, things change. People don't like you for you a lot."

"Well, they do here. So maybe it's good you came back."

"And frankly, people are looking for a down-and-out story. That's why I have to get back up and running as soon as possible."

Hadley shook her head. "I completely disagree with jumping on some bandwagon as fast as you can just to avoid scrutiny."

He shrugged. "I don't want my story to end with my football career."

She stood in front of him and put her hands on his shoulders. "I've *always* known you were more than football."

"That means a lot." He took her hand. "Here's the thing, Hadley," he said, twining his hands with hers. "You remind me of what's the best in me. Every minute I spend with you, I want you more. I miss you. I miss...us."

"I miss you too," she said, her voice practically a whisper.

They'd both leaned in, her lips close, a kiss tempting and inevitable, but he forced himself to say what he needed to say. "I can't lie to you," he said. "I'm off balance, off my game."

"*I'm* off balance," she countered. "I...Well, there's no way I'm ready for another relationship right now. Not to mention if we started one and...and it didn't work out. We're both not in the best place."

She seemed as nervous as he was. "Those kisses on the beach...I haven't felt that way with anyone but you." He paused and looked straight at her. "But I don't want to hurt you."

She stroked his mostly cut hair, then smoothed a hand down his cheek. Her touch was so pleasurable he closed his eyes.

He pressed his forehead to hers and they stayed there for a long moment. Then he drew back and looked at her.

"We still have a building between us." This time, he had to make sure all the cards were on the table.

Neither of them moved. Seconds ticked. In the corner of the patio, Bowie rolled over in his bed, his tags making a soft *chink*. In the background, the waves gently rolled.

He should let her go, but instead of dropping her hand, he tugged on it. Her eyes widened in surprise.

"Despite everything, I want you so badly I can't think of anything else." There. He'd spilled what was in his heart.

"Me too." She wrapped her arms around his neck. "Except I've never kissed a man with a bad haircut before. You really should speak to your barber."

"You're fired," he said. And then he kissed her.

* * *

Their lips met in a clash of passion, so different than the more tentative kisses on the beach. Cam's lips were hungry and devouring, his mouth possessing hers with every kiss, every stroke. And every single one left her dizzy and trembling, her heart pounding, her breath running ragged. She kissed him as if they had years to make up for in a few short minutes.

They sort of did.

"I think you're holding back." He smiled against her skin as he dropped a line of kisses all along her neck.

She made light of it, but truthfully, there'd never been any holding back with him. Nothing had ever felt like this, no one. *No one but him.*

That was the kind of thinking that could get her in big trouble. So she pushed it out of her head and told herself to just enjoy the moment.

She'd started to untie the tablecloth cape around his neck when he reached up and took her hands. "You don't have to say it," he said, his voice low and ragged. "I know."

She pulled back, frowning a little. "Know what?" she asked, a little breathless.

"That I'm a really good kisser."

"Excuse me?" she said with mock outrage. "*I'm* a really good kisser. I hope our competitiveness doesn't extend to the bedroom."

"I'm just messing with you." He chuckled, his eyes full of warmth and mischief.

She pulled herself back from completely falling under his spell. "Look I ... This is just for fun, right?" Because they were thrown together, they couldn't help but be reminded of old times.

That was all.

In response, he wrapped his arms around her and pulled her close. So close she could feel the rock-hard wall of muscle surrounding her, the taut planes and valleys of his chest, the solid body built for blocking. "Right," he whispered as he swept back her hair and kissed the sensitive skin below her ear. "Neither of us is ready to start something. I get it."

She stood and took his hand. "Come inside now."

He took her hand but didn't budge. "That doesn't mean this doesn't mean something to me." He brought her hand up to his mouth and kissed her knuckles, each in turn.

That made her eyes threaten to tear up. And made her melt into him as he kissed her again, slowly and languidly, until the patio began to spin and the world around them faded away.

"I can't fight this anymore, Hadley. I just wish I had more to bring to you."

She shook her head. "It's you I want. Nothing more or less. Just you."

On hearing their footsteps, the dogs, who'd been passed out in the corner of the patio, woke up begrudgingly. Jagger shook his head, his tags clinking, and Bowie yawned widely. Cam let them out into the grassy part of the yard to do their business, then rounded them up. The letting in of the dogs, the turning off of lights, the sliding shut of the glass patio door—it felt like a routine, a ritual that seemed natural and seamless.

"The kids are settled in." Cam gave a nod to the two dogs who'd curled up on opposite sides of Gran's couch in the living room.

"I think Jagger's pretty excited about having an overnight guest," Hadley said. "I know I am."

"Wait," Cam said. "Doesn't Jagger somehow always end up in your bed? Because Bowie has that habit too."

"Yes. But maybe since they have each other they'll stay out here."

"We can hope." Cam pulled her close and kissed her, slow and deep, leaving her shaky and wanting. "Can I take you to bed now?"

She nodded and started to guide him down the hall, but he suddenly scooped her up instead. She gave a little yelp as he slung her effortlessly over his shoulder and carried her to Gran's spare bedroom. "Amen to that."

* * *

It was a little primal, being slung over Cam's shoulder, being carried by a man who'd blocked other guys with his body—for a living. But despite all the impenetrable muscle, he set her down on her bed as gently as a snowflake.

He lay over her, whispering to her how happy he was to be with her, how he'd missed her, and of course, everything he wanted to do with her and to her. And despite her resolve to hold back, she believed him. Every word.

And then he showed her, kissing her slowly and deeply, running his hands over her curves, peeling off clothes layer by layer. She ran her hands under his shirt, over the smooth hills of muscle, surprised at how soft his skin was over the hard, toned flesh.

Hadley swallowed, struggling against the heat that was building inside of her. Cam kissed her cheek, her temple. "I want to kiss every part of you," he murmured as he pressed his lips to her neck, making her head drop back on the pillow. She was becoming boneless, heat rising everywhere, and she was adrift somewhere, aware of nothing but his kisses, completely transfixed under his spell.

"You can... You don't have to do a lot of... warm-up. I'm... I'm ready."

He drew his head up and, frowning a little, assessed her.

"What? What is it?" she asked.

"You never tell a tight end how to catch the ball," he said softly, stroking her hair. "So let me do what I know how to do, okay?"

"I just didn't want to take too much time."

He scowled. "First I'm going to explore every inch of you. And then I'm going to do that over again. All. Night. Long. So there is no such thing as taking too much time."

"You're a little cocky," she said, a fierce blush overtaking her at his words.

"I never brag," he said solemnly. "I let my actions speak for themselves."

"I know how to do a few things, too, Mr. Tight End," she said, running her hands over the contoured muscles of his butt.

He tossed his head back and laughed. From his position over her, he looked at her, quietly assessing. "You're quivering," he whispered.

"Just a little," she said.

He placed her hand on his arm so she could feel the soft covering of hair, the tense length of flexed muscle. "I am too."

Their gazes locked, and that familiar feeling—connection, acceptance, honesty, despite everything between them—was nothing short of terrifying, and it shook her to the core. "You're so beautiful," he said, bending his head to kiss her. She was trembling under his touch, restless, struggling to give him pleasure, too, but he gently brushed her arms away.

"Your turn right now. Let me...let me do this, okay? Tell me if you don't like it."

Her hands grazed restlessly over his pecs, his stomach, his back. He was so gentle, so loving, and the worst, most devastating thing...so kind and familiar. Long ago, he'd treated her with the same...reverence—the exact same care he demonstrated with her now—and he was slowly driving her mad.

"I'm ready," she said, trying to fight the waves of pleasure that were mounting inside of her. "You don't have to keep—"

"Oh, I'm just getting started." He flashed a boyish grin. "I have to show you that I learned a thing or two in all this time, don't I?"

Then the world's most famous tight end showed her how good he really was at catching the ball and running it over the goal line.

* * *

A long time later, they lay together in the dark, the dogs fast asleep at their feet. Bowie's soft snores filled the room, and Jagger, who took up almost the entire bottom half of the bed, twitched his limbs, probably dreaming of chasing seabirds in his sleep. But Cam didn't mind. Hadley lay her head on his shoulder and wrapped her arm around his waist, their fingers laced together. For the first time in months—since his injury, really—all the noise in his brain had stopped. The noise that told him to *hurry up, make a plan, divide and conquer*. And the silence had brought a sense of calm that he hadn't felt in ages.

He glanced down to find her looking up at him. "You've gone quiet."

He always knew when her moods changed, something she'd always had a hard time hiding from him. She gave him a squeeze. "Just thinking how that was pretty good."

He laughed. "Pretty good? Hmmm. If you're only going to give me a B, I'm going to have to try harder. Like, right now."

In one quick move, he rolled them over so he was on top and kissed her neck until she started laughing. "Okay, okay," she said. "I just didn't want you to get a big head. It was amazing, all right?" She bit her lip. "How was it for you?"

Couldn't she tell by the dumb, contented expression that must be all over his face? He'd known good sex but this was great sex coupled with an insatiable, desperate desire to please her in every way he knew and to stay here with her body curled into his. He was dazed. He was drained. He was stupidly happy. "Let's just say I'm lying here plotting what I can do to get you to call out my name like that again."

That earned him a punch in the arm.

He saw she was waiting for a real answer. One he was afraid to give. But then he thought that she *deserved* one. Especially if, as he suspected, that ass Cooper had also been an ass in bed.

He smoothed her hair back and cradled her beautiful

face in his hands. "When I was eighteen, I thought I was the luckiest guy alive to be with you. What we had between us was always easy and fun and...natural."

"We were just kids," she said with a shrug. "What did we know?"

"We knew we cared for each other. And maybe that's what made it so...good."

"Thanks for saying that. But you didn't really answer the question about...now."

"Footballers have great instincts," he said. "Sometimes you just know."

"Know what?" she asked.

"Every baller has their sweet spot. Where in their hand the ball feels just right." He gathered her in. "You're *my* sweet spot." He kissed her forehead before lying back on the bed beside her, a little anguished that he'd been so honest—and that she'd gone completely quiet. "*Now* what are you thinking about?"

"No one's ever compared me to a football before but...I like it." She reached up and smoothed his hair.

He shot her a grin. "Any time a baller uses a baller analogy, that's pretty profound."

She chuckled. He lay there with her in the quiet, happiness rolling over him. After a while, she spoke. "Actually, I am thinking of something. Christine and Drew." *Christine and Drew? Now?* "He came back after college and started coaching, and she came back to work at the library. I was wondering...what that would've been like, if we hadn't lost all those years."

"I was thinking that could've been us," he admitted as he absently played with a lock of her hair.

They could've had three kids, a house...and a lot of years together.

"I'm not sure if you would've been happy with me," he said. "We probably would've ended up back here after college. My career might've dominated everything, including the choices of where we lived. We would've bought a house, probably oceanfront, and you would've been a football wife. I can't really see you being a football wife."

"Me neither."

"There's a positive side, you know," he said. "We left. We learned things. And we found each other again. Besides," he said, "with me, the best is definitely yet to come."

"How do you know that?" She looked at him with a puzzled expression.

"Oh, I just do." He raised himself up on one elbow, the sudden movement causing both dogs to scatter off the bed. Then he kissed her, thoroughly and slow, sending a deep shiver running through her.

He lifted his head. "Had?" he asked.

"What is it?" she managed.

"Think you'd mind finishing my haircut before I have to have my picture taken tomorrow?" He chuckled deeply.

She laughed, and he went back to business.

Chapter 23

THE NEXT MORNING, the summer sun was slanting through the blinds, spilling warm beams across the quilted seahorse comforter in Gran's spare room. Caught in the pleasant fog of sleep, Hadley wondered why she was sleeping in so late. When *had* she slept in last? She couldn't even remember. But then consciousness hit her like an avalanche, causing her to bolt upright in the bed. It all came back to her in flashes. Cam's lean, strong body over her, his whispered words making her laugh or blush. The low growl of pleasure in his throat.

Tears came to her eyes. Ones that shouldn't come for just a lighthearted summer fling. Cam was...Tony was...both of them together were...well, she had no words. All she knew was that the pain and sorrow of the past six months had faded, and her heart was bursting with happiness. With a rightness she hadn't felt for a long time.

He hadn't slickly manipulated her grandmother into selling him her building. He loved his sister, his niece, his family, and his community. He'd protected her from the photographers' vile questions and sacrificed something big.

And he just…got her. He'd encouraged her passion for working with animals even though doing that very thing worked against what he wanted the most.

If only Cam understood how amazing he was. Hadley certainly did.

Her eye caught a flash of bright yellow next to her pillow. It was a sticky note with Cam's handwriting and read:

> Good morning,
> Princess.

Smiling and suddenly feeling flushed, she left the bed, sticky note in hand, and found another on the floor right in front of the bathroom doorway. This one said:

you're pretty when you
sleep.

Aww. This was melting her. Another one over the closed toilet lid said that he'd made coffee, to which she thanked her lucky stars, and the fourth, stuck on the faucet, said:

Meet me at my dad's at
11.

And just like that, her aversion to sticky notes evaporated.

She didn't have a clue why he wanted her to meet him at his dad's, but she hoped Cam's whole family would be there. And she hoped that, given the Cammareris' love of feeding people, possibly lunch would be involved too.

A worry crossed her mind. What were they—she and Cam—in front of his family, in front of the town, the world? And what exactly did sleeping together make them?

She decided to do herself a favor and not define it, just enjoy the happiness of being with him. Because it felt too wonderful not to.

She spent the morning making sure everything on her half of the gala list—flowers, PR/media, favors, programs, music, and speeches—would go on tomorrow night without a hitch. Cam was working on the food, parking, tables, and lighting. Somehow it would all hopefully come together and be awesome.

At eleven on the dot, she pulled up in front of the little Craftsman-style house where Cam grew up, not far from the square. It looked the same, tidy with neat trim, a big covered porch full of comfy furniture, and Angelo's giant vegetable garden growing like crazy in the backyard. There was a metal contraption standing in the driveway that she thought might possibly be a smoker.

So maybe there really would be one of Angelo's delicious lunches after all.

"Hey," Cam said, greeting her at the door, his blue eyes soft and eating her up with that same hungry look of his, which made her feel . . . a little terrified.

Because suddenly she wasn't sure how they were going to handle this—whatever *this* was—in front of each other, let alone in front of everyone else.

She loved that he wanted her. But she knew in her heart that what she felt for him went way beyond desire. Maybe it always had.

He was wearing an apron. The same red-and-white checked one as at the festival. Which was odd but cute. Cooking today, when there was so much to do?

"Hey back," she said. For a second they stood there, grinning awkwardly at each other. She wanted to throw herself into his arms but...should she? Would he want her to do that on his dad's doorstep?

"I...um." Okay, she needed to start again. "We never talked about how we should behave in public." She glanced around to make sure no one was watching. "I don't want to do anything you feel uncomfort—"

Before she could finish, he stepped down and gathered her into his arms, dragging his mouth over hers, his fingers lacing into her hair. It was a wonderful, wholemouthed kiss that made her feel like she was going to slide down to the ground in a puddle at his feet. Finally he broke the kiss, releasing her. She backed up and nearly fell off the step, his strong forearm pulling her back on balance.

Oh my. He'd turned her into a dizzy, breathless mess.

And he stood there, grinning from ear to ear, clearly pleased with himself. "Did you just say something about behaving in public?"

"Oh," she said, grasping for words. "I was thinking maybe we should let the benefit be the story for now. Once people catch wind of something going on between us, you'll be headlined as my rebound romance."

"And you'll be my hometown honey fling." He chuckled. "I can probably behave until after the benefit...but that doesn't mean I'm not crazy about you."

Her stomach gave a tumble. She was inordinately thrilled despite telling herself not to be. But how could he know how much she'd needed to hear that?

She was still in a daze when Lucy popped her head up behind Cam. "Did you tell her? Hurry up, time's flying!" She nudged Cam out of the way. "It's time for taste testing. Come in as soon as you're ready."

"What's going on?" she asked. She saw Nick race out the side door and fiddle with the smoker. "Why is everyone...cooking?"

"Okay," Cam said. "I'm just going to give it to you straight. But know that I'm already working on solutions to our problem but I haven't finalized anything yet and never would without you."

This was sounding ominous. "Cam, you're scaring me," she said. "What problem?"

He took her hand and led her down the steps to the yard. "Lars the caterer had to cancel. There was an electrical fire in his prep kitchen. Everyone's okay. The building made it, too, but the appliances got damaged. So...no food."

Hadley's head whirled. "I'm glad no one got hurt. But...no food for two hundred people by tomorrow?"

"Lars gave me the name of his brother over in Chesterton and I called and gave him a heads-up. He said he could help us out."

Hadley blew out a breath. "Thank goodness. An alternative."

"My dad knows him and says he's a nice guy. But my dad thinks we can do better."

Wait—Angelo thought he could do better than the caterer? She was having a hard time following. "What do you mean?"

"My dad and Lucy think they can handle it. Or, I should say, they're *dying* to handle it."

She dropped her voice to a whisper. "Tony, are you insane? We have to feed a crowd the size of a small wedding. I know your family loves to cook but we need *professionals*. I'm in PR. I know all about what it takes to carry off big events like this. And I can tell you—"

"I know that, Had, but... but well, when I told my dad and Lucy what happened, they were all over it." He paused. "Even Nick rallied."

"Hey! I heard that." Nick came up from checking the smoker. "So I'm not a born chef like everyone else around here. But I work hard." In true Cammareri fashion, he flexed his biceps.

"*Hardly work*, you mean," Cam shot back, chuckling.

"Guys!" Hadley said, wanting them to focus. Because... two hundred people. *Tomorrow.*

"So we've got a few things prepared," Cam said. "You know my dad was a cook in the army, right? He knows how to feed a crowd. And Lucy has the catering experience."

"And I've got the brawn." Nick did more flexing.

Cam immediately fake-punched him in his rock-hard abdomen while Hadley tried to take calming breaths. Is this what brothers did?

"Even if your family *can* do this," she said, "your dad's kitchen is tiny. It would be... impossible."

"Lucy's catering boss told us we can use her kitchen, and even some of her staff if we can pay them."

Well, they'd thought things out, that was for sure.

"You can be the judge of the food," Cam continued. "If it doesn't pass your muster, we go to Plan B, okay?"

She met his gaze. It occurred to her that he didn't look stressed. He looked...excited. Yes, that was it. "You want this, don't you?"

He walked her back to the door. "I loved learning how to make homemade pasta with my dad. He knows what he's doing. Just...just come see, okay?"

He looked...different. Yes, that was it. Like he was on a mission. Like he was having fun. Unlike Hadley, who was imagining a huge crowd of hungry, angry people wanting to drive to the next town for burgers. "Okay. Fine. Impress me."

"I thought you'd never say that." He put a hand on her back to guide her into the house and dropped his voice. "I'll take that as a challenge in more ways than one."

* * *

Cam carefully placed a couple of cappellacci di zucca onto a plate and spooned some pan sauce over them as his dad hovered right behind him making sure he did it right. It was an old family recipe from northern Italy, and Cam wanted to give it the respect it was due. Lucy and his dad had done all the prep work, but they'd taught him how to run the pasta through the laminator and cut it, then stuff it with pumpkin filling and form it into little hats.

Everyone gathered around the old oak table with forks in hand. Even Bernie, locked and loaded in her high chair and ready for some pureed pumpkin, seemed to sense the solemn air.

Cam's eyes were on Hadley, waiting expectantly for her to lift the fork to her mouth. It wasn't that he didn't know if the pasta was good. He'd watched his dad make it just as he had a thousand times before, going through the painstaking steps of mixing flour, water, and oil, rolling and cutting the dough and filling it with cheeses, frying pancetta, and drizzling a butter sauce over the still-warm pasta.

But this time he found himself holding his breath. He wanted her to be pleased. No, thrilled. He wanted to share the family heritage. He wanted to *feed* her.

He was proud of his family and their food traditions. Proud of his dad, and how his face had lit up about this challenge. Lucy's too.

"Are you ready?" he asked as he placed more cappellaccis on a plate.

"Very nice," Angelo said from behind his shoulder.

Lucy brought over orange-and-yellow frothy drinks and passed them around.

"Is that what I think it is?" Hadley asked. They'd asked Lars to create a special drink for the benefit. Something appropriate for the tropical theme and symbolic of Seashell Harbor. Lucy had taken the assignment and run with it.

Lucy smiled. "This will help take the edge off from dealing with my brother."

Nick broke out laughing.

"I should've said *both* my brothers," Lucy said, frowning.

"It's really pretty," Hadley said, examining the fancy drink. "What's in it?"

"Take a sip," Lucy said proudly.

Cam was ecstatic to see his sister so excited.

"I call it a Tequila Sunset," Lucy said. "The party is *right* on the boardwalk, so everyone will be watching the real sunset."

Cam passed out the food as everyone exclaimed over the drinks. When the meal was finally served, Hadley lifted her fork to her mouth but noticed no one else was taking a bite. "Why aren't you all eating?"

"Because you're the guest of honor," Cam said pointedly. "It matters what you think here."

Hadley shook her head and laughed. Then she speared a cappellacci with her fork and—Cam had to give her credit—ate it with everyone watching.

"Wow," she said, chewing slowly. "It's...incredible. It melts in my mouth. Are there more?"

"There are a *lot* more," Angelo said. "It's a traditional family recipe. We'd be proud to serve it."

"I'd be proud to have you serve it," she said, holding up her plate. "Now, may I please have more?"

That's what Cam was waiting for. He blew out a pent-up breath.

"You can sit down now," Angelo said to him. "She likes it."

"There's nothing like family and food," Cam said, finally sitting down to dish out some for himself. If only his investors would allow him to serve food like this in his restaurants. But a homemade, fresh recipe like this would be too complicated and time-consuming for a chain.

"I think you were born to serve food like this," Hadley said. "Cooking food and being with people is your calling." She speared another bite on her fork. "Hey, you should open a restaurant."

She was half joking, but her words made him choke up. He did love food—*this* food. His family's traditional recipes. Without thinking, he reached over and placed his hand on top of hers on the table.

She sucked in a breath. The only other sound in the room was the baby babbling as she dropped peas on the floor. Everyone else's eyeballs were focused on what he'd just done.

Which was to show everyone exactly how he felt about Hadley. He'd done it without thinking.

Was she okay about that? Was he? A glance across the table showed her to be carefully watching his next move. He couldn't tell what she was thinking.

"Hey, what's that about?" Nick finally asked.

"Nothing, Nick," Cam said as he removed his hand. "It's nothing." He weighed his options. She might be upset with him if he spilled their secret. But if he stayed silent, she might think he didn't care enough to tell his family about them. Which was worse?

"But I saw—" Nick seemed to be thinking about it. "Well, that certainly explains that stupid expression you've been wearing on your face all day."

Angelo looked up from his pasta, his fork in midair. "It's not every day a woman can do that to a man, you know what I'm saying?"

"What, embarrass him?" Nick chuckled.

"No, make him blush," his dad said wisely.

Nick could barely hold in a belly laugh.

"I hope we can be sisters one day, Hadley," Lucy said, no doubt just to get Cam's goat. "Because I'm way too outnumbered around here."

"I hope you all have had your fun," Cam said, "but I have to say you're right. Hadley means a lot to me." He met her gaze across the table. "I'm really glad you're here with me to enjoy this great meal."

As they all dug into the great meal, Cam felt something he hadn't felt in a long time. *Thankful.* He might've lost football, but he had his siblings, who would torment him until his last breath, of that he was sure.

And most importantly, he had Hadley, something he'd never dreamed of. He looked up to find her staring at him from across the table. And then she smiled.

He gave her a wink, dug into his plate, and ate the delicious food.

Chapter 24

THE NIGHT OF the gala couldn't have been more ideal if fairies had sprinkled magical dust to paint the evening sky in hues of salmon and orange and the glassy ocean in deep midnight blues. There was even a full moon over the boardwalk.

The stunning color show made Hadley emotional and breathless with wonder. Or was it that her heart was so full, every sense seemed to be heightened?

In front of her on the grass of the beachside park, a sea of tables was set with bright yellow cloths. The boardwalk, which was doubling as a dance floor, was lined with rows of white lights. And the calmly rolling ocean served as the dramatic soundtrack to a picture-perfect setting.

Hadley had just complimented Maggie Hakutani and her daughter on the gorgeous orange and white gladiolas in tall glass vases on every table that were lit inside with tiny lights.

Everything was ready. It was as if the entire harbor were holding its breath, waiting for the guests, who were starting to arrive.

"Um, excuse me," a voice said from behind her. "Are you the person in charge?"

She whirled around to find Cam standing there. He wore a simple black collared shirt, khaki shorts, and nice flip-flops, casual attire that most men would be wearing this evening. Darkly handsome, confident, and elegant, he simply took her breath away as he leaned against a tree, looking like everything she'd ever wanted. And he happened to have one of Lucy's fancy drinks in his hand, which she hoped was for her.

"Hey there," she said.

"Well, hello," Cam said, giving a low whistle as his gaze traveled over her. She was wearing a simple black dress overlaid with black lace and cute sandals. Nothing special. But the way he looked at her made her feel... beautiful.

He held out the drink. "They told me to bring this to the badass lady with the headset."

She shrugged. "All in a day, Cammareri." Adjusting her headset, she took a sip of the drink he'd brought her and sighed. "That's delicious. Better take it away until later."

He snuck a quick kiss.

"I thought there was no PDA." Not that she was protesting.

"That was just for good luck," he said. "My way of being helpful."

She laughed nervously. "That kind of help makes me forget *everything* I have to do."

He straightened her headset and took back the drink. "You're too good for that."

"Are you nervous?" she asked.

"Yes," he admitted. "But I'm also really excited. I

can't wait to see people enjoy our food. Thanks for letting my family do this. It meant a lot to my dad and my sister."

"What does it mean to *you*?" she asked.

"I know what you're trying to get me to do. Say I love feeding people."

"Well?" she asked.

"Okay, fine. Yes. I'm really excited. I'm headed to the food tent now to help out. I think everything else is in control. You need anything?"

They'd agreed she would stomp out fires while he went to check on his family. "All is well—so far, anyway. We worked hard on this."

"We worked hard on this *together*," he amended. "See you after dinner?" He whispered something in her ear as they parted ways.

"See you," she said weakly as she waved him off. When she finally got her wits about her, she walked over to the boardwalk, where a local band was setting up.

"Your cheeks are blazing," Kit said with a wide smile.

Darla hugged her. "We saw him kiss you," she reported like they were back in high school. "On the *lips*."

Kit suddenly looked teary.

"Kit! What?" Hadley said.

"It's...it's wonderful to see you happy," she said.

"I'm afraid to say it, but I *am* happy," Hadley said. "But I'm not calling this anything. We're just...we're just..."

"Completely smitten," Darla said, letting Hadley take a sip of her gin and tonic.

"Taking it one day at a time," Kit suggested.

Hadley nodded, swiping at her own eyes. "Both of those."

"I'm thrilled for you," Kit said. "I've always liked Cam."

"But Darla was ready to hang him up by the balls a few weeks ago," Hadley said.

"I know but…I've decided he deserves a second chance." She gave a resigned sigh. "He gave my mom some Giants wear, and she can't stop talking about how wonderful he is."

"Speaking of second chances," Kit said to Darla, "I've heard Nick's been working at your house every day this week."

"He convinced me to let him fix my porch roof."

"That's pretty impressive considering the Cammareris don't usually touch any house less than a century old," Kit said. "Has he offered to do anything else for you?" Kit nudged Darla with her elbow.

"It's not like that," Darla said, but her fingers flitted nervously around her drink. "I'm just glad we can hold a conversation without getting angry with one another."

"Nick helped my parents remodel their powder room and only charged them the cost of the materials," Kit said.

"He's a nice guy," Hadley said. "Funny too."

"He's the same old Nick," Darla said. "I mean, I get why I fell in love with him in the first place. He still tells the stupidest jokes. And he still has that same ratty vintage baseball cap collection. One day he showed up with one he bought on our honeymoon in Savannah. Weird, huh?"

Weird. That was one word for it…

"Speak of the devil," Kit said, nodding toward the boardwalk.

And suddenly there Nick was, walking across the grass near the boardwalk. He stopped to speak to Cam, who was chatting with the valet parking staff. Hadley couldn't help but notice Darla looking with interest but pretending not to, a move they'd all perfected well during their teenage years.

"Maybe he'll ask you to dance later," Kit said.

"What is this, high school?" Darla waved a hand in dismissal. "I don't want to dance with him."

As they talked, a woman walked up to Nick and kissed him. He laughed and put his arm around her.

Darla's eyes grew wide for a flash of a second.

"Oh," Kit said. "Lauren. I'd forgotten about her."

Darla tore her gaze away. "I'm definitely not interested in rehashing anything with him. And I hope he's happy with her. Really. I wish him the best."

Darla exercised her usual restraint about showing her feelings, but Hadley could tell from the way she forced a convincing tone and the way she suddenly fidgeted with her phone, that she was affected more than she let on.

"Oh, there are my mom and dad, standing by the fountain waving," Kit said, waving back. "My first night in a century without Ollie and my parents are here to watch my every move."

"Maybe they'll leave early," Darla said hopefully.

"I hope so," Kit said, "because I'm really looking forward to those pineapple drinks with all the froth."

"You mean piña coladas?" Darla said.

"Um, they're called Tequila Sunsets," Lucy said as she flew by with a large tinfoil-covered pan.

"They're delicious," Hadley said. "Lucy created them just for tonight."

"You did?" Darla asked.

"Not only is it orangey and frothy," Lucy said, "but it also has a little kick. Let me know how you like it." She was out of breath as she rushed past them to the food tent.

"I want one," Darla said. "Right now."

"Parents or no, I'm planning on having two." Kit looked across the greenspace, where her mom and dad were both still waving and smiling and trying to attract her attention. They all waved back while Kit let out a telling sigh. "I'd better go. See you both in a bit. Everything looks fantastic, Hadley."

"Thanks," Hadley said. "I hope you have a nice time tonight." Kit deserved to have a little fun, and Hadley vowed to help her more in the future. Maybe she could introduce her to someone. Or babysit Ollie on the weekends.

As she walked off, Hadley asked Darla, "Are you okay?"

"Of course." Her go-to answer. She survived cancer—she could survive anything. "I know better than to get my hopes up about Nick, okay?" she said. "I was just trying to be his…friend. Since I'm living here now." She looked Hadley in the eye and gave that smile she always gave when she was trying to be tough and upbeat, which was nearly all the time. Finding Hadley still staring, she sighed hard. "I think I'm just a little…lonely, you know? And sometimes I wonder if coming back here wasn't such a good idea after all. It stirs up…things."

"Want that drink?" Hadley asked. It was the first thing that came to her mind. Because she sure wanted one, too, as soon as her responsibilities were done.

Darla grinned. "You read my mind. I'll go get us some." She paused. "You and Cam did an amazing job," she said, changing the subject. "He's a good guy, Hadley. I hope everything works out with you two."

"I still have a lot of things to figure out. Like my future. And whether or not it includes him, I...I just don't know."

"But you're figuring it out," Darla said. "Bravo for you."

Hadley left to check out the food tent, which was a crazy flurry of activity. Angelo and Lucy were plating food, Nick was hauling trays, teenagers were serving, and Cam...was nowhere to be found. "Can I help?" she asked Angelo.

"Yes," he said, looking at her over his glasses as he spooned out pasta and then breaking into a giant smile. "You can go sit down and enjoy a nice dinner. We've got everything covered."

"I second that," Lucy said as she loaded plates onto serving trays.

Well, like father like son. And daughter, she thought.

Outside Cam was serving tables, smiling and laughing, joking. Everyone seemed delighted to have a famous football player not only serve their food but chat them up as well.

Feeling her responsibilities begin to dwindle, Hadley sat down with Darla. Only to have Cam serve their food himself. "Well?" he asked with concern. "Is it warm? Is it good?"

"It's perfect," Darla said, savoring a bite of pasta.

"Darla," Cam said. "I can't believe you said that."

She shrugged and took another bite.

"Save room for dessert," he said quietly to Hadley

with a look that made her blush *again* before he ran off to serve more people.

"Somehow, I have a feeling he wasn't talking about the tiramisu," Darla said.

Hadley was glad she didn't have to respond to that, because the band started playing. They both happened to look over at the light-strung boardwalk, where Kit was standing near the dance floor...with a *guy*.

"Parents or no parents, look at that," Darla said.

"Is that Hal? The insurance adjuster from work that keeps asking her out?" Hadley asked. "She doesn't look very happy."

Kit was standing with her arms crossed and shaking her head. A Caribbean-beat song was just getting started, and the lit torches gave a fun island vibe as everyone flocked to the boardwalk.

The guy took her recklessly by the elbow and, laughing, headed to the dance floor. The gesture wasn't overly rough, and they probably wouldn't even have noticed except for the fact that Kit wasn't laughing.

The guy was large and muscle-bound and clearly had already had too much to drink. "I'm going over there," Hadley called over her shoulder, already rushing away, Darla following right behind her.

"C'mon, Kit," the guy was saying as they neared. "Quit being a tease. You know you want me."

Hadley, infuriated, was about to do *something*—not quite sure what the depths of her outrage would come up with—but someone else got there first. A tall, lean guy with a military cut and his own set of muscles wore an expression thunderous enough to freeze Hadley in her tracks. She suddenly recognized Kit's rescuer as Alex de la Cruz, Carson's best friend.

"I don't think the lady wants to dance," Alex said, inserting himself between Kit and Hal.

Hal held up his hands defensively. "I just wanted to dance, I swear it, nothing else. I just thought—"

Alex hovered over him. *Way* over him. "Okay, no thinking. If you don't back off, you're going to be dancing *with me*. And I don't think you're going to like my rhythm. You get what I'm saying?"

Hal shook his head, backed away, and vanished into the crowd, leaving Kit to stand there, openmouthed.

"Are you all right?" Alex asked.

"I…um, yes," Kit said, crossing her arms. "Just a little disappointed."

His brow rose in surprise.

"…because I might've liked to see you dance with him."

He squinted into the distance. "I can still arrange that, if you'd like."

"I'm swooning," Darla whispered to Hadley. "I love a guy in uniform."

"He's not wearing his uniform," Hadley whispered back.

"That's okay," Darla said. "He's still going in my next book."

"Thanks for helping me," Kit was saying to Alex. "He's harmless, just a little drunk. When…did you get into town?"

"Just got here," Alex said, glancing around. "Thought I'd come check out the celebration."

"I emailed you," Kit said. "I told you not to come on my account. I really don't need help with the McKinnon house. I'm sorry if you didn't receive it."

"I got your email," he said. "I'm actually back home

to visit my mom. I'm still on active duty until next spring."

Kit frowned and opened her mouth to say something but Alex interrupted.

"It's a shame to waste a good song. Want to dance? I promise I'll do better than our friend there."

Kit's eyes widened in shock. "Dance? Now? With you?"

Say yes was the look that passed between Hadley and Darla. Say yes *now*.

Alex started to sway to the music. "I love this song. C'mon."

Kit scanned the crowd, maybe to see if her parents were watching. But then she took his hand.

"I can't believe she just did that," Hadley said.

"Me neither," Darla said. "But just FYI, I'd let him work on *my* house anytime."

"Is that Alex?" Cam asked, walking up. "Maybe we need to worry more about him than that jerk who was bothering her. I was ready to give him a piece of my mind until I saw you all had it covered."

"All I know is I never did get that drink," Darla said. "Shall I bring three?"

Hadley glanced at her watch. "Thanks anyway, but I'm on the clock for another half hour."

"I'll get you one," Cam offered to Darla.

Darla placed a hand on both their arms. "Go dance. I'll handle it."

"Shall we?" Cam asked. "Unless there's something we need to do in the next five minutes?"

"I did want to check with Lucy one more time. But to be honest, the last time I did that she kicked me out of the kitchen." She set down her clipboard and removed her headset. "I'd love to dance."

Cam didn't hesitate to take her hand and lead her onto the boardwalk.

"We haven't danced together in a long time," Hadley said as Cam wrapped an arm around her waist.

"Prom, senior year?"

"Father Martin told us not to dance so close that the Holy Spirit couldn't fit between us."

He chuckled and held her close. He was wearing... shaving cream and soap, her favorite aphrodisiacs. "No chaperones tonight," he said with a smile.

"Just the whole town watching us," she said. But she couldn't bring herself to look at anyone but him. For that moment, there was just the two of them on a warm summer night, the stars peeking out above their heads, lights twinkling from far out in the ocean.

"Hi, sweetie," her mom said, suddenly sailing by on the dance floor with her dad. "Hi, Cam. So nice to see you again."

"You two are a cute couple," her dad said, winking before turning to her mom. "Shall we show them our moves?" he asked.

"Moves?" Hadley asked with a creeping sense of horror she hadn't felt since she was a teenager.

Her mom shrugged. "We've been practicing." Her dad pulled her mom in, released her, and spun her around. After which they both giggled and spun away, leaving Hadley shaking her head in wonderment.

"Your parents are pretty cute." Cam chuckled, pulling her close again. "Speaking of unexpected, look at that." Hadley craned her neck to follow his gaze.

Cam's dad was dancing with Mayellen.

"I totally called that," Hadley said.

Cam didn't look surprised. "There must be magic in

the air tonight. There's your grandmother and Paul." He nodded in their direction. "Let's dance by and say hi."

"Are you sure you want to do that?" Hadley asked. "I'm afraid we're going to get a giant I-told-you-so."

Cam spun them around just in time for Hadley to see Paul chuckling as he slow danced with her grandmother, who was actually *dancing*. Cautiously, but nevertheless dancing. She was smiling radiantly into Paul's eyes.

"Well, look at you two," Hadley said. "Hi, Paul. I love the bow tie. You look terrific, Gran."

"Well, look at *you* two," Gran said. "You make a great team. Everything turned out amazing. Thanks to both of you, I'm certain we've raised a ton of money for the new pediatric outpatient building."

As they were separated from Gran and Paul by the sea of dancers, Hadley asked Cam, "Do you ever wonder if my gran devised our 'punishment' for a reason?"

Cam smiled down at her, his blue eyes twinkling. "Well, it turned out not to be punishment after all. Maybe she knew all along."

"Knew what?" Hadley asked, looking up at his handsome face. "That we could work together without killing each other?"

He shrugged. "Maybe she knew we just needed a reason to set aside our differences."

She nodded. "I haven't even thought about the build—"

"Don't say it," he warned. "Not tonight."

"How did we manage to forget our differences?" she asked.

"People grow and change?" he offered.

Maybe so. Despite all the upheaval and the broken

heart that brought her home, Hadley felt...like herself for the first time in a long time. She closed her eyes and gave in to the moment as they swayed slowly to the music.

"Do we have more things to do?" Cam asked softly as the song wound down.

Did the music have to end? Did she have to open her eyes? "I should see if Lucy needs anything," she murmured against his shoulder, "but I think everything's taken care of."

"Good. Because I want to take you home."

She looked up to find him staring at her, his gaze filled with heat. "Better be careful, Cammareri. If you kiss me on the dance floor, tongues will be a-flapping."

As the music ended, she stepped back. He looked...amused. With the tiniest gleam in his eye that she was coming to recognize well.

"Well, I should probably do a final pass and thank all the workers and make sure that someone puts the chairs—"

"We'll get it done together," he said. Before she knew what was happening, he'd planted his lips on hers and kissed her until she was boneless, until she couldn't hear that the music had stopped or that people around them had stilled.

And then she heard clapping. And saw the faces of all their people—her mom and dad, Nick and Lauren, Mayellen and Cam's dad. And the very pleased and overjoyed face of her grandmother, who was standing next to Paul one step away from jumping for joy. Even Mayor Chaudhry and the members of the town council were yelling, "*Bravo! Bravo!*"

Cam, completely nonplussed by the fact that he'd

outed them to the entire town, bent and whispered in her ear.

She somehow got her wits about her enough to whisper a few choice things back. And this time—she swore she saw it—*he* blushed.

Chapter 25

CAM MADE A mental note to thank his sister personally for shooing Hadley out of the food tent. He took advantage of the opportunity by taking her hand and running with her to his car. As soon as they reached the beach cottages, they picked his place so they wouldn't have to deal with the dogs right away. Cam wasted no time keying the door. Or at least tried to.

"I can't see the lock," he said, fumbling the key for the second time.

"I'm not blocking your line of vision," she said innocently.

"No," Cam said, "but you're kissing my neck and running your hands up and down my...back."

She wrapped her arms around his waist. "That's what happens when you take too long to let us in," she added. As soon as he finally got the door open, she hustled him in and kept on with the kissing before he could get the door closed behind them.

Not that he was complaining. Not at all. He let her back him up against the wall. Putting his hands up in surrender, he let out a soft, "*Whoa.*"

"Do you want me to stop?" she asked, pulling back.

"Not a chance," he managed. "Maybe we need to oversee big events more often if this is the result."

"We make a great team," she said, kissing his chest.

He pulled her up to kiss her lips deeply and thoroughly. "What did I do to deserve you?"

"Nothing," she said, her eyes warm and dancing. He had to agree. He'd done nothing special to deserve all her warmth, her laughter, her honesty and kind spirit. He felt in his bones that whatever this crazy thing was between them, it was rare. Special.

He cradled her face in his hands and stared at her. She took his breath away. Astoundingly, she saw him for who he really was, not a superstar, not someone struggling to reinvent himself. And she wanted to be with him anyway. He didn't have to be anything or do anything or prove anything.

When he was with her, he felt that it might be possible to sort through his confusion and find a path forward.

The fevered kisses continued, deep and breathless, and somehow they ended up on the floor.

"Don't move a muscle," he said, a little out of breath.

"Why not?" She gave him a puzzled look.

He smoothed back a wisp of hair and gazed at her, a little awestruck. "Just that...I want to remember this forever." The moon was shining in, beams thrown across the floor, highlighting her hair like a halo. She looked down on him, the strap of her dress falling over her shoulder, her hair tumbling around her. "You want to go somewhere more comfortable?"

She traced a finger lightly over his brows. "I kind of like the floor."

He tossed his head back and laughed, even as the pleasure from her touching him flushed through his veins. He was losing his mind, his sense, his . . . heart . . . to this woman.

"Then the floor it is," he said as she kissed him again.

* * *

Afterward they lay tangled up in each other, a gentle breeze washing in from the screen door, the constant slow churning of the waves suddenly seeming loud and present. She rested her head on his shoulder, and he bent and kissed her hair.

"Sweet Hadley," he said. Her hand rested on his chest, and he took it, intertwining their fingers. When she looked up at him, he couldn't help but smile.

"That was terrible," he said, closing his eyes and holding her hand over his heart.

She popped up and scanned his face. "Horrific," she said, her eyes glistening a little. She gave him a quick kiss and nestled in, fitting perfectly against him.

He didn't laugh. Or move. Just enjoyed being with her.

She glanced around the room. "You do realize we're on your living room floor."

"Hey, be grateful the dogs aren't here. They'd be all over us, thinking it was playtime."

"I never thought I'd say this," Hadley said, "but I'm a little sad the gala is over."

He'd been thinking the same thing.

"I haven't had time to tell you this," she continued, "but I've been contacting a lot of people about starting a rescue. I have a meeting with the head of the state SPCA next week. And Fuller got his veterinary training program to agree to allow the residents to spay and neuter animals. And I met someone online from a popular no-kill shelter in New York who's going to talk to me about their business plan."

"Hadley," he said, "I know that whatever you decide to do, you'll do an incredible job." He believed it wholeheartedly.

"I was thinking the same about you," she said. "I think maybe you were born to own a restaurant. You love cooking and feeding people. Whatever happens, I want you to know that."

They were both quiet, listening to the familiar, soothing rhythm of the waves as they crashed to shore and receded, over and over again.

He told himself they'd started this just for fun. Or because they couldn't help it. Or any of a number of reasons he could try and convince himself were true.

He pushed those thoughts out of his head, determined to celebrate every moment with her. "So I want to know why you only call me Tony during... certain times."

"Well, that *is* your name," she said with a laugh. "*Someone* should call you that."

"But you haven't called me that in a really long time. Well, except the other night..."

"Now you're just embarrassing me," she said, but she was smiling. "If you don't like it, I'll stop. I've gotten used to calling you *Cam*."

He lifted his head and looked at her. "I love it when you call me Tony." He felt like it was his real name, his real self. The one that she somehow saw.

"Well, I suppose I can try it out again outside of the bedroom. Or living room," she added with a chuckle.

"I *do* have a bed, you know."

"Can we just stay here for a little longer?" She smiled up at him in a wistful way that made his heart twist with feeling.

"As long as you want to." He tightened his grip around her. He understood the feeling of wanting to slow down time. Of wanting this moment of peace and contentment to last.

They lay like that a long time, enjoying the quiet lull of the ocean and the sounds of the soft velvet night. And his heart was fuller than it had ever been.

* * *

Sometime in the middle of the night, Hadley bolted upright in bed. Cam stirred, his arm falling from around her waist. "You okay?" he asked in a sleep-laced voice. Nothing seemed amiss, both dogs snoozing happily at their feet, Bowie's snores following their usual rhythmic pattern, Cam's big body curled comfortingly around her.

Yet something seemed amiss. Hadley blinked, half awake, the gray room coming into focus. "I had the weirdest dream," she said, still groggy. "It was about puppies."

"You *would* dream of puppies." He rolled to his back. At some point they'd brought over the dogs, who immediately thought it was a slumber party and climbed right into bed with them. Bowie, who was lying on his calves, stirred. "Was it a good dream?"

"No, they were crying. Like—"

The faraway sound of whimpering suddenly filled the room. Hadley exchanged a did-you-really-hear-that glance with Cam, then jumped from the bed. Jagger, who'd been asleep near the edge, lumbered to the floor. Bowie sat up and shook himself, ears flapping. Hadley ran to the window in a flash, throwing it open. "Like *this*."

Distant strains of mewling drifted in from somewhere at the back of the house, brought in by the gentle breeze. Suddenly she felt the radiant warmth of Cam's body right behind her. "What is it?" he asked. "Cats, maybe?"

She turned from the window to face him. He was adorably disheveled, his hair sticking out at odd angles. "Something newborn. Puppies or kittens would be my guess." Grabbing her robe from a chair, she ran out of the bedroom, but Cam got to the kitchen first. By the time she caught up, he was standing at the door, his hand resting on the knob. Jagger was pacing back and forth, sensing something exciting out there. "Let me go first, okay?" Cam said, in full protector-warrior mode.

"Okay." She found it easiest to give in to those tendencies, which she secretly loved.

"Sorry, guys," Cam said, making sure the dogs stayed inside. "You'll have to miss the fun, but we'll be right back."

He was the first one out, using his phone flashlight to illuminate the little brick walk, following the soft noises next door to underneath Gran's patio table. Pulling out the nearest chair revealed a large cardboard box, the kind you'd use when you were packing up a house. They cautiously bent to see inside.

Hadley gasped as two flashes of silver shone back at them. The eyes of a dog, solemn and frightened. She was black and white, a collie mix with silky fur. And she was surrounded by five tiny nursing newborn puppies.

"Brand-new," Hadley said incredulously, studying the naked-looking babies, some tan and white, some black and white and brown, all with eyes closed tight.

"Well, I'll be." Cam flashed his light around, then walked to the side of the house and peered at the road. "Someone must know about you. About the shelter."

"Don't even bother looking," Hadley said. "I'm sure they're long gone. This has happened to Gran over the years. People find a dog that's given birth or else they can't handle their own dog with newborn puppies, and they drop them off. I'm not judging. I'm glad they brought them here rather than let them die." She bent to examine the mother dog, who appeared to be trembling. The pups were all still latched on, drinking. Except...her breath hitched. "Wait...Oh no. Can I see your light?"

She took the phone and shone the light. The five puppies were lined up against the mother dog. But off to the side was one more, a tiny black-and-white puppy curled up and shaking. She clutched Cam's arm.

"What is it?" he asked, struggling to see in the pitch darkness.

"I'm afraid the mom has rejected that one. It happens sometimes."

"What do we do?" It touched her that he was pacing the patio, poised to help.

"They need blankets and a heat lamp. I've got to get them to the shelter. The little guy needs milk replacer. And I need to call the vet." Her head was spinning.

"Milk what?" Cam said, a little sleepily. "Never mind, let me get my keys," and he was gone before she could even thank him.

Then he was back, quietly moving the chairs and gently sliding the box out from under the table. He gave

Hadley a little shoulder squeeze and flashed her an *I-know-you-got-this* look. She certainly hoped so. "On three, okay?"

She nodded, and together they gently lifted the box without a word.

* * *

To Cam's chagrin, Fuller came in a flash. But to his credit, he brought a big supply of milk replacer solution for the little runt puppy. "Don't get your hopes up too high," he said to Hadley. "Sometimes puppies don't eat because they're sick or frail or predisposed not to make it, you know? Sometimes the mama dog senses that and lets nature take its course."

Cam saw Hadley tear up even as she took a tiny syringe from Fuller and stood next to him at the counter while he explained what to do with the puppy milk. Cam set up a chair so Hadley could sit near the heat lamp and try to feed the puppy, while Fuller set to checking the mama dog.

Cam, completely out of his element, had never felt so helpless in his life. "We're going to think positive on this one," he offered to Hadley, not knowing what else to say. "And just do all we can."

Hadley shot him what he thought was a grateful look.

Still, Fuller and Hadley spoke a language he didn't. With words he'd never heard before, like *milk replacer*, *latching on*, *whelping pen*, and *rejected pup*. Still, he was determined to do whatever Hadley needed. Even if all he could do was simply be there for her.

So when there was a knock on the door, he ran to get it. It was Maddy, standing there with a cane and a worried expression on her face. "Over here." He gestured to where Hadley was struggling with the puppy.

"Oh, Gran," Hadley said. "I'm so glad you're here. It's been a long time since I've done this."

"You're doing fine," Fuller said as he stood next to Hadley and beamed. *Ugh.* Fuller should not count on staying fine himself unless he backed up a few paces. Cam crossed his arms and pasted on a friendly expression, but his muscles were twitching in readiness if Fuller moved one inch closer to her.

Gran, looking over Hadley's shoulder, smiled and rubbed her back. "You're doing a great job. Have you fed her yet?"

"The syringe is warming up in that bowl of water," Hadley said, placing the puppy stomach-down on her lap. "Cam, would you mind getting it?"

Cam found a small syringe with a rubber nipple attached to the end floating in the bowl and handed it to Hadley.

"I think you should do it, Gran." Hadley's face was riddled with worry. "I have no idea what I'm doing."

Maddy smiled a careful smile. "I'd rather watch you and be here in case you need me."

Hadley gently held the syringe up to the puppy's mouth.

The room had gone silent. Everyone seemed to hold their breath waiting to see if the puppy would drink.

"Point it toward her cheek," Gran said. "And squirt in just a tiny bit."

Milk promptly dribbled out of the puppy's mouth. The puppy stirred then went limp. Hadley looked to her grandmother for help.

"Try again," Maddy said. "Just squeeze out a tiny bit more."

This time the puppy stirred but still didn't suck. Milk dribbled down her chin and onto the towel again. But then she swallowed.

"Oh, you brilliant little girl," Maddy whispered. "More now, Hadley. Just a little bit."

More dribbling, but another tiny swallow.

The room's collective sigh was audible.

"Okay, Gran." Hadley held up the syringe. "That was a whole two cc's."

Maddy, who had walked over to the utility sink, clapped her hands. "A perfect first meal. You know what to do next."

Hadley gently turned the puppy over and unwrapped the blanket. Gran handed her a washcloth she'd run under warm water.

Cam, who felt a little shaky himself, asked, "You're going to give it a bath?"

Hadley used the washcloth to gently massage the puppy's crotch. "Nope. I have to get it to pee and also maybe poop."

Maddy added, "It's the mother dog's job to lick each puppy to get it to go to the bathroom."

"You're kidding," Cam said, incredulous.

Fuller shot him a look that Cam read as *stupid football player*. "We'll have to do it every two hours."

Cam raked a hand through his hair. "Every two hours?"

"Mmm-hmm," Maddy said, eyeing the puppy. "Every time she eats."

He caught Hadley's eye, and she gave him a little smile. Despite being worried, she seemed to take this all in stride. "We'll do everything we can to save her," she said.

Fuller, who'd gone into the pen, stepped out and pulled his stethoscope from his ears. Cam couldn't help noticing the way he looked at Hadley. Like he was just as infatuated with her as Cam was.

Infatuated. No, Cam suddenly realized as he fought a sudden pressure in his chest, that wasn't it at all. Even he couldn't deny that his feelings for her had grown roots and spread deep and wide, through every part of him.

"Everybody looks·good," Fuller said, "mama dog too. Now we just have to wait and see."

"It was kind of you to come," Hadley said. "I can't thank you enough."

"My pleasure." Fuller wound his stethoscope around his neck and leaned against the countertop. He was a tall, confident, good-looking guy, Cam thought. And the way he was looking at Hadley was making his stomach twist.

"I've got more milk replacer in my trunk," Fuller said. "And do you need a pet heating pad?"

"No, thank you, Fuller," Maddy said. "I have two of them."

"We can take it from here," Cam said, anxious for him to leave.

Fuller didn't pay Cam much heed. He glanced at his watch and said to Hadley, "It's almost six a.m. I'd like to stop by again before I go home tonight, if that's okay?"

"Of course," Hadley said. "Let us see you out."

"I can take a shift for you so you don't get exhausted," Fuller offered.

That left Cam clenching his fists. "She'll have plenty of help, Fuller." Cam set the record straight once and for all. "Thanks anyway." He scrambled to his feet and made sure he got to the door first.

As he saw the vet to the door, took the extra puppy formula, and sent him on his way, Cam couldn't shake a sense of worry that had begun to seep in. It was watching Hadley with these dogs, finding her way, finding *herself*. It was crystal clear to him that she was in her element, loving every minute. Making a difference, just as she'd wanted to do.

His phone pinged off with an email, unusual for this time of day. It was from Dolittle, saying that they wanted him to announce their partnership during his upcoming interview, which was scheduled for two days from now.

A sick feeling turned his stomach. He'd been dragging his feet for as long as possible, but there was no avoiding it. He would have to talk about his restaurant plans in some concrete way. But how?

One thing was clear: Hadley belonged here. But he was bound to Dudley and Dolittle.

Chapter 26

THANKS FOR COMING to play with Bernie until my sitter shows," Lucy said on Monday, at around 6:30 in the morning.

"No problem," Cam said, feeding his sweet niece a bottle while sitting in Nick's souped-up desk chair. Bernie had put her tiny hand over his and was staring lovingly up at him while she finished her breakfast. A great opportunity for him to make faces. "You're with Uncle Tony now," he said. "It's party time, even at this ungodly hour."

He was up early because today was the day of his interview. And he still had to figure out exactly what he was going to say. *How do you feel about never playing football again? What are your plans for the future?* He had no answers. At least, not the kinds of answers that people would want to hear from him eight months after his injury. All he knew was that last night had demonstrated something: Hadley had found her joy. He'd seen it from afar this past month but last night he'd seen it up close. And it had really thrown him.

He wasn't a jealous man. He was happy for her.

Make that *thrilled*. But on some complicated level, it made him feel more bereft and out of sorts than ever.

"Okay, Uncle Tony," Lucy said as she settled in at her desk. "Bernadette would love to sit on her quilt in the back room and play. There's a basket of toys next to the diaper bag. And just to warn you, she usually poops right after she eats." She glanced nervously at her watch. "I have an hour and a half before Dad gets here and I've still got to run all these numbers to see where I messed up. And did I say thank you?" She rolled her chair over and kissed him on the cheek. "My sitter usually shows up at eight."

"We'll be fine." He got up to leave his sister to her work. "C'mon, Bernie, let's go play." He stood by the window and scrolled through his phone while Bernie finished up her bottle.

His sister was stressed because of some inventory spreadsheet problem he didn't completely understand, only that it had caused a misordering of some construction supplies. And Lucy had gotten up early to sort it all out.

After a few minutes, it was clear she was very frustrated. She got up and went for the coffeepot. "Want a cup?" she called over to Cam. "My eyes are crossing."

"You did an awesome job at the gala," Cam said as she handed him a coffee that, thanks to her, was a gourmet blend. His dad preferred a generic bulk brand that tasted like castor oil. "Everyone's still talking about how great the food was."

Lucy shot him a look of death. "I had a lot of fun doing it. But my job is here."

"Dad and Nick would get over it if you quit," Cam said, unable to stop pressing her. "I know you feel loyal to the family business but—"

"Cam." She stopped him in his tracks. "I can't talk about this now, okay?"

"It's just that it seems like an opportunity to get you doing something you really enjoy." Dudley and Dolittle's restaurant ideas struck him as a lot of compromise, but at least it would be worth it if Lucy could get something out of it. If she'd only see the light.

"I'm just having a bad morning, okay?" she said. "Just because you're not afraid to plunge in with both feet and go off on crazy business ventures doesn't mean everyone else is made that way. I need to think things through. Plan. Decide what's best for Bernie."

"Well, don't wait too long," he said, despite knowing he should shut up. "Because one day you'll wake up and it might be too late."

Her face paled. "Cam, you aren't listening to me. You keep trying to get me to do something that *you* think is right for me, but you're not me. You need to go now, okay?" She walked back to her desk and put her mug down so forcefully the coffee sloshed over the edge.

He'd done it now. Upset her when she was already stressed. He was an idiot.

"I'm sorry," he said, but she ignored him. "And...I don't have things as figured out as you think."

She waved him off over her head and he finally took the hint and headed for the back.

In fact, he really didn't have them figured out at all.

* * *

Cam showed up at seven at the shelter with fresh coffee and Bernie, full and changed and snoozing in her stroller, feeling like he'd handled things with Lucy completely wrong. When he opened the door, he found Hadley standing in the middle of the puppy pen. "Now," she was saying to the mother dog, "I know you've been through a lot. And abandoned on top of everything. But I want you to know you've done a fantastic job. And you're going to love it here. It's warm and there's plenty of food and a nice comfy bed and...and we're going to help you with those puppies. Don't you worry, sweetie." She petted the dog in long, soothing strokes while the dog watched her with wary eyes. "I know," Hadley said. "You think I'm crazy, right? Must just be the sleep deprivation." Then the dog lifted her head and licked her on the face, making her chuckle.

Just then the phone rang. "Oh, good morning, Mayellen. Thanks for calling back. Hey, I wanted to ask if you and Ivy can do my dog walks today? Not to mention we've got the puppies and Bubba and Hershey and Jagger and Bowie here, and I've got a meeting at ten with the state coordinator of the SPCA." As she talked, she prepared to feed the little pup, gathering the syringe and warming the replacer and fetching clean towels.

"She's quite a multitasker, isn't she?" a voice behind Cam said.

Cam turned to find Maddy there, leaning a bit on her cane.

"Morning, Maddy. I...I like watching her. How she talks to the mama dog, and answers the phone, and takes care of that one little runt puppy, and—"

"She's using all her PR skills, that's for sure."

He nodded. "Except doing more good, I think."

"She's always been that way. Wanting to do good. To leave things better than how she found them."

He nodded and smiled a little, mostly to himself. Because she'd done that with *him*.

"I hope she understands that she *is* doing good here," Maddy continued. "I hope she doesn't get swayed back to her big-city life. But maybe I'm just being selfish. I love having her near."

Me too, Cam thought.

"Hadley was born to do this," Cam said, watching her feed the tiny puppy. The look on her face was exhausted, determined, and...happy. She went about her work joyously; there was no other word for it.

"People can't seem to stop talking about the gala," Maddy said. "The food and the music and the way everything went off without a hitch. You two made it a perfect evening. And you raised over a hundred thousand dollars for the hospital."

Great. "So what's the verdict with the town? Me or Hadley?"

Gran sighed. "Both of you. A toss-up." She threw up her hands. "People can't seem to stop talking about you two as a couple. Apparently, everyone thinks you're just adorable."

Cam smiled a little. "Well, that's good—and not good."

"Listen, dear." Maddy patted his arm. "Sometime soon all three of us need to sit down and come to a decision together about this building." She looked at him steady and direct. "I love you both, you know. But it can only go to one of you."

It wasn't a surprise. With the diversion of the benefit over, it was time to get back to business. He thought again of Dudley and Dolittle's request for him to discuss the restaurant during his big interview. As if to emphasize the unnerving countdown to 10:00 a.m., the hand on the wall clock made a clicking sound.

"Come here, you," Hadley said. Cam glanced over to see her chasing Jagger around. He appeared to have a baby blanket in his mouth.

Hadley looked over and saw him and Maddy. "Hey, you two! Jagger's such a stinker, aren't you?" The dog's good ear drooped, knowing full well he was being scolded. "He keeps pulling the blanket away from the pups. I think he's a little jealous!" She laughed and almost caught him, but he zigzagged under a table and ran for the back.

Hadley said, "I give up!" and beckoned them over as she took another phone call.

Yep, *joyous*. There was no other word for it.

"No need for a meeting," Cam said to Maddy. "I've come to a decision."

"I know that," she said softly. A glance over at Hadley showed her busy talking on the phone, tucking in an errant puppy, and carefully wrapping the tiny one up in a bundle for its next meal.

"Hey, Maddy." Cam pulled two coffees from the stroller and set them on the counter by the door. "I brought these for Hadley and me but I'd love for you to take mine. I...I've got something I need to attend to. Tell her I'll see her a little later." He turned to push the stroller out the door.

"Does Hadley know?" she asked, stopping him in his tracks.

"Know? About the building?" he asked.

"No," Maddy said softly. "That you love her."

Love? This was not a romantic decision. "Hadley deserves to have it. She's found the thing she should be doing in the world."

"Well," Maddy said, resting a hand on his shoulder.

"I always knew you were a good egg. But sometimes I'm not sure you realize it yourself."

"I haven't done anything to get credit for."

"You've put her needs before yours. Don't you know that's what love is all about?"

* * *

Later that morning, Darla was holding the bundled puppy and gently squirting formula into her mouth. "Look at her," Darla said. "She's swallowing more every day!"

Kit stood up from a chair, and Hadley climbed out of the puppy pen to see.

"Oh, I've never seen anything so tiny and sweet," Kit said, bending down to watch. "Why did the mom reject her?"

"Fuller couldn't say for sure." Hadley blotted the milk from the puppy's fur. "But the mom was moved right after she gave birth, and really stressed, so she was probably very frightened. Plus this one is the tiniest of the litter."

"She won't be little anymore if she keeps eating like this." Darla held up the drained syringe. "She took five cc's!"

"That's a whole teaspoon," Kit said.

Hadley grinned. "That's a great meal for a brand-new puppy, actually."

"Do I have to burp her?" Darla asked. "Or can I just cuddle with her?"

The bell tinkled as Ivy and Mayellen entered, back from the morning dog walk.

"It's nearly time for Cam's live interview," Ivy said as

she turned on an old-model TV that sat on the counter. "Come on over, everybody."

Hadley was dreading the interview almost as much as Cam was. She felt a stab of guilt because if it weren't for her, he wouldn't have been forced to do it. And what would he say about his restaurant? It had been an amazing couple of weeks not thinking about it, but now the topic couldn't be avoided.

She'd passed out early last night but asked Cam to stop by this morning to discuss things before the interview. She'd been so consumed with the puppies she hadn't noticed when he'd stopped by with coffee, and he'd had to leave before they had a chance to talk.

Ivy fiddled with the remote and smacked the side of the old set a few times to find the interview was already in progress. They gathered around to see Cam on camera, dressed in a shirt and tie and looking like the sexiest man alive. Which he definitely was, Hadley thought with a pang. She knew how uncomfortable he felt but also knew he'd handle himself well. And maybe he'd see that not having his life perfectly in place wasn't the big deal he thought it was. That would be a good thing, right?

The popular local sports reporter who scored the national interview sat beside Cam at a desk. Cam made the nervous gesture of tugging at his tie as the reporter began. "We heard you and Ms. Wells are in competition for a downtown building owned by a longtime business owner, Maddy Edwards."

Hadley gasped and held her breath. Her friends glanced anxiously at her and then the TV. The pounding of her heart was so loud that she had to lean forward to make sure she heard Cam's reply.

"Not anymore," Cam said.

"What do you mean?" the reporter asked.

"Hadley Wells, Maddy's granddaughter, has created a dog rescue in the building that's really unique—it will provide spay, neuter, and vaccination services at a very reduced rate. It'll also be a fantastic place to go volunteer if you love dogs or even want to foster a dog. This is going to provide a valuable service that's greatly needed in our part of the state, and it's a way for our community to get involved with an important cause. So I hope everyone will check it out."

Wait…what? Hadley reached for the nearest chair and managed to sit.

"Well, look at that," Ivy said proudly. "Cam just did a commercial for us!"

"And he gave you all the credit, honey," Mayellen said to Hadley.

"Not to mention the *building*," Darla said.

Kit just stood there, grasping Hadley's hand while Hadley stared incredulously at the TV.

"So what will you do next?" the reporter asked.

"I've partnered with a group of investors who want to roll out a chain of my restaurants," Cam said. "As far as location, I'm keeping all my options open at this point. But as soon as I decide, you'll be the first to know."

"Well, we love having you back in town, Cam." The reporter held out his hand, which Cam shook firmly. "Best of luck."

Darla turned off the TV. Hadley sat, stunned, unable to move. Cam had eloquently minimized all his big plans in order to showcase her rescue. He'd given up the building, the fight for his restaurant location. *For her.*

Chapter 27

I HEARD YOUR interview," Hadley said that evening as soon as Cam walked into her grandmother's cottage. Gran was out of rehab and claiming she'd rather stay with Paul so he could help her out when she needed it. Hadley knew she'd have to make a decision soon about another place to stay. But for this evening, she planned a special dinner for her and Cam to celebrate the end of their competition. And what she hoped would be the beginning of another phase in their relationship.

It was a rare rainy evening, and she'd been sitting reading in one of the cushy yellow flowered chairs by the tiny fireplace, letting her made-from-scratch spaghetti sauce simmer until he got home. She'd gotten them a lovely bottle of wine and a crusty loaf of bread from Mimi's. The dogs, who had been passed out on the rug in front of the fireplace, immediately rose to greet Cam at the door.

The only thing was, she hadn't heard from him all day. He'd texted:

Crazy day, see you tonight

But that was it. Radio silence after the interview.

Hadley reassured herself that everything was okay, that maybe he really was just busy, that he'd done an incredible thing for her, and she shouldn't dwell on negatives.

"The phone at the Palace has been ringing off the hook," she said to fill the silence as he walked in, setting his keys down in the little basket on the table by the door. He seemed full of energy, restless, his smile seeming a little forced. "People are donating to the shelter from all over. Someone even started a GoFundMe page. And ESPN wants to interview *me*. Can you believe it?"

She stood there, wanting to race into his arms and smother him with kisses. Wanting to tell him how much his gesture meant, and how she was going to turn the shelter into something wonderful, and now that they weren't competing for the building, they could focus on their future together, no-holds-barred.

She wanted to tell him *I love you*.

He squatted down to greet the dogs, but not with his usual round of roughhousing and general riling up. At last he straightened up and faced her.

"Tony, I—" She started to say a thousand things, but he spoke instead.

"I watched you with those puppies," he said, his voice subdued. Hadley pushed her anxiety away. She wasn't going to assume the worst. He was here, wasn't he? And they both had the whole night off. They would celebrate! "You're a natural," he continued. "It's what you should be doing, Had."

His words made her breathe a little easier. And she took comfort in the fact that he'd called her *Had*. "Well, maybe I'm crazy, but you're absolutely right. I really love the shelter. I have so many plans. But...are you okay with this?"

He nodded firmly. "One hundred percent."

She blew out a pent-up breath. *There, you see?* she told herself. *He's fine with it.*

"Thank you," she said with all her heart as she walked over and wrapped her arms around him. "I know how much it cost you to give up the building as the location for your restaurant." He seemed tense but rested his cheek against her hair, and she heard him suck in a deep breath. She opened her mouth to say it—to say she loved him—but they both started talking at the same time. "I love the way you smell," he said.

There was something about the way he said it—his tone, his inflection, *something* that sounded like he was saying it for the last time. Hadley shook off the sinking feeling in her stomach that was growing by the second. He'd just surrendered his plans to open a restaurant in Gran's space. He'd just given up everything for *her*. *Thank you* had sounded awkward and inadequate. But what else could she say?

She went for lightening the mood. "That's funny because I probably smell like puppy milk replacer and a few more unpleasant things." As she chuckled and drew back, she prepared to ask him, *What's next? What are your plans?* But something in his eyes scared her. "You know, I could help you scout out another location for your restaurant. Maybe beachfront. We could have Carol make a realty portfolio for us and take a whole day—"

"Hadley," he said in such a flat tone she stopped midsentence. "Sit down a minute, okay?" He tugged her gently to a wooden bench near the door that her grandma used for pulling off shoes and boots.

"Cam, wh-what is it? Are you okay?" Because *she* wasn't. Suddenly she was shaking all over. A flashback to Cooper, no doubt. She remembered what it had felt like just before he dropped the Maeve bomb on her. Somehow, even then she'd known something bad was coming. Call it a sixth sense. But the radar of her soul could predict crushing disappointment a mile away.

She reminded herself to *just calm down*, that this was *Cam* and she trusted Cam. Cam was not Cooper. Cam was...wonderful.

As soon as she sat down, Jagger bounded over, Bowie fast on his trail, certain that it was time for a walk, since everyone was congregating around the spot where the leashes were hung on the wall. "Jagger, no." She gave him a quick pet. "It's not time for a walk." But at the sound of his favorite word, he began doing a happy dance.

"Later, Jaggy, okay?" Hadley patted him on the head while starting to panic inside. Cam wasn't being...Cam. He sat stiffly, fidgeting with his fingers, acting...weird.

He leaned over and took her hands and looked at her directly. But his eyes were...empty.

"You do everything with all your heart and soul," he said. He didn't sound angry. He was complimenting her, after all. But he wasn't really looking at her—he was looking *through* her. The kind of look a person gives you when they don't want to hurt you...but they have no other choice.

"Listen to me." He squeezed her hands, tension radiating off his muscles. "I know what that feels like, having something that you love more than anything. Having something you wish would never end."

He was talking about football, right? Not her?

"I know you'll turn your grandma's business into something impressive. The building is yours. You deserve it."

"What will you do?" she asked. Because he certainly wasn't volunteering any info.

The pause was so long she actually heard her grandma's old kitchen clock, the one shaped like a teapot, *tick-tick-ticking*.

"Hadley." He looked up quickly and then down at the floor. "I'm leaving in the morning for LA."

Ah, yes. There it was. "LA." Wow. That was far. Across-the-continent far. "What for?" she said, way too fast and way too cheerily. Because maybe there was the tiniest chance that he was not telling her goodbye. Her heart pumped cold dread all through her veins, sending chills down her spine.

Yet, she knew what it was like to be left.

He was leaving her.

"I told Dudley and Dolittle the building deal was off. So they want to scout for the flagship restaurant out West. I'll be gone a couple of days, but if all goes well, I'll relocate there so I can help get the project off the ground and give input on the next sites."

Out *West*? To LA of all places?

When Cooper had told her he loved Maeve, she'd been blindsided. She'd lost her words. She'd promised herself never to lose her voice again.

"You're leaving," she managed. "You're leaving me." She cleared her throat and pushed herself forward. "You're leaving *us*." She forced herself to look at him because she wanted to see his face. She wanted to read what he was thinking. And she wanted him to see her when she asked, "Why?"

"I can't fail at this. It's an important business decision at a critical time."

"That's not the right answer," she said, poking him in the chest. Which may have been childish but...

He turned to her then. "We never said there was an *us*."

She blinked in stunned surprise. Silly her. She'd believed *feeling* that there was an *us* was sufficient. But clearly he hadn't thought so. Would she ever learn?

"I told you I'm not in a good position to have a relationship."

Her head was whirling. She was trying to understand the sudden change in him. Just a few days ago they were cuddling in bed, talking about forever...or had she just assumed all of that? Had she dropped her walls and trusted him so completely...because that's what she always did? She hadn't protected herself enough. She'd tried, but it had been useless. Because she loved him. She really, really loved him. "Because you don't have this restaurant thing figured out?"

"That's part of it." He sounded a little defensive. "I succeeded at something once, and I will again. It's just going to take some time. Time I need to take— by myself."

"Wait a minute. You're leaving me to go to LA because you need time to yourself?" He was bolting. Leaving her. Just like he did before. Just like Cooper had. On to bigger and better things.

"Look, we said we were going to keep this light." He barely made eye contact. "I have things I need to figure out."

She folded her arms. "And whether or not you love me is clearly one of them."

She waited, but the *I love you* never came. "Maybe Fuller is better for you anyway," he said.

Her stomach took a roller-coaster plunge. "You're seriously going there?" She bit her lip to avoid saying more. She didn't get it. She didn't understand why his restaurant was more important to him than...she was. She just knew that it was.

He shook his head as he got up and headed toward the door.

She stood but didn't follow him. Because it suddenly occurred to her what was happening here. He wasn't a stupid teenager dumping her on a sticky note. And he wasn't Cooper, who didn't have the capacity to know what real love was. "You can't run away from yourself, Tony."

That made him halt, his hand on the doorknob. Jagger and Bowie nearly tripped over each other in their race to get to the door, ready to break free for playtime.

Her head was whirling but she had to speak. "I never cared about how famous you were or whether you play football or *any* kind of ball. But I do care how kindly you treat everyone around you. How you care about people. How you always have a nice word even if it's the hundredth photo you've taken that day. How you lead your life with character and dignity and without bitterness. I don't need you to prove that you're worthy of my love. I just love you for who you are." She bit her lip, but tears were already leaking down her face. "I love you."

"I'm sorry, Hadley." The misery in his eyes made her anger fizzle. "I have to go."

He turned the knob and walked out. She watched

him pick up a duffel bag he'd left by the door. A duffel bag, already packed! He walked down the sidewalk and tossed it in the back seat of his car, just as they had the cute little picnic basket not long ago.

He could not be leaving. She could not be left again, this time by the one man she would always love with her whole heart.

"Fine," she said, anger welling within her in a great wave. "Enjoy LA." Then she shut the door.

Chapter 28

GOOD THING THESE puppies needed her. Well, the runty little one anyway. That's why Hadley had volunteered for another night shift, shooing off Ivy and Mayellen, who had already done their share of night duty but had offered to stay anyway because she was upset.

The place was practically glittering from cleanliness. She'd done three loads of puppy towels, scrubbed everything from the counters to the sinks to the floors. She would have swept the parking lot, too, if she'd thought that wouldn't have attracted some strange looks from passersby.

And when she ran out of work, she sat down next to the puppy pen and cried. She cried for the little runty puppy, who was still weak and drip-feeding every last cc. And she cried for the business she was trying to get off the ground, because there was so much to do. She'd been so eager to do it all—the PR, the partnerships with local businesses, the adoption days, the volunteer program for teens—but now she felt exhausted and overwhelmed.

Actually, everything was overwhelming. Eating, sleeping...living without Cam.

But mostly she just cried for her broken heart. For how good it had been with him. Who'd have thought she'd get the building but lose him for good?

Sometime in the middle of the night, she leaned back against the wall. The mother dog and the pups were settling. She was trying to latch her mind on to something productive when Jagger lay down beside her and put his head in her lap. She scratched behind his ear and kissed his head, grateful for a buddy who understood when she needed him. "Hey, Jaggy. Don't worry, I'll stop crying, I promise." But more tears leaked out.

Hadley had finally dozed off, it seemed, because she was awakened by rapping at the door. A glance out the window between the hardware store and the flower shop showed that the sky was glowing with the salmon colors of another summer dawn.

She sat up and rubbed the sleep out of her eyes, threw off the sweatshirt she'd been using for a blanket, and found her grandmother at the door. *Sans* cane.

"What time is it?" Hadley asked, rubbing her eyes.

Her grandmother perused her in that efficient way she had and handed her a coffee. "Six a.m. You look terrible."

"Probably because it's six a.m." Hadley's mouth felt like chalk and her head felt like a bowling ball from crying.

Gran gave a little chuckle at the bad joke and sat down. "I heard about Cam," she said, coming straight to the point. "I'm sorry."

For some reason, that made Hadley start crying all over again. "I'm fine, Gran," she said.

With that, her grandmother pulled her into a giant hug. "It's all right, Hadley. You don't need to be strong all the time."

Hadley blew her nose. "I suppose I could be really angry with myself for getting involved with someone so quickly after Cooper, but you know what? I'm not. I'm...sad. I love him, Gran. I love him so much." Her grandmother reached out a hand to pat her back.

"Maybe he just needs time."

"He's off to LA to start his restaurant there. He chose his restaurant over me," she said, her stupid eyes leaking again. "And I'm so angry with him, but he's hurting, I can tell. I just don't know how to help him."

"He gave you the building," Gran said. "That means something. I believe he was planning to do it for quite some time."

"It means he wanted to move on. Away from here. Away from *me*." Her voice cracked on the last word despite herself. She looked up at her grandmother. "I'm staying in Seashell Harbor. I'm going to throw all I've got into this business and make it thrive. I love it." Cam was right. She'd never felt better about anything. Except him. But even without him, she'd be all right.

Gran blew out a breath. "Hadley, I've always secretly imagined you taking over because you understood and loved the dogs as much as I did. But I didn't dare to dream it. And I didn't ever want you to feel coerced by me." She took a breath, teary-eyed.

"Gran, no. Don't cry." Hadley hugged her grandma.

Gran hugged her back but then pushed back a little. "Let me cry my happy tears. I'm just so proud of you. Not just because you took a scary leap in a direction that seems right for you."

Hadley shook her head. "I've made a lot of mistakes along the way."

Gran patted her arm. "It's called living, my dear. You've had the courage to be daring. To go out in the world and find yourself."

Hadley twirled Darla's ring, which had reminded her to be brave as she tried to figure out her life. Sometimes that strategy had worked, and in other ways it hadn't at all. But she was determined to focus on the positive. "I'm excited about starting a rescue in a way I've never been. But... I might need your help occasionally. Would that be okay?"

"I think I might like retirement," Gran said. "But I'll always want to spend time with the dogs. When I'm not traveling. Paul and I have got a trip planned. For our honeymoon."

Her grandmother was beaming. "Gran! I'm so happy for you." Hadley hugged her—again.

"You're the first one I've told."

"Well," Hadley said, nearly speechless. "That's incredible."

"I know." She shrugged. "Who knew?" She stepped back and touched Hadley's cheek, like she'd done so many times before. "I know you'll find happiness too."

"I'll be fine," Hadley said, determined not to ruin her grandmother's wonderful news. "When's the wedding?"

"We're thinking this fall. It's going to be very simple so I'll have plenty of time if you can use a hand some days."

"Any days you want. On your schedule. I still need plenty of your expertise."

The puppies were stirring, and the little one was starting to squeak pitifully.

"How's our little girl?" Gran asked.

Hadley started to prepare the puppy's meal. "I'm still squirting the milk into her cheek without any help from her. I'd feel a lot better if she'd start sucking it down herself."

"Maybe she just needs time too."

Hadley shot her a look.

"Don't give up on the puppy—or on Cam yet." She walked over to Hadley and held out her hand for the syringe. "And now I want you to go home and take a shower and a nap."

"Look, Gran." Hadley smiled a little. "Just because you're showing off your excellent walking skills does not mean you have to come back and work yourself to the bone. I'm fine."

"Hadley Marie, if I hear *I'm fine* one more time, I swear . . ." Gran took the syringe from the bowl of warm water, scooped up the puppy with her other hand, and sat down.

"Mayellen will be here at four," Gran said firmly. "After dinner, I'll come back and sleep over."

"No, Gran."

"Don't worry about me," she said. "Paul's bringing me an air mattress. I'm not sleeping on the floor like you do. Now shoo." She waved Hadley off. "Go and come back tomorrow."

Hadley felt puffy and groggy and rumpled. And she knew when to accept a favor. "I love you."

"I love you too." She looked down at the puppy and startled. "Oh my goodness, take a look at this."

Hadley bent to check out the puppy, who was vigorously sucking on the syringe.

"I am *not* pushing this," Gran said, pleased as pie. "*She* is."

Hadley dropped to her knees to see better. The puppy was tugging at the syringe, visibly extracting the milk from it. When the five cc's was drained, she pulled back, her chin covered with a dribble of milk.

Gran glanced from the puppy to Hadley. "Sometimes things aren't quite as bad as they seem."

Hadley gave her grandmother a squeeze. "Not when I have you for a grandmother."

* * *

Cam tried to take the red-eye from LA, but because of rain delays and some minor mechanical problems, it was 7:00 p.m. the next day when he finally got back to Seashell Harbor.

On the drive home, he answered a call from his sister, the seventh one, even though he'd texted her earlier and let her know he was on the way back. She'd been calling him constantly, unlike Hadley, who not only hadn't called him but also hadn't answered any of his calls.

"Cam!" Lucy said, her voice riddled with worry. "Why haven't you picked up? I've been calling you!"

"I texted you before I took off and I just got off the plane. I'm fine." He fell into his usual big-brother tone.

She wasn't having it. "I know you told me you were headed back but I'm worried about you."

"Nothing to be worried about." Nothing that he wanted to talk about anyway. And it wasn't like he'd had an eventful day and a half. He'd spent it flying across the country—twice—and eating bad airport food in between. And thinking. A lot.

There was a long pause. "I stopped by Pooch Palace to check to see if Bubba the bulldog got adopted yet and Ivy told me you and Hadley broke up. I'm coming over."

As Cam pulled onto the tiny street of beachfront bungalows, he noticed that Hadley's car was gone. But his dad's black SUV was parked in his driveway.

"Wait a minute," Cam said. "Did you tell anyone I was on the way back? Because I did tell you I needed some space, didn't I?"

"I...um." Dead silence. "Well, maybe I did tell Dad."

Cam rolled his eyes. "I take it back. You're not my favorite sister."

"He was worried about you too."

"So you sent him to my *house*?" Just what he didn't want. To be accosted by caring people, whom he loved but...couldn't a guy have some alone time?

"Not exactly. He asked me where you hid the spare key."

He let out a deep sigh. "I have to tell you something."

"What is it?" she asked, her tone wary.

"I'm...sorry. For trying to control your life. For not listening. I think you're the best mom in the world and I know you'll do what you want when the time is right. And if I gave you the impression I've got things all figured out, that's absolutely wrong. That's all."

"Oh," she said. She seemed to take that in for a moment. "That means a lot. But don't worry about me. Just get your head out of your butt and get Hadley back."

"So you're giving *me* advice now?"

"When you need it, yes." There was a sudden loud crash in the background. "Okay, that was a plate of cookies that Molly is now scarfing up whole. Gotta go."

"Luce," he said.

"Yeah?"

"Thanks for worrying about me. I love you."

"I love you too. And, Cam?" he heard just before he was about to hit the end button.

"Yes, Lucy."

"I might have told Nick about your being back too. Also, I love you too. Bye!"

The line went silent just as he parked on the dirt road in front of his cottage. Great, so now Nick would probably be calling him any minute too.

The truth was, he had a great family and could use their support. He'd been pretending for too long that he was okay. That he could figure everything out on his own. That he was Cam, tough enough to plow through anything, from a monster defensive line to handling a career-ending bad knee all by himself.

Well, Cam might be a plow but Tony was...just Tony. He'd made it all the way to LA before it had dawned on him that he didn't want to forge ahead with the restaurant across the country. In fact, he didn't want to forge ahead with a subpar restaurant chain with his name on it at all.

"Dad." Cam walked through the kitchen door and found his father dusting flour off his hands. His kitchen smelled like...fresh bread. *Warm* fresh bread. A far cry from the single granola bar he'd eaten three airports ago.

"You're alive," his dad said in his usual deadpan voice. But Cam could read the concern in his eyes. He hated that. For years, Cam had done everything in his power to *not* get that look from his dad. "If you're looking for Hadley, she's not home. I already checked."

"Oh," Cam said. "Well, I'm glad you're here." He

noted a stack of clean dishes in the dish rack, the tidy table. He'd left a mess behind him, in more ways than one. "You didn't have to do my dishes."

The response was a grunt as his dad checked the oven. "This oven is a piece of crap," he said. "When *you* bake this dough, it better be in one of those fancy-schmancy wood-fired ovens, okay?"

It dawned on Cam that his dad was making The Dough. For *him*.

His dad opened the fridge, revealing two bottles of beer and an old carton of milk. He took out the carton of milk, smelled it, and made a face. "Geez. How you live."

That made Cam laugh. "You weren't really going to pour me a glass of milk with pizza, were you?"

Angelo brought two glasses of water to the table. "You look like you need milk, not beer."

Cam wished it was that simple. The smell of the pizza was familiar and comforting. Finally his dad pulled it out of the oven and sat down across from him. Steam rose up from the perfectly golden homemade crust, and his dad had sliced onions and Italian peppers for the toppings, his favorites.

Angelo sliced the pizza. "Eat," he said simply.

For the first time in days, Cam found he was hungry. "It's incredible," he said, two pieces later. "Thanks."

They ate in silence. Then his dad put down his napkin and said, "What else do you need—besides food?"

Cam sat back in his chair. *Hadley* came immediately to his mind.

He wasn't used to having heart-to-hearts with his dad. Or more accurately, he'd *avoided* them. Why tell anyone when you've messed up instead of just fixing the problem?

But this time his strategy hadn't worked.

"The knee injury threw me for a loop," he finally managed. The words made him cringe.

"Maybe," his dad said.

Cam looked up from his water.

"Yes, the injury cut your football career short," his dad said in a matter-of-fact tone that, with his gray hair and Italian features, reminded him a little of Al Pacino in *The Godfather*. But a lot kinder. "Yes, it threw you a big curveball. But it made you come home. It gave you a second chance to really think about what you want. And it brought you Hadley. Trouble is, your head's been in your rearview mirror."

Cam crossed his arms, not really wanting to hear his dad's take on what he already knew but fearing that he was right. "How so?"

"You haven't slowed down enough to take time to think. And you're letting ghosts from the past take the driver's seat."

"*I* always take the driver's seat in my life."

"Well, this time you took the wheel and crashed the car," his dad said.

Ouch.

Just as he was reeling from that, his dad reached over the table and patted him on the cheek like he was twelve years old. "You're my tough kid," he said. "My rebel. You always wanted to get out of here and see other places, do things."

Cam shrugged. "I'm glad I saw the world. But I like being back home."

"You've made us all proud. There was a time I wondered if I was even capable of raising good kids. I'm thrilled you all turned out okay."

He flicked his gaze up at his dad. "What did you just say?"

"When your mother left, you were eight, Nick was five, and Lucy was one and a half. That was *my* curveball."

Of course it was. How had he not even thought of that? His dad had been left alone to raise three kids. And he'd never complained, never talked about how that—*they*—had altered his life.

His dad drummed his fingers on the table. "Maybe I never told you this, but I wanted to start a restaurant."

That made Cam sit straight up. Yes, his dad was a phenomenal cook. Yes, he often cooked for fun. But a *restaurant*?

His dad nodded. "I'd been saving up for a down payment, but after your mother left, I put it toward a college fund for you kids. The restaurant business has bad hours for a single parent, you know?"

"Why didn't you ever tell me this?" Cam asked. A *restaurant*? How could he not have known?

"I'm not complaining about how my life turned out. I'm happy with our business. But maybe I should've told you more about my struggles. And dreams. You and I are alike in some ways. We don't talk about our own issues."

"Maybe we need to do a little more of that." A *lot* more.

His dad nodded. "After she left, you kept watch by the front window. Do you remember that?"

Cam shook his head. Thank God he didn't.

And then he realized his dad was talking about his mother, and he *never* did that.

"Every night, you'd leave your bed and drag your

blanket out to the living room and fall asleep by the window. You told me you wanted to be the first one to see her when she came back. Imagine, having to break a young child's heart and tell him his mother wasn't ever coming back."

Cam winced. "That must've been terrible for you."

Angelo nodded. "That's when you started to do everything perfect. You fixed your bed without a wrinkle. You got the highest grades. You excelled in all the sports. Looking back, I thought, I don't have to worry about that kid. You were so driven, such a hard worker. But truth is, I should've worried about you the most."

"No, Pop, no." He put a hand on his dad's shoulder. "I did fine. You raised me fine." Geez, his eyes were watering.

And, to his shock, his dad's were too.

"Maybe you thought that if you were perfect at everything, she'd come back and love you again."

Cam rubbed his neck. The conversation was uncomfortable. "I got something good out of it," he said. "I'm determined."

"Maybe too determined."

He lifted his head. "What?" He'd never heard that before. *Ever.*

"Yeah. I mean…maybe taking a step back for a while is a good thing," his dad said in a musing tone. "Maybe take a little time off."

"I've had eight months off." An eternity.

"All I'm saying is, it's okay not to know where you're going for a little bit." His dad spoke animatedly, with lots of hand gestures, reminding Cam of advice his dad had doled out to all three of them over the years, especially when they were teenagers. Probably the last time they'd sat and talked like this. "But that doesn't mean you should turn everyone away until you're perfect again. There's no such thing as perfect. People who love us, love us for our warts."

"Hadley pretty much told me the same thing."

"I knew I liked that girl," his dad said.

"I love her too, Dad." That had slipped right out of his mouth without thinking. Yet it felt exactly right.

It was a long time before either of them talked. "I've been thinking," Cam said. "If I take some time off, will you take me and Nick fishing? We haven't done that for years."

"Of course."

All right, then. Fishing it would be. He looked around the kitchen. "Thanks for the pizza. And for being a great dad."

His dad waved him off, too choked up to answer. But then suddenly he was next to his chair, and Cam was standing up to meet him, although his knee caught a little, getting wrapped up in a warm hug. "You're a good boy, Anthony."

"I love you, Dad."

His dad patted him on the back. "I love you too."

"Don't clean up, okay?" Cam said. "I'll do it later. There's something I've got to do."

His dad picked up the pizza stone and started putting away the leftovers. "Good luck," he said with a wise smile. "And tell her I love her too."

Chapter 29

TWENTY MINUTES LATER, Cam found himself at the Sand Bar, the last place he could think of where Hadley might be.

"Hey, Darla. Hey, bro." He nodded to his brother, who was drinking a beer with his ex. That might've been interesting if he weren't on a mission. "Has anyone seen Hadley?"

"You look like death," Nick said.

"I was supposed to take the red-eye last night but a few of my planes were delayed," he said.

Nick reached over and pulled out the chair next to him. "You look like you've taken *two* red-eyes."

"Thanks," he said drily, sitting down. "How's everybody doing?"

"Great," Darla said.

"Fantastic," Nick said.

He had no idea why they were sitting together. But right now, he didn't care.

"We were just having a drink and talking about you and Hadley," Nick said.

They were bonding over him and Hadley? Weird. He telegraphed his brother a *don't-even-go-there* look.

"I'm going to go there," Nick said, setting down his beer. "Darla and I were just saying how lucky it was that you found each other again. And we hope you don't let that go."

"Nick's right," Darla said. "We hate to see you screw this up."

Wow, they were actually agreeing with each other. "Thanks," Cam said, scanning the place. "Hadley wasn't at home or at the shelter and Maddy said she might be here but I..."

"I know where she is," Darla said, taking a sip of her fruity drink. "But I'm not sure I should tell you. I keep trying to like you, but you keep messing up."

Cam just looked at her. "I *did* mess up."

"Oh." Darla looked up from her drink. "Well, then, that's different. And since my mother's still talking about her free team wear, I'll tell you." She leaned forward. "Hadley said she was going for a walk. That-a-way." She pointed a thumb down the beach. "Toward my house. If you run, you might catch up with her."

"Thanks." He tried not to sound too incredulous, but frankly, he was shocked that Darla actually helped him out for once. He responded with a quick hug, which shocked the heck out of her, then waved to her and his brother as he took off down the beach.

* * *

Hadley's friends had arranged for a night out at the Sand Bar. That was the plan. But she wasn't in the mood for company, even the company of dear friends who were trying their best to see her through this.

The sky was lit up with streaks of salmon and pink,

sunset about a half hour away, and the evening was mild and clear. The urge to walk and walk, sinking her feet into the warm sand, pushed her onward. That and Jagger's enthusiasm to have free rein to sniff whatever he wanted.

She passed Darla's gorgeous house but wasn't ready to stop. Jagger seemed up for more (when was he not?), so she continued down the beach, past the line of modern homes that lined the oceanfront.

Suddenly the houses ended and before her stood the rocky outcropping that marked the end of the beach.

That rocky outcropping. Near the Crab Shack. Near...their place. Hers and Cam's.

"C'mon, Jagger," she called. "We've walked far enough. Let's turn around."

But Jagger apparently was of a different mind, pulling so hard on the leash that it flew out of Hadley's hands as he took off running across the sand.

"Come back here, stinker," Hadley called, certain that the usually chill dog had caught the scent of an animal and had torn off in pursuit. Her words faded in the sound of the current.

"Jagg-*er*," she called, a little annoyed now. She didn't want to be walking around the rocks when night was coming. Plus, Jagger always stuck close by—it wasn't like him to just take off, and it was nearly dark. What if she lost him?

Having no choice, she climbed over and around the boulders until she came to the familiar path that led to the little strip of hidden beach. She *definitely* didn't want to be here after dark, especially if there were teenagers sneaking around.

"Hey, is this your dog?" a too-familiar voice called.

She spun around to find Cam standing on the sand, Jagger's leash in hand, the traitorous dog sitting at his feet, staring up at him adoringly.

And Cam looked...well, a bit on the scruffy side. Dark circles ringed his eyes, and his face was unshaven. He wore an old T-shirt that read NICKELBACK from a concert they'd gone to together in *2005*.

Something about his unusually unkempt appearance gave her a heart pang.

And hope. The tiniest little trickle of hope. Because he looked about as miserable as she felt.

"Hi," she said.

He stopped petting the dog and walked over to her, placing his hands in his pockets. "Hi."

"Jagger missed you," she said, suddenly needing to sit down on a rock.

"Oh yeah?" he said, noting the dog following fast at his heels. "How do you know?"

"Well, he looks all over the house for you. Then he jumps up on your side of the bed and looks for you before he settles in."

"Always an opportunist, huh, Jag?" He ruffled the fur behind the dog's ear.

"Yeah, but he does seem to feel a little guilty for it."

Cam put his hands back in his pockets. "My dad says I have issues."

"Everyone has issues," Hadley said with a shrug. "Like, I keep picking the wrong men."

He came and sat down next to her on the rock. "No. I...I'm going to show you that you didn't." He turned to her, scanning her face carefully. "If you'll let me."

He had her at hi. But she needed to hear what he came here to say. "I thought you were in LA," she said.

"I was. Long enough to catch another plane back."

"Oh." Her heart hammered crazily in her chest. He was here. He was *back*. For good?

"My first impulse was to do something, anything. I wanted to run from this terrible feeling that I was failing on every level. When it was clear to me you've found your place."

"Not *every* level," she said quietly.

"I don't have everything figured out, but I do know that I'm not a chain restaurant kind of guy. And I don't want to be in California."

"Why not?" she asked, her heartbeat pulsing in her ears. "It's wonderful there. Sunshine. No Nor'easters."

"Nothing would be wonderful without you." He grasped her shoulders. "And, Hadley, I'm so proud of you. I'm proud of everything you've accomplished. And I know you're just getting started."

Oh, there went the waterworks.

"I was an ass," he said. "I'm sorry. I love you. Forgive me."

"Forgiven," she said, waving her hand. He was. Because he'd come back. For her. Hearing the *I love you* was pretty spectacular too.

"I tried not to be as stupid as I was when I was eighteen."

"I love you back," she said.

"I told you I missed football. That it was something I loved more than anything. Something I didn't want to end."

"It was a hard blow," she said. "One it's going to take a while to—"

He took her hands in his. "No, I'm trying to say that I was wrong about that. *You're* who I love more than anything. You're who I can't live without. Not football. *You.*"

The tears were streaming freely now. She was completely overcome. "I'll try to open up more," he said. "I'll do my best to figure it out. But I want to do it with you."

"I want to do it with you too," she said. "It's okay to lean on somebody a little. You know what else might help?"

"What's that?" he asked.

"That little puppy. She's eating like a horse right now. Want to see her?"

"Yeah," he said, his voice low and gravelly. He was smiling at her, and his eyes were full of warmth and...love. "A little later." Then he bent his head and kissed her.

She wrapped her arms around his broad back, getting lost in the feel of his lips on hers, of his big arms holding her, and she felt with a certainty that bowled her over like a sudden wave crashing that *this was it*.

This was where the buck stopped. This was where her search ended.

This was *her future*.

Somehow they ended up leaning back against a big rock.

Cam kissed her forehead and wrapped his arms around her. She rested her head against his chest as the sun performed its nightly color show and the salt-scented breeze blew through and the little waves churned quietly behind them.

"I'll love you forever, Had," he said. "I always have."

His arms came around her more tightly. "I love you too, Tony."

Epilogue

October

JAGGER, NO, SWEETIE!" Hadley pulled the dog out of the patch of petunias running along the old stone walkway of what used to be the Millers' house. Jagger's ear and tail instantly wilted as he gave her a stricken look that made her want to tell him he could eat all the petunias he wanted, except she wasn't sure that was a good idea for a dog. "I know you love your new yard, but doggies don't eat petunias, okay? Let's go in and get you a cookie."

That made him jump for joy. She reached into her shorts pocket and tossed him a dog biscuit to keep him away long enough so that she could lift the sign she was painting on the patio out of reach. But the wind blew off the ocean just then, ruffling the sign, and Jagger, thinking she was playing a game, came and sat right on it, smearing the paint.

"Oh!" Hadley said, biting down on the *No!* that almost spilled from her mouth. Jagger was a sensitive soul, and she always tried her best not to yell.

She succeeded today. She ran the sign into the screened porch and set it on the old picnic table, Jagger at her heels. "Well," she said to the dog, "glad you put your artistic touch on it. Butt painting just might catch on." Besides, there was nothing she could do about it now. She had a big surprise for Cam, and she couldn't wait to show him.

* * *

The first thing Cam saw as he walked up the path to the house at the end of a long day were petunia heads strewn all over. He couldn't help smiling that Jagger was at it again. In the past few months, he'd settled in enough to be his usual slightly naughty self, which Cam felt was a good sign.

Hadley might not agree, especially insofar as her carefully tended flowers went.

He lugged the samples he carried—boards of tile, chips of paint, a hunk of granite—up to the screen door. He was exhausted, in a good way. He'd spent most of the day speaking with contractors and reviewing plans. The old Crab Shack was no more, and in its place was a half-constructed vintage-inspired building that would one day become his restaurant. The ton of samples he was dragging home were for Hadley because his knowledge about decorating could probably fit on the head of a straight pin.

It was their four-month anniversary, and he had a surprise for her. They'd packed a lot of living into those months. First, they'd bought the Millers' house and moved right in. An impulsive move, yes, but they'd both figured they'd wasted enough years apart.

Every night as they chilled with a glass of wine on the porch, listening to the ocean, they talked about their plans. A brand-new kitchen. Real patio furniture, not the aluminum folding chairs they'd scrounged up and the old two-seater glider his dad had given them that Hadley had spray-painted a bright aqua blue. They'd been too busy with their respective businesses to agree on what they exactly wanted for the house, and they'd decided not to rush it.

Sitting next to her on the squeaky glider, sharing a bottle of wine, looking into the sea and into their future, was as close to his idea of heaven as it got.

They didn't need fancy furniture for that.

He opened the screen door to find newspapers strewn over the picnic table the Millers left behind. On top was a bell jar full of paintbrushes sitting in murky-colored water.

"Hadley?" he called. No Hadley, but Jagger was there, of course, always ready to greet him at the door. And from the near distance came the yipping of a much tinier dog.

Freddie, the once-runty puppy, was scratching at the bars of her crate and immediately began jumping and twirling her tiny tail as he blew through the kitchen. He stopped to love her up a little before he checked his cell for a text. It wasn't like Hadley to not tell him where she was. Tonight they'd planned to go to Ollie's Tee Ball game and then maybe get some takeout with whoever wanted to come back with them.

He hoped this house would one day be a gathering place for both their families.

He hoped it would be overrun with children.

And he *knew* it would be overrun with dogs. "Jagger's

been a little lonely since Gran took Bowie back," Hadley had said one night while snuggling up during one of their glider talks. And that's how Freddie had come to live with them.

The runty puppy was now an adorable, roly-poly sixteen-week-old who'd been taken in by another nursing mother dog thanks to Fuller, who it turned out wasn't so bad after all. Apparently being fostered was critical to help the rejected puppy learn how to get along with other dogs. It hadn't taken long for both him and Hadley to fall in love with her. The first of many puppies, Cam feared.

Whatever she wanted.

His heart had never been so full.

As he wandered back to the porch, he found Hadley standing at the door. She wore one of those sundresses he had so much fun helping her out of and her hair was up in a high ponytail.

"There you are," she said, a little out of breath from running up the path. "You're late."

"Sorry, but the decorator gave me a ton of samples," he said. "She wants us to talk them over, then meet with her tomorrow at lunchtime. Can you make it?"

"Sure." She seemed a little nervous. She was looking around, checking her watch, shifting her weight from one leg to another.

"Everything okay?"

"Yes. I...uh...maybe we should take the samples over to the restaurant and look at them there."

"Good idea." He checked his phone. "But I don't think we have time before the game."

"Why don't we drop them off now anyway? Then we can maybe get takeout and look at them on the way back?"

He drew her into his arms for a moment, not able to go too long without touching her. His want for her was endless.

"How did I get so lucky?" he whispered into her sweet-smelling neck. Jagger wiggled his skinny—but not as skinny as before—body between them, wanting to get in on the affection too. From the kitchen, Freddie barked.

"To get me and this wonderful dog?" She spoke to Jagger, reaching down to pet his head. "You *are* wonderful, aren't you?" Jagger showed his agreement by promptly dropping to the floor and rolling over for a belly rub.

"Jagger's really sweet with the new puppies at the shelter," she said. "He has a favorite. A fat little brown one that's so stinking cute."

Uh-oh. "You know how I feel about getting another puppy."

"The more the merrier?" she said.

"How about *less is best*?"

Hadley chuckled. "But I've already thought of the perfect name."

"What's that?"

"Stevie."

"Stevie?" Cam said. "That goes against the theme of rock star names, you know." Cam had felt it was a stretch to name a dog *Frederica Mercury* but somehow *Freddie* had worked just fine.

"Actually, it doesn't." Hadley rolled her eyes. "I'm not sure I can be with someone who doesn't get this."

Cam rubbed his chin thoughtfully. "It's a girl puppy, isn't it?"

Hadley nodded. "Mmm-hmm. You're getting warmer."

"Nicks. Stevie Nicks." He grinned widely, pleased he'd got it.

She looked pleased too. "Thank goodness. Relationship saved."

He lifted a brow. "But now I need a reward."

"A reward for what?"

"Getting you in so many ways." He tugged her close and started kissing up her neck. Until she sighed and melted a little into his arms.

"We're going to be late for Tee Ball," Hadley said weakly, arching her neck so he could have better access.

"Ollie's four," Cam said, lifting his head. "Do you think he'll notice?"

"Please don't stop," she said, curling her arms around his neck and tugging his head back toward her lips. "I suppose a little late won't matter."

Cam, giving in to her kiss, whispered, "That's just what I was thinking."

That made her grin. "I guess we get each other, then."

* * *

It had been fun to be spontaneous, and Hadley had been watching the time carefully, but now Cam was making her sweat bullets because he wanted to just throw the samples in the car for later instead of drop them off at the restaurant construction site.

And she really needed to get him over there.

When they were in the car, she said, "Cam, I really want to see the samples in the natural light. Let me just run them in, okay?"

"Oh, okay, sure," he said as he pulled into the old Crab Shack parking lot. "If it's important to you, we'll do it."

Yes. She did an internal fist-pump.

The old asphalt parking lot was gone, and in the Crab Shack's place stood a wooden frame covered with sheets of Tyvek. Stone that would soon give the outside its aged look sat in stacks around the perimeter. The scent of freshy cut plywood greeted them on the way up to the building.

Cam halted as he saw the sign that Hadley had draped over the top of the open framed doorway. In big black letters, it read CAM'S PLACE.

A puzzled frown furrowed his brow as he looked from the sign to her. "What's this about?"

Her heart skipped a little beat, hoping that surprising him had been the right thing to do. "Well, it's our four-month anniversary and I thought it might be nice to go out to dinner."

"Nice." His mouth quirked up in a little smile. "But...there won't be any food here for quite a while."

"That's not a problem." Hadley walked him through the rectangular opening and gestured for him to follow her.

"What have you done?" he asked, taking the hand she held out to him. "This may lead to some repercussions later."

"*Rewards*," she corrected. "Definitely rewards. You're going to love it." She hoped.

As soon as Cam walked through the doorway, a chorus of all their family and friends yelled "*Surprise!*" All standing in the openly framed room, in what would one day be the restaurant proper, and spilling out onto what would eventually become the back deck. In the middle of all the people they loved was a long folding table, filled with a sea of enticing-looking food.

Nick came forward with a champagne bottle. "I'd tell you to break it against the doorway or something like that but we want to drink it instead. Okay to open it?"

"Of course," Cam said, greeting and hugging everyone.

"Tony, will you help me carry the coolers out?" Hadley asked, gesturing him into what would soon become the kitchen.

"I didn't tell them about our four-month milestone," she said in a low voice. "But I thought it would be fun to celebrate that the place is finally framed."

He pulled her into his arms. "I love it."

"You didn't mind the surprise?" she asked. Because he was awfully quiet. He usually loved a crowd but maybe this was too much.

"I always love a reason to celebrate."

"Okay, well, I just wanted you to know," she said. "Shall we go back and join everyone?"

He tugged her back. "Not just yet. Now I have a surprise for you."

One look in his eyes showed her that he'd somehow turned the tables on her. His expression was a mix of gravity and...nerves. A cold sweat broke out over her skin despite the afternoon heat.

Then suddenly he went down on one knee—his good knee—and pulled out a little box. "Open it," he whispered.

With trembling fingers, she pried the little velvet box open to find a yellow sticky note in his handwriting. Which she had to blink back happy tears to read.

Marry me.

And underneath...a beautiful emerald-cut diamond with two baguettes on either side, sparkling in the late afternoon light.

"Take a chance on me," he said, "even though I still don't have my life all figured out. Come live in a house that overlooks the bluff where we first made love all those years ago. So that every day we can look out the window and be reminded of where we began. Will you marry me, Hadley?"

"Yes," she said, jumping into his arms. Easiest answer of her life.

Suddenly a big crowd of people—*their* people—began to cheer. But she was too busy kissing him to notice.

When a flash went off, her first thought was paparazzi, but it was only her dad, taking some photos.

"Congratulations, honey." Her dad hugged her first and then shook Cam's hand. "Welcome to the family, son."

"Thank you, sir," Cam said as Hadley's dad hugged him too.

"We couldn't be more pleased," her mom said. "We're going to start line-dancing lessons now so we can get good for the wedding. Maybe we can all sign up together!"

"Oh, that sounds like so much fun." Mayellen clapped her hands. "Doesn't it, Angelo?"

Cam's dad blanched. "I haven't danced in thirty years."

"Well, then"—May took his hand—"it's high time someone got you out there, don't you think?"

Cam's dad laughed, shaking his head and flashing May a smile. "So what's the name of the restaurant?" he asked Cam.

Cam looked up at the banner, then lovingly at Hadley. "*Cam's Place* sounds perfect to me."

"Perfect," Hadley said, meeting his gaze and getting a little teary again. Yes, the name suited him just right.

Nick popped the cork, and Kit and Darla handed out glasses of champagne all around.

"To Hadley and Tony," Angelo toasted. "May they have a wonderful, loving life together."

"Hear hear," everyone cheered as Cam took her in his arms.

* * *

Later, Hadley sat down with Darla and Kit while Ollie finished a piece of cake. Hadley, on the other hand, was still sampling the spread of hors d'oeuvres, which included crab and avocado toast, bruschetta with olive tapenade, and grilled shrimp. She fully believed it was going to be a treat to belong to a family who loved feeding people.

"We're so happy for you," Kit said, swiping at her eyes. "Let us see the ring."

Hadley held out her sparkler for them to exclaim over. "Oh, I almost forgot," she said, twisting off Darla's ring from her other hand. "Darla and I talked about this. I've had my summer of adventure." She pushed the ring across the table. "Now it's your turn, Kit."

Kit looked up in surprise. "I don't believe in superstition."

"But you believe in love," Darla said. "You're the most romantic of all of us. Put it on."

"It really is a beautiful ring." She slipped it onto her finger.

As Cam walked over, Darla rose and gave him a hug. "Congratulations," she said.

"Thanks, Darla," Cam said. "I appreciate your vote of confidence."

"But if you hurt her," she warned, "I'll come after you. And I can cover my tracks really well."

"That won't be necessary," Cam said warily. "But thanks."

Nick whizzed by with two pieces of cake. "There was only one piece left that was half chocolate, half white, so I snagged it for you, Dar," he said. "And I brought one for you, too, Kit."

"Thanks," Kit said.

"You remembered that?" Darla asked, clearly pleased. Hmm. Hadley was getting the same vibes with these two as she had with Angelo and May.

"Of course." He turned to Cam. "The place is looking great, if I do say so myself."

Cam slapped his brother on the back. "I'm glad you're branching out into doing some new construction. I love it."

"As long as the look is vintage," Nick said.

Later, when they were all gathered around a few round tables set on the future deck overlooking the water, Hadley asked Cam, "You knew about the surprise, didn't you?"

He chuckled. "Lucy knew about the catering order you put in for the food and accidentally let it slip. So then I thought it would be fun to have everyone with us when I popped the question."

"Lucy knew about the catering order?" Hadley asked.

"I hope you don't mind that I spilled the beans," Lucy said.

"Of course not," Hadley said. "I can't believe I was the one who got the surprise."

Cam looked very pleased with himself. "In the spirit of our recent competition, I can say it's not often that I get a chance to one-up you."

"I guess I can let you win once in a while." To Lucy, she said, "The food's amazing, by the way." She grabbed a bacon-wrapped scallop.

Cam hugged his sister. "But not as amazing as you."

Lucy made a face at her brother. "I'm ecstatic for you two," Lucy said. "And you might be happy to know I put in my notice with Dad. Lars heard so many good things about the food at the gala, he asked me to join his catering business. As his associate."

For once, Cam was speechless. He put an arm around his sister. "Well deserved."

"You handled that really well," Hadley said after Lucy had moved on. "You didn't say a thing about cooking school."

"She'll decide about that on her own time. But, hey, this could be a start."

Hadley's mom and dad pulled her aside. Which sort

of freaked her out. "Sweetheart, I couldn't be happier for you and Cam," her mom said. "But I . . . just wanted to say something that's been on my mind."

"What is it, Mom?" Hadley held out her plate of hors d'oeuvres. "Have a grilled shrimp. It's got some kind of citrusy coating on it. Delicious."

"Sweetheart, I think I sold you and your grandmother short. What you're doing with the business—how you're starting a rescue from scratch—well, it's impressive. I just wanted to tell you how proud I am of you. I don't think I've said that nearly enough."

"I don't think *we've* said that enough," her dad said, joining her mom. "I think we're learning that hard work is nothing without passion. Maybe that was the piece we forgot when you were growing up."

"And there's more to life than work," her mom said, threading her elbow through her dad's arm. "And one more thing," her mom added. "Can we have Bubba?"

"Bubba's a medical train wreck," Cam said, walking up.

"I have a soft spot for him," her mom said. "I don't know why. That lolling tongue, that drooly mouth. He's too adorable."

Cam laughed and looked at Hadley. "Now I know the soft spot is genetic."

"We're so proud of both of you," her mom said, "and so happy."

Hadley hugged her parents. "Thanks, Mom and Dad, for teaching me all about hard work. I love you. And Bubba is all yours."

Gran joined them, walking up with barely a guarded step. "I just knew you two would hit it off again," she said. "I'm so thrilled."

"Yep," Ivy said. "That idea you had to get them together really worked, Maddy." She clapped a hand over her mouth.

Mayellen's hard stare did not go unnoticed. "What idea?" Hadley asked, exchanging a look with Cam.

"Oh, it's nothing, really." Maddy scanned the room. "Has anyone seen Paul? This has been so much fun, but we really should be going."

Hadley was at her grandmother's side before she could escape. "Come clean," she said.

"Retirement was a huge decision," she said, looking a little nervously from Hadley to Cam. "But I made it a long time ago."

"Is that right?" Cam said.

"I obviously wasn't planning on breaking my hip. And I honestly was going to sell you the building, Cam. But that was before Hadley was so determined to help me through everything. You know how I've always loved you two together. I just felt you needed a little nudge—and everything fell together so naturally. Hadley was defending me and wanting to make sure I wasn't being pressured to stop working, and all I had to do was tell a teeny-tiny little fib."

"What fib, Mom?" Hadley's mom asked.

"You know Mayor Chaudhry is the sweetest thing. And her little dog *did* get away and I *did* fall but...she wasn't angry with me at all. And I didn't lose all my boarding business because word got around I was too old. We stopped taking bookings right before you came, Hadley, right before I fell. So it looked a lot worse than what it was."

"Gran!" Hadley said. "I really thought the business was in trouble."

"That's quite the plot twist," Darla said with an appreciative smile.

"It was the only thing I could think of to force you together," Gran said. "I hope you're not angry with me. Really, the only thing I'm sorry for is making you think the mayor was a little evil."

"Love won," Paul said, taking Gran's hand and lifting his glass before anyone could think about that too hard. "Let's have another toast."

Everyone raised their glasses. "To Hadley and Tony," Hadley's dad said. "May all your years be happy ones."

"Are you angry with your grandmother?" Cam asked.

She looked up at him and smiled. "Not at all." She looked at him a little worriedly. "Are you?"

He took her hand and kissed it. "How could I be angry with someone who helped me find my way back to you?"

Hadley clinked her glass with his. "Helped us to find our way back to *each other*," she amended.

"Amen to that," Gran said.

"I love you, Gran," Hadley called, still looking into Cam's eyes.

Amid the cheering of family and good friends, Hadley kissed the man she loved.

This was her life, a life she never would have found if not for all the pain of the past. Strange that it had been right here at home, waiting for her all along.

As soon as they sat down with their plates, Ivy came up to Hadley. "I feel so bad about lying," she said. "I'm sorry if I caused any trouble. We just wanted to see you and Cam together so badly."

"No, Ivy, not at all," Hadley said. "Don't even worry about it."

Ivy smiled. "Good. Because we have another tiny problem."

"What is it?" Hadley asked. Why was the back of her neck suddenly starting to prickle?

"Someone left a box by the front door."

"Wait," Hadley said, setting down her wine. "*This* front door?"

Ivy nodded and pointed. "Right outside."

Cam set down his fork. "Not more puppies," he said with a groan. "You've finally caught up on your sleep," he said to Hadley.

"Um, not exactly," Ivy said.

Ollie came running over and tapped her on the leg. "Aunt Hadley, Aunt Hadley."

"Hey, Bud." His hair was too short to ruffle. "What is it?"

"I just petted the kitties! They're so funny. Come look!"

Kitties?

"I know we don't take cats," Ivy rushed to say, "but all the foster homes are full because of all the kittens born in summertime and—"

Mayellen rushed over, nuzzling a black-and-white kitten against her cheek and crooning to it. Angelo trailed close behind, carrying a box.

So adorable and helpless. But there was no room at the shelter. There were dogs everywhere now.

"There are two more just like him in the box," Mayellen said.

Everyone was gathering around, exclaiming at whatever was in the box.

"Keep that box away from Hadley," Cam warned, a giant grin spreading over his face.

"I'd take one but I already have three cats," Mayellen said. "What do you think, Angelo?"

Cam's dad peered into the box at a tiny orange-yellow

head that popped up to peer at him. "Well, look at that," he said.

"Do you like cats, Hadley?" Cam asked, petting a kitten.

He was egging her on, she knew it. "Of course I do," Hadley said. "But we have no room for cats. The whole shelter is full of dogs."

Mayellen said, "Poor kitties."

Ivy wrung her hands. "Wish there was a no-kill shelter nearby."

"Of course we'll take them," Hadley said. "But only until we find a better place for them. They'll have to go in the back room for now."

"Wonder what it would cost to expand the back room," Mayellen mused.

"I could give you a good quote on that," Angelo said with a grin that looked an awful lot like Cam's.

"Everyone, stop!" Hadley said, holding out her arms. "We have a major construction project going on here. And we're going to be planning a wedding. It would be crazy to take on more!"

"Right, right," Mayellen said.

Cam pulled Hadley into his arms, which seemed made just for her.

"I've seen crazier." He kissed her on the forehead.

"I'm so glad you've both found each other again," Gran said. "Together you can accomplish anything!"

Hadley kissed Cam in the midst of everyone she held most dear. "You're my first love," she said, "and my last. I love you. So much."

He placed a kiss on her lips and touched his forehead to hers. Grinning widely, he put his lips to her ear and whispered, "I love you more."

Author's Note

Dear Readers,

I am writing this on a historic day—the first precious doses of the COVID-19 vaccine are being given to a few lucky health-care workers around the United States, the first vaccinations of many to come.

It is nothing short of a miracle.

Some of you have asked me throughout this year how I've been able to write lighthearted fiction when the world seems to have been coming down around us.

It hasn't been easy. There were times when I opened my computer gritting my teeth. When I've stared helplessly out the window, unable to type a word. When there wasn't a drop of humor left in my brain to squeeze onto the page. When I wondered if what I was doing day after day made any difference at all in a world that has seen so much tragedy in the past year.

But then I thought of the kind messages I've gotten when something I've written has made someone smile.

That's a simple thing. A smile, and a little

time to escape into a place where your worries fade for just a little while.

My mom used to tell me when I was sad or upset, "Pick up a book." Yes, she didn't exactly say, "*write* a book." But you get the message, which I still take to heart.

It ultimately became therapeutic for me to escape into a wonderful, sunshine-filled world. Where your friends have your back, where your family might drive you up the wall but know you better than anyone, and where you just might rediscover the love of your life. And where somebody always provides a quip or two (intentionally or not) to make you laugh.

This book was written as a love letter to you. Thank you for choosing to read it! I pray that by the time this is in your hands, we are out of the worst of this pandemic. That we can now visit our friends, hug our family, and head to the grocery store without shaking a little inside.

I pray for you and for everyone who has suffered hardships, big and small, this past year. And I will continue to do so as our world struggles to regain its balance and our lives slowly return to normal.

In the meantime, we can still have a laugh to lighten the load. And love will always go on.

Miranda
December 2020

Please turn the page for a preview from Miranda Liasson's next novel in the Seashell Harbor series, *Sea Glass Summer*.

Ever since her husband's death, Kit Blakemore has been focused solely on raising her precious little boy. But with her friends' encouragement, Kit is ready to start living again, beginning with selling her house to finance her college education. But when her husband's best friend comes to town with an offer to renovate the property, Kit fears accepting Alex's help would be the first step in losing her newly returned independence. This time, she's depending only on herself—it's the *only* way to keep her heart safe.

AVAILABLE JUNE 2022

"DID YOU JUST say I *don't* have a reservation after tonight?" Alex de la Cruz asked the clerk at the Seaside B and B, a big, historic inn right on the waterfront.

And...he was screwed. He could tell by the clerk's face.

Actually, he'd known that already, even if he had a place to stay.

Not that Seashell Harbor wasn't a beautiful, unique place to grow up, and not that his childhood hadn't been great, ever since he was adopted into a big, loving Hispanic American family with plenty of love to spare. It was just that he was constantly reminded of the best friend that he had lost. Every street invoked memories of cheeseburgers they'd eaten, balls they'd thrown, good times they'd had. The memories were as inescapable as the ocean that churned a steady rhythm alongside their picturesque town.

His heart was wrung out with sadness. Both he and Carson had set out as air force fighter pilots to do their patriotic duty, but only Alex had come back. He couldn't imagine being here without Carson.

He couldn't imagine being anywhere without his best friend. Now a little boy was fatherless, and Carson's wife was left on her own.

Your fault, a voice within him whispered.

The deep pain in his heart made him rub his chest in desperation, but it would not be erased.

He tucked his LSAT study book into his bag. That was Part 2 of his post–air force discharge plan. After he took care of Part 1. Which had to do with Carson.

The kindly gray-haired clerk glanced up at him over her rhinestone-studded spectacles. What was her name again? She used to volunteer with his mom over at the county mental health and addiction recovery center. "Our system says you booked one night, sweetie." She smiled, and he remembered her name was Lina Amari. "That's it."

He called up the confirmation email on his phone, swearing he'd booked the room for the entire weekend. His heart sank as he discovered she was right. "Mrs. Amari, any chance you've got a room for the next two nights?" That might be enough time to find a more permanent arrangement for the two months he planned to be here.

Again, the look. Kind but with a touch of *Are you sure you're from here?* "It's the season. Every rental on the island is booked. But let me see what I can do."

He wasn't going to get a room. He knew that. This was not the usual way he operated; as his mother would say, *Siguiendo los indicadores del gluteus maximus*.

Which translated to *Leading with your butt instead of your head*.

He always had a plan. Plus a backup. He kept lists, obsessively filed on his phone. His middle name was Control.

Actually it was *Constantino*, but close enough.

He never thought he'd be the one to spearhead the renovation on the turreted, old Queen Anne that Alex used to often tease Carson about.

"There's a house behind all that mess?" Alex had asked one time several years ago as they both stood looking at it.

"This is a gem," Carson had said, pride—and maybe a touch of insanity—in his voice. "Four bedrooms and a wraparound porch. Right on the harbor. If you're nice to me, Alex my man, maybe one day I'll let you come and watch the Fourth of July fireworks from my backyard."

"You mean that overgrown jungle back there?"

He smiled at the memory. Carson had always looked on that house as an opportunity. He'd had a clear vision of what could be.

Alex, in contrast, had never been able to see it as anything but a disaster, a teardown on a great piece of property. It knifed him, knowing that his closer-than-blood-brother would never be here to fulfill his dream. Or watch his son grow up. Or be reunited with his wife.

His wife, Kit, who was surely going to kick him out as soon as she laid eyes on him. She'd already warned him not to come.

But he'd come anyway. Because Stubborn was his second middle name. Actually it was Sebastian but...whatever.

He hadn't asked his old buddies about a place to stay for fear it would get back to her, preferring the forgiveness-rather-than-permission route. He had, however, scouted all the Airbnbs in Seashell Harbor. But every single one was full.

"I'm sorry, Captain de la Cruz," the clerk said. "We're all booked up. But I can put you on a wait list. Also, can't you stay with your mom?"

Actually, she'd been his very first stop when he got back in town. She'd hugged him until he couldn't breathe, said many tearful prayers of thanks for his safe return, and filled his belly with delicious Puerto Rican food. "She's staying above the art gallery for the summer," he said. Lots of folks rented out their quaint old homes for the season. Since his dad had passed away from cancer back when he was in college, his mom had made a great profit staying in the little efficiency apartment during the summers. It funded her extended visits back to Puerto Rico to visit their family.

He didn't want to worry her about his arrangements. If worse came to worst, she'd find him a place in a heartbeat with one of her many good friends, his adopted *tias*. But he really didn't want anyone knowing his business.

"How long is the wait?" For the first time, Alex noticed the polished wooden desk with its intricate carvings. It smelled faintly of lemon oil. Which was the other reason he'd chosen this place. He'd wanted to see the restoration work. And it was all first-class.

"You'd be fifth in line. It's possible something could open up."

Alex's gaze wandered around the lobby of the meticulously renovated hotel. It boasted a grand staircase with a gleaming oak banister, a giant fireplace just made for cozying up during a chill, and killer views of the ocean through enormous floor-to-ceiling leaded glass windows that people had been gazing out of for a century and a half.

Unlike a lot of the Victorian buildings in their town, this one was light and airy. And not too pattern-crazy. That's what he was going to aim for in his own work.

If that was what Kit agreed to. If she didn't boot him out on his aforementioned *gluteus maximus*. She disliked him, something he'd cultivated on purpose over the years. Except that wouldn't serve him very well now. "Did the Cammareris do the renovation?"

"They're the best," she confirmed.

Growing up, Alex had worked with the Cammareri brothers, Nick and Cam, and their dad for three summers and counted them among his good friends. He'd spent the past months before his discharge studying journals and blogs, watching YouTube videos, and keeping an online file of photos.

He was going to make that old house shine until it brought in a price big enough to provide a nest egg for his buddy's widow. So she could send their kid to college or get herself a house or a car or whatever it was that she needed.

And maybe then the awful anvil of guilt would leave his chest. He doubted it, but he hoped it would make the weight a little more bearable. At least, that was what his therapist had recommended. She'd also told him not to isolate himself, something he'd also been pretty good at doing since the accident.

"I know you're military," the clerk said, "and I'd do anything to help you, but we're completely full. I can call around to a couple of people who might be willing to rent a room if that would help."

"Sure, thanks." As she began writing something down, he added, "You wouldn't know of anyone in town offering a short-term rental? Like, for a couple of months?" *The cheaper the better*, he almost added. He wanted to invest his capital into the project, not in his own accommodations.

That was the idea. Fix up the disaster and recoup his expenses for materials when it sold. Kit would rather die than take charity, but even she would have to admit that was a fair deal to cut.

"Here you go, Captain." The clerk scrawled down some names and handed him a piece of paper. "Those are the names of a few other B and B owners off the beaten track. Good luck."

Alex thanked the clerk, pocketed the information, and left. Tossing his duffel bag into his car, he walked the few blocks to the McKinnon property and set eyes on it for the first time in a very long time.

His stomach plummeted, a feeling of foreboding seeping steadily into his veins. Carson had talked about this place like it was fricking Tara. In the front stood a couple of raggedy, half-dead pines instead of a stately allée of grand old oaks, and the great big porch was sagging so badly it wouldn't support a tall pitcher of iced tea, let alone a bevy of wooden rockers.

What he saw was a turreted, old, wood-framed Queen Anne, every inch peeling, its chimney crumbling. The stone steps leading up to the porch were as crooked as a six-year-old's front teeth. The grass was cut but the flower beds were unruly. And the landscaping...ugh. Shrubs and once-decorative small trees had grown into a tangled, matted mess that obliterated most of the forlorn exterior.

Carson, buddy, what were you thinking? Of the two of them, Alex had been the dreamy, poetic one. Carson had been firmly grounded in reality. What on earth had he seen in this train wreck?

He tried to focus on the fact that you could see the historic Seashell Harbor lighthouse jutting out from a cove in the near distance—a million-dollar view.

Ha. And a million-dollar reno job.

A memory jolted him then. Kit running around the side of the house and flinging herself into Carson's arms while Alex carefully averted his gaze. The two of them had been crazy and silly and totally in love. The tragedy of that lost happiness hit him hard.

Alex would conquer this house. He would beat it into submission with every muscle in his body. He would restore and renovate and tear out and rebuild.

He would do it from the depths of his anger and his grief at losing his best and oldest friend. It would be the last thing he could do for Carson. He'd put his heart and soul into this project. And then clear out of here as fast as he possibly could.

Decided, he turned his back on the house. And prayed that the spell that Kit Blakemore had cast on him long ago had faded with time.

* * *

Kit dragged herself into her parents' kitchen at 6:30 a.m. that Saturday to find her parents sitting around the table drinking coffee, her dad reading the newspaper—in his preferred form, paper—and her mom reading a library book. The gentle *tick-tick-tick*ing of the oven filled the air, as did the warm and welcoming smell of cinnamon. Ollie, who usually had no trouble following after the early rising habits of the Admiral was, surprisingly, nowhere to be found.

Kit poured herself some coffee and sat down, blowing on it so it would be cool enough to mainline. Unlike her parents, she tended more toward the night owl side. Ever since Carson died, all her anxieties seemed to get chatty when the house was settling into quiet, preventing a good night's sleep. So, down the hatch.

"Mom, you made cinnamon rolls?" Kit stared at the plate of steaming pastries with icing melting and dripping down the sides. "How long have you been up?"

"Well, Ollie loves them," she said, closing her book. She was already dressed, in a cute shaker sweater and jeans. And did she have lipstick on? "And he had a hard day yesterday."

The vision of Ollie's distressed face at Tee ball came rushing at her. As did the realization that her friends might make her jog five miles this morning, but just inhaling that buttery, cinnamony smell was enough to undo all her willpower.

"Why are *you* up so early?" her dad asked over his spectacles. He really couldn't understand why anyone would want to waste the morning by sleeping past 7:00.

Kit stifled a yawn. "I'm going for a jog with Hadley and Darla." She tried, but failed, to put some levity in her voice.

"That right?" her dad said, assessing her more thoroughly this time. Maybe he was checking to see if he'd heard right.

"It's a crisp spring morning." Her mom sipped her coffee. "I'm sure you'll have an invigorating run."

"It's thirty-nine degrees," her dad reported. He knew the weather better than their local meteorologist, thanks to having minute-by-minute updates from three weather apps on his phone, so Kit totally believed him. "Better dress warm."

"I will," she said automatically, feeling a little bit like a teenager in her parents' home. Then she tapped her nails nervously against her mug. *Might as well just come out with it, Kit*, she told herself. "Mom and Dad, I've been thinking of making a few changes."

That made her mom look up. "Do you mean taking up jogging? That's wonderful, dear."

"Yes. Physical fitness clears the mind," the Admiral said, his newspaper rustling as he flipped a page.

"Actually, I-I'm thinking it's time Ollie and I moved out." Both of their heads jerked up. "It might be time to get our own place."

"Why on earth would you want to do that?" Her mom's stone mug hit the table with a definitive *thunk*. "We love having you and Ollie here."

"It's been two years," Kit said. Not to mention she was thirty-five. "I think you both have taken care of Ollie and me for long enough."

"Nonsense," her mom said. "You've both been through a tremendous trauma. We'd never want you to go through that alone. That's what family is for."

"Your mother is right." Her dad put his paper down and folded his hands. "Now that we're retired, we enjoy having you and Ollie around. And living here has helped you save up for your future."

She grabbed both her parents' hands. "I love you both so much, you know that. And I'm so grateful for everything you've done. But I think it's time for me to get my life going again."

"What do you mean?" Her mom seemed genuinely puzzled.

"Yes, so, about that," Kit said. "I...I was thinking about signing up for this new program the community college is advertising for nontraditional students. It would involve taking a summer class or two to get back into things and see how I do."

Her dad's thick gray brows knit down, the first subtle sign of disapproval that Kit knew well.

"Maybe Ollie should be your first priority," her mom said, not unkindly.

When was Ollie *not* her first priority? "Do you mean because he's been a little anxious lately?"

"Well, there will always be anxieties," her mom said wisely. "But he's just going to be starting kindergarten in the fall. And how on earth are you going to move out on your own and take college classes and work full-time?" Her mom patted Kit's hand. "I know you must be restless. But changing everything all at once seems hasty."

"I have to agree," her dad said. "But being restless is a good sign. It means you're taking steps to move on."

Her mom nodded. "There's no need to try to do everything on your own when you have a great support system right here."

"But what about you two?" Kit asked. "Now that Dad's retired, you two should travel. Join clubs, volunteer. Have fun." Last year, they'd talked about traveling to Greece for their anniversary but stayed. Surely they wanted their house and their life back?

"Ollie is a joy," her mom said. "Right, Hal?"

"Absolutely." Her dad nodded.

So many times over the past two years Kit had accepted her parents' sage advice. And their help. It had been easy to do when she'd felt so unsure and unsteady and...sad.

But Kit could see herself years from now, still leaning

on them like a pair of crutches while all her friends lived their very full lives. She needed to plan a solid future for her son, and all she had was a decrepit old house that hadn't sold in forever and a boss who hated when she left for lunch and grumbled every time she asked if she could go to one of Ollie's preschool programs, even though she was a stellar employee.

Was it selfish to put some of her needs before Ollie's? Sometimes? She wasn't sure if her mom ever had. A military wife, she'd quit teaching school long ago and had devoted herself to volunteer projects, being a classroom mom, making amazing Halloween costumes, and always having healthy snacks and making great dinners every evening.

Kit helped all she could around the house, and insisted on helping with expenses, but her grade as a mother, split as she was in seventeen different directions, always seemed to pale in comparison.

"Just think about it," her dad said. "You'll figure out the right thing to do."

Now didn't seem to be the time to ruffle more feathers. But what was one more teensy-weensy, slightly more upsetting detail? She took a big breath and plunged in. "I've been looking at small houses and duplexes to rent."

Her mom and dad exchanged a grave parental glance. "Oh, Kit," her mom said.

Uh-oh. Her mom hadn't used that tone since she and Carson announced they were marrying at twenty-one. Her dad put down his paper *and* his glasses, an equally bad omen.

That did it. She was definitely going to chuck the jog and all this stress. Just as she lifted a big gooey roll to her lips, there was a rap on the back window.

Hadley and Darla walked in, making themselves at home as they had for the past thirty years.

"Hey, Mrs. Wendell, hey, Admiral," Darla said.

"Have a seat, girls," Kit's mom said. She'd probably still be calling them *girls* even when they were eligible for AARP membership. Her dad pulled out a chair.

"We can't sit," Darla said.

Kit's mom nodded to the empty chairs. "Sure you can," she said. "Come chat for a few minutes."

Hadley took the cinnamon roll from Kit's hand and returned it to the plate. "Later," she said, pulling her up. "Grab a sweatshirt. It's a little chilly."

"And a hat," Darla said, then examined her hand. "And while you're at it, get the ring."

Before Kit could protest, her mom said, "Darla, your hair's getting long." Today Darla wore it pulled up in a high ponytail.

Darla tugged on it. "Finally. It's been a year and a half."

What she didn't say was *from the chemo*, which she'd had for Hodgkin's lymphoma and was successfully cured of. Thank God.

"It's so pretty." Kit tugged a little on her ponytail. Darla's hair was a shimmery shade of pale blond that Kit had always envied, very different from her own dark hair.

Tugging on Darla's ponytail suddenly brought a strange thought to Kit's mind. Fixing a little girl's hair. Would Ollie ever have a brother or sister? Being an only child was...lonely; she could attest to that. And Ollie was a sensitive soul, loving books and art. While she did all she could to help him have friends, she worried about him having too much alone time.

As her friends chatted about Hadley's upcoming wedding and the newest thriller Darla was writing, Kit felt the same unsettling tug inside herself. The one that told her there was more out there for her and Ollie. How was she going to open up the possibilities of anything happening in her life if she didn't go out and look for them?

Darla, always the taskmaster, glanced at her watch. "It's almost seven," she told Kit. "You ready?"

Kit had no choice but to run down the hall to the mudroom and grab Carson's old Air Force Academy sweatshirt and the first hat she found. And yes, she fished the old-fashioned filigree ring with the diamond-like stone out of her purse. No, she wasn't ready, but she was presentable enough as she let her friends hustle her out the door.

About the Author

MIRANDA LIASSON is a bestselling author who writes about the important relationships in women's lives as well as the self-discovery and wisdom gained along the way. Her heartwarming and humorous romances have won numerous accolades and have been praised by *Entertainment Weekly* for the way she "deals with so much of what makes life hard...without ever losing the warmth and heart that characterize her writing." She believes that we can handle whatever life throws at us just a little better with a laugh.

A proud native of northeast Ohio, she and her husband live in a neighborhood of old homes that serves as inspiration for her books. She is very proud of her three young adult children. And though every day she thinks about getting a dog, she fears a writer's life may bore the poor animal to tears.

When she's not writing or enjoying books herself, she can be found biking along the old Ohio and Erie Canal Towpath trails in the beautiful Ohio MetroParks.

Miranda loves to hear from readers!

You can contact her at her website, MirandaLiasson.com or at the following:

Facebook.com/MirandaLiassonAuthor

Twitter: @MirandaLiasson

Instagram: @MirandaLiasson

Pinterest: @MirandaLiasson

For a bonus story from another author that you'll love, please turn the page to read *Only Home with You* by Jeannie Chin.

In this sweet second-chance novella, a free-spirited accountant's infatuation adds up to love for her brother's best friend.

FOREVER

New York Boston

To the members of the organization formerly known as the Capital Region Romance Writers of America. I can't imagine having gone on this journey without you.

Acknowledgments

Thank you to everyone at Forever who helped bring this story to life, including my lovely editors Amy Pierpont, Sam Brody, and Madeleine Colavita, and to my incredible agent, Emily Sylvan Kim. My support network of fellow writers—especially the tea ladies and bad girlz—were invaluable.

Thank you as well to my husband and my daughter, and to her preschool teachers, without whom I could never have found the mental space and peace of mind to focus on telling stories about people kissing.

I am also grateful to the Asian American and biracial communities who have been a well of strength and support in these difficult times.

Finally, a big thank-you to *you*, the person reading this book. You are the secret ingredient that keeps the storytelling magic alive.

Chapter One

TWENTY-EIGHT MORE months.

Devin James silently repeated it to himself with every crack of his nail gun. He moved to the next mark on the beam, lined up his shot, and drove another spike of steel into the wood.

Based on the numbers he'd rerun over the weekend, twenty-eight months was how long it was going to take him to save up for a house of his own. Still too long, but he was on target, putting away exactly as much as he'd budgeted for, paycheck after paycheck.

"Take that," he muttered, sucking in a breath as he kept moving down the line.

His dad had told him enough times that he'd never amount to anything. Devin tightened his grip on the nail gun and sank his teeth into the inside of his lip. What he'd give to get that voice out of his head. To show his dad he wasn't too stupid to do the math, and he wasn't too lazy to do the work.

He'd buy those three acres of land from Arthur. His mentor—and his best friend Han's uncle—had been saving the lot for him for three years now, and he'd promised to sell it to him at cost. Once Devin had the deed in his hand, he'd start digging out the foundation the next day. Between the buddies he'd made at construction sites and the favors folks owed him, he could be standing in his own house within six months. A quiet place all to himself on a wooded lot five miles outside of town. He'd get a dog—a big one, too. A mutt from the animal rescue off Main Street.

He'd have everything his useless old man told him he could never have. All he had to do was keep his head down and keep working hard.

He finished the last join on this section of the house's frame and nodded at Terrell, who'd been helping him out. The guy let go, and they both stood.

Adjusting his safety glasses, Devin glanced around. It was a cool fall day in his hometown of Blue Cedar Falls, North Carolina. The sun shone down from a bright blue sky dotted with wispy clouds. The last few autumn leaves hung on to the branches of the surrounding trees, while in the distance, the mountains were a piney green.

He and his crew had been working on this development for the better part of a year now. It was a good job, with good guys for the most part. Solid pay for solid work, and if he had a restlessness buzzing around under his skin, well, that was the kind of thing he was good at pushing down.

"Hey—James."

At the shout of his last name across the build site, Devin looked up. One of the new guys stood outside the trailer, waving him over. Devin nudged the protective muffs off his ears so he could hear.

"Boss wants to see you before you clock out."

Devin nodded and glanced at his watch. The shift

ended in thirty. That gave him enough time to quickly clean up and check in with Joe.

He made a motion to Terrell to wrap things up.

"What's the hurry?" a voice behind him sneered. "Got to run off to Daddy?"

Devin pulled a rough breath in between his teeth. Head down and work hard, he reminded himself.

No punching the mayor's son in the face.

But Bryce Horton wasn't going to be ignored. He stepped right in Devin's way, and it took everything Devin had to keep his mouth shut.

"Isn't that what you call old Joe?" Bryce taunted. "*Daddy?* You sure come fast enough when he calls."

Devin's muscles tensed, heat building in his chest.

He kept himself together, though. Bryce had been like this since high school, putting everybody down and acting like he was the king of the hill. The entire hill was all sand, though. The guy never did any work. If *his* daddy didn't run this town, he'd have been out on his rear end ages ago.

As it was, Bryce'd been hired on as a favor to the mayor's office, and getting him fired would take an act of God. Didn't stop Devin from picturing it in his head. Daily.

Devin ground his molars together and brushed past him.

"Oh, that's right," Bryce called as Devin showed him his back and started to walk away. "Your real daddy left, didn't he?"

Red tinted Devin's vision. He flexed his fingers, curling them into a palm before taking a deep breath and letting them go.

It'd be so easy, was the thing. Bryce wasn't a small

guy, but he wasn't a particularly strong one, either. Two hits and he'd be on the ground, snot-faced and crying. That was how bullies were.

That was how Devin's dad had been.

Without so much as a glance in Bryce's direction, Devin shucked his glasses, muffs, and gloves, stowed his stuff, and headed over to the trailer. As he walked, he blocked out the sound of Bryce running his mouth. He blocked out the surly voice in his own head, too.

By the time he got to the door, his blood was still up, but he was calm enough to show model employee material, because that was what mattered.

With a quick knock, he tugged open the trailer door and poked his head inside. Joe was at his desk, big hands pecking out something or other on the keyboard.

"Hey." Devin kept his voice level. "Heard you wanted to see me?"

Joe glanced up and smiled, the lines around his eyes crinkling. "Yeah, hey, have a seat."

Devin closed the door and sat down. While Joe finished up what he was working on, Devin half smiled.

Joe was a good boss because he was one of them. He'd worked his way up the ranks from grunt to site supervisor over the last twenty-five years.

Didn't make the sight of his giant frame squished behind a desk any less funny, though.

After a minute, Joe squinted and hammered the return key before straightening and turning to Devin. "James. Thanks for coming in."

"No problem, boss."

"I'll cut to the chase. You're probably wondering why I called you in here."

Devin shifted his weight in his chair. He'd been so

distracted by Bryce and then by watching Joe pretend he didn't need reading glasses that he hadn't given it that much thought. Business had been good, and Devin never missed a day. He hadn't screwed anything up that he knew of. Which left only one thing.

Something he'd dismissed out of hand, even as he'd thrown his hat in the ring.

"Uh..."

"You know Todd's retiring at the end of the month."

Devin nodded, his mouth going dry. He fought to keep his reaction—and his expectations—down. "Sorry to see him go."

"We all are, but he's earned it." Joe let out a breath. Then he cocked a brow. "Big question of the day is who's going to fill in for him as shift leader for your crew."

"You made a decision."

"Sure did." Joe kept a straight face for all of a second. When his face split into a wide smile, Devin mentally pumped his fist. Joe extended his hand across the desk. "Congratulations."

Devin didn't waste any time. He shoved his hand into Joe's with fireworks going off inside his chest.

Yes. Holy freaking hell, yes.

"I won't let you down, sir."

"Oh, believe me, I know it, or I woulda picked somebody else."

As he pulled his hand back, Joe started talking about responsibilities and expectations, and Devin was definitely listening.

He was also mentally updating all the numbers in his budget.

He'd never really expected to get the job of shift leader. There were older guys who'd put their names in. Heck, Bryce could have gotten it, and then Devin would have been looking for another job entirely.

But he knew exactly how much his pay was going to go up by. Every cent of it could go into savings. Twenty-eight months would be more like fourteen. Maybe even twelve.

One year. One year until he'd have enough for the land and the materials.

He couldn't wait to tell everybody. Drinks with his buddy Han would be on him tonight.

Arthur was going to be so proud.

Joe paused, narrowing his eyes at Devin and making him tap the brakes on his runaway thoughts. "It won't be an easy job, Devin."

Devin swallowed. "I'm up for the challenge."

"You don't have to convince me," Joe repeated, holding his big hands up in front of his chest. He set them down on the desk and fixed Devin with a meaningful look. "Just. Stand your ground, okay? Do that and I have every confidence you'll be fine."

Right.

Moving up would also mean being responsible for an entire shift crew of guys.

Including Bryce Horton.

That same hot, ready-to-fight instinct flared inside him, followed right after by the icy reminder to push it down. He smiled tightly. "Not a problem."

"All righty, then." The matter seemed settled as Joe stood. "I'll get the paperwork sorted. You start training on Monday."

Devin rose. "Thank you. Really."

Joe gestured with his head toward the door. "Go on. Have a beer or three to celebrate, you hear?"

Devin had no doubt he'd do exactly that—eventually.

With a spring in his step, he headed for the parking lot. He smacked the steering wheel of his beat-up bucket of bolts as he got in and slammed the door behind him. As the old truck lurched to life, he cranked the stereo and peeled out, triumph bursting inside him.

This was it. The break he hadn't dared to hope for but that he needed, the thing that was going to get him on the fast track to his goals.

And there was only one place he wanted to go.

The Harvest Home food bank and soup kitchen stood in a converted mill on the north end of town. Business in Blue Cedar Falls was generally good, and it had only been getting better since tourism had picked up on Main Street.

Main Street's cute little tourist district felt a long way away, though. Devin's wasn't the only rust bucket truck parked outside Harvest Home. On his way in, he held the door for a woman and her four kids who were coming out, each armed with a bag. He didn't need to peek inside to know they were filled with not just cans but with fresh food, too. The kind of stuff that filled your belly *and* your heart.

Goodness knew Devin'd had to rely on that enough times when he was a kid.

He ran his hand along the yellow painted concrete wall of the entry hallway, his throat tight. He couldn't wait to tell Arthur.

But when he turned the corner, it wasn't Arthur standing behind the desk. Oh no. Of course it wasn't.

Devin's blood flashed hot. For one fraction of a second, he let his gaze wander, taking in soft curves and softer-looking lips. Dark eyes and long, silky, ink-black hair.

A throat cleared. A brow arched.

Like he'd been slapped upside the head, he jerked his gaze back to meet hers. She smiled at him mischievously, and he bit back a swear.

"Hey, Zoe," he managed to grit out. Silently, he said the rest of her name, too.

Zoe *Leung*. Devin's best friend Han Leung's little sister. Arthur Chao's beloved niece.

The one person on this earth he should *not* be getting caught checking out. Especially by her.

"Hey, Dev." The curl of her full lips made his heart feel like a puppy tugging at its leash to go run off into traffic. Only a semi was barreling down the road.

The past few months since Zoe had moved back home after college had been torture. Fortunately, he had lots of practice keeping himself from doing anything stupid around her. He'd been holding himself in check for years, after all. Since she was eighteen and he was twenty-two.

Because if he ever let go of that leash on his control? Gave in to the invitation in her eyes?

Well.

It'd probably be a whole lot easier if he just got run over by a truck.

Chapter Two

ZOE LEUNG'S HEART pounded as heat flared in Devin's eyes.

Only for it to flicker and then fizzle in about two seconds flat.

The whole thing made her want to tear her hair out.

Because she was a realist, you know? Sure, she'd had a crush on Devin since she'd realized that not all boys were slimy and gross (her brother Han definitely excluded). But she'd never expected anything to ever come of it.

To him, she was the bratty kid who used to follow her brother and his friends around all the time. Skinned knees and messy ponytails and oversize hand-me-down T-shirts did not bring any boys to the yard, and she'd made her peace with that.

Right until her high school graduation, four and a half long years ago.

Her mom had made such a big deal of it. Her last kid graduating from high school had combined with menopause in some pretty unpredictable ways. Finally, the nagging about wanting a good picture had gotten to be too much. Fed up with it all, Zoe had gotten her sister Lian to help her figure out how to do her hair and her makeup, and she'd actually worn a dress for once. It'd been a big hassle, but she'd had to admit that she felt and looked great.

At the party after, while Han and Devin and a few of their friends were tossing a football around in the backyard, she'd gone up to them to let them know the pizza was there.

She could see it all in her head so clearly. Devin had looked up. His eyes had gone wide.

Only to have a football smack him right in the head.

He'd never looked at her the same after that. Every time his gaze landed on her, it would darken. His Adam's apple would bob, and that scruffy jaw would tense, his rough, hardworking hands clenching into fists at his sides.

Exactly the way he'd been looking at her about two seconds ago.

An angry flush warmed her cheeks as he jerked his gaze away—probably checking to make sure her overprotective big brother, Han, wasn't going to materialize out of nowhere and throw another football at his head.

It was infuriating.

When he didn't have any interest in her, she could totally handle it. But now? This weird, intense game of sexual-attraction chicken he was playing?

What a bunch of bull.

The last time they'd run into each other at the drugstore, he'd done the same thing, heat building in his gaze right until the moment she'd stared back at him. She'd played it cool, hoping he'd say something.

Instead, he'd grabbed the first thing he saw off the shelf and darted toward the checkout. Either the guy was super eager to get home with his novelty sunglasses or he was avoiding her.

After months of being back home spinning her wheels on her doomed job search, she was tired of spinning her wheels on whatever was going on between the two of them, too. She wasn't expecting him to drop down on one knee and ask her to marry him or anything. But she was into him, and it sure seemed like he was into her. While she was here, couldn't they, like, *do* something about it?

Enough playing it cool. Clearly she was going to have to be the one to make the first move.

Abandoning subtlety for once, she sauntered over to him. She put a little swing in her hips, just for fun. She'd come out of her shell a lot during the four years she'd been away. She could still rock a messy ponytail and an oversize T-shirt, but the snug top and short skirt she was wearing in preparation for her shift at the Junebug tonight were just as comfortable—and she knew how to use them.

"How's it going?" she asked, coming to a stop a foot away. Too close, for sure. The air hummed. He was tantalizingly warm, pushing heat into the tight space between them and making her skin prickle with awareness.

Licking her lips, she gazed up at him. She was all but batting her lashes here.

The darkness in his eyes returned as he stared down at her.

He had always been good-looking. Back in the day, it had been in a loping, gangly teenage way. His spots on the baseball and football teams had put some muscle on him, but whatever he'd been up to at his construction job had done even more. Under his jacket and tee, he rippled with muscle. His jaw had gone from soft to chiseled, and he kept his golden-brown hair shorter, too.

"Uh." He swallowed. "Good. Great, actually."

"Yeah?"

He still hadn't backed away. That was a good sign, right?

"Yeah." He nodded almost imperceptibly.

Something turned over, low in the pit of her belly. He smelled so good, like man and hard work and wood shavings.

She wanted to ask him what was going on that was so great. She wanted to sway forward into him, tip her head up or put her hand on his broad chest and find out if it was as hard and hot as it looked.

He swallowed and shifted his weight, edging ever so slightly closer to her. Her heart thudded hard. Maybe he wanted her to do all those things, too. Maybe...

"Devin? What are you doing here?"

Crap.

The instant Uncle Arthur's gently accented voice rang out, Devin jumped back as if he'd been burned. The hot thread of tension that had been building between them snapped. A flush rose on her cheeks, almost as deep as the disappointment flooding her chest.

"Arthur! Hey, um." Devin glanced around wildly, looking at everything but Zoe. Honestly, it would have been less conspicuous if he'd come over and put his arm around her. "Do you have a second?"

"For you?" Uncle Arthur smiled, pleased lines appearing around his eyes and mouth. "Of course." He looked to Zoe. "You don't mind?"

Zoe forced a smile of her own. "Of course not."

With a smile of thanks to Zoe, Uncle Arthur led Devin back to his office. Zoe was tempted to follow and listen at the door, but that would be childish.

Instead, she sighed and retreated to the front desk. This was a slow hour. All the appointments for people to pick up goods from the food bank were over, but the soup kitchen hadn't opened for dinner service yet. Down the hall, pots and pans banged, though, so Harvest Home's two staff cooks, Sherry and Tania, must already be at work.

That didn't mean there wasn't anything to do, of course.

Ever since she'd slunk back to Blue Cedar Falls with the useless accounting degree her mom had talked her into, she'd been splitting her time between scrolling social media, waitressing at the new bar in town, and helping out here. Working at Harvest Home barely paid a pittance, of course, but she didn't mind. Uncle Arthur might be her mom's brother, but he was her exact opposite in terms of how he treated Zoe. He was cool and relaxed, and he trusted Zoe with real responsibilities. Watching him work his rear end off here—even though he was in his sixties and on three different high blood pressure medications—made her want to live up to his example.

She liked helping people. Sending folks off with whatever they needed to help get them through tough times gave her a warm feeling inside. Even the boring administrative stuff felt important.

With a sigh, she plunked behind the desk and got to it, confirming pickups, arranging deliveries, and checking in about volunteer shifts. When the crew of said volunteers helping out with supper tonight showed up, she showed them to the kitchen and placed them in Sherry's and Tania's capable hands. On the way back, she definitely did *not* linger outside Arthur's office, staring at the closed door as if she could burn through it with her laser eyes and find out what he and Devin were going on about.

Okay, maybe for a minute, but that was it.

As she returned to the front room and started in on labeling bags for the next day's pickups, the door swung open.

A telltale *tutt*ing sound announced who it was before Zoe could so much as look up.

"Zhaohui." Her mother came in carrying a box of extra produce from their family restaurant, the same way she did every Tuesday—the one day of the week the Jade Garden was closed. She set the box down and came straight over, her tone as disapproving as ever as she snatched the marker from Zoe's hand. "You know Arthur likes black ink."

Zoe rolled her eyes. "Well, I like purple, and do you see Arthur doing the work?"

"I think the bags look great." Han had come in behind her, hauling another crate of soon-to-expire vegetables.

"See?" Zoe told her mom.

Her mom made that noise in the back of her throat that said nothing and everything as she waved a hand at Zoe and let her grab the marker back. She drifted away, and Zoe met her brother's gaze over her head.

"Hey." Han wrapped an arm around her shoulders to give her a quick squeeze in greeting. She rolled her eyes the way she was contractually obligated to as his little sister, but she appreciated the affection all the same. "How's it been today?"

"Not bad." Zoe finished labeling the bags—in dark, entirely legible purple—as she gave him a general rundown. She glanced at the clock. She didn't need to leave for her shift at the Junebug for another few minutes. Normally, with Han and her mom here to take over, she'd head out and get a few minutes of quiet in her car to decompress, but she eyed the back office again.

Before she had to make a decision, the door swung open, and her breath caught. Devin came out first. Uncle Arthur followed, patting his back. Both of them were all smiles.

As Devin spotted Han, his grin grew even wider. "Dude, I didn't know you were going to be here."

"What's up?" The two traded bro-hugs and smashed their fists together, and for a second it was like being twelve years old again, watching them and feeling completely outside it all.

Devin stepped back. "Guess who's moving up to shift leader next week."

"Whaaaat?" Han held his hand out, and they high-fived.

"That's awesome," Zoe interjected.

Devin's gaze shot to hers only to dart right back away.

Uncle Arthur clapped Devin's shoulder. "I knew it would happen."

The corners of Devin's mouth curled up, even as he shrugged and looked down.

Zoe's ribs squeezed. He might be trying to act cool, but Devin had been following her uncle around for even longer than Zoe had been following Devin. She knew the praise and faith meant the world to him.

"Your company hiring?" her mom asked Devin, her tone way too innocent. "Maybe in accounting department?"

Zoe glared at her.

"What?" Her mom put her hand over her chest. "I'm just asking." She raised her brows. "Someone has to."

Sure, sure. So helpful. Zoe clamped her mouth shut against the instinct to remind her mom that she'd been the one to push Zoe into accounting in the first place. Well, that or medicine or law, and accounting had definitely been the easiest option of those.

Zoe hadn't exactly had a strong sense of what she wanted to do, but it wasn't sit behind a desk crunching numbers all day. The fact that she hadn't been able to find a job in the field was salt in the wound. Did her mom really need to remind her of it constantly?

"I'll check, Mrs. Leung," Devin promised. He cast Zoe a sympathetic glance, and she couldn't decide if that was better or worse than him totally ignoring her.

Her mother cocked a brow, silently saying, *See?*

Zoe huffed out a breath.

Diffusing things the way he always did, Han turned back to Devin. "We *have* to celebrate."

"The Junebug does two-for-one drinks before eight tonight," Zoe blurted out. Self-consciousness stole over her as all eyes turned to her, but screw it. She doubled down. "Plus, you know." She pointed her thumbs at her chest. "Employee discount."

Han looked to Devin, brows raised.

"Sure," Devin said slowly. He let his gaze fall on her for all of a second. There was that flare of heat again. But as fast as it had come, it disappeared as his eyes darted away. "Who doesn't like cheap beer, right?"

"Right," Zoe agreed. She smiled tightly.

Thanks to her entire freaking family showing up, this round of "Poke Devin Until He Cracks" was a stalemate.

But the good news was that she'd just earned herself another shot.

Chapter Three

"SO, HOW'S IT feel?" Han asked. "Mr. Fancypants promotion."

Devin shook his head. "I'm still having a pretty hard time believing it."

After a brief stop at home to change, he'd met Han at the Junebug on Main Street for the cheap drinks Zoe had promised them. Add in some burgers and the owner Clay's famous cheese fries, and this was basically Devin's ideal night out. He snagged another stick of greasy goodness from the basket in front of him and popped it in his mouth. It tasted like victory.

And cheese.

But mostly victory. After years of careful planning, everything he'd been working for finally felt like it was within his grasp. Arthur'd taken the time to rerun the numbers with him in his office, and twelve months was a solid projection. For years now, Arthur had been holding on to that lot on the outskirts of town for him. It was one of a handful of shrewd real estate investments he'd made decades ago. He'd been slowly selling off the rest of his plots as Blue Cedar Falls had grown and tourism had boomed, but not that one. It made Devin's throat tight, just thinking about it. The guy had so much faith in him.

Sure, he'd also somehow gotten Devin to commit to mustering up a volunteer squad from Meyer Construction to serve Sunday supper at Harvest Home—some church group had apparently made the finals in a choral competition and had to pull out at the last minute. But that was just more evidence of how much he trusted Devin.

Well, Devin was going to show him that he'd put his faith in the right man. He'd get enough guys from work to show up on Sunday—no problem. And twelve months from now, he'd make good on his promise to buy those undeveloped acres.

His own land, away from the crappy apartments where he'd grown up. Someplace quiet just for him, no nosy roommates or noisy neighbors upstairs. A home he'd build with his own two hands.

Just don't screw it up, a voice in his head whispered.

Devin bit the inside of his cheek. Ignoring the doubt in the back of his mind, he reached for his beer and took a good swig.

"How're you boys doing?" Zoe appeared at the side of their table in the corner. Heaven help him. She'd put on some lipstick or something since he'd seen her at Harvest Home. He couldn't stop looking at her red mouth, and his best friend was going to *murder him.* Oblivious, Zoe glanced between the both of them. "Y'all ready for another round?"

Devin drained the last gulp from his glass and thunked it down in front of her. "Sure am."

"Awesome."

Devin should probably be pacing himself. He had an early shift in the morning. But he was celebrating. Letting loose for one night wouldn't hurt.

Just so long as he didn't slip up and let himself look at Zoe's chest.

Crap. Too late.

He jerked his gaze away. "Maybe some water, too," he croaked.

Zoe nodded. "Probably a good call."

"Whatever he's having, put it on the house." Clay Hawthorne, owner and proprietor of the Junebug, wandered over. He clapped Devin on the shoulder, then shot a narrow-eyed glance at Han. "Not this guy, though."

"Hey," Han protested. "After all the free food I give you."

"Fine, fine." Clay held his hands up in front of his chest. "It's all on the house, but, Zoe, don't give them any top-shelf stuff, you hear?"

"Only the worst for my brother," Zoe agreed. "Got it, boss."

"You know I'm just giving you free stuff because it means I don't have to write a receipt, right?" Clay told them.

Han shook his head. "You have really got to figure that stuff out, man."

"I know." Clay scrubbed a hand through his red-brown hair. "But math is hard."

Devin gestured around. "When you get to big numbers like this it is."

"Doomed by your own success," Han sympathized.

Clay was a relative newcomer to Blue Cedar Falls, but you'd never know it. Devin didn't make it out to Main

Street all that often, but whenever he did, the Junebug was hopping, drawing in the tourists that flocked to the area and locals alike. Clay seemed to know everybody on a first-name basis—or if he didn't at the start of the night, he did by the end.

He'd become good friends in particular with Han, which was great to see. Han had been Devin's best friend since they were kids. He was a good guy—maybe the best. But he was so serious, carrying the weight of the world on his shoulders. He didn't get out a lot. The guy could use another friend in his corner.

"Tell me about it," Clay grumbled. "This place was supposed to be small, you know. Just a hole in the wall for me and maybe ten other people."

"Guess you should have told June that." Han tipped his head toward the front door, which had just swung open to reveal the lady in question.

Clay's complaining ceased, his whole demeanor changing as he lifted a hand to her in greeting. She smiled, too, broad and unreserved, as she crossed the space toward him.

Devin shook his head, rolling his eyes fondly as Clay swept June up in his arms. He'd never get over a big, gruff guy like that turning into a teddy bear whenever his girlfriend was around.

As they kissed, Devin looked away, because wow. They were really going at it. He happened to meet Zoe's gaze, and they shared a stifled laugh at the PDA.

Then Devin had to look away all over again, because sharing anything with Zoe—especially something related to kissing—was a terrible idea.

"Get a room." Han threw a napkin at Clay and June, and they finally broke apart.

Zoe swatted lightly at Han. "Don't listen to my brother," she told June. "He's just jealous."

"Ew." Han recoiled. "I definitely am not."

And okay, yeah, considering Han had dated June's sister May for approximately all of high school, that made sense.

"How's it going?" June asked, ignoring him.

"Fine," Zoe told her. "Just commiserating with Clay about how you ruthlessly turned his dive bar into the most popular spot on Main Street."

June shook her head and patted his arm. "Pretty sure that was mostly your doing." She gestured around. "Everything here was your idea. I just helped you put it all together."

"Okay, fine, it was a group effort," Clay said, his smile wry. He then pointedly steered the conversation away from how business was booming—and, Devin noticed, away from the jabs Han had been making about how he needed to get his accounting figured out.

If anybody else noticed, they didn't make a big deal of it, so Devin kept mum, too. They all made small talk for a few minutes. Inevitably, Zoe had to excuse herself to go check on her other tables. "You got everything under control?" Clay asked.

Zoe gave him a thumbs-up as she walked away. "On top of it all, boss."

"Guess we should head out." To Han and Devin, he explained, "Date night."

"Have fun," Han told them.

"And thanks again for the grub," Devin said.

Clay tipped an imaginary hat at him before turning and steering June toward the back.

Devin returned to his burger, but after a minute, it

registered with him that Han's attention was decidedly elsewhere. And that he wasn't happy.

He followed his buddy's scowling gaze.

And kind of immediately wished he hadn't.

Zoe stood over by a table on the other side of the bar, her head tipped back in laughter as a group of guys gave her their orders. One of them had sidled his chair awfully close to her. Another winked.

Devin fought not to sigh.

"Don't do it," he warned.

Han's voice came out gruff and pinched. "Do what?"

"Whatever it is you're thinking about doing to those jerks."

The guy next to Zoe leaned over as if to pick something up off the ground, only there was nothing there.

Han bristled.

Zoe neatly sidestepped the creeper, but none of the tension left Han's frame.

"Seriously, dude." Devin shifted his chair to block Han's sight line. If it also meant he couldn't see Zoe anymore, well, that was just a bonus. "She can handle herself."

The opening night of the Junebug had proven that. Han had lost it on the guys leering at his little sister, and she'd put both them—and her brother—in their places.

"I know," Han grumbled. "But those guys are out of line."

He wasn't wrong, but still. "When it comes to Zoe, you think everyone is out of line."

"I do not."

"You absolutely do." Devin's throat tightened.

Han had always been overprotective. When they were

kids, it was cool. No one at Blue Cedar Falls Elementary could mess with either Zoe or their middle sister, Lian. But as the girls had gotten older—and after Han's father died—Han's overprotective instincts went out of control.

"I just..." Han picked at his fries before pushing them away. "I know she's an adult, okay?"

"You sure about that?"

Han ignored him. "She's an adult, but she doesn't act like one. At her age, I'd taken over the restaurant. I was paying the mortgage, you know? She's living in the basement."

Ouch.

That wasn't exactly fair, though. Their father had died during Han's first term at the Culinary Institute in Raleigh. It'd been his decision to leave and help his mom out after.

It'd also been his decision to make sure Zoe and Lian wouldn't have to make the same sorts of sacrifices.

Devin raised a brow. "You think she shouldn't have gone to school?"

"Of course not." Han blew out a breath. "It's not even that I mind her living in the basement. It's just—those guys are dirtbags."

"Maybe dirtbags leave good tips."

"It's more than that," Han insisted. "It's like she *likes* dirtbags. You remember all the losers she brought home in high school. And none of them lasted."

"So she dated a few guys." Devin stared at Han pointedly. "*Most* people did."

Han narrowed his eyes right back. "This is not about me. Or May."

Han had been practically married to May Wu for the entirety of high school, and everybody knew it.

As Devin saw it, Han had never gotten over her, either. Just because he'd mated for life didn't mean he should expect everybody else to.

"Uh-huh."

"I didn't go nuts on Lian, did I?"

Lian had also been a lot less of a wild child than Zoe growing up.

"I'm telling you," Han insisted. "You know how Zoe and Mom would go at it. She's always been rebellious. Mom says turn left and Zoe heads right. Mom says get a job in your field, and Zoe ends up waitressing in a bar."

"In a job you got her."

"Beside the point—I just wanted to get her out of the house, and Clay needed the help." Han picked up a fry and pointed at Devin with it. "The guy thing is just a part of it. She'll bring home anyone she thinks will piss Mom off."

Was that it?

Devin fought not to squirm. If so, how far did it go? Their mom had her opinions, and yes, she and Zoe bumped heads about them. But was Han any different with his overprotective crap?

Would Zoe do something just to piss her brother off, too?

Suddenly, Zoe going all seductive temptress on Devin back at Harvest Home that afternoon took on a whole new light.

Something in his stomach churned. He'd known better than to act on her flirtations—for a whole host of reasons. But if she'd been doing it to get a rise out of Han?

Devin took a big gulp of his water to wash down the bitterness creeping into the back of his throat.

It didn't matter. Han was Devin's best friend. If he didn't want anyone dating his little sister, Devin would respect that.

That didn't stop him from asking one final question.

"So what if she brought home someone you *did* like? Someone with good intentions, a decent job. Treated her well." Devin's voice threatened to tick upward, but he wrestled it down. "What would you do then?"

Han chuckled. "Sure. That'll be the day."

"For real, though."

"Look, I just want her to be happy. She brings home someone great, fine. But I don't see it happening. She's immature and messing with fire just to see if it'll burn. I'm protecting her from douchebag guys at bars, sure. But I'm also protecting her from herself."

"Who are you protecting from herself? Someone new?" Crap, where had Zoe come from? She set a fresh beer down in front of Devin. She snagged the other one off her tray and held it over the table like she was seriously considering throwing it in her brother's face. "Or just me, like usual?"

Han reached out and grabbed the pint glass, but she pulled it away, keeping it out of his grasp.

"Way to prove how mature you are." Han stood.

She set the glass down with a thud. Beer sloshed right to the edge, but it didn't spill over. Clenching her jaw, she asked, "Anything else I can get you gentlemen?"

"Zo, don't be like that."

She ignored Han. "Devin?"

"Nah," Devin said carefully. "I'm good."

"Great, well, anything you need, you just let me know." She smiled at him way too sweetly.

He swallowed hard, his heart pounding. The full

force of her attention on him affected him way more than it should. He didn't want Han getting a whiff of him being interested. He didn't want her getting an inkling about it, either.

Maybe her earlier flirting had been genuine. But her being sunshine and roses to him now?

Yeah. That was definitely for Han's benefit.

Which cast everything else in doubt, too.

Chapter Four

"STOP."

Zoe screeched to a halt with her hand mere inches from the knob on her family home's back door.

So close.

Her mother cleared her throat, and Zoe prayed for strength before turning around. "Yes, Mother?"

Her mom stood in the kitchen, brows raised, arms crossed. Ling-Ling, the shepherd mix Han had adopted after Zoe left home, sat at her heels. If it was possible, the dog bore the same judgmental glare. "How many résumés did you send out today?"

"Mom—"

"How many?" her mother repeated, firm.

Zoe blew out an exasperated breath. "I didn't, like, count."

"And why not? We paid for a degree in *accounting*, did we not?"

"Would you like me to send you a spreadsheet?"

Her mom scowled, and Ling-Ling made a little growling sound. "No need to take that tone."

Zoe could say the same herself. "Look—"

"You remember what we talked about earlier, right?" How could Zoe forget?

"Yes, Mom." Zoe wasn't applying herself enough, wasn't taking her future seriously, wasn't considering enough options, blah, blah, blah. "Can I go now? I promised Uncle Arthur I'd open up Harvest Home for him."

The severe line of her mother's frown finally softened. "Fine." She made a little shooing motion with her hand. "Go, go."

Zoe turned to leave. "I just fed Ling-Ling, so don't let her con you into a second dinner."

Her mom never cut Zoe an inch of slack, but the dog walked all over her.

"You send me that spreadsheet tomorrow," her mom called.

"I was *obviously* kidding about that," Zoe cast over her shoulder, opening the door.

She kept walking right on through it, too, blocking out any further replies from her mother by swiftly—but gently!—closing the door behind her.

Still annoyed by the whole thing, she got into her sensible pre-owned Kia and started it up. Her fingers itched on the steering wheel, and the urge to put the pedal to the metal as she pulled onto Main Street tugged at her. She mentally shook her head at herself. The last thing she needed was Officer Dwight pulling her over and giving her a lecture, too.

As she begrudgingly maintained the speed limit, she ran over her mom's words again in her head. With every iteration, she got more worked up. Wasn't it bad enough that her mom had pressured her into going into accounting in the first place?

"Think about your future," Zoe mumbled, imitating her mother's voice. "You want good job, right?"

Fat lot of good the accounting degree had done her in that respect.

To be fair, Zoe hadn't exactly had a better idea about what to do with her life. But it would have been nice to have had some options other than doctor, lawyer, or bean counter.

She chewed on the inside of her lip. At a stoplight, she impulsively hit the button on the dashboard to make a call.

Her sister, Lian, picked up on the second ring. Long and drawn out, her voice came out over the car's tinny speakers, "Yes?"

"How did you know what you wanted to do with your life?"

"Well, hello to you, too."

"I'm serious," Zoe insisted.

Despite facing more or less the same pressure from their mother, Lian had forged her own path. She had a job as a teacher in the next town over, with a 401(k) and health insurance and everything and an apartment where no one harassed her every time she tried to get out the door.

Basically, living the dream.

"I can tell," Lian said dryly. There were rustling noises in the background. "Give me a second to think."

Zoe didn't have a second. The drive to Harvest Home took only ten minutes, and she'd squandered at least seven of them stewing. "I mean, you must have felt pretty strongly about it. Goodness knows it wasn't Mom's idea."

Lian laughed. "No, that it was not." She hummed

in thought, then said, "I guess... When you know, you just *know*. You know?"

"Clearly not." Zoe groaned.

"Sorry, that's what I've got."

"You are so useless."

"Uh-huh. Which is why you always call me first when you're stuck."

"I'm not stuck." Okay, she was. Kind of.

She just didn't know what to do with her life or how to get her mother off her back. But other than that, she was fine.

No, she hadn't made any progress on Operation: Seduce Devin Until He Breaks, but she had her job at the Junebug, which was fun and paid well. Her leftover free time—when she wasn't applying for jobs or making pointless spreadsheets for her mother—she spent at Harvest Home, and it was... well, great.

She sighed. If only she could convince Uncle Arthur to take that well-earned trip to Fiji he was always talking about and let her take over there full time. She'd miss him, sure, and it wouldn't exactly be a fancy corporate accounting job. But if she could rustle up enough grants to pay herself a salary, even her mother couldn't give her a hard time about that.

As she turned into Harvest Home's parking lot, she finished up her conversation with her sister. Sherry and Tania arrived just as she was heading toward the door.

"Good afternoon, ladies," Zoe said, swinging her hair out of her face as she found the right key.

Sherry grinned. She was an older white woman who'd been cooking for Harvest Home since Arthur had founded it back in the late nineties. "Hey, Zoe."

"Arthur finally take a day off?" Tania asked. Tania

was newer, hired when the place had expanded a few years ago, but now it was hard to imagine how they'd gotten along without her. She was Black and maybe twenty years younger than Sherry, and the two were a powerhouse team.

"Fingers crossed."

Tania threw her head back and laughed. "I give it an hour."

"Swear I'm going to tie that man to his recliner." Zoe shook her head and pushed open the door.

Uncle Arthur was tireless, and getting him to take an entire day off—much less a trip to Fiji—was a rare victory. She swallowed hard. The only person she'd ever known who worked harder was her dad, and everyone knew how that had ended. If he'd rested and relaxed more, would that have prevented him from dropping dead of a heart attack at forty-eight?

Who knew. Probably not.

But Uncle Arthur was sixty-five with high blood pressure. The guy deserved a break.

Heading inside, Zoe flicked on the lights and fired up the computer to check messages at the front desk. Sherry and Tania made their way to the kitchen. Absently, Zoe pulled up the volunteer schedule. It took its sweet time loading, so she called, "Any idea who's serving tonight?"

As paid employees, Sherry and Tania were the backbone of the organization's meal service, but they couldn't pull off feeding fifty people a day without an equally dedicated crew of volunteers. Businesses, churches, and schools fielded teams that came out to make the magic happen every night.

Sherry and Tania must have been out of earshot.

Frowning, she wiggled the computer mouse and re-loaded the schedule. Before it could come up, the door swung open. Zoe darted her gaze toward the entryway.

Only to be met with a pair of gorgeous blue eyes, a broad set of shoulders, a trim, muscular frame, and a bright smile.

"Meyer Construction, reporting for duty," Devin said.

Zoe's heart did a little jump inside her chest as she straightened up. "Oh, hey!"

"Hey." Just like he had the last time he strode through that door, he raked his gaze over her. She swallowed. She wasn't dressed to get good tips at the Junebug today. A flannel shirt over a T-shirt and jeans was hardly what she'd call sexy, but it didn't seem to matter, based on the way his eyes darkened.

"I didn't know you all were serving today."

Devin moved forward into the space, making room for a half dozen folks to file in after him. He shrugged, tucking his thumbs into the belt loops of his dark-rinse jeans. "Arthur talked me into it when I was here telling him about my promotion." One corner of his mouth curled upward. "Said it'd be a good use for my new leadership skills."

The last guy to come in groaned. "Are we ever going to hear the end of that?"

Devin stiffened and flexed his jaw. "I haven't even started yet, Bryce."

Ah, okay, now Zoe recognized the guy shouldering past Devin. The mayor's son, Bryce Horton, had been a couple of years ahead of her in school, but Lian had complained about him plenty at the time. He'd been a royal jerk, and it didn't seem like much had changed.

"Then why am I even here?" Bryce asked, pulling out his phone and plunking down in one of the chairs meant for patrons.

Devin's whole frame radiated tension, but however angry he was, he kept it out of his tone. "Come on. Kitchen's in the back."

Bryce rolled his eyes, even as he kept his gaze glued to what sure looked like a dating app he was swiping through. Zoe resisted the urge to sneak a peek at his username—just so she could avoid it if she ever ended up on the same site.

Devin's voice dropped. "Now."

Grumbling, Bryce lurched out of the chair and followed Devin down the hall.

"Right behind you," Zoe called. She just had a couple more quick things to take care of out here.

Bryce looked over his shoulder at her and made a super-gross kissy face. Glancing back, Devin caught him, and his eyes narrowed, his hands curling into fists at his sides.

Interesting. When her brother shot his death glare at guys who were hitting on her at the bar, it made her want to strangle him. But when Devin did it?

A warm little shiver ran up her spine.

She probably shouldn't like it so much, but she did.

She swallowed, fighting to calm the flutters in her chest as she shot Bryce a glare of her own. No matter how much Devin's protectiveness gave her the warm fuzzies, she could handle herself. "Wasn't talking to you," she informed Bryce.

"Sure." He clicked his tongue and brought his hand to his ear like a phone and mouthed, *Call me.*

Devin bustled him along, thunderclouds in his eyes.

The coiled strength in him gave her even more little flutters inside.

As soon as they disappeared around the corner, she put her head in her hands to muffle her groan. Getting the butterflies over this guy was pathetic. She was acting like a swooning schoolgirl with a crush again.

Sucking in a deep breath, she dropped her hands from her face. She was too old for this pining nonsense.

Resolve filled her. Devin showing up to volunteer tonight might have taken her by surprise, but it was a golden opportunity. Han was working at the restaurant tonight, so he couldn't appear from out of nowhere, football in hand or no. Devin would have his guard down.

With so many people around, Zoe couldn't exactly seduce Devin. But maybe this was her chance to show him that she was so much more than a kid with a crush now.

And that the spark between them was real.

* * *

"Need any help?"

Zoe sighed and cast her gaze skyward but didn't stop busing dishes. "I thought you were taking the day off."

Uncle Arthur smiled. "Was just in the neighborhood and thought I'd stop in." He craned his neck to peer into the dining room. "Decent crowd tonight."

"Fifty-seven."

"Impressive." He pursed his lips. "Terrible, but impressive."

Nobody wanted to be put out of business more than Uncle Arthur. When his family had landed in this country nearly sixty years ago, they'd relied on soup kitchens. He'd come a long way since then, and he'd had some good luck with investments that had allowed him to found this place. He loved having a way to give back to the community here in Blue Cedar Falls that had taken him in. But if hunger and unemployment just disappeared, he'd be delighted to be out of a job.

Stir crazy and climbing the walls, looking for his next venture, but delighted.

"Late fall is always tough."

The weather here was warm enough that construction and tourism carried on year-round, but whenever the weather turned chilly, the number of people showing up at Harvest Home climbed.

"True." Uncle Arthur came over to squeeze her arm. "Knew you could handle it, though."

Her chest contracted. With no one else in her life trusting her to handle anything more than her TikTok account, that was way too nice to hear. She chuckled to hide the tightness behind her ribs. "Which is why you felt no need to check up on me at all."

"He's not checking up on you," Tania said, coming in from taking a load to the compost pile out back. "He just can't stay away from me," she teased.

"You know me," Uncle Arthur agreed indulgently, dropping his hand.

Sherry was right behind Tania. She shook her head at Arthur. "Held out longer than I thought you would."

Ignoring her, Uncle Arthur gestured toward the dining room. "I'm just going to quick make the rounds."

Zoe waved him along. On his way out, Arthur nearly bumped right into Devin, who had a crate filled with dirty dishes in his arms.

Devin's eyes lit up. "Thought you were taking the night off."

"Don't you start in on me, too." Uncle Arthur waggled a finger at him.

"You're working yourself to an early grave," Zoe called after him.

Uncle Arthur's finger shifted to point at her, but she just shrugged. She wasn't going to apologize for trying to remind him to take a break once in a while. He continued out to the dining room to do his usual thing, thanking volunteers and checking in on the guests. Sherry and Tania followed him with more milk crates to help with cleanup.

Rolling her sleeves to her elbows, Zoe started running the water.

Devin brought his crate of dishes over to her. "He's unstoppable, huh?"

"Seems it." She frowned. Her uncle definitely gave that impression, but he was getting up there, and she did genuinely worry about him.

"He's fine. There's a reason he showed up at the last possible second." Devin tipped his head toward the dining room. "He's not going to do any work. He just likes talking to everybody."

His voice was soft and full of affection.

"Right." Sometimes Zoe forgot that Devin's road to practically becoming a member of their extended family began right here at Harvest Home. Uncle Arthur didn't like to talk about it, but Devin had started out as a guest, coming by with his dad every week. Then by himself even more often than that. Sure, he'd become best buddies with Han by then, but it went deeper than that. Devin knew better than anyone how dedicated Uncle Arthur was to making people feel welcome here.

As he started unloading the dirty dishes, Devin's arm brushed hers, and a shiver of warmth ran through her skin.

Her throat went dry as she glanced up at him. They'd been working in close quarters all night, but any efforts to either seduce him or change his impression of her had taken a back seat to the task of getting dinner on the table for almost sixty people. In the end, this was the closest they'd really gotten, physically.

As if he could feel her gaze, he looked down. When their eyes met, heat flushed through her. How could a person's eyes be so blue? She got lost for a second, just staring at the gold-brown scruff on his sharp jaw, the soft red fullness of his lips, when everything else about him was chiseled and hard.

"Do you—" The huskiness of his voice only distracted her more.

"Huh?"

He pushed a plate toward her more insistently.

A different, embarrassed flush rose to her cheeks as she grabbed it and ran it under the water. "Right, right. Sorry."

He didn't need to stand so close as he passed her the next one, but she didn't tell him that. Wasn't she the one who'd started the game of trying to make him break? With the way he'd been looking at her, she'd taken it as a personal challenge to get him to make a move or at least admit that there was something brewing between them.

Now here she was, right on the cusp of cracking herself.

What would he do if she did? If she made the real first move and turned to him. Reached up to graze her fingertips along his cheek.

If she leaned forward on her tiptoes and tugged him down so she could taste his mouth...

She shuddered inside, blushing furiously as she placed another plate on the rack inside the dishwasher. She'd been harboring these kinds of fantasies since she was a teenager. It was hard to tell how much was actually possible and how much was just the same nonsense she'd been imagining for years.

Unwilling to shatter the moment, she set it all aside and concentrated on cleaning up. He seemed content to do the same. Even if his presence was making her heart do weird flips behind her ribs, she tried not to let it show.

They fell into a rhythm, like they'd been working together like this forever. That made sense—they'd both been volunteering here for years, but it still felt unfairly kismet, somehow.

"Thanks," she said after a couple of minutes. "By the way. For bringing in the folks from your company tonight."

"Happy to do it." He let out a rough sigh. "Well, for the most part."

It was clear who he was talking about.

Chuckling quietly, she shook her head. "Yeah, Bryce is still a piece of work, huh?"

"You have no idea."

The guy had barely lifted a finger the entire time he'd been here, and he'd eaten a solid dinner's worth of food meant for the guests.

"How does he get away with it?"

"You know." A dark undertone ran through Devin's words.

She shivered, reminded again of how much strength

Devin kept contained inside himself. He never used it, though, no matter how frustrated he got.

It made her feel...safe. It always had. Even when they'd been kids messing around in Uncle Arthur's basement. Any time the other boys his age had gotten too rough around her, he'd stepped in and said something.

Which was probably part of how she'd ended up with this stupid crush on him in the first place.

"Yeah, I guess I do."

People filed in and out of the kitchen, bringing new loads of dishes through. Zoe was indulging herself, spending this time rinsing plates when she should be out there directing traffic, but between Uncle Arthur, Sherry, and Tania, there were enough people running the show for her to dawdle a little longer. And the chance to stand so close to Devin was just too good to pass up.

"So you've really gotten involved here, huh?" he asked, moving to her other side to help her start loading the second washer.

She shrugged and passed him a stack of silverware. "I have the time right now. And I like helping out. Working with the guests. Getting to spend more time with Uncle Arthur."

A smile stole across her face as she talked about it all. She'd missed everyone in her family while she'd been away at college, but her uncle was the only one who didn't carry any baggage—or seem to have some sort of agenda for what she should do with her life.

Devin hummed in acknowledgment, giving her space to keep talking. It was refreshing.

"This place," she continued, trying to sum it up.

"The work we do here, the people we serve. It feels important."

"I get it," Devin said quietly.

He would.

But then one corner of his mouth tilted down. "You said you have the time 'right now.' You see that changing soon?"

"Ugh." Zoe huffed out a breath as she scrubbed at a particularly stubborn spot on a plate. "I don't know. Apparently, at some point I'm supposed to get a real job."

He chuckled and passed her another dish. "What? Overrated."

"Says the guy who just got the big promotion."

"It's not that big a deal," he said, rolling his eyes, but his posture straightened slightly. It was definitely at least a medium-size deal. Humble as he might be, she hoped he was getting some satisfaction from his work.

She considered for a second before asking, "How did you know? That construction was what you wanted to do?"

It was the same basic question she'd asked Lian earlier—unhelpful as that conversation had been.

"I don't know," he answered slowly. "I didn't exactly have a ton of options."

"Smart guy like you?"

He laughed, only it didn't entirely sound funny. "I like working with my hands. Got a decent eye for it. Pay's good, relatively speaking. Arthur was able to help me get my foot in the door when I needed—when I decided it was time to find a place of my own."

There was something he wasn't saying, his voice dipping low and pulling at something in her chest. Before she could probe any deeper, though, he looked at her.

"So, how are things going with the whole real job thing, then?" he asked.

Well, that was certainly a way to kill the mood.

"Ugh. Terrible." Her mom had laid into her just that afternoon, telling her she wasn't sending out enough résumés or casting her net wide enough, prompting her to waste a good hour or two rage-scrolling Monster. "I'm putting in applications for jobs pretty much all over the state at this point. A few in Atlanta, too."

His eyebrows pinched together. "You'd really go that far?"

"I don't want to." She liked it here. She always had. Things here were easy. Comfortable. Being close to her family—when they weren't driving her up a wall or dictating her love life and her job search, anyway—was nice.

But she'd do what she had to do. She'd always wanted to get out on her own, and this extended period of being between things was making her itch to be independent again.

It wasn't like it was with her brother. Han had come home when their father died and had taken over—well, everything. His sense of duty was giving him white hairs.

She'd choose to stay here, too, if it worked out. But she had to keep her options open. She couldn't just be *stuck* here because she couldn't make it on her own.

"We'll see how things go." She shrugged. It was such an annoying platitude, but that was her life now.

"Well, I hope you stay close." The way he said it was so genuine, she jerked her gaze up to meet his, but he was pointedly studying the dishes. After a second, he smiled, his tone lightening as he darted a teasing glance her way. "I mean, how can Han kill anyone who dares to look at you if you live far away?"

That was it. She shoved him, and he laughed, plates clanking together as he bumped into them where they were so neatly stacked in the racks. He playfully pushed back, and then what choice did she have, with her wet hands and all, but to flick some water in his face?

He sputtered, the droplets clinging to his skin in interesting ways, and her breath sped up. She went to do it again, but she must have telegraphed her intentions too clearly, because he grabbed her wrist before she could. Her heart hammered in her chest.

She stared up into his eyes, and for a second, everything around them faded, because she had seen that look before.

About two seconds before he got hit in the head with a football.

"Someone wanna tell me why we're out there doing all the work while these two are messing around in here?"

Devin straightened, pulling away from her so fast, she had to catch herself from falling over.

Apparently, playing the part of the football tonight, Bryce came over holding one measly dish, which he popped—still caked in drying potatoes—straight into the dishwasher. Struggling not to let on how flustered she was by the unwelcome interruption, Zoe plucked it out and set it in the sink, shooting him a glare.

"Thank you, Mr. Horton," Arthur said delicately as he hauled a crate in and set it on the counter. He caught Zoe's gaze, and she huffed out a breath.

Bryce's dad was the mayor. The town gave Harvest Home a bunch of money and support every year. She would do well to remember it.

But wasn't that just how a jerk like Bryce got so...jerk-y? Everyone giving him a free pass because his father was a powerful guy?

She glanced at Devin. How did he do it? Constantly keeping a lid on himself when the guy kept asking to get punched in the face?

Before she could suss it out, a few more of the Meyer Construction volunteers came in with the last of the supper service cleanup.

Bryce gawked at the towering piles of dishes. "How are we supposed to get all this done? Some of us have places to be tonight." Winking, he elbowed one of the other guys, who subtly moved to put more distance between them. Not that Bryce noticed. With a leering smirk and a waggle of his phone, he added, "If you know what I mean."

Devin exhaled roughly. He threw his shoulders back. Instead of answering Bryce, he looked around and held his hands out expansively. "With a crew like this? We all pitch in and we'll have it done in no time."

"Uh-huh." Bryce kept scrolling on his phone.

"What do you say we put a little wager on it?" Devin's smile rippled with challenge. "We get out of here within the hour, and the first round at the bar is on me."

Chapter Five

THIS WAS GOING to cost Devin a small fortune.

It was worth it, though. At the hour mark, pretty nearly on the dot, his team had put the last clean pan on its shelf. The fact that Arthur, Sherry, Tania, and Zoe had thrown their backs into it, too, had helped a ton. Heck, even Bryce had cleaned a few tables. Free drinks were some powerful motivation.

Powerful, expensive motivation.

As the last guy put in his order, Clay whistled, punching in the numbers on the register.

"This sure seems like a nightmare for the bookkeeping," Devin tried in vain. "You should probably just give them to me for free."

"Nice try." Clay printed off the bill and handed it to Devin. "You wanna settle up now or start a tab?"

"Settle up now." Passing over his debit card, Devin eyed Bryce, who was standing by the pool table in the corner. Devin had promised the first round, and he was going to see it through, but he wasn't going to make it easy for anyone to try to turn it into two.

"Good choice."

He signed the slip, then joined the rest of his crew. He tried to pay attention to what they were saying, but his gaze kept drifting to the table in the corner where Zoe sat with Arthur, Sherry, and Tania. All four of them had been only too happy to take him up on the free drink offer, too, and he was happy to have them.

Probably too happy.

Working side by side with Zoe tonight had been an eye-opening experience. While her sexy waitress outfit had bowled him over the other day, this afternoon it had been her maturity—the way she'd known how to handle every situation that arose as they'd cooked and served. Even now, while he and his buddies from work stood around, shooting pool and playing darts and talking about yesterday's game, she was engaged in what looked like a deep conversation with Arthur, Sherry, and Tania. They regarded her with all the respect she deserved. Which he was starting to realize was a heck of a lot.

She'd really rolled up her sleeves tonight. She knew Harvest Home as well as he did, and despite mostly working in the front office, she wasn't afraid to get her hands dirty. Her eyes went all soft when she talked about the place, too. She might be the only person besides him and Arthur who understood it for the miracle it was.

She was funny and smart and beautiful and...

He cut off his train of thought before it could pull any farther out of the station. Jerking his gaze away from her mouth as she laughed at something Tania was saying, he took a big gulp of his beer.

Han wasn't here tonight, but the two of them had been friends for so long that the guy lived rent-free in his head. If anybody else was staring at Zoe the way Devin had been just now, Han would've been ready to deck him. Devin wasn't some dirtbag trying to get a peek up her skirt, but he needed to do a better job keeping his eyes to himself.

Before too long, Bryce gave one of the other guys a noogie before sauntering Devin's way. Devin crossed his arms over his chest, but his body language wasn't enough to keep Bryce from coming over and slapping him on the biceps.

"See you tomorrow, *boss*." He said it like an insult, but Devin wasn't going to take it that way.

"Bright and early."

The instant Bryce was gone, it was like someone had undone one of the knots in Devin's back. A few others filtered out not long after, and he thanked them each for coming out and giving a part of their day to volunteer.

Eventually, he and what was left of his crew drifted toward the pool table. They played a couple of rounds, but it was tough to focus. Every time he lined up a shot, he either had to face Zoe or put his back to her, and he had to get this under control. Being this aware of her wasn't right.

But it did give him a heads-up when she and the others started to gather their things.

Arthur was the one to approach first and clear his throat. Devin turned to find him jacket in hand.

Arthur clapped him firmly on the shoulder. "Good work tonight, Devin."

"Anytime." Then he remembered how Arthur had somehow managed to get him to agree to find a crew for this afternoon without his even fully realizing he'd committed until it was too late. "I mean, not *any* time, but..."

"I know what you mean."

Devin nodded at Sherry and Tania, who stood behind Arthur, clearly ready to go, too. "Glad you all could come out."

Tania grinned. "Any time you feel like footing the bill, you let us know."

They said their goodbyes, and the three of them made for the exit.

Which left Zoe. He scrunched his brows together. She wouldn't have just snuck out, would she? He would have noticed.

"Boo," she said from just behind him, poking his shoulder.

He didn't jump, but it was a near thing.

"Oh, hey." His voice came out rough. God, she smelled good. She was doing that thing again, getting up in his space, but unlike the other day, it didn't feel forced or unnatural. It felt like where she was supposed to be. Half hopeful and half ready to be disappointed, he asked, "You taking off, too?"

She had her flannel shirt draped over her arm and her bag slung across one shoulder, but there wasn't any sign of her keys. She cocked a brow and glanced behind him. "Actually, I was about to call winner."

Oh.

Oh, okay. This he remembered.

Devin and Han and some of the other guys used to play pool in Arthur's basement, days they couldn't mess around outside. Zoe would hang out there, too, and of course they couldn't tell Arthur's niece to scram. They only ever let her play if they needed an even number for a team. She was short and she scratched half her shots, and when she called winner, everybody had to pretend not to groan.

Unconsciously, he flicked his gaze over her form. His throat bobbed.

She was still short, but the confidence in her expression told him she'd learned a couple of things since she was twelve.

It was late. He should probably tell her he was just wrapping up here and ready to call it a night. If he was serious about not jeopardizing his friendship with Han, spending more time with his baby sister was *not* a smart strategy.

But there was something about the challenge in her eyes that was too enticing to resist.

For old times' sake...

Before he could second-guess himself any further, he lifted a brow to match hers. Without a word, he turned. He surveyed the table. His team was in good shape—just the eight ball left to sink, while stripes had three balls on the table. Sucking in a deep breath, he pointed toward the corner pocket.

He could feel her behind him as he lined up his shot. His skin tingled with awareness, but his vision went sharp. He pulled his cue back and nudged it forward, once, then twice.

The cue ball went spinning off across the felt, straight as an arrow. It rebounded, narrowly missing the ten before smacking straight into the eight. The eight shot toward the corner pocket, where it hovered for half a second on the edge before sinking right in.

He couldn't have done it better if he'd tried.

His partner held out his hand, and Devin slapped their palms together. He nodded at the guys he'd beaten. They shook their heads, but they took it just fine. He grabbed his beer and swallowed the last of it down.

Then he turned. He met Zoe's gaze again, and the heat in it went straight to the center of him.

"You want winner?" he asked, throat raw.

Her head bobbed up and down, her pretty pink mouth parted just the tiniest bit.

"Well." He swallowed deeply. This was a monumentally stupid idea. But he was in it now. "What're you waiting for?"

* * *

Zoe was seriously starting to lose track of who was egging on who. After she'd called winner, the other guys Devin had been playing with decided to head out. At least one of them had shot him a knowing look. Another had patted him on the back and winked at her. She'd rolled her eyes and sent them on their way.

Was the tension between them as obvious to the people around them as it was to her? If so, it was a good thing her brother wasn't around. She glanced toward the bar. Clay didn't seem to be paying them any attention. His girlfriend, June, had shown up a little while ago with her friends Caitlin and Bobbi, and between pouring drinks for everyone and chatting with them, he had his hands full.

Zoe still didn't completely trust him not to rat her out to Han—intentionally or otherwise.

Whatever. All along, she'd said her brother should mind his own business. She was a grown woman, and she could do as she pleased.

And at the moment, what she wanted to do was Devin.

Only it wasn't quite that simple anymore, was it? Her

advances had sort of been a lark at the beginning, but after spending time talking to him while cleaning up tonight, she was starting to wonder if there might be more between them than simple attraction. This wasn't a schoolgirl crush, and it wasn't leading to just a single night of fun.

As to what it was leading to?

Little sparklers fired off inside her. She'd love to have the chance to find out.

After she schooled him at pool.

She took a second to select a cue and chalk the tip as he went ahead and racked the balls. The sight of him in those jeans had her sucking her bottom lip between her teeth.

The guy was really just unfairly handsome, with that golden tan skin and clear blue eyes. The short-cropped hair that shone under the hanging lights and the scruff on his deliciously sharp jaw.

He smiled at her and gestured toward the table. "You wanna break?"

"Be my guest." That had been her plan, right? Getting him to break.

He grabbed his cue from where he'd leaned it. He set the cue ball down just to the right of center, leaned over, and lined up. She let her gaze move over his entire body as his muscles tensed.

With a sudden surge of motion, he fired off his shot. The crack of the cue ball hitting the one dead center rang out through the air. Balls scattered everywhere, while the cue ball spun in the middle of the table before coming to a halt.

"Nice."

He winked. "I've been practicing a bit."

Oh, she liked him like this. She'd always appreciated his serious side, but seeing him loose and playful and—dare she say flirty? It warmed her insides, even as it ratcheted up nervous anticipation about where this evening was going.

He called a shot and made it with ease. He sank two more before finally missing.

Zoe gripped her cue more tightly as she walked the perimeter of the table. Devin's gaze on her was distracting as hell, but she kept her focus.

He might have missed, but he'd done a good job setting her up for failure. Nice to know he wasn't going easy on her. She finally selected her shot and grabbed a bridge off the rack.

"You don't need that," Devin told her.

"Speak for yourself, tall person."

"Seriously." Then he was there, wrapping his hand around hers. "May I?"

Heat zipped up her arm. His warm scent surrounded her, and she got dizzy for a second, having him so close.

Which was her only explanation for why she let him take the bridge away. He guided her to the other edge of the table. She lined up her shot, and sure, she was closer to the ball now, but she didn't love the angles.

"I don't know." She shook her head, ready to stand and go back to her original plan, but he stopped her.

"Let me show you?" he asked.

Her whole body locked down as he stepped up behind her. He was so hot, bracketing her frame. His height swamped her, making it hard for her to breathe, and she was going to die before she even so much as managed to seduce him.

"See?" he asked.

Did he know what he was doing to her? She clenched down inside against a powerful wave of desire.

But he was still talking about pool. He placed his hand over hers on the felt, realigning her shot a few degrees to the left. Her breath caught.

Seriously. She was Going. To. *Die.*

She hovered there for just a second, soaking in the feeling of his body blanketing her, fluttering her eyes shut to bask in his closeness.

But as good as it felt—and as much as she never wanted to move again, ever in her life—she couldn't stand there and take a crummy shot just because a hot guy was scrambling her brains.

Carefully, she stood up again. He moved with her. She glanced at him over her shoulder, and his face was inches from hers, his kissable mouth *right there*.

She stepped away. She got the bridge down from the rack. Her face flushed hot as she set up her original shot again. If she missed, she was going to feel like twice the idiot now, but she knew herself, dammit all. She knew her own mind, and she knew her body and her abilities.

No guy was going to waltz in out of nowhere and try to tell her differently before he'd even seen her play.

She ignored the pressure of his gaze. Then, with a breath and a prayer, she pulled the cue stick back.

The ball careened forward, banking off the far rail before heading straight for the nine. Everything in her tightened as the nine rolled toward the side pocket, slower than she would have liked. It hovered on the edge for an agonizing instant.

And then it tipped right on in.

She wanted to shout and scream—maybe jump and dance. As it was, she restricted herself to a single pump of her fist before locking her gaze with Devin's.

"Watch out," she told him, breathless—and not just from the score. "I've been practicing, too."

Chapter Six

"OKAY, FOR REAL, though, where did you learn to play like that?"

Zoe laughed as she braced her elbow against the bar. Devin settled onto the stool beside hers. His knee rested against hers, and she shivered.

They'd been getting closer and closer all evening. She wasn't complaining, but there was a tension inside her chest. This didn't seem like it could last. A half dozen games of pool and almost as many drinks between the two of them had them both loose-limbed and happy. After their last match, when someone else had asked them for the table, she'd kind of expected him to call it a night. It was late, after all. But when she'd started making her way over to the bar, figuring she'd check in with Clay before heading out herself, Devin had come on over, too.

Now here they were. Sitting together, fresh drinks in hand.

Zoe shrugged and took a sip of her cosmo. "There was a pool table in the basement of my dorm my first year of college."

"And a shark there to teach you all?"

"Don't underestimate bored teenage girls trying to avoid writing term papers."

He chuckled. "Fair enough."

She stirred her drink, probably a little too forcefully. "Turns out, hustling pool is one of the most useful things I learned at school."

"Oh?"

"I mean..." Releasing the tiny straw, she gestured around. She couldn't quite keep the sour note out of her tone. "See how far that degree has gotten me?"

"I don't know. Doesn't seem so bad."

She shook her head. "Try telling that to everyone else."

"You mean your mom?"

"Among other people. Han and Lian don't seem super impressed, either." Sighing, she looked away, to the bottles of liquor on the shelf, the taps, the specials she'd written on the big black board the day before. "I mean, I had a great time at college—don't get me wrong. But the whole grand compromise of it all—me going so far away, to a school that cost so much..." Even with aid and a bunch of money from her mom, she was going to be paying off loans forever. "Mom let me follow my dream, but she hammered home that if I didn't pick something practical, I'd end up penniless in a gutter somewhere."

"And that's how you ended up going into accounting?" Devin asked, leaning his elbow on the bar.

"Pretty much." She pinched the little straw from her drink again and stabbed at an ice cube. "I'm good at math, and after the first year, none of the courses were before noon. Seemed like a good deal at the time."

"What if you could do it all over again? Without your mom hanging over your shoulder. Would you pick something different?"

The question barely computed. Zoe's parents had always had strong opinions about her life. After her dad had died, her mom had become even more aggressive in trying to control Zoe's future. She'd clearly been grieving. Zoe had been, too. She'd fought back about some things, but on others, she got worn down and just got used to going along.

"I don't know," she said quietly. "Maybe? There wasn't anything I was super passionate about at school."

"Was there anything you were passionate about outside of it?"

"Not really." Usually, when people asked her questions like this, it made her uncomfortable, but Devin's expression was so open as he gazed at her. He'd known her practically their entire lives, but it felt like he actually wanted to know more. So she dug deeper. "I liked normal stuff—hanging out with my friends, watching TV."

"Making friendship bracelets."

"Shut up." She flapped a hand in his general direction as if to swat at him. Her cheeks flushed warmer.

One corner of his mouth lifted. "I still have mine."

"You do not." Oh wow. She'd made them for everybody one summer. She'd found a ton of old embroidery floss from some kit her mother had never finished. Bored, she'd gone to town.

She'd picked the colors for the one she'd given to Devin so carefully. Blue for his eyes, orange and brown for the Blue Cedar Falls team colors. Red for the hearts she secretly drew around his name in the back of her diary. Because she was super, super cool and not a dork at all.

"I do," he promised, and for some reason, she actually believed him.

Her throat tight, she looked down at her drink again. Silence held for a second. Then she continued. "But yeah. Just normal teenager stuff, mostly. I mean, I liked volunteering at Harvest Home, too, but if I'd told my mom I wanted to work at a nonprofit or go into social services or something, I think she would have flipped her lid."

"Did you ever try?"

"What? No." The idea had never occurred to her.

But maybe it should have.

That was too much food for thought for this late into the night, though.

"How about you?" she asked. "You said construction was sort of something you fell into. Did you ever think about doing anything else? Going to school?"

The question seemed to take him off guard. Furrows appeared between his brows. She wanted to reach over and smooth them out, but even with the soft intimacy that somehow surrounded them now, it felt like too big of a line to cross.

"You mean college?"

She nodded, sipping at her drink.

"Sort of?" He lifted one shoulder before setting it back down. "Mrs. Jeffries in the guidance department thought I should, but it was never in the cards for me."

"How come?"

"Money." He said it without any bitterness to his tone. "There's a reason I started going to Harvest Home, you know."

Right. Crap. "Sorry—"

"It's fine. I could have maybe gotten financial aid or something, but I needed to be out on my own."

"I can drink to that." She lifted her drink, and he clinked his glass against hers before taking a deep pull at it and setting it down.

He still seemed calm, but a familiar stiffness settled into his shoulders. A far-off look came into his gaze. "My mom died when I was young, you know. Really, really young. I don't even remember her. But my dad— he was..."

As he searched for words, Zoe sat up straighter. A girl couldn't hang around her big brother and his best friend all the time without overhearing some stuff. She knew Devin's home life wasn't great, but he'd never talked about it in front of her directly.

"Yeah?" She held her breath and reached out, brushing her hand against his. His skin was warm and rough, and she wasn't oblivious to all the other, different ways she wanted to touch him. But she dropped her hand away after one quick, encouraging squeeze.

The point of his jaw flexed. His bright eyes met hers for a second, shadows forming behind his irises. Then he looked away. "He wasn't a good guy—let's just leave it at that."

He picked up his glass again. Zoe bit her lip. She should probably leave well enough alone.

But the book he'd started to crack open didn't feel shut quite yet. She couldn't shake the sense that he *wanted* to talk about this. How many times had she caught him holding himself back? Was this just more restraint?

What would it be like if he let go?

And honestly. Poking the bear had gotten her this far.
"You don't have to."

He lowered his drink and stared at her in question.

She took a deep breath. "You don't have to leave it
at that. If you don't want to." Her face warmed, but she
wasn't backing down. "I'm happy to listen."

He regarded her for a long, silent moment. The
sounds of the bar around them filtered in. It had felt
like they'd been in their own little world this whole time,
but there were other people here. Not many. It really
was late. But a few. Clay was still kicking around here
somewhere.

No one else mattered, though.

As the moment stretched on, she held her ground,
waiting patiently.

Finally, he grabbed his beer and tossed the rest of
it back. He gestured at her drink. She was tempted to
finish it, too, especially when he put on his jacket. The
taste of it soured in her mouth. She'd pushed too far,
huh? Sometimes she did that. She set her half-full glass
on the bar.

But then he tipped his head toward the door.

"Come on. Let me walk you home."

The offer took her by surprise. Neither of them had
had so much to drink that they couldn't drive. She
probably *should* drive. Getting her car in the morning
would be a hassle.

But walking home...walking home was good.

Letting *Devin* walk her home. Well, that was downright great.

When he extended his hand to help her up? No way
that was an invitation she could refuse.

His calloused fingers were warm against hers. He

gripped her tightly as she popped down from the stool. Was she imagining it when he held on for a second even after her feet hit the floor?

He let go, and she dropped her gaze. She untied her flannel from around her waist and shrugged it on.

Then she followed him out into the night.

It was chillier than she was prepared for, but between the Asian flush from the little alcohol she'd had and the heat Devin radiated at her side, she didn't mind. She crossed her arms over her chest.

Devin didn't have to ask where she lived, of course. He'd been hanging out at the Leung house for a decade or two. They were both quiet as they headed north on Main Street.

The crisp air smelled like fall, the last few leaves of the season just clinging to the trees. She hugged herself more tightly. The dark sky above shone with stars and a half-full moon. Twinkling lights draped over the white fences all along Main Street gave everything a cozy feel.

She sighed. When she'd first realized she'd have to move home, she'd spent most of her time thinking about how annoying it would be to have to camp out in her mom's basement. She'd been right about that. Her mother's constant, snide comments about her prospects had only added to the ambience.

She hadn't been thinking about this, though. Blue Cedar Falls was beautiful by day, with the bright blue sky above and the mountains all around them. At night it was quiet and still, and it just felt like...

Home.

A tiny shiver racked her, followed by a pang. Getting a real job would be great, but the more time she spent here in Blue Cedar Falls—and with Devin—the less eager she was to leave.

Misunderstanding her shiver, Devin glanced down at her. "Cold?"

"I'm fine."

Stupid, chivalrous boy. He whipped off his jacket anyway, leaving his arms bare. Really hot, sexy, muscular arms, but it still seemed unpleasant for him.

"I'm fine," she protested again, but he was having none of it.

He draped the jacket over her shoulders. Instantly, heat blanketed her. Oh wow. His delicious scent wrapped around her even more thoroughly, making her whole body come into another, deeper level of awareness.

"Looks good on you," he said, his voice rough. He snapped his mouth closed as if he hadn't meant to say that, but it was out there now.

There was clearly no point arguing anymore, and anyway, now that she had his jacket, it wasn't as if she wanted to give it up. "Thanks."

"No problem."

They hit the end of the downtown strip and turned right together. As the businesses faded away into little houses, the quiet grew. She glanced up at him.

She met the soft blue gaze staring back down at her, and warmth fluttered inside her chest.

"Thanks," he murmured. He pointed with his thumb in the direction of the Junebug. "For what you said back there."

Right. Talking about his not-a-good-guy father.

She got her head out of the clouds of teenage crush land and mustered a smile. "I meant it."

"I know." He directed his gaze forward, ducking to

avoid a couple of low-hanging branches on an old oak. "Sorry it took me by surprise. I work with too many guys. Some women, too, but they act even tougher than the men. Nobody gets touchy-feely on the job site."

"What about friends?"

"You mean your brother?"

"Okay, yeah, never mind."

Han was a cool guy, deep down. To hear Clay talk about it, he'd offered all kinds of great relationship advice back when he and June were getting their act together. But Han had never gotten over their father. He'd died suddenly, almost ten years ago. All Han's plans for his life had gone up in smoke when he'd rushed home, eighteen years old and determined to take up the mantle and become the man of the house.

The loss still hurt in Zoe's heart, too, of course. She missed her dad. Losing him had changed the entire family. It had harshened her mom and aged her brother. Fortunately, she'd had Lian and Uncle Arthur to lean on, both during that first tough year and after.

But Han hadn't seemed interested in leaning on anyone. He was too busy taking over the business and the house. Deep down, though, she knew her brother too well. He'd been devastated.

Talking about someone else's issues with their father? He couldn't have handled it. He probably still couldn't.

Devin's gaze focused on something far off in the distance. His jaw hardened before going soft—like he was building walls around himself only to have to consciously decide to let them down.

"He was a bully," he said quietly. "A mean old drunk who told me I'd never amount to anything in my life."

Zoe's heart squeezed. "Devin... That's awful."

"When high school graduation came around, I still half believed him." His smile was pained. "I told myself I didn't, but asking for people to give me money so I could go fail out of college just the way he always told me I would? Nah."

She shook her head, but he kept talking. As they turned onto her street, his pace slowed.

"It was all stupid head games, I know. In the end, it didn't matter. The best route to getting out of his house was getting a job." The sharpness in his gaze finally eased. "Arthur hooked me up, actually."

"Sounds like him."

"Yeah, it does." Unguarded affection colored his tone—with maybe a little hero worship mixed in there, too. "I was always handy. He got me an interview at Meyer, and the rest is history. I got a good-paying job and an apartment." His jaw flexed. "And I never looked back."

A different kind of darkness shadowed his eyes now. He clenched and unclenched his hands at his sides.

"Devin..."

"It's for the best. I'm saving up for a house of my own, too. In another year, it'll be just me and some mutt out on the edge of town, and no one will ever be able to bother me like that again." He looked down at her and blew out a breath. "I'm glad. Honestly."

"Okay." There was more to the story than he was telling, but even she knew when a bear had been poked too much. "Well, I'm glad you're glad, too." With a soft smile of her own, she bumped her elbow against his arm. "For what it's worth, I think you turned out pretty great."

His lips curled upward. "You didn't turn out so bad yourself, Itch."

"Hey!" She swatted at him. That's what he and Han and their friends had called her when she was really bugging them.

"Sorry, sorry!" He put his hands in front of his face as she swung at him again.

And she was just goofing around—really, she was. He was, too. But she rose onto her toes and reached up, aiming for a good smack upside his head. "Take it back."

"I take it back. I take it back." He grabbed her wrists in his big, strong hands. He held on to her, stopping her from taking another shot at him.

He was breathing hard. She was, too.

Suddenly, it dawned on her exactly how close they were standing. Her chest was practically brushing his. Heat radiated off his body, soaking into hers, and out of nowhere, she couldn't get enough air.

She darted her gaze to his. Surprise colored his eyes, like he'd just realized the position they were in, too.

But he didn't let go.

Forget fluttering. Her whole chest was on fire. She was dizzy with the unexpected rush of contact.

Of his gaze darting down to her lips.

A pang of wanting hit her so hard it took her breath away. She looked to his mouth, too, red and soft. She'd been dreaming about this since she was twelve, but this was real. Devin James was really standing here with her, looking at her.

"Zoe…"

Before he could move, a bright light suddenly blinded them. Devin jerked away, shielding his eyes. Zoe cursed.

Right. Without her even really noticing, they'd arrived at her house.

And the floodlights outside had just turned on.

Humiliated anger swept across her cheeks. She looked at Devin, but he was backing up—fast.

"Sorry. Good grief, Zo."

"What—"

"You should go in." His throat bobbed as he gestured at the house.

And it was hard to make out, given the glare of the lights. But yeah. That was her mom standing just inside the door.

She cursed beneath her breath. "Look—"

"You should go," he said again, firmer.

She wanted to laugh. Almost as much as she wanted to cry.

Five seconds ago, he'd been looking at her like she was anything but the little girl she used to be. His gaze had been hot as fire, his hands grasping at her wrists like he had no intention of letting go. He'd been about to kiss her.

Her. A grown woman, fully capable of making her own decisions.

"Devin." She hated the shakiness in her voice.

"Keep the jacket," he told her, backing away. "I can grab it from Han. Later."

"Devin," she called again.

Regret flashed in his eyes.

And that was what did it.

She couldn't decide which was worse—him regretting getting caught or him regretting almost letting it happen in the first place. Either way, if he regretted it already?

It didn't matter how much she liked him—how much she had liked him since she was twelve freaking years old.

She deserved better than that.

He turned and walked away. She watched him go for a long minute.

Fuming, she turned and stormed toward the house. The door swung open before she could get to it, which only pissed her off more. With her mom holding the thing, she couldn't even slam it behind her.

"Late night," her mom observed.

"I've been home later." She worked at a bar, for Pete's sake.

"Zhaohui…"

She rounded on her mom. "Save it."

Her mom regarded her. Zoe was vibrating with anger. At her mom for interrupting. At Devin for walking away.

At every freaking person in her life who treated her like a kid, who didn't trust her to know her own mind.

Her mother made a soft *tutt*ing sound in the back of her throat. She let the door swing closed. Lifting one brow, she leveled Zoe with her most skeptical gaze. "I hope you know what you're doing."

"Believe it or not, Mom," she gritted out, "I usually do."

Only in this case, even she wasn't sure that was true.

Chapter Seven

"YOU WANT TO talk about it?"

Devin looked up to find Arthur gazing at him across the worktable in the back of Harvest Home. He fought not to snap at him. Arthur didn't deserve any of his crap.

The only one who deserved that was himself.

"About what?"

Arthur just raised his brows, shifting his gaze pointedly to the mangled box Devin had been destroying in a vain effort to rip it open with his bare hands.

Okay, yeah, fine, so he was acting a little off.

Scrubbing his hand across his face, he grabbed the box cutter from the other side of the table and got back to work.

But Arthur wasn't going to leave this one alone. "Let me guess. Girl trouble."

Devin narrowly avoided slicing his finger off. Stupid. More carefully, he started again. "No."

"Boy trouble, then?"

Devin scrunched up his face in confusion. "What?"

"Never hurts to ask," Arthur said, waving away

Devin's reaction. "Zoe yelled at me the other day, saying I'm too"—he snapped his fingers a couple of times before finding the word—"'heteronormative.'"

"Believe me, I still like the ladies." There was nothing wrong with being gay, obviously, but Devin had known from day one that he was into women.

And what he was into right now, apparently, was a girl who was too young for him, a girl who got under his skin like nobody else. A girl who made it easy to talk about things he never talked about. His dad, his life, everything.

A girl with dark, sparkling eyes, silky hair, and the softest hands. A girl he'd come so close to ruining everything with on Sunday night.

He swallowed hard, putting down the knife and clenching his hands around the edges of the box. Ever since he'd been a kid, this place had been a second home to him. The Leung house had become a third. Arthur, Han, and everyone else in their family trusted him. How would they look at him if they found out he was having wildly inappropriate thoughts about the youngest member of their family?

What would happen if he got with Zoe for real? Even if everyone accepted it...if it didn't work out, if their relationship hit the rocks or went down in flames...

Arthur and Han cared about him. Deeply. But at the end of the day, faced with the decision, they'd choose their flesh and blood over some stray they'd taken in.

Acting on his attraction to Zoe was a nonstarter. It couldn't happen.

So why couldn't he stop thinking about it?

Even a couple of days later, he could feel her skin, smell the sweet scent of her wrapping around him and turning him inside out. In the driveway of the Leung house—right where he and Han used to hang out when they were kids, when Zoe was *literally* a kid—he'd been inches from kissing her. The moment they'd shared kept playing in his head on repeat, and all he could think was, what if those lights hadn't gone on? What if Zoe and Han's mom hadn't caught him ready to claim those soft, rose-colored lips?

When would he have stopped?

How much would he have risked?

He shook his head. Fury burned in his chest, almost as hot as his arousal whenever he let his mind drift back to that almost-kiss. He was an idiot to be even thinking about it, much less actively imagining it.

So why was he torturing himself like this?

And why was Arthur just sitting there instead of trying to get him to talk?

"Okay, fine," he exploded. He glared at Arthur. Patient bastard had always been good at waiting him out until he finally told on himself. "Let's say there is a particular lady in question."

Arthur set aside the inventory sheet he'd been working on and gave Devin his full attention. "Okay."

"But it's a terrible idea."

"Most love usually is," Arthur said with a sly smile.

Devin shook his head, gesturing wildly with his hands. "Like, natural disaster kind of terrible."

Arthur just raised his brows.

"Okay, fine, maybe not that bad, but bad. It would cause big problems."

"What sort of problems are we talking about? Legal trouble?"

"No." Though a half dozen years ago, it would have. "Work trouble?"

"No."

"Then . . . ?"

Devin cast about for a second before landing on "Her family."

Of which Arthur was a member. This was so messed up.

"I can't believe they wouldn't approve of you."

"It's more complicated than that." Devin raked a hand through his hair. "But they'd have good reason to think it's a bad idea."

The Leungs had welcomed Devin with open arms. Here at Harvest Home, Arthur had taken Devin under his wing. As Han's best friend, Devin had free run of the Leung house. Sleepovers, afternoon hangouts. They trusted him.

Han trusted him. Han, who was so obsessed with keeping his family safe and secure. He'd always been protective of his baby sister. How many times had he confided in Devin about wanting to basically go check Zoe into a convent?

Devin hadn't been lusting after Zoe that entire time, but his attraction to her had grown and grown, from the spark he first felt at her high school graduation to this inferno now. The other night, first at Harvest Home and then later at the bar, he'd kept losing sight of who she was. She stopped being his best friend's sister or Arthur's niece. She'd become just . . . Zoe. Gorgeous, easy-to-talk-to, smart, funny, empathetic Zoe.

While Devin's thoughts spun out, Arthur kept regarding him with that steady, patient gaze of his. Finally, he sat back and exhaled long and low.

"Have I ever told you the story of how I ended up here?"

Only about a million times.

Devin managed not to thunk his head against the table. "Yeah."

"All of it?"

"I don't know," Devin said carefully.

"My family, when we came over, we started in San Francisco."

"Right."

"Moved to New York from there. It was crowded. Dirty. We worked hard, lived in a tiny apartment. Huilang and David and me with our parents." Huilang being Han, Lian, and Zoe's mom, and David their distant uncle.

"Okay…"

"I was the one who decided to set out and go somewhere else. Not an easy decision."

"I'm sure." There was no stopping Arthur now, so Devin strapped in for the ride.

"My father. He told me it would be big trouble if I left."

Devin perked up. This was a part of the story he hadn't heard before. "Really?"

Arthur nodded. "He had so many reasons it wouldn't work. He thought I was betraying the family by leaving them behind." He smiled, knowing and maybe just a little smug. "But I knew. There were more reasons to go. And you know what?"

"What?"

"I was right." He waved a hand around. "Look what I've been able to accomplish. I had a great career." He had, starting the Jade Garden restaurant. Socking away cash and making a whole series of unlikely investments that had enabled him to open this place and grow it year after year. "Brought my sister and her husband down here with me, and they've had happy lives. We all have."

"Okay..."

Arthur fixed him with a gaze like he could see right through Devin. Could he? Did he know more than he was letting on?

If he did, he kept it to himself. "You can't let fear push you around. Worrying about what other people will think, what other people will do. It leaves you miserable. This girl—if she means enough to you, you go to her. You find a way to make it work. No matter what anybody else says, you hear me?"

For a split second, Devin considered it. He let go of all his concerns about Han and Arthur and Zoe's mom.

He let himself imagine going for it. Being with Zoe. Having her in his arms, talking to her the way he had the other night. Celebrating a great game of pool with a kiss.

Taking her to his bed.

A jolt of electricity zipped down his spine.

Yeah. He wanted that. All of it.

But before he could really talk himself into believing he could have it, a deep voice broke in.

"Wait—Devin's got a girl?"

All the hope that had started to rise in Devin's chest came crashing down. He turned to find Han in the doorway.

Right. Crap. It was Tuesday. Han or his mom or both—they always came by in the late afternoon.

Stupid. How could he have forgotten? How could he have asked Arthur of all people about Zoe—even in the most veiled of terms?

How could he have imagined this could work?

He forced out a laugh, but it was hollow to his own ears. "Nah, man. Me and Arthur—we were just talking."

Devin stood up, anxious, restless energy making it impossible to sit.

"Really?" Han asked, setting down a crate of leftover produce from the restaurant before wiping his brow. "Because it sounded like—"

Mercifully, Arthur stepped in to save him. "Your friend. He was talking in"—he cleared his throat—"hypotheticals."

Devin directed an appreciative glance his way. Leave it to Arthur to make Devin sound innocent without telling a single untruth.

But Han wasn't going to be deterred. "I don't know, man." He sized Devin up. "You have been a little weird lately."

"Work stuff." That wasn't an untruth, either. Taking over as shift leader had been great, but it had come with all the headaches he'd assumed it would.

Namely managing Bryce Horton.

But he wasn't here to complain about Bryce. Especially when Han was still regarding Devin with suspicion, and Devin was trying not to sweat.

Finally, Han gave him a playful shove on his shoulder. "Well, whoever the *hypothetical* girl is, I hope you win her over. Your dry spell has been going on for *way* too long."

"Like you're one to talk."

Han's gaze darkened. The fact he hadn't had a serious long-term relationship since he and May broke up after high school was a sore spot, and Devin had aimed right for it. "Whatever. Keep your secrets."

"No secrets to tell." And he was going to make sure it stayed that way. Needing some air after that close call, he grabbed a stack of inventory forms they'd already gotten through. "Gotta hit the head. I'll swing these by the front office."

"Thanks," Arthur said.

Han got to work. Relieved there wasn't going to be any more third degree, Devin headed out.

He had an ulterior motive for swinging past the office anyway.

The second Zoe came into view, his heart did something funny in his chest. She looked as beautiful as ever. She had when he'd first arrived, too.

She'd avoided his gaze in a way that was new, though. There'd been no flirty banter. She hadn't gotten in his space. She definitely hadn't come close enough for him to slip up and almost kiss her, and that was a good thing.

So why did it feel so awful?

Arthur hadn't known all the facts, so his advice hadn't been right, but there was one area where he'd been on the nose. Zoe did mean something to Devin. That meant he had to make this work between them. Not the kissing part, but the rest of it. He'd really started to think they were becoming friends. He wanted her, sure, but he also just plain liked her.

If almost kissing her meant losing her smiles and the way she looked at him and talked to him, then he'd screwed up worse than he'd realized. He had to make it right. Fast, before he messed this up for good.

He walked right up to the desk and put the inventory sheets in the bin. She glanced up at him. Her eyes sparkled for a second before darkening. Glowering, she looked away.

No smile. No "hello," even.

Guilt churned in his gut. She really was mad, and she had every right to be.

"You have a minute?" he asked. He couldn't keep the urgency out of his tone.

"Nope."

"Come on, Zo." He reached for her hand, only for her to snap it away.

"Uh-uh. No way." She darted her gaze around, but they were definitely alone out here. She still lowered her voice. "You of all people do not get to do what you almost did on Sunday night and then 'Zo' me."

Anger flashed in her gaze, only it was more than that. She was trying to hide it, but she was hurt.

Was it possible to feel even worse?

"Just hear me out," he begged.

She narrowed her eyes. "Fine."

Crossing her arms over her chest, she stared up at him, fire and defiance in her gaze, and that really shouldn't get him feeling hot under the collar, but it did.

He didn't care that she'd just verified that they were alone. He did the same thing she had, glancing around, but he couldn't talk to her like this, one eye constantly looking over his shoulder.

"Come on."

He tipped his head toward the spare office behind the desk. Keeping her feet planted, she cocked a brow at him, and he shot a glance skyward before holding out a hand. "Please?"

With a gruff sigh, she rolled her eyes but then consented to follow him. Once they were both inside, he closed the door and flipped the lock.

He turned to look at her. Her posture was still closed

and defensive, and he hated that. But what could he do? How could he get them back to the place they'd been the other night—all smiles and quiet confidences—without going too far?

"Look, Zoe." He was making this up as he went along, barreling ahead without a plan. "I'm sorry. Really."

"For what?" She tipped her chin up, the stubborn set to her jaw driving him to distraction. She started counting things off on her fingers. "For almost kissing me? Because if so, screw you. Or for jumping away from me like I'm a leper? Because if so, also screw you." She started advancing on him, her voice rising. "Or for treating me like a freaking child, the way everybody in my life does?" She was right in his space again, her eyes on fire. "Because if so"—she reached out and jabbed him in the chest—"screw"—she did it again—"you."

He grabbed her by the hand, and oh no. This was too much like the other night. She'd been swatting at him for his teasing then. She was righteously angry now. Guilt churned in his stomach, but his skin was prickling, her hand warm in his. He stroked his thumb over her palm, holding on even though he should let her go.

He should walk right out of this office. Out of this building and maybe off a short pier, but her cheeks were flushed, her eyes bright, and her soft red lips so wet and kissable, he was losing his mind.

"I can't," he said. "Your brother—"

"Isn't my keeper." She went softer against him, some of the anger fading out of her.

And it was like he couldn't stop himself.

He drifted closer to her, erasing the gap between them, licks of flame darting across his skin. "I don't want to be a bad guy."

He didn't want to take advantage. He didn't want to mess things up between them and lose the fragile friendship they'd been building—the one that had already come to mean so much to him.

What could they even have together besides friendship? Her time here in Blue Cedar Falls was clearly a stopgap. She was on her way to bigger and better things. His biggest goal in life was a house in the woods alone. If they crossed this line, it would change things forever. With her. With her family.

Keeper or not, he didn't want to violate Han's trust.

She gazed up into his eyes. The liquid brown of her irises melted something inside him. Reaching up, she grazed her fingertips across his cheek.

"You're not a bad guy, Devin." Her hand settled tentatively on the side of his neck, and the intimacy of it was almost too much. "I've been back home for months, and I swear you're the first person who's made me feel like you're actually listening to me. You care. A lot." She shook her head gently. "Bad guys don't do that."

He swallowed, scarcely able to think with her so close. Without his permission, his arm moved to wrap around her, and that felt so good. She was practically flush against him, warm and soft and smelling like heaven.

All his resolutions went up in smoke.

"This is a terrible idea," he rasped.

"Probably."

Then she rose onto her toes.

He was going to hell, because he met her halfway. Their mouths crashed together, and that was it. Something snapped inside him. Hauling her in against him, he let himself really feel her. Light exploded behind his eyes. Forget all his worries about the fact that she used to be a kid to him—Zoe Leung was all woman now. Her soft curves fit to his body like they were made to press together. She kissed like the spitfire she was, opening to him, nipping at his lips with her teeth, sucking on his tongue.

Groaning, he picked her up and sat her on the edge of the desk. This whole place was a disaster—the place they put stuff when they didn't know where it should go. Something clattered to the floor, but he didn't care. With a hand at the back of his neck, she reeled him in, and he went so happily. He lost his mind to the heat of her mouth, the warmth of her hips in his hands. Scooting backward on the desk, she folded her legs around him.

Alarm bells went off in his head.

What was he doing?

He tore himself away, only for her to drag him back in.

"Zoe," he gasped, kissing her again, but he had to stop.

She raked her nails through his scalp. "If you say one word about my stupid brother, I swear—"

"No." He laughed. "Just no."

But as he drew away, the kiss-bitten redness of her lips, her tousled hair, and her flushed cheeks told him the truth. They'd crossed a line. He knew how she tasted now, how perfectly she fit in his arms.

There was no going back.

But he wasn't a complete idiot.

"My place," he panted. "Not here."

She hooked her ankles behind his rear and pulled him in, and he saw stars.

He pulled away again and fixed her with a gaze that brooked no argument. "Not here."

She pouted, breathing hard, but she released him. He stepped away, and she hopped down off the table.

"Fine," she relented. She narrowed her eyes at him, but her voice shook. "No take-backs, though, okay?" She reached up to tap him on the head. "Don't over-think this."

Yeah. Like that was going to happen.

He grabbed her hand again. But instead of brushing her away, he held her gaze and brought the back of her palm to his mouth.

"No take-backs." He kissed the soft skin of her knuckles.

And seriously. He was going to hell.

But if the smoldering look in her eyes was any indication?

It was going to be worth the ride.

Chapter Eight

NERVOUS ANTICIPATION AND wary disbelief warred in Zoe's gut as she pulled up to Devin's building an hour later. Staying at Harvest Home and finishing the tasks she usually enjoyed had been pure torture—especially when Devin had slipped out. The dark look he'd given her on his way to the door had made her clench down deep inside.

But he'd been hot and cold over the past few days, to say nothing of the past few years. She had no idea what she was walking into here.

Still half expecting him to have changed his mind again, she got out of the car and headed up the walk. Bubbles formed and popped inside her chest. She was trying to keep her expectations in check, but his kiss had set her on fire. An hour of waiting had only stoked the flame. By the time she hit the top of the stairs, she was a riot of desire and nerves—if he turned her away after all that, she really was going to deck him. She reached the apartment number he'd given her, lifted her hand, and curled it into a fist.

She took a deep breath, then steeled up her nerve and knocked.

The door swung open instantly.

Behind it stood Devin, and Zoe's stomach did a loop-the-loop.

Good grief, he was gorgeous. His sandy-brown hair was all mussed, exactly the way she wanted it to be after she'd been raking her hands through it all night. If it was possible, his jaw was sharper, the scruff there even more masculine. He stood there in a T-shirt and jeans, his feet bare on the hardwood.

His eyes shone midnight black with want, and just like that, all the doubt disappeared from her mind.

"Devin—"

"C'mere."

He reached into the space between them to drag her in.

She crashed into him with the same passionate, desperate need that had overcome them in the back office of Harvest Home. The kisses were just that bright and stinging, and she couldn't get enough. The door slammed closed behind her. With all his bulk, Devin pressed her into it, and oh *God*.

She'd known he was ripped, but feeling all that hard muscle awakened a need inside her. Wrapping her arms around his neck, she used what leverage she had to climb his body, and he helped her, lifting her up. She curled her legs around him.

The hot bulge of him against her center sent fireworks off inside her. He let out a noise that was pure sex as they ground together. She'd never gone from zero to sixty so fast. She was dizzy with it, barely able to think.

He moved them away from the door, holding on to her as he turned to carry her through his apartment.

She got only the most glancing impression of the place. It was neat but spare, no pictures on the wall. A plain beige couch, a glass coffee table, and a sage-green rug.

And then she didn't have time to even think about his interior decorating, because that was his bedroom door he was hauling her through.

She pulsed deep inside as he practically tossed her down onto the big bed. He stood over her for a long moment, breath coming hard. Her entire body flushed. She liked being seen like this, liked the dark glint in his piercing eyes as he ran his broad hands along the tops of her thighs.

But the moment stretched and stretched. That same nervous flutter from earlier returned. "No take-backs?" she reminded him. She hated how it came out like a question.

He inhaled deeply. Then he nodded. "No take-backs."

Resolved, he climbed on top of her. As he kissed her again, slower this time, she wanted to pinch herself. There was no hesitation in him, and when she put her hands on his skin, under the hem of his shirt, he pushed into her touch. This wasn't some frantic, impulsive rush.

This was real.

Savoring every moment, she opened to him, curling her legs around his hips. The hot weight of his body settled over her. Every lick of his tongue and scrape of his teeth across her lips set her ablaze. Molten desire bubbled up inside her, and she wanted to take her time, but she couldn't wait.

She pushed his shirt up. Rising onto his knees, he grabbed the fabric by the back of the neck and tore it off, and holy crap. His muscles had muscles, all of him golden tan and smooth. A trail of hair led down to the button of his jeans, and she had to stop herself from ripping those open right away, too.

When he kissed her again, it was with a new intensity. A flash of burning arousal shot through her when his rough hands dipped beneath her top. She helped him take it off. Her bra followed, and he groaned.

"I've been trying not to think about these for so long." He buried his face in her breasts, and she laughed.

It didn't stay funny for long. Not when his hot mouth sealed over that tender flesh. Aching for more, she arched into him, running her fingers through his hair. Everything he did felt so good. Triumph had her flying high.

Until he started kissing lower down her abdomen.

"Devin," she moaned when he got to the waistband of her leggings.

Staring her straight in the eyes, he pressed one firm kiss to the very center of her through the fabric, and she practically came right then and there.

She reached for him.

He raced back up her body, sucking and biting at her all the way. As soon as he was close enough, she kissed him hot and deep, scrambling at his fly. She finally ripped it open and pushed his jeans and underwear down. The hot, hard length of him sprang free, and they groaned as one. He was huge in her hands, and she still couldn't believe this was happening.

As she stroked him, he tore at her clothes, too. She kicked off her boots, and it was all a mad dash until they were both naked. He paused just long enough to get a condom on. When he lined himself up, she had no doubts.

Still, he paused. "Zo..."

She sucked in a breath. Cupping his face in her hands, she brought his lips to hers for another, softer kiss.

"I want this," she promised him, and it was too true. With emotion she couldn't name, she told him, "I want you."

He closed his eyes.

His body sinking into hers turned her inside out. He felt so perfect as he ground against her, sending sparks surging through her.

"Zo," he repeated.

"I'm here." She was babbling. What was she saying? "I'm here, I'm here, I want you. I want this."

He pulled back, and she pushed into him until they fell into a rhythm. Pleasure started at the apex of her thighs, spreading outward until all she could see and feel and touch and taste was him. Over and over he drove into her, faster. She scrabbled at him, running her hands all up and down his back and shoulders.

"Zoe, Zo, I can't—you feel so good—"

"Devin, come on, please, I want—"

He slammed into her another half dozen times.

Her climax tore through her out of nowhere. Her vision flashed to black, and she squeezed every part of herself around him. Driving in deep, he called her name a final time. He pulsed inside her, and her entire world shattered.

Because this was *real*. She'd had sex with Devin James.

What had started as a challenge to see if she could get him to break had turned into a breaking down of her conception of the natural order of the universe.

She still had no real delusions that this could be more

than a fling, but the impossible had already happened the instant he'd touched his lips to hers.

As she stared up at his ceiling in wonder, she pressed a hand to the center of his back.

Who knew? Maybe all her notions of what she could and couldn't have in this world were wrong.

Chapter Nine

"WATCH OUT!"

At the sound of Terrell's shout, Devin jerked his gaze up from his clipboard.

Half his people were raising a section of the house's frame, Terrell and Gene up on ladders while the rest supported and spotted from below, only something wasn't right. Devin shot to his feet, gaze swinging wildly, the entire site going into slow motion. There—crap.

Off to the side, Bryce had let go prematurely, and Devin lurched forward, calling his name, but it was too late. Terrell's grip slipped without anyone to back him up.

The whole thing came crashing down.

Devin raced over. "Is everybody okay?"

"Yeah." Terrell scrubbed a hand over his face.

Devin checked in with everybody else, and no one had gotten hurt, thank goodness. He appraised the rest of the scene. The damage to the section that had fallen wasn't that bad, either, but it was still going to set them back a couple of hours—and that was before the headache of writing this up.

"I swore I had it," Terrell said, climbing down. His eyes narrowed as he glared silently off to the left.

Following his gaze, Devin flexed his jaw. He patted Terrell on the back. "It's just about lunch time anyway. Take a break, and then we'll get this cleaned up afterward."

He and the rest of the crew nodded.

Reassured that they were all okay, Devin stalked to the other side of the building, grinding his teeth together hard enough to crack.

A week had passed since he'd moved up to shift leader, and for the most part it had been going great. The team listened to him, and he'd handled the couple of issues that had arisen without much trouble.

Except Bryce.

Mostly it was little things like unauthorized breaks or screwing around on his phone when he was supposed to be working. Some of it was more serious, like using inappropriate language when talking to the women on the crew. Devin had documented it all, slowly building a case that even the folks who protected him couldn't ignore.

But this?

"Horton," he growled.

Bryce looked up from his phone. "What?"

"Don't 'what' me." Devin wanted to grab the guy's phone and chuck it in the cement mixer, only that would make a defect in the next house's foundation. Workers on the site weren't forbidden from being on them or anything; this wasn't high school. But when your eyes and hands needed to be on the job, they needed to be on the job. "Where were you?"

"Right there." He gestured toward where the crash had happened. "Weren't you watching?"

Old anxiety rose in Devin. His dad used to do that, too—reframing everything to make it out like Devin was the one to blame. He had to remind himself that wasn't true today. Devin had been doing his job, keeping an eye on his team while also seeing to the rest of his duties. "You weren't paying attention, and somebody could've gotten hurt."

Bryce rolled his eyes. "Terrell's butterfingers aren't my fault."

Forget a headache; the incident report was going to be a full-on migraine. Enough other people would back Devin and Terrell up that Bryce had been the one to let go, but the fact of the matter was that this never should have happened in the first place.

"You not doing your job is your fault." Devin kept his voice restrained but barely. "I'm not going to turn a blind eye to this BS."

"Sure you won't." Bryce's smile was mocking as he patted Devin on the shoulder.

Devin shoved him off automatically. He clenched and unclenched his jaw.

He walked away, hating the hot feeling in his chest and the hotter one in his face. The sense of helplessness ate at him, making him feel like he was twelve years old all over again.

Sure, he'd document this entire thing, but there was no satisfaction in that.

How did he protect his people? Stop giving Bryce any jobs where he could put the other members of his crew at risk? Stop giving him jobs at all? Bryce would love that.

The unfairness made him want to punch something.

Instead, he drew in a few deep breaths, trying to calm himself down before getting back to it.

On impulse, he popped his phone out of his pocket for the first time all morning. A handful of alerts greeted him, and he scrolled through them. When he got to the couple of texts from Zoe, the remaining tension bled out of his body, and he couldn't hold back the warm smile that curled his lips.

Ugh, remind me why I'm shacking up with a morning person again? I need coffee and it's all the way over theeeeerre

A photo came with the message, showing her in his bed, her hair a mess where it lay splayed out across his sheets, and he had to suck in a breath. There wasn't a single inappropriate thing about the shot, but it didn't matter. The sight of her, all rumpled and gorgeous and soft from sleep...It did things to him.

He just wished he could be there to take advantage of it. To roll her over and kiss that red mouth until they were both breathless.

Or maybe—if it was a day when he wasn't working...to go make her coffee. Pancakes. Breakfast in bed.

He mentally shook his head at himself. What a sap.

A week now they'd been doing...whatever it was they were doing together. Giving in to the overwhelming force of attraction between them had been the easiest thing in the world. When she was around, it was like all his worries disappeared.

He'd thought it would be weird, going from her brother's best friend to her friend to maybe something more, but it hadn't been. At all.

They'd never had to have any intense conversations about what was going on between them, either. Even that first time, when he'd been nervous about risking everything for a night of fun, it was like she'd been able to see right through him. Proving just how well she knew him, she'd just climbed right back on top of him and kissed him senseless, then wandered naked into his kitchen to fix herself a sandwich. She'd called out to ask if he wanted anything, too. Casual—like it was the most normal thing. And you know, he had been kind of hungry after working up an appetite like that.

So she'd just slipped into his life. When they weren't having mind-blowing sex, they were sharing takeout pizza or introducing each other to their favorite shows. He still wasn't quite sold on *The Bachelor*, but watching her yelling at the TV made him grin, and she was surprisingly receptive to reruns of *This Old House* playing in the background the rest of the time.

His crummy, boring apartment felt warm when she was in it. So warm that he almost forgot for hours at a time that his entire goal in life was to build his house in the woods and get out of here.

His only regret was the same one she had. She worked nights and he worked days, and so there she was waking up at—he checked the time stamp on the message—ten in the morning, while he was up at six.

Shaking his head at himself, he tapped out a quick reply. *Wish I could've gone and grabbed you one.*

Her answer came seconds later. *It's ok, I managed.*

The picture that followed was of her at Bobbi's bakery on Main Street. She was seated at one of the little tables inside, a latte and an empty plate set next to her open laptop.

His smile faded slightly. She'd kicked it up a notch on the job search of late. That or, now that he got regular updates about her life, he was just more aware of it.

Every time she talked about it, a little pit formed in

his stomach. Which was stupid. He'd known from the minute she moved back home that it was temporary. She was only here until the right opportunity came along, and he could be a big enough man to hope it showed up for her soon.

Even if, deep down, he never wanted her to leave.

"Hey, James." Bryce's voice had Devin jerking his gaze up. "Your girlfriend's here."

For a second, Devin's heart lurched into his throat.

No way. Zoe had just texted him from the bakery, and even if she hadn't—they hadn't exactly talked about it, but the one time he'd tried to bring up how he'd prefer to keep whatever they were doing together quiet, at least for the time being, she'd just rolled her eyes.

"Don't worry. Your secret is safe with me," she'd said before kissing his cheek. "My brother murdering you would be a real bummer."

And then she'd started kissing *other* parts of him, and well, that'd been the end of that.

Long story short, she wouldn't just show up at his work unannounced, and Bryce wouldn't know to call her his girlfriend.

Before he could work himself up any further worrying, he spotted Han's car in the lot—not Zoe's. Relief swept over him, even as a new kind of nervousness started to intrude.

Flipping Bryce off for being a homophobic prick, he started crossing the site toward the lot. As he approached, Han got out of his car and held up one of the same chopped-up liquor boxes he used for Jade Garden deliveries, and Devin managed a smile.

"Hey, buddy," Han said as he hauled the food over to the picnic table by the trailer, where they usually ate.

"Hey."

He and Han did this once a week or so. Their schedules didn't match up much better than Devin's and Zoe's. Lunch on the job site was one of the easier ways to get together most weeks.

As Han started unpacking the containers he'd brought, Devin pulled apart a couple of paper plates. His stomach growled as the mouthwatering scents of whatever Han had cooked up today hit him.

"The mango pork's new," Han said. "And I tweaked the ginger on the veggies."

"Yeah?"

Han might've had to drop out of culinary school when his dad died, but you'd never know it. He cooked all day, and then he cooked some more on his days off. He tried out new recipes—fancy "fusion" stuff that he and his mom had agreed didn't fit with the Jade Garden's brand, though he did manage to sneak a few of the tamer test recipes into the Chef's Specials "secret menu" now and then.

As Han plated up the food, he tipped his head toward the guys eating sandwiches and leftovers at the other tables. "So, how's it going?"

Devin rolled his eyes. "Same as usual."

"AKA, Bryce is being a jerk?"

Devin glared, but he knew there had been no one close enough to hear Han. "Yeah, pretty much."

Han scooped meat and vegetables onto a bed of noodles, then went ahead and sprinkled sesame seeds and scallions and drizzled some sort of orange sauce over it all, because the parking lot of a construction site was a five-star restaurant in his eyes. He passed the plate over, and Devin smacked his lips.

"I'm telling you." Han opened a set of wooden chopsticks and pointed them at Devin. "You gotta stand up to guys like him."

The same old discomfort churned in Devin's gut, but he pushed it down. "Sure, just like you did with all the mean kids back in high school."

"Shut up, man."

Neither of them had gotten picked on too badly when they were kids. Han stuck out, one of maybe four Asian kids in the school at the time, but he'd been as charming then as he was now—the bastard. Devin had held his own. He never started any fights, but when any came his way, he finished them. The two of them and the rest of the gang they ran with—they were fine.

But Han's girlfriend, May, had gotten savaged by the mean girl squad. She acted like it was no big deal, but whatever had happened, it had been bad enough that May had taken off after graduation. She'd come back for Han's dad's funeral and a visit or two here and there, and that was it.

Han scowled and nodded at Devin's food. "So? You gonna eat or just give me crap about things that happened a decade ago?"

"Like I can't do both." He tore open his own chopsticks. He'd never be as good with them as Han was, but he managed okay. He eyed the food. "Nice presentation."

"Obviously."

He tried the pork first, because how could he not.

"Get some mango with it," Han urged him.

Devin raised a brow. He didn't ignore the advice, though. He scooped up a noodle for good measure and shoveled the whole thing into his mouth.

His eyes slipped closed and he thumped his fist onto the table.

"Uh…"

"Shh." Devin put a finger to his sealed lips as he chewed. Once he swallowed, he opened his eyes.

"Well?"

"Man, that's good." Salty and sweet, rich but not heavy.

"The mango really makes it, huh?"

"Yup."

"You getting the garlic?"

"Uh-huh."

"But not too much."

"Close—I wouldn't do any more. But seriously. It's a keeper."

"Try the veg."

Devin forced himself to stop cramming delicious, delicious pork in his face. The vegetable was some weird green thing Han had been messing around with. It'd been a little bitter for his taste last time, but it'd probably go pretty well with the pork. He gave it a shot and nodded. "Yup. Cutting the ginger helped a lot."

"Thought so." Han flashed a smug, ever-so-slightly-secretive smile as he dug into his own plate.

"What're you up to?"

"Nothing."

"Yeah, I don't buy it."

Han had always had fun messing around with new recipes, but he'd been more intense about it of late. There was definitely something going on.

"You don't have to." Then his smirk deepened. "But maybe someday someone will."

Devin put down his chopsticks. "You aren't finally doing it."

Han had always idly talked about opening his own restaurant. It never came to anything, though. He was too busy at the family business.

"No." Han shook his head. "Not yet. But let's just say I'm working on something that might be a first step."

"Okay, you keep your secrets. As long as you keep the awesome grub coming, too."

Chuckling, Han nodded. "That I can do." He took a bite of his own lunch and seemed pleased. "Speaking of which, I've got a few other things I'm ready to guinea pig. Dinner at my place tomorrow?"

Normally, Devin would jump at the chance, but heading to the Leung house made all the hairs stand up on the back of his neck. He cleared his throat. "Who all's going to be there?"

"Does it matter? Free grub, remember."

"I know. I'm just asking."

Han shrugged. "Bobbi and Caitlin probably. Clay if I can pry him away from the Junebug for a minute, and you know he'll want to bring June." He listed the names of a couple of other guys they hung out with regularly. Then he grimaced. "I think Zoe has the night off, so she'll probably invite herself."

"Oh?" Devin's voice came out strangled to his own ears.

"Maybe. Who knows."

Not good enough. But he couldn't probe any deeper without sounding suspicious. He rummaged around in his brain, trying to think of excuses why he couldn't go, but he came up with squat.

Zoe was a firecracker. She said their secret was safe with her, but she loved to push him, and he had to admit it—he kind of loved it when she did. But interacting with her at their family home, with Han right there? What lines would get blurred?

It wasn't just her he didn't trust. His fingers twitched. He was getting too comfortable hanging out at his apartment with her. They spent half their time naked or snuggled up or both. Reaching out and putting his hand over hers and pulling her into him was becoming second nature.

Would he be the one to slip up and give them away?

Oblivious to Devin twisting himself into knots, Han pursed his lips. "Then again, she's been going out a lot recently."

"Yeah?" Devin's throat threatened to close again.

"It's super weird. She bummed around the house all the time when she first moved back in, but now it's like she's never there. I think she's sneaking out at night, too."

Devin tried not to choke on a piece of mango and pork. He coughed into a napkin.

"You okay?" Han asked.

No.

"Yeah, yeah." Fighting both to breathe and to come off as casual, Devin asked, "Is it really sneaking, though? She's in her twenties, right?"

"Fine, fine, whatever. It's still weird. I didn't think she had a lot of friends around here." He narrowed his eyes. "I'm pretty sure she's not dating anybody."

"Maybe she's just working late? The Junebug is a bar."

"Maybe." Han frowned. "You're right—it's none of my business. I just hope she's not doing anything stupid."

Devin's stomach flopped around inside his abdomen. She was doing something stupid all right.

Namely him.

"I'm sure it's nothing," he lied.

Only he wasn't so sure of that.

He wasn't so sure at all.

* * *

"So...do you want me to stay away?" Zoe had her back turned to Devin as she brushed her hair, but her gaze flicked to his in the bathroom mirror.

He was a little groggy, still splayed out on the mattress, naked and boneless. She hadn't had to close the bar tonight, so she'd come over after her shift, which was great—he loved seeing her. But it was past his bedtime, and that last round had been particularly athletic.

There was something in her voice that told him he needed to pay attention, though.

He rose onto his elbows and rummaged around in his skull for enough brain cells to rub together. "What do you mean? It's your house."

Their pillow talk had inevitably turned to a discussion of the dinner party Han was holding at the Leung house. She'd seemed surprised to hear he was trying to find a way out of it.

"Yeah," she allowed. She set down her brush—one of a couple of her things that had somehow found a home for themselves in his bathroom this week—and came back over to the bed. As if she could tell that he wasn't at his best when she wasn't wearing any clothes, she pulled the covers up over her chest. "But Han is your best friend. I don't want to get in the way of that."

He wasn't quite tired or stupid enough to laugh. He'd only resisted her as long as he had because he hadn't been willing to risk Han's friendship or Arthur's welcome. Of course his being with her now was going to affect his relationship with her family.

He reached for her hand and held it in his, running his thumb along the lines of her palm. He should be stressing out right now, but it was hard to be anything but relaxed when it was just the two of them. She made talking about his feelings easy in a way no one ever had. "You aren't in the way. I'm just nervous he'll catch on to something being weird between us."

"Yeah..."

He closed his fingers around hers more firmly. "You know I don't like keeping this secret, right?"

"I know." She wasn't looking at him, though.

"It's just..."

"I get it. I'm probably not going to be here for long." She huffed out a breath and pitched her voice higher, putting on the fake-happy smile she always used when talking about her job search. "Fifteen more applications submitted today." She deflated back to a more natural tone. "No point rocking the boat for something temporary, right?"

Sourness coated the back of his tongue. This was good, them being clear with each other like this. It was smart and mature.

So why did he hate it so much?

He couldn't bring himself to agree with her, so he barreled on. "Look, I don't want you to feel like you have to stay away."

"And I don't want you to feel like you do."

"So we won't," he decided. "We'll both go—if that's what you want to do. And we'll just try to be normal. It'll probably be fine."

Her expression finally brightened. "Sure. We can do this."

"Of course we can."

"So, what do you think?" She scooted closer to him, and he breathed a little easier. "Does Han just keep living with our mom out of sheer martyrdom? Or is it because he's using her for her kitchen?"

Devin tipped his head back and laughed. Leave it to Zoe not to mince words. "He'd probably say it's to take care of your mom and save money."

"Martyrdom." She poked his arm with her index finger.

He took her hand in his and kissed her knuckles. "But you might be onto something with the kitchen." Devin had helped them redo it back a few years ago. "He'd never find an apartment with one as nice."

Gazing down at their joined hands, Zoe asked, "What about at your loner house in the woods? Any plans to build a giant kitchen there that he can use?"

"It'd be worth it just for the free food," he mused. But he shook his head. "I don't know. It's going to be a small place. Just me kicking around it."

"You don't think there'd ever be anybody else?" she asked quietly.

The question settled on him heavily. She was still studiously looking down. He brushed her hair back from her face, but it didn't let him see her eyes any better.

The answer should be simple. His whole life, he'd been dreaming of the day he could have a home of his own.

He glanced over at the bathroom, though. At the hairbrush and the toothbrush and the little bottles of lotion and soap.

He shrugged, noncommittal. "How about you? Gorgeous kitchen a must-have for your Realtor when you land your dream job?"

He kept his voice light, but forget heavy. This question sank inside him like a stone.

"Nah." She put her head on his shoulder. "It's not like Han would ever leave to come visit me."

I would, Devin didn't say. But her kitchen wouldn't have a thing to do with it.

Silence hung between them for a minute. He twisted his neck to press a kiss to her temple, but before he could come up with anything smart to say, a yawn snuck out of him.

She laughed and kissed him back before ruffling his hair. "Come on. Let's get you to bed. You have incident reports to write in the morning."

"Don't remind me," he groaned, flopping backward into his pillow.

She got up and turned off the lights, and wow, she was so great. As she slipped back into the bed beside him, he curled his arms around her. Even the prospect of dealing with more paperwork and more people letting Bryce off the hook couldn't bring him down.

Nope. Apparently, the only thing that could do that was the reminder that his time with her was temporary.

Which sucked. Because he was pretty sure he was going to get even more of those when he was pretending not to be sleeping with her at Han's party tomorrow night.

Chapter Ten

"Y'ALL—DON'T even get me started on weird customers." June held a hand in front of herself, palm out.

Zoe raised a brow and took another sip of her wine.

Ten minutes into Han's dinner party, she, June, and
June's friend Bobbi were standing around the island in
the center of the kitchen, trading work stories. Over
by the stove, Han prepped ingredients while trying to
keep Ling-Ling from stealing any of them—with mixed
success. Between fond rebukes to the dog, he kept a
light conversation going with Clay, Bobbi's girlfriend,
Caitlin, and a couple of guy friends.

"Ooh." Bobbi rubbed her hands together. "This is
going to be good."

June smiled. "Let's just say there's a reason the
Sweetbriar Inn now has an official policy prohibiting
birds."

Zoe snickered, but before June could dive any deeper
into whatever guest at her family's B&B had prompted
that new rule, the doorbell rang, setting Ling-Ling off.

Zoe's pulse raced, and she put her glass down with a
thunk. "I'll get it!"

"Seriously," Han called after her, "nobody's fighting you for it except the dog."

And okay, yeah, she was a little eager, racing to get the door each time a new person arrived. But this time, she had extra reason to run. Devin was the only person they were still waiting for. This had to be him.

She skidded to a stop in the entryway, making sure her body was blocking Ling-Ling from getting out before flinging open the door.

And there Devin was. All six foot something glorious inches of him, his cheeks flushed from the chill outside, his blue eyes sparkling, and what was it about the way he lit up when his gaze fell on her? Her heart pounded, her ribs squeezing around it.

Her over-the-top reaction made no sense. He was just a guy, and she was in a weird, temporary place in her life. They'd basically agreed that whatever they were doing together was just for fun. The very sight of him shouldn't turn her to goo.

But she liked him so much.

She cast one backward glance over her shoulder before closing the door and launching herself at him. He caught her in his arms. Pausing only to set down the six-pack he'd brought, he pressed her into the freezing-cold siding of the house, and she didn't care about the temperature or the fact that he was so worried about getting caught.

His mouth was hot as it covered hers, his tongue commanding. She kissed him back with a hunger that had nothing to do with the promise of the upcoming meal. Running her hands through his hair, she soaked up every second of contact with him.

It wasn't enough. He jerked away, his breath coming

fast, the darkness in his gaze pure torture considering what was coming next. "We should—"

"Go make out some more in your truck?" she suggested helpfully.

He buried his face in her shoulder, and she wrapped her arms around him as tightly as she could. "Don't tempt me, woman."

"Why not?" She gazed up at the stars and breathed him in. "It's so much fun."

"For you, maybe," he said, but there was a hint of darkness in his tone.

The corners of her mouth turned down. "I was just messing around."

"I know." Did he, though?

The mood broken, he gave her one last quick peck before letting go.

Stepping away, he gestured at his face. "Do I have any...?"

"Just—" She reached up on her toes to swipe at the little smudge of lipstick at the corner of his mouth. Considering how they'd just been sticking their tongues down each other's throats, it wasn't bad. This long-wearing stuff was the best.

"Thanks."

"No problem."

He picked up the beer he'd set down and they headed inside. She stole another glance at him under the entryway light as he stopped to give Ling-Ling a quick scratch behind the ear. There was no sign that anything was amiss. The way she'd run her fingers through his hair could have easily been the wind. No one would know.

She tried to remind herself that that was a good thing.

"I'll, uh, show you where to put your coat." She started to lead him down the hall.

"Please," her brother scoffed, appearing at the top of the half flight of stairs. "It's just Devin. He knows." Han smiled at Devin. "What's up, man?"

"Nothing," Devin replied.

"Was starting to think you'd gotten lost out there."

"Nah." Devin brushed past her. Out of her brother's sight line, he gave her fingers a reassuring squeeze before continuing on. He held up the six-pack. "Almost forgot these in the truck and had to run back for them."

"Nice." Han accepted the beers.

But as Zoe followed Han and Devin into the kitchen, she caught June gazing at her appraisingly. Crap—she'd checked Devin for lipstick smudges but she hadn't checked herself. She casually glanced at her reflection in the hallway mirror. Nope—she was basically okay.

Well, whatever. June could give her weird looks if she wanted to. Zoe wasn't going to act like she had anything to hide.

To prove it, she snagged a fried wonton strip off one of the appetizer plates. She dragged it through the plum sauce dip and popped it in her mouth. She really didn't know what that was supposed to prove, but it was freaking delicious, so it didn't matter.

Around her, all signs showed this to be a successful dinner party. Han was doing his thing, cooking and putting on a show. If it weren't so clichéd—and if they were Japanese instead of Chinese—he could've had a heck of a career at one of those hibachi places.

Zoe shook her head, trying not to stare at Devin, who had joined the loose cluster hanging out over by her brother. Han's parties were never formal or anything, but people usually put in a little effort. Devin had traded in his work clothes for a sharp blue button-down that made his eyes look even brighter.

She wanted to peel it off him.

"So, you wanna talk about it?"

Zoe tried not to jump when June spoke from right beside her. "Talk about what?"

June's friend Bobbi snickered.

Zoe's face went warm. Crap. She was really bad at this secretly banging her brother's friend thing, huh?

"There's nothing to talk about," she said, more firmly this time.

June didn't seem convinced. "Uh-huh."

"He's one of Han's friends." Zoe swallowed past the lump in her throat. "Gross."

"Gross? I mean—" Bobbi gestured with her wine-glass at the guys. Her girlfriend, Caitlin, stood over beside them. "I don't even like dudes, and I can admit he's hot."

"They're all hot," June said.

Zoe recoiled. "Ew. My brother is not hot."

Shrugging, June took a sip of her wine. "May would kill me for saying it, but it's true."

"Seriously, though," Bobbi said, leaning in. "Devin's been sneaking looks at you almost as much as you've been sneaking looks at him."

"Really?" Her voice came out too high. She retreated to the side a bit to reclaim her wineglass and took a gulp.

"Really," June confirmed.

Zoe had to stop herself from glancing over at him to verify. "It doesn't matter. Even if he weren't gross." He was so, so not gross. "It's like I said—he's my brother's best friend, and you know how Han is." Her mouth felt dry despite the wine. "If either of us made a move, he'd flip his lid."

"I don't know..." June mused.

"Well, believe me, I do."

Devin and Han had both been plenty clear. A bitter taste formed at the back of her mouth.

At first, the whole off-limits thing had been kind of fun. But the more time they spent together, the more it twisted her up inside.

Being someone's dirty little secret wasn't great for the ego.

Not that that was stopping her from developing— ugh—*feelings* for the guy.

Yeah, she might be in denial about a lot of things, but that was a tough one to get away from. She wasn't an idiot. The way his touch made her feel all warm and squishy inside, the way her thoughts kept drifting to him throughout the day... It was like her teenage crush, only times a million, because now she knew he liked her, too.

Maybe not as much as she liked him, but more than enough to keep throwing gasoline on the fire in her chest.

She was saved from having to downplay things to June and Bobbi any further by Han flicking off the burners with a flourish. "Okay, y'all, grub's up."

Zoe downed another gulp of her wine before excusing herself. This was old hat. Positioning herself at her brother's side, she passed him plates, and he portioned out the food.

Her mouth watered. Han had been refining his stable of experimental dishes for ages, and they just kept getting better. Tonight's menu included a rice dish with pickled ginger and edamame, plus seared scallops in a basil sauce she never would have thought would work, but it did. Baby bok choy that he'd cooked over a little electric grill, and some mystery egg tarts he'd done in the oven. He scattered the lot with a drizzle of vibrant green and white sauces, chopped nori, and sesame.

Devin stepped in to pass the completed dishes out.

"Wow," Caitlin said as she received the first plate.

"Let me know what you think."

Zoe frowned at her brother. His voice had a different pitch to it. He was always proud of his cooking, but the nerves jangling around in there were new.

She didn't have much time to think about it. Before she knew it, everyone had a plate in hand. As they found places to sit or stand, appreciative moans and compliments sounded out around the room. Han shone a sly smile as he started eating, too, Ling-Ling parked hopefully at his feet. He made a running commentary— he always did. What worked and what hadn't, though as far as Zoe was concerned, it was all a hit.

The regulars in Han's guinea pig squad were easy to spot as they echoed Han's comments. Devin was a down-to-earth guy, but he'd been hanging out with Han long enough to mention something about the butter-to-shortening ratio in the crust of the savory egg tart. Zoe shook her head and just kept shoveling it in.

One of Han and Devin's buddies, Terrell, snapped his fingers. "I know what this reminds me of. That thing you made for my sister's wedding."

Han tipped his head to the side. "Did I do shrimp for that?"

"No, but the sauce."

"That was totally different," Han said.

Devin scrunched up his nose. "It was kind of the same."

"You know what it reminds me of?" June interjected.

"What?" Han asked. "And please tell me you have a better memory than these guys."

"She usually does." Clay chuckled, and Devin elbowed him in the ribs.

"Graduation," June said, sure of herself. "Your year. That meal you did at our place."

"Oh." A shadow crept across Han's gaze.

Right. Any meal he would have made at the Wu-Miller house would have been because of May.

Devin looked at Han with the same concern Zoe felt.

As if realizing her mistake in bringing that up, June continued. "Though this is way better. I mean, the graduation meal was amazing, but these egg tarts are next level. What's in them again?"

Han rattled off some of the ingredients.

Devin cleared his throat. "I think it's more like that Thanksgiving you cooked—what was it? Twenty seventeen?"

Han pulled a face. "That menu was totally different."

"Yeah, but the basil—"

"Oh man," Terrell said, elbowing his buddy. "New Year's Eve, like, five years ago."

"Yeah!" The dude's eyes lit up. He waved a hand at Han. "The one you did at the park."

"Fried turkey," Han agreed. "Seriously, guys, that was nothing like this."

"Didn't you have little pastries? I swear there was, like, basil in them like this."

"The basil is in the sauce." Han was smiling again now, which was something.

"Oh! Oh!" Terrell held up a finger. "Wasn't that the year we were picking gravel out of the cupcakes?"

"Man, who baked those?"

"Pretty sure it was me." Bobbi grinned.

"They were so good, it was totally worth it, even when—"

Devin slammed his plate down on the counter. His fork clattered against the china. Ling-Ling whined.

Suddenly, everyone got quiet.

Zoe sucked in a breath. Devin's face had turned a shade of purple. Thunderheads colored his eyes.

"What?" she asked.

Devin's gaze connected with hers for a fraction of a second, and it was like an iron band closed around her heart.

Devin glanced away. "Excuse me."

He stalked off. Zoe put her plate down. The band around her heart released, but it was replaced by a freaking jackrabbit, jumping up and down on the insides of her chest so fast, she could hardly breathe. She gripped the edge of the counter she'd been leaning against until her knuckles turned white.

Everything in her told her to follow him. His gaze was seared into her. His eyes had looked so *angry*.

But more than that, he'd looked so...

Lost.

A door slammed in the distance, and Zoe squeezed the counter even tighter. Han smacked himself in the forehead, then reached over to cuff Terrell on the back of his head, too.

"Ow—"

"Devin's dad," Han hissed. "Remember?"

"Wait." Zoe should shut up, but she couldn't. "What—"

Han shook his head.

Wincing, Terrell scrubbed at his face. "Oh, right. Crap."

Quietly, Bobbi turned to Zoe. "Devin's dad showed up drunk. He knocked over the cupcakes."

"Said some really awful stuff, too," Han added.

Zoe stared toward the corner Devin had disappeared around. It was like she was being yanked in that direction. He'd told her the other night that his dad wasn't a good guy, but seeing his reaction to someone bringing up that memory now...

She bit the inside of her lip.

Was he okay? No, of course not. How could he be?

She wanted so badly to chase after him. If she were really his girlfriend, she would do just that. She'd put her arms around him and hold him tight, and maybe—maybe he'd even let her.

Her stomach plummeted to the floor.

The only problem was that she wasn't. If she gave them away, he'd be even more furious—furious at her.

But she couldn't ignore this *pull*.

"Shouldn't someone go after him?" she asked.

Han shook his head. "Just makes it worse."

Everyone seemed to take that as definitive.

Slowly, people started eating and talking again, but Zoe couldn't hear any of it. She was listening so carefully for any sort of sound from the hallway. When she heard the bathroom door open, her heart leaped.

Speaking to no one in particular, she said, "I have to..."

She pulled out her phone as if that would explain her needing to step away.

June gave her a knowing glance that bordered on

encouragement. Accepting that unexpected morsel of support, she took off down the hall at a measured pace, but as soon as she was out of sight, she couldn't help it. She broke into an all-out sprint.

Only to almost crash into Devin. His jaw was set, storms still brewing in his eyes, and she'd just come out here to check on him.

But she couldn't stand this.

She grabbed him by the wrist and hauled him down the hall.

"Zo—"

He resisted, but he finally let himself be dragged into the next available room with a door. It was Lian's old room—now her mother's sewing room, but it would do. Her mom was working at the restaurant tonight, so she wouldn't notice.

As soon as the door was closed behind them, she launched herself at him. She wrapped her arms around his chest, but he was stone.

"You don't have to—" he gritted out.

"Shh."

He shook his head, but she wasn't having any of it.

She shushed him again. He stayed as stiff as a board for a long moment. Crap. Maybe she'd misread this entire thing. Maybe he didn't need comfort.

Maybe he didn't want any from her.

Well, too bad. She was giving it to him anyway.

She'd give him anything.

She clenched her eyes tight. That was probably so stupid of her. He wasn't in this with her for real. Even if he were—what kind of future could they have? He'd never be willing to face Han's wrath or risk Arthur's judgment. There wasn't any place for her in his lonely loner's house in the woods. Who knew how long she'd be staying in Blue Cedar Falls anyway? Getting invested was a waste, but she couldn't seem to fight it anymore.

Finally, Devin let out a sigh. He curled his arms around her, too. His posture softened as he pressed a kiss to the top of her head. "I'm fine," he told her.

"I know." People banging dishes on counters and leaving in a huff—that was always a sign that they were fine.

"I just..."

She leaned back so she could look him in the eye. The anger had faded from his gaze, replaced by something that made him look tired and older than he was. She sucked in a breath. "Han said it was something to do with your father?"

Devin nodded grimly. He pulled her back into a hug, her face pressed to his chest. Normally, she wouldn't mind being snuggled up with his firm pecs, but it was clearly a way for him to avoid her gaze. She allowed it for now.

Exhaling, he said, "Yeah. Told you he wasn't a good guy."

"You didn't tell me he was the 'shows up drunk to parties and knocks over cupcakes' kind of bad guy."

He shrugged, but she could practically feel his wince. "They told you that, huh?"

"Yup."

"They tell you the part about him smacking me around?"

She drew back. "No."

His grimace deepened. "Can we forget I just admitted it, then?"

"Seriously?"

"He was a jerk," he said, as if that were some kind of explanation.

"But he hit you?" More rumors and hushed conversations floated into her memory. She hadn't understood them then. But Devin telling her this...It slotted an awful lot of things into place.

Devin rubbed his hands up and down her arms, and she didn't need him to comfort her. Not when he was telling her about his pain. "It's okay. I'm fine now."

"How?"

His throat bobbed. "I got out."

"How?" An intense need to understand this man clawed at her. She shouldn't pry, but she wanted to know everything. "I mean—if you don't want to talk about it—"

"Your family, for one." His gaze connected with hers, a little light coming back to his eyes. "There's a reason I was always at your place or hanging out in Arthur's basement."

"Right."

"And then, as soon as I was out of high school, I packed my bag. Started working. Got an apartment. The rest is history."

Was it, though? The pain of it still seemed to live inside him.

She put her hands over Devin's chest, trying to take in the breadth of him. This strong, incredible man, who'd dealt with so much and who still stayed open and kind.

It occurred to her again, just like that night he'd walked her home after they'd hung out at the bar. Did he ever talk about what had happened to him? How did the pressure of keeping it all inside not make him explode?

Gazing up at him, she took a deep breath. "What happened to him?"

"I have no idea," he said quietly, ghosts in his eyes. "I assume he rotted in that house for a while. I never went back. He never came looking for me except a couple of times when he was trashed." He shrugged. "When he did, I just called Officer Dwight to take him home. Otherwise, I had nothing to do with him. Year or so after I left, I got a drunk dial from him. Said he was set up in a trailer park in Florida."

"You think he'll stay there?"

"Honestly, I don't care."

He meant it, too. The pain in his voice was like a hand reaching into her chest and squeezing.

Zoe's family was her bedrock. She defied them and fought with them, but deep down she loved them fiercely. She never in a million years could doubt they loved her, too.

Devin...he didn't have that.

Slowly, she skated her hands up his chest. She took his face between her palms. His scruff was rough against her skin. She stroked her thumbs just beneath his eyes. "I'm so sorry," she told him quietly.

"It's nothing. Old history."

She repeated it. More firmly this time. "I'm sorry." She reached up onto her tiptoes, pulling him down to meet her. She kissed his lips. "I'm sorry."

"Zo..."

"I'm sorry." She kissed him again, soft and slow.

He melted into it, wrapping his arms around her. Holding on to him, she tried to pour everything she was feeling into the motion of their lips. He didn't want her to comfort him or to let her tell him how her heart ached for him, and that was fine. She'd make him understand like this.

Because any of her ideas about not getting invested? Not growing *feelings* for this man?

They were out the window. She'd tossed her sense of self-preservation right along with them.

All she could do was hang on.

And wait for the crash when they all hit the ground.

Chapter Eleven

A COUPLE OF weeks later, Zoe sat on the kitchen counter, texting with June about grabbing coffee, Clay about whether or not she could open the bar tomorrow, Lian about how she wanted to bang her head against the wall over her job search, and a group of high school friends about a time to meet up for drinks later that week—all without accidentally sending any messages to the wrong person. She snickered to herself as she sent a reaction gif to Lian. Take that, accounting firm looking for "attention to detail."

No sooner had the thought occurred to her than her screen went blank, a call from an unknown number appearing over her fifteen messaging threads.

Her first impulse was to ignore it—she'd talked to quite enough people excited to offer her a free time-share or help her with a problem at the social security agency. But one of the worst things about being on a job hunt was having to answer every call.

Bracing for the worst, she tucked her hair out of the way and brought the phone to her ear. "Hello?"

A male voice replied, "Good morning. Is this Zoe Leung?"

She sat up straighter. "It is."

"Hi, I'm Brad Sullivan from Pinnacle Accounting, following up on a résumé we received."

"Oh, hi!" She scrambled down off the counter and over to her makeshift office set up on the end of the dining room table. Pinnacle, Pinnacle—oh, right. It was a firm in Atlanta she'd applied to last week.

"I was hoping to talk to you about your interest in the position. Do you have a few minutes?"

She blinked about fifty-seven times. "Of course."

"Great." With that, he launched into a quick overview of the job she'd applied for as well as a series of questions about her experience and training, which she somehow or other managed to string together coherent answers to.

Slipping back into the accounting persona she'd honed during her coursework and internship was harder than it used to be. Once upon a time, it had felt like a second skin. Now it felt like a wet suit that was three sizes too small.

"All right," Brad said, "sounds to me like you're an excellent candidate. Let me just talk to a few people and we'll get you set up for an interview with the rest of the team."

It was a good thing the chair she was sitting on had a back, because otherwise she might have tipped right out of it. "Oh wow, okay, great."

"Just one last question—this job does require you to be on-site in our Buckhead office. Looks like you're in North Carolina right now, but I'm assuming you're prepared to relocate?"

"Yes," she said, but as she did, a stone lodged in her throat.

"Perfect." He rattled off a few more details, and they said their goodbyes.

The whole while, the tightness in her windpipe grew and grew.

Atlanta was a four-hour drive from here. A few months ago, she might not have cared. She'd lived away from home when she'd gone to college. She'd always assumed she'd have to leave again to get a decent job that was in her field.

But her time back here in Blue Cedar Falls had changed her perspective.

She liked being home. She liked seeing Han all the time and being able to meet up with Lian now and then. She liked Clay and June and working at the bar. She loved getting to spend time with Arthur and helping out at Harvest Home.

She loved...

She clenched her phone so tightly she worried the screen would break.

She and Devin had told each other that their time together was limited. He wasn't interested in anything serious; all he wanted in this world was a house of his own outside of town, and he never imagined sharing it with anyone, least of all her. He definitely wasn't interested in upsetting the balance of his relationship with her family.

Ever since Han's dinner party, when he'd opened up to her about his dad, she'd known that eventually he'd break her heart.

She just hadn't been prepared for it to happen so soon.

Maybe it didn't have to. A bubble of hope filled her

chest. Maybe she wouldn't get the job. Maybe she could just stay here forever, working at the bar and helping Arthur run the food kitchen and sleeping with Devin and it would all be okay.

Right.

The bubble popped almost instantaneously. She needed this job. If it was offered to her, she'd have no choice but to take it and go. This was the moment she'd been waiting for, working toward, training for.

So why did everything about it make her feel so terrible?

Before she could even begin to get it all sorted out, the front door opened.

"Crap."

Instinctively, she scrambled to look busy, but sitting at her laptop with her spreadsheet open was about as busy-looking as she could get.

"Oh, look, you're awake," her mom said, deadpan.

Zoe drew in a breath and forced herself to smile. She hadn't gotten home until two a.m. yesterday after closing up the Junebug. The fact that she was up before ten was a miracle.

Try telling her early-bird mother that, though.

"Han went to the restaurant already?" her mom asked.

Zoe shook her head. "Took the dog for a hike first."

"Good. Ling-Ling needs more exercise."

"Ling-Ling needs you to stop slipping her extra treats."

"Me?" Her mother put her hand to her chest dramatically. "Never."

Right. "How was brunch?"

Zoe's mother ate with May and June's mom and a

few other old ladies almost every morning down at the Sweetbriar Inn on Main Street.

Her mom waved a hand dismissively. "Same as ever." She headed into the kitchen to start a pot of tea. Managing to sound both casual and pointed, she mentioned, "Mrs. Smith's son got a big promotion. Branch manager."

"That's great." Zoe dug her nails into the meat of her palm.

The competitive instinct in her told her to brag about the interview she'd just landed, but she knew better. Her mom would get obsessed with it and have her cramming for it like the SATs. Better to keep mum.

But as her mother puttered around, getting everything together for her tea, Zoe kept running around in circles inside her head. She wanted to talk this out with someone. Devin, namely. He was so grounded, and he asked her questions that made her see things in a new light. Could she bring up her mixed feelings about moving without letting on that she was getting too attached to him? Probably not. He was working right now anyway. So were June and Lian and pretty much all of her other friends she might try to talk to about this.

Which left her with her mom.

With her teapot and little porcelain cup and saucer balanced on a tray, her mother returned to the table and took her usual seat at the head. She put on her reading glasses and opened up the newspaper.

Zoe fidgeted, glancing between her open laptop screen and her mom, but she couldn't quite figure out how to open up her mouth and say what was on her mind.

Talking—really talking—with her mother had never been easy. Her mom had this unique way of shutting

Zoe down and making all her ideas seem foolish. Sometimes Zoe had enough force of will to barrel right through.

And sometimes she ended up picking a stupid major she didn't even like anyway.

She still couldn't decide who she was more upset with about that—her mother or herself. Clearly her mom wasn't entirely to blame. Yeah, Zoe had gotten a different version of her mom's weird guilt-trippy style of parenting, considering how much younger she'd been than her siblings when their father died. But Han and Lian—they were doing what they wanted to do. Or at least some variation on it. They were happy.

"Something on your mind?" her mother asked, not looking up from her paper.

So many things.

But the one she ended up blurting out was, "How come you always rode me so much harder than Han and Lian?"

Her mother's rapid blinking was the only sign that the question took her by surprise. With deliberate slowness, she set her teacup down and dabbed at the corner of her mouth with a napkin.

Stalling. Zoe was used to it.

That didn't make it any easier to wait her mother out. Chewing on the inside of her lip, she put her hands under her thighs, literally sitting on them to try to give herself patience.

Finally, her mom put the napkin down. She fixed Zoe with an appraising stare that lasted way too long for comfort. Inside, Zoe squirmed a little, but she remained firm.

Shaking her head, her mother let out a breath and

looked away. "I ever tell you about the first day I picked you up from nursery school?"

Zoe deflated. She pulled her hands out from under her legs. "Probably."

"You were a mess. Glitter everywhere. Your teacher apologized, but I knew. It wasn't her fault."

Great, so Zoe had been a disaster since she was four. Good to know. "Look—"

Her mom talked right over her, slow and steady. Like a Zamboni. "Whole ride home, you never stopped talking. Told me all the friends you made, everything you did. You couldn't decide if you liked Joey best or Kim. Or costume party or building with blocks. Everything was your favorite."

"Right, right. I was a happy kid. I know."

Her mom's lips curled into a smile. "Ray of sunshine." She turned her gaze from the past and back to the woman in front of her. Her smile faded. "You remember what you told me you wanted to be when you grew up?"

Had she ever known? "No."

"I remember. Clear as yesterday. 'Princess astronaut veterinarian ballerina.'"

Zoe's face flushed warm. "I mean, I was, what? Four?"

"But you believed it. With all your heart."

"Mom..." She was beginning to lose her patience.

Her mother's voice rose by a fraction, her tone growing serious. "Your brother, Han. Only thing he cares about besides his family is cooking." Her mother jabbed her pointer finger into the table. "Han is easy."

Zoe frowned. She wasn't so sure about all that.

But her mom was on a roll now. She tapped the table hard again. "Lian wanted to be a teacher since she was six. Easy."

"But what about all the stuff you told me?" Zoe asked. Bitterness seeped into her tone. "Pick any career you want, just make sure it's comfortably middle class."

How many times had Zoe come home from school excited about some project in her communications elective or jazzed about a fundraiser Uncle Arthur was going to let her help out with at Harvest Home, only to be met with her mother's dismissive *tut-tut*ting?

"You." Her mother shoved that finger in Zoe's direction this time. "You were never easy."

"Great," Zoe grumbled.

"You weren't. Still aren't."

Zoe's cheeks warmed, and she squirmed inside. Clearly she'd been selling her mom's passive-aggressive streak short, because this direct insult approach was no peach. "Okay, okay, I get it."

Her mother shook her head. She was fluent in English, but she still muttered a few words to herself in Mandarin. It was one of her only tells that she was getting flustered.

"That's not a bad thing, Zhaohui. You always make it out like I'm attacking you."

"Uh, you kind of are." How else was she supposed to interpret her mom telling her to her face that she was, always had been, and always would be difficult?

"You were not easy, because you actually wanted to be princess astronaut veterinarian ballerina!"

"Who wouldn't?" That sounded awesome.

"You have your head in the clouds. Someone has to help keep you here. On earth where you belong." Fire burned in her mother's gaze.

And okay, Zoe knew her mom loved her and that she'd fight off an invading horde for her. But she occasionally forgot that the overbearing stuff was love, too.

Annoying, frustrating, occasionally infuriating love.

"You don't have to," she insisted.

"I do." Her mother reached across the table, and for the first time in what seemed like a long, long while, it felt like she was looking at Zoe. Not past her. No snide remarks, no judgment. She held out her hand. "I know it, because that's what your father did for me."

Zoe's eyes flew wide. Her mom almost never talked about her dad. "Wait—"

Her mother shook her head, her whole expression softening. "So like me, sometimes, my Zhaohui. I don't want you to learn lessons the hard way like I did." She extended her hand an inch farther, and Zoe slipped her fingers into her palm. "You have to be practical. You have to survive."

And Zoe would probably never fully understand her mother, but for one moment, she wondered if maybe she was right. If maybe they did have more in common than had ever been keeping them apart.

Her mother gave her hand a gentle, reassuring squeeze. "Look. I make you a deal."

"Okay..."

"You ever find job opening for princess astronaut veterinarian ballerina *with* pension and health insurance? I promise I stop riding you so hard."

Zoe laughed, and she swabbed at her eyes. This was making her way too emotional—especially considering her mom had basically just promised to never, ever give her a break.

She had about a bazillion other questions, but before she could figure out a way to give voice to them, the actual, honest-to-goodness phone on the wall started ringing.

Her mother patted Zoe's hand before letting go to stand and answer it.

"Hello—" She barely got through the word. A muffled voice came over the line.

Then all the color drained from her face.

* * *

"For crying out loud, James." Bryce looked up from the same set of joists he'd been supposedly assembling for the last hour now. "Your mommy calling you or something?"

"Mind your own business." Devin ignored his phone buzzing in his pocket again. This was the third time, and no, it wasn't his mommy. Dead women didn't call.

He was starting to get a little worried, though.

He drove the last nail home in his set and looked up, meeting Terrell's gaze. "You got this for a second?"

"Sure, man."

"You heard him," Bryce said, dropping his nail gun. "That's five, everybody."

"You already had your break, and you don't have time to take another." Devin gestured at the work still to be done.

Bryce pantomimed a yapping mouth, and Devin gritted his teeth.

The guy had been giving Devin a hard time since high school. Ever since Bryce had come on at Meyer Construction, it had been the same—like Bryce resented that a guy as powerful as the mayor's son had to stoop so low as to be working alongside schlubs like Devin. Devin's promotion had been salt in the wound. The backtalk had gotten worse and worse, and Devin had tried to turn a blind eye to it. He'd focused on the job and the work and let the personal stuff slide.

Goodness knew there was enough to focus on work-wise. Ever since the disaster the other week when Bryce had let half a wall collapse, the higher-ups had taken a personal interest in Devin's crew. Devin had shown Joe all the documentation he'd been gathering about Bryce's sloppy work, and Joe had been clear that Devin had his support. He just needed to keep collecting evidence to build a case that could hold up against whatever scrutiny they might get if and when the time came to finally give the boot to the mayor's son.

Ignoring Bryce, Devin made sure he was out of everybody's way before pulling out his phone.

Only to find three missed calls from Zoe.

His heart thunked around in his chest, thrown by a whole warring set of reactions. Pleasure at hearing from her. Surprise, because she never called unless it was too late to come over and she still wanted to tell him something dirty.

Worry.

He tapped on her number and brought his phone to his ear. As it rang, he glanced around. The rest of his crew was still working. Bryce was continuing with his little tantrum, but he'd actually nailed two pieces of wood together, so who cared.

On the third ring, Zoe picked up.

"Hey—" he started.

"Devin."

He straightened, adrenaline rushing his system. Her voice was all breathy and watery and wrong. "What happened."

"Uncle Arthur. He had a heart attack."

A ten-ton weight fell right on Devin's chest. He changed direction midstride. "Where is he?"

"Pine Ridge."

"I'll be there in ten."

"You don't have to." She sniffled. "I just—I thought you should know. Arthur—"

Arthur was like a father to him. A better one than his own had ever been, but Devin couldn't focus on his own concern right now.

Zoe put on such a front. She acted carefree, like nothing could touch her, but under all that she was tender and soft, and he knew her well enough now. The raw emotion in her voice reached into his chest and squeezed.

"Who's there with you?"

"Just my mom. She's trying not to freak out, but it's not working. Han's on his way, but Lian's car broke down, so he had to drive out to Lincoln to get her."

Right. "I'll be there in ten."

"Devin . . ." The way her voice broke made him stop.

He exhaled out, deep and rough. He covered his eyes with his hand. "Do you not want me to come?"

Everything in him was itching to go. A crisis demanded action. This was Arthur they were talking about.

"I just . . . If you don't . . . You're working."

She'd called him three times. She'd reached out.

"Tell me not to come."

"I—"

"Tell me explicitly, specifically, that you do not want me there, or I am getting in my truck."

Silence held across the line. A sob broke it.

"I want you to come," she whispered.

He dropped his hand from his face. "Ten minutes." His voice was still too hard. With a deep breath, he forced himself to be soft for her. "Hang on, baby."

Then he hung up.

It was fifty yards to the trailer. He crossed it in big strides.

"Hey, James, you okay?" one of the guys called.

"Family emergency," he barked out. He tossed open the door to the trailer, but it was empty. He backed right out. "Where's Joe?"

The couple of guys gathered around shook their heads and shrugged. "Maybe down at corporate?" one of them offered.

Devin shucked his safety gear. "When he gets back, tell him I had to go."

"Okay..."

"Terrell? You're in charge."

And then a voice came from behind him. A stupid, teasing voice. "What did your mommy want, James? Need you to come home and have your bottle?"

Devin ignored Bryce. He didn't have time for this.

But as he headed for his truck, Bryce followed him. "Real nice, ignoring your employees while you're running out the door halfway through your shift. Super responsible. I can see why you got the promotion over me."

Real nice, ignoring your father. Worthless sack of—

Devin's father's words had no place in his head. Not now when he was on his way to help Zoe, to help her family, who had been better to him than his own flesh and blood had ever been.

"Maybe I'll fill out one of those write-up forms you keep doing for me—not that anybody reads them."

Bryce leaned against the side of Devin's truck as Devin went to open the door. "You know that, right? That nobody listens to you?"

Just try to report me. Devin's dad had been stumbling, slurring. *Nobody's going to listen to you.*

"Get out of my way." Devin managed to keep from growling, but it was a narrow thing.

"Make me."

Devin hauled open the door of his truck and got in, but when he went to pull it closed behind him, Bryce was still there.

"Seriously, James. I want to see you do it." Bryce was in the way now, making it impossible to close the door. "Or are you too weak? Weak guy trying to boss everyone around." His voice dropped. "Not a great look. Think all of them will still respect you when they see me walk all over you?"

Devin looked past Bryce's shoulder before he could stop himself. Terrell and the rest of the team were back at work, but people were looking. Was that Bryce's angle? Trap him like this? Make him back down? Rub it in his face the next time Devin tried to call him out?

When would it end?

All Devin's life, he'd tried to keep his head down, work hard, stay out of trouble, and for the most part, it had panned out just fine. He had a great job, great friends. For the moment, at least, he had Zoe.

But what if it wasn't enough to keep quiet and do things the way they were supposed to be done?

What if he'd stood up to his dad a long, long time ago?

Righteousness surged through Devin's veins. "Move." When Bryce didn't budge, Devin turned. He got out of the truck, and that put him right in Bryce's face, and he didn't care. "Go back to work now or pack up your things."

"Whatever—"

And that was it. Devin was done. "You're fired."

For the first time, Bryce flinched. "Wait."

"Get off my site. Don't come back."

"You can't—"

"I can." Devin took a step forward, and as Bryce retreated, power filled Devin's chest. He didn't have to keep his head down. He didn't have to stay silent when people were treating him like crap. He was in charge. People trusted him to make the right calls.

And this was one of them.

"Terrell?" Devin shouted.

"Yeah?"

"Call security to escort Mr. Horton off the property."

"With pleasure."

"My father—" Bryce tried.

"Doesn't have any authority here. And if he shows up and tries to pretend he does, then I'll stand up to him just the same."

Devin had heard enough. This guy didn't deserve his time. He had to get to the hospital, had to find out if Arthur was okay. Zoe needed him.

He climbed back into his truck and slammed the door shut behind him. He put the key in the ignition, and the engine roared to life.

From the other side of the window, Bryce shouted, "My dad is going to destroy you. One word from me and you can kiss this job goodbye. That little piece of land you've been saving up for? You can forget it. My father—"

Terrell appeared behind Bryce, two security officers in tow. "Oh, shut up already, Bryce."

One corner of Devin's lips curled up. They'd all been tiptoeing around Bryce forever, but a dam had just broken.

He should have told Bryce off years ago. It hadn't even taken a punch or a shove. Just evidence and words and an unwillingness to be pushed around anymore.

But he didn't have any more energy to waste on that guy now.

Arthur was in trouble. Zoe was reeling. Han was on his way.

The most important people in his life were waiting for him.

And he'd do anything for them.

Anything.

Chapter Twelve

OK, CLASS IS covered, Han's here, be there in 20

The text from Lian allowed Zoe to let out a sigh of relief.

Drive safe, she replied. She trusted her brother and all, but the look in his eyes as he'd taken off to go get their sister had shaken her.

It was the same look he'd had after their father died. Devastated. Determined. Hard.

She put her phone away, only to pull it back out again two seconds later. She couldn't focus on anything. The waiting room wasn't big enough for her to properly pace, and if she drank another cup of stale coffee, she'd shake right out of her skin.

The elevator at the other end of the room dinged, and she looked up. This was getting ridiculous. She'd been snapping her gaze to see who was arriving every time, but inevitably it was a group of doctors or nurses. Maybe another worried family with food from the cafeteria, a bouquet of flowers, or balloons.

Except this time, when the doors slid open, they finally revealed the face she'd been waiting for.

She leaped to her feet as Devin scanned the area. He spotted her immediately. Their gazes connected, and something inside her broke down. He ate up the space with huge strides and pulled her right into his arms.

A sob erupted from her. She clung to him, which was stupid—everyone could see.

When she started to pull away, he only held her tighter, though, and she couldn't help herself.

She'd been trying to keep it together since the moment the phone had rung.

Uncle Arthur was in his sixties. He had high blood pressure. He was fit enough, but he never stopped, never took care of himself. Others always came first.

"Shh, I got you," Devin murmured.

Tears were leaking down her face. She breathed through them. "He's fine. He's going to be fine."

So why was she losing it like this?

Maybe it was because she finally had the option to.

On the way to the hospital, she'd had to be the one to drive. Her mother had been even more of a wreck than her, so Zoe had been strong. It made sense. Uncle Arthur was her mother's big brother, after all. They'd been through so much together.

Devin rocked her back and forth, whispering reassurances into her ear the entire time, and she melted into him.

It seemed like it took forever, but Devin's steady strength slowly seeped into her. The tears ebbed. She pulled away, reaching into her purse for yet more Kleenex. Dabbing at her eyes, she shook her head. "Sorry."

"Don't be."

She blew her nose, but her mouth started wobbling

all over again. He was being so nice to her, when he must be all shaken up, too.

Sitting back down, she beckoned him to take the seat beside her.

"What happened?"

"Heart attack. Partial, they said?" She gestured at the door her mother had disappeared behind a few minutes before. "They let my mom go see him before he heads up to surgery. They're doing that—that balloon thing." Angioplasty? "And a stent. They think his prognosis is good." She waved her hands at herself. "I don't know why I'm freaking out."

"Hey, hey." He grabbed her hand out of the air and squeezed it. "It's okay."

"I just—" She forced herself to stop and take a few deep breaths. As she stared up into his eyes, an unshakable sense of safety wrapped around her. It made her mist up all over again, but it was better this time. Shaky, she buried her face in his shoulder. "I'm just really glad you're here."

Too glad. Good grief. She needed to pull herself together. Han would be back with Lian soon. Her mother would be coming out before she knew it. The moment any of them returned, Devin would pull away. The idea of having him so close but unwilling to actually touch her made a fresh wave of misery crash across her chest.

"Come on." He held her close, rubbing her back. "You said it yourself. He's going to be okay."

"I know," she said, but the reassurances rang hollow. The only thing that helped was him holding her, so she clung to him, trying to soak in his strength while she could.

Far too soon, the elevator let out another chime. When she looked toward the opening doors, a different sort of nerves stole over her.

There they were. Han and Lian. Ten minutes ago, she would have been trembling with relief.

Ha.

She dropped her face into Devin's neck for one last breath. Then she tore herself away, and it actually hurt. She met his concerned gaze, and she hated having to do it, but she nodded toward her brother and sister.

Devin glanced in the direction of the elevator. He had to see them, but he didn't let go. Instead, he turned to Zoe. He stared deep into her eyes. A dozen emotions flashed across his face.

But the last one—the one that remained . . .

It was resolve.

* * *

Enough.

It was the same feeling that had come over Devin back at the construction site. When he'd been pushed too far, and he finally pushed back. He'd made himself heard.

And it had worked.

A strange, ringing silence eclipsed the riot of voices in his head.

He wasn't powerless. He wasn't unworthy of love or acceptance.

He wasn't going to hide what he wanted. How he felt. From anyone.

Least of all his best friend.

Least of all when it was going to hurt someone he cared about, someone he . . .

Well.

For a long moment, he gazed down into Zoe's deep brown eyes. She was shaking. Just minutes ago, she'd been crying. She'd gone soft in his arms, molding herself to him, leaning into him, and this wasn't about sex anymore. This wasn't some game to her. All his doubts about what she was doing with him finally melted away.

He held out his hand to her.

Without hesitation, she slipped her fingers into his palm, her eyes going wide as she sputtered, "But—"

He shook his head and raised his brows.

Her mouth snapped closed.

Like she understood him, she wordlessly rose to stand beside him. Their gazes held, and the rightness in his chest was so hot it burned. He curled an arm around her. Bending down, he pressed his lips first to her forehead. Then to her mouth.

He turned forward.

Lian spotted them first. Her eyes flew wide, and she started to divert Han, but Devin shook his head.

The second Han caught sight of them, he waved. A relieved grin crossed his face, only to fade in the next instant. His pace slowed, his brows furrowing.

A few feet away from them, Han came to a stop. "Devin." His mouth drew into a frown. "Zoe."

Zoe fidgeted the way she did when she was nervous, but Devin felt steady as a rock. He gave her fingers a reassuring squeeze.

"Hey there, Han."

Slowly, deliberately, Han darted his gaze between the two of them and their joined hands. "What's going on?"

Lian practically bounced up and down.

Maybe that shouldn't have given him confidence, but it did.

"Before you say anything," he started.

Han's complexion darkened. "Say anything like what?"

"We're in a hospital," Zoe interjected. "You try to murder us and they'll fix us up." She snapped her fingers. "Like that."

"Devin."

And Devin was standing his ground. He was refusing to let anyone push him around anymore. He wasn't going to live in fear of his best friend, and he wasn't going to hide the way he felt. He couldn't.

"I didn't mean for this to happen," he prefaced.

The vein in Han's temple started to bulge. "She's my *sister*, man. You were supposed to help me protect her."

"I am," Devin said helplessly. "I will." A lump formed in his throat.

Because he would. He'd protect her from anything that could possibly threaten her.

Even Han.

"I don't need protecting," Zoe insisted, because of course she'd never step back and let two men argue about her.

In the far reaches of Devin's brain, he registered the sound of Han laughing, but he couldn't focus on that right now.

This was Zoe he was talking about. The little girl he'd bickered with as a kid and the feisty, incredible, kind, wonderful woman he'd come to know since. She'd drawn him out of his shell over these past few weeks.

She'd helped him let down his guard and see the world beyond the little piece of it he'd carved out for himself.

She made him happy. She made him want things he'd never even considered before.

He wanted them all with her.

"I love her," he blurted. The pressure behind his ribs popped, and he could breathe again.

Lian squealed, her hands over her mouth. Han looked like he might need heart surgery, too, but they were in a hospital. He'd be fine.

Zoe whipped her head around to gawk at him.

This wasn't how he'd wanted to tell her. He hadn't realized he wanted to tell her how he felt in the first place, but now that it was out there, he wouldn't take it back. Its truth radiated through him.

"I do," he confessed. "Sorry, but—"

"Oh my God, shut up, I love you, too, you idiot." Zoe flung herself at him, and if Han murdered them this second, it would be worth it.

Devin caught her in his arms and kissed her hard and deep. All this time, they'd been acting as if they were both okay with being casual, but apparently the only person he'd been fooling had been himself. Nobody made him laugh or turned him on or pulled him out of his head like she did.

For years now, he'd had dreams of building a house in the middle of nowhere, but those dreams had been about running away from the unhappy home he'd grown up in.

He wasn't running away from anything now.

At the sound of Lian clearing her throat, Devin tore himself away from Zoe. All around them, people cheered. Zoe hid her face in Devin's shoulder, blushing but happy.

He looked to Han.

The man had been Devin's best friend since they were in elementary school. They'd been through everything together.

But Devin had never seen Han's jaw come unhinged like this before.

"Wait—" Han held up a hand in front of himself. "Who said anything about love?"

"This guy." Zoe jabbed a finger into Devin's chest.

"Ow." He caught her hand and brought it to his lips.

He couldn't quite get a real lungful of air, though. Not while Han was looking at them like this.

"How long has this been going on?" he finally asked.

Devin looked to Zoe, who lifted a brow. "About a month?" he answered.

"Or maybe forever," Zoe said.

"Uh, but not like creepy forever, right?" Lian asked.

Devin scrunched up his face. "No."

"No." Zoe rolled her eyes. "Definitely not 'creepy forever.'"

He'd never laid a hand on her until this fall. But the truth of what she was saying smacked him upside the head all the same. He'd been looking at her differently since her high school graduation. Every time they'd hung out in the years since, he'd enjoyed her company more and more. The way they felt about each other now—yeah, it had been building for a lot longer than a month.

"I'm not even going to touch that one with a ten-foot pole." Han scrubbed a hand over his face. Then he let out a rough breath. "You're both happy."

"Yeah," Devin answered, automatic and sure. He glanced down at Zoe, and she nodded.

"Really, really happy," she promised.

"Well, that's good enough for me." Lian broke the tension by swooping in and hugging them both. She whispered something to Zoe that made her blush deeper. Pulling back, she smiled at Devin. "Welcome to the family."

Oh wow. That part hadn't even occurred to Devin. He'd been too busy worrying about how pissed Han would be.

His gaze shot to Han. It was too early to be thinking about this stuff, but if he and Zoe worked out... if they went the distance...

They'd be brothers. For real.

Han shook his head. As Lian backed away, he held out his arms. There was still a certain wariness to him, but any fury had left him. "Dude. You've always been family."

With that he came in and awkwardly hugged them, too, and it was like a ten-ton weight suddenly floating off Devin's chest.

Zoe squirmed away from her brother, leaving Devin and Han in a weird side-to-side bro-hug. Han took advantage of the opportunity to haul Devin down into what Devin was going to choose to assume was a joking headlock. He ruffled Devin's hair, and yeah. He was definitely playing at the edge between teasing and menacing.

"Seriously, though," Han muttered under his breath as he let Devin go. "You ever hurt her, and I will kill you."

Devin straightened up and cleared his throat. Han's smile was warm, even as he cocked a brow in genuine warning.

Devin looked at Zoe. It was so clichéd, but his heart swelled.

Beautiful, incredible Zoe. Whom he loved and who loved him. He couldn't help but smile.

Devin bumped his hand against Han's. "I'm going to hold you to that."

Something in Han's gaze shifted. His mouth curled at the corners. He bumped Devin's hand right back, and even more relief flooded Devin's chest.

They were going to be okay.

It wasn't going to be easy, but for the first time since Zoe had arrived back home...Devin was starting to think this all just might work out.

Chapter Thirteen

"READ 'EM AND weep." Zoe laid her cards down on the table, showing her three of a kind.

"Ugh." Han tossed his cards aside.

Devin groaned and pushed the impressive pot of five sticks of gum and a half dozen of the wrapped hard candies her mom kept in her purse Zoe's way.

"Your deal." Her mom nudged the deck toward Lian. The two of them had been smart enough to fold as soon as Han and Devin started raising each other peppermints. Knowing exactly what she had in her hand, Zoe had stayed quiet and let them bid each other up.

Uncle Arthur had been in surgery for an hour or so now, and they'd had to dig deep into the well of ways to distract themselves—if for no other reason than that their mom was going to get herself kicked out if she bothered the nurses station any more.

As Lian started shuffling, Zoe's phone buzzed in her pocket. She pulled it out.

Oh crap. "Sorry, gotta take this."

"Sure, sure," Han said. "Wipe us out and then walk away."

"I'll be right back."

Devin tilted his head in question, but she shook her head, telling him that everything was okay.

Despite the thread of dread spinning in her gut, she was even pretty sure it was true.

Demonstrating exactly how distracted she was, her mom didn't even question her retreating toward the elevator bank. Zoe turned away from her family before accepting the call. "Hello?"

"Hi, Zoe. It's Brad from Pinnacle Accounting again. I just reviewed your file with the team, and we're excited to get you scheduled for that interview. How does Thursday morning work for you?"

Zoe opened her mouth. All the mumbo-jumbo accountant-drone speak she'd managed to summon to the tip of her tongue while talking to him earlier that morning was right there, ready to come spilling out again.

But she closed her mouth.

She turned, looking back across the waiting room at her mom eyeing the clock, her brother and sister fighting over a couple of Werther's.

Her Devin, who was holding his cards close to his chest, literally. But figuratively, he was staring right at her with all of them right there for the entire world to see.

Sudden certainty filled her chest.

"Zoe?" Brad asked. "You still there?"

"Yeah, Brad." She gripped the phone more tightly. "I'm right here."

Still holding eye contact with Devin across the space, she took a couple of deep breaths.

Every time she'd discussed her job search with him, he'd asked her questions she hadn't been ready to answer. Questions about what she wanted, what she loved, what had motivated her to go down the roads she'd chosen. She'd answered the best she could, but deep down, she'd known that she'd been hiding the truth, both from him and from herself.

She didn't care about some big corporate accounting job. She didn't want to go to Atlanta or Charlotte or Savannah.

She wanted to be here. With him. Working with Arthur and Clay and just living her life. Not the one her mother had charted out for her the second she'd been born.

She may be a dreamer, just like her mom said, but her head wasn't in the clouds. Her feet were firmly planted on the ground, and she was ready to stand tall.

"I'm sorry, Brad," she said. "But I've decided not to pursue this opportunity after all."

As she said the words, the rightness of them sank into her bones. There'd be consequences to this decision, but she was prepared to face them.

If Devin could stand up to Han for her, then Zoe could stand up to her mom. She could fight for her own happiness—and for a chance at a future for the both of them, here in Blue Cedar Falls, where they belonged.

* * *

"How is he?" Zoe practically bounced to her feet as Han and Lian returned to the waiting room after getting to go in and see Uncle Arthur in person.

"He's good," Han assured her.

"If already getting annoyed at Mom." Lian rolled her eyes.

Zoe could only imagine. She'd spent enough sick days at home with her mom—and her delightful bedside manner—to empathize.

"Can we...?" Devin asked, standing and gesturing toward the door. Zoe's mom had wrestled her way back to sit with Uncle Arthur the second he got out of recovery, but outside of her, they were only letting folks in one or two people at a time.

Han nodded. He reached for his jacket. "I should go check on the restaurant."

Thank goodness they had employees who could open the place.

"Call if you need anything," Devin told him.

"Will do." Han looked to Lian. "You want to stay or go?"

"I'll stay awhile." She tipped her head toward the door before sinking into one of the seats near where Zoe and Devin had been sitting. "Go on."

As he pulled out his keys, Han paused for a moment. "Hey, Zo?"

"Yeah?"

"Thanks." His gaze met hers, and it wasn't as if it was the first time he'd made eye contact with her since he'd found out about her and Devin, but there was something different about the way he regarded her. Like he was acknowledging her as an equal and not some kid sister he had to protect. "Mom told me how you held things together this afternoon, when I was off picking up Lian."

Zoe smiled. "No problem."

Han nodded, new respect in his eyes, and it was too much to hope that he'd start letting the rest of his family help carry some of the responsibility he was always lugging around with him. But a girl could dream, right?

As Han took a backward step toward the elevator, Devin held out his hand. Another little thrill ran through Zoe as she slipped her palm into his.

And hey, the vein in Han's temple bulged only a little, so that was progress, right?

A nurse was kind enough to show Zoe and Devin to Uncle Arthur's room, but they didn't really need the guide. Her mother's voice rang out as clear as day the moment they rounded the corner. "*Jeopardy!* gets you too worked up."

"*You* get me too worked up." Her uncle muttered a more colorful rebuke in Mandarin.

Zoe shook her head and sighed. Well, at least it was good to know he was feeling better.

She knocked on the door, eyebrows raised. "You two playing nice in here?"

Her mother and her uncle both looked up and smiled. Zoe didn't miss the way they were still silently wrestling over the remote, though.

"Zoe," Uncle Arthur said, swatting at his sister's hand. "Devin." Then he seemed to notice the fact that they were holding hands, and his head tilted in question.

"Uh…" Devin rubbed the back of his neck.

Her mother followed his gaze and did a double take, though she recovered quickly. Letting Uncle Arthur have the remote, she stepped back, one brow raised.

With Han finally in the know, Zoe and Devin hadn't held back on the casual PDA while they'd been hanging out in the waiting room, but they hadn't made an announcement or anything, either. Her mom was usually uncannily observant, but apparently she'd been too busy pacing a hole in the carpet to notice all the shared glances or the occasional moments when Devin would put a hand on her back or her knee.

Zoe's face warmed, but she held her head high, meeting her mother's gaze.

Her mom clicked her tongue behind her teeth and shook her head fondly. "Guess you did know what you were doing after all."

Zoe huffed out a breath. "Sure did."

"Good," her mom said, firm. A sly smile curled her lips, and Zoe's throat went tight.

It would scarcely count as approval from anybody else's parent, but for Zoe's mom? She might as well have thrown her a "Congratulations on Nailing the Hot Guy" party.

Uncle Arthur's reaction wasn't nearly as subdued, his pale face eclipsed by a bright grin. "About time."

"Hey," Devin protested.

"'Theoretical,'" Uncle Arthur scoffed, tucking the remote under his leg to make air quotes.

Zoe didn't know what they were talking about, but that was all right. Letting go of Devin's hand, she stepped forward to kiss her uncle on the cheek.

He squeezed her palm and winked. Quietly, he murmured, "Good choice."

"I know."

She moved aside, and Devin took his turn giving Arthur a careful hug.

Her mom slung her purse over her shoulder. "I'll give you two a minute."

"Really?"

She patted Zoe's hand. "Just a minute. I'm starving.

Did you know vending machines here charge two dollars for a Kit Kat bar?"

Okay, yeah, her mom running to the car to grab a free snack from the stash she kept there made a lot more sense than her actually giving them privacy. "Outrageous."

Her mom made a disapproving sound in the back of her throat, calling out Zoe's sarcasm, but with a quick pat to Zoe's shoulder, she kept walking.

Zoe turned her attention back to Devin and Uncle Arthur, who were engaged in a little sidebar of their own. She rolled her eyes. "You don't have to threaten Devin if he hurts me. Han's already got that covered."

"You?" Uncle Arthur huffed out a breath and waved a hand dismissively. "You can fend for yourself. I was telling Devin that if you hurt him, you'd have to deal with me."

Devin looked kind of embarrassed about it, if secretly pleased.

Good. He deserved someone looking out for him.

Zoe dropped into the chair her mother had set up on the other side of Arthur's bed. As she did, Arthur struggled to sit up. She shook her head at him. "Relax."

"Your mother wouldn't let me have my phone."

"Nor should she have."

"I have to call Sherry." He scrubbed a hand across his forehead. "Ten people had appointments at Harvest Home today. Supper service—"

Zoe grabbed his hand and held on tight. "Is handled."

"The key—"

"Sherry already came by to pick up mine."

"Deliveries—"

"Have been postponed until tomorrow. All today's pickups, too."

"But—"

"Uncle Arthur." She gripped his hand in both of hers. "I've got it."

She sucked in a deep breath. Instinctively, she glanced up at Devin, but he just stood there, silently supportive. Because he was the awesomest dude in the world, and she was so freaking glad to have him at her side.

"Zoe..." Uncle Arthur started.

"Trust me." That's what she'd been asking everyone in her life to do since she graduated.

She could make her own decisions about who she wanted to date.

And about what she wanted to do with her life.

"I've been doing a lot of thinking." She stopped her uncle before he could interrupt again. "Not just today, but for the past few months. About my future."

That finally got him to let her speak. His mouth drew down into a frown, but she had his attention.

"You've been doing too much."

He shook his head, but she looked pointedly at the hospital bed he was all but strapped into.

"You do too much," she insisted again, "because you care too much. You take care of everyone all the time. Well, it's time we all took care of you." She cleared her throat. "It's time I did."

"Zhaohui?"

"I'm taking over Harvest Home." She kept going, putting it all out there before he could try to contradict her. "You'll still be in charge, obviously. It's your baby. But from now on, the day-to-day operations are on me."

"But your job—"

"Will be fine." She'd already talked to Clay about

adjusting her schedule. It wouldn't be a problem. And she had some other ideas she was going to run past him, too.

Arthur started again. "Your job *search*. You had all those leads in Atlanta, Charlotte—"

Zoe shook her head. "My job search is over."

"But—"

"I don't want to be an accountant. And I don't want to leave Blue Cedar Falls," she said firmly. She looked at Devin, asking him to hear the weight of her words.

She was done worrying about what everyone else expected her to do.

Devin's own actions, telling Han about them, had been an inspiration. He wasn't going to let other people's opinions hold him back anymore. So neither was she.

"I like it here." She squeezed Uncle Arthur's hands. "I'm happy here. I have friends, family." Leaning in conspiratorially, she murmured, "And a really nice boyfriend."

Devin smiled, and her heart glowed. He wasn't going to fight her on this. Good.

Because she would fight. For her family and for her future and for her vision of how she wanted to spend her life, now that she'd finally figured it out.

"You don't have to..." Uncle Arthur put his other hand on top of hers.

"I want to. So you just focus on getting better. Leave all the worrying about Harvest Home to me."

Uncle Arthur finally smiled. "I wouldn't trust it to anyone else."

The warmth in her heart only grew.

"There are some grants we can apply for," he said, that gleam appearing in his eyes, exhausted as they were. "So we can get you a salary. If you go to my desk in the back office—"

"After you get out of the hospital," she assured him, reaching in to fluff his pillows. "Until then, you just rest." She nodded, both to him and to herself. "I've got everything under control."

Epilogue

One month later...

"SO, AS YOU can see in Figure C in your handout." Zoe clicked a button on the remote for the LCD projector she'd borrowed from Lian. She arched a brow toward her audience as the spreadsheet she'd meticulously compiled came into view. "Taking into account average rent for a one-bedroom apartment, food, gas, personal expenses, and an acceptable rate of savings for a person in my age bracket..."

At the back of the room, June silently wiggled her hand, reminding Zoe about the laser pointer in her other hand. Right. Thank goodness the two of them had practiced this together last night.

She aimed the little red dot at the total at the bottom of the column. "Projected monthly expenses can be satisfactorily accounted for with projected earnings."

"Hold on a second." Clay held up his hand.

"I know exactly what you're going to say, Mr. Hawthorne." Zoe flipped to the next slide. "Income is broken out in Figure D." As the assembled crowd all turned the pages in their handout, she moved the laser pointer to highlight each number as she explained it. "Earnings fall into two major categories. The first is the modest salary I'll be able to begin drawing from Harvest Home once our grant applications to expand our staff are accepted."

Uncle Arthur nodded, leaning forward to agree. "The grant proposals are very good."

"Thank you, Mr. Chao." Zoe shifted the pointer. "The second category is income from my part-time position in the hospitality industry."

"You mean waitressing," Clay said.

"Waitressing, hostessing"—she set down the pointer and remote to begin counting on her fingers—"bartending—"

"Okay, okay," Clay interrupted. "You're good, but—"

"And bookkeeping."

His mouth snapped closed. "Wait."

"Admit you need the help," June said from the back.

"Hey—"

"With these additional responsibilities, I've determined that I'll be earning a twenty percent raise."

"Twenty percent!" Clay balked.

Zoe's pulse ticked up, but she had full confidence in her value to him. She arched a brow. "You think you can find a new server who's as good as me *and* who can start doing your books for you?"

"She's got a point, man," Han agreed.

"This is a setup." Clay looked around at everyone with suspicion in his gaze. There wasn't any malice, though. The guy had been to war and ended up with a knee full of shrapnel and so many trust issues he might as well have gotten a subscription, but he knew he was among friends here.

"Of course it's a setup," Zoe's mom agreed. She gazed at Zoe with a knowing curl to her lips. "But you're not the one she's setting up."

Zoe's heart pounded harder as she met her mother's gaze.

Oblivious, Clay continued, gesturing at the screen. "She just gave herself a twenty percent raise."

"That I'm going to earn," she promised, still looking at her mom.

"You sure about this, Zhaohui?" her mother asked.

Clay sat back in his chair, arms crossed. "I'm not sure about it."

"Yes, you are," Zoe and her mom both said as one.

"I guess that settles that," Clay said.

June stepped forward to put her hands on his shoulders. She pressed her lips to his temple. "Accept when you're beaten, dear."

"Fine, fine."

As they spoke, Zoe and her mom continued their silent staring contest. Zoe could hear all her mother's doubts, and she expressed her confidence back to her, even as neither of them said anything at all.

This plan was going to work. She'd draw a low but respectable salary managing the day-to-day operations of Harvest Home. She'd augment it by continuing to work at the Junebug and taking over Clay's accounting. She liked both jobs. Her work at Harvest Home fulfilled her, while waitressing at the bar was both lucrative and fun. Doing a little bookkeeping would maintain her skills and her résumé in case she ever changed her mind. Uncle Arthur would be less stressed, and if he ever decided to retire, she'd be ready to step up and slide right into his place. It was a win-win-win-win.

Finally, Zoe's mother raised a brow. "Princess astronaut veterinarian ballerina?"

"Princess astronaut veterinarian ballerina." Zoe let out a rough breath as lightness filled her chest.

"Well, then." Her mother smiled. "I suppose I can't argue with that."

* * *

"Hey—James!"

At the sound of his last name, Devin looked up. Joe stood outside the trailer, waving him over.

"Got a sec before you head out?"

"Sure." He finished the last couple of joins he'd been working on before nodding to the crew. It was a few minutes early, but they'd made good progress today.

He helped with cleanup, but once it was all in hand, he patted his buddy Terrell on the back and gestured at Joe's office.

Terrell nodded. "See you in the morning, boss."

Devin took off, a spring in his step.

It still amazed him how peaceful the entire site felt now that Bryce was gone. The guy had talked a big game about getting his father to retaliate, but it had been precisely that: talk. Sure, the mayor's office had made a few overtures, hoping to get management to reverse his dismissal, but Joe had stood behind Devin's decision. In the end, Bryce had been more of a liability than he'd been worth. Last Devin had heard, the guy was heading back to community college. Devin hoped he learned some things while he was there, but as long as he didn't show up on Devin's job site again, he honestly didn't care.

Inside the trailer, Joe was perched behind his computer,

same as always. He smiled when Devin knocked and let himself in, gesturing for him to have a seat.

Joe folded his big hands on top of the desk. "Just wanted to ask how things are going."

"Good." Devin pointed his thumb toward the door behind him. "We're on schedule out there, maybe even a little ahead."

"I know that. I meant with you."

"Me?" Uh... "I'm good."

Great, actually. He couldn't stop the little smile that curled his lips.

Work was less stressful. The bump in his pay from the promotion had finally started showing up in his bank account. Arthur's recovery was going well.

And then there was the conversation he and Arthur had had the other night.

His leg bobbed up and down in anticipation.

He couldn't wait to tell Zoe about it. He was leaving after his shift to go pick her up, and he was going to do just that.

It had only been a month since he and Zoe had gone public, but it had been the best month of his entire life. It was like the thing with Bryce; Devin hadn't grasped how much strain all the secrecy and sneaking around was putting on them both.

But that was behind them now. They were happy and in love. Han was still his best friend—even if he did look at him kind of funny now and then.

Well, he'd get used to it. Devin was in this for the long haul.

And after what he planned to show Zoe this evening, hopefully by the end of the night he'd know she was in it for the long haul, too.

"All right, all right." Joe shook his head. "I get it— you're a private guy. Well, I just wanted to let you know that we're real pleased with how you've taken over as shift leader. Your crew's doing good work. Word on the street is you've really turned things around."

"Oh. Thanks."

Joe's raised brows were pointed. "Wasn't an easy situation you inherited with Horton on your crew. But you handled it like a pro." With that, Joe pulled open the top drawer of his desk and fished out an envelope. He passed it over. Nodding at it, he said, "Little token of our appreciation."

Devin blinked in surprise. He glanced at Joe, who motioned for him to go ahead and open it. The check inside stared back at him, and his jaw dropped. "I— I mean—"

People got bonuses pretty regularly around here when things were going well, but this was generous, to say the least. He sputtered for another few seconds before Joe took mercy.

"'Thank you' is the phrase you're looking for, I think."

Right. "Thank you."

"You earned it." Joe closed the drawer and gestured toward the door. "Now get on out of here."

"Will do." Devin tucked the check in his pocket. He rose, turned to leave, then stopped and twisted back around. More fervently, he repeated, "Really, Joe. Thank you."

Devin didn't think he'd ever fully get rid of his old man's voice in his head, telling him he'd never amount to anything. But he had a lot of evidence to say otherwise of late. This bonus...the pride in Joe's eyes...They were the icing on what was already a pretty flipping amazing cake.

By the time he got back outside, the cleanup job was basically done, and folks were getting ready to head out. Devin gave everything one last check over before making his way to his truck. He drove the familiar route to Harvest Home, where Zoe stood outside waiting for him.

She hopped in the cab of the truck and leaned over the gearshift. He threaded his fingers through her silky hair, closed his eyes, and kissed her, and he was really never going to get over that, was he? How good she felt, how sweet she tasted.

How much he loved her.

"Hey," he managed when she pulled away.

"Hey, yourself."

The flush to her cheeks and the glazed darkness in her eyes almost derailed him, but he managed to keep his focus. "How'd it go?" he asked. "Your presentation?"

"Good. Really good." She rolled her eyes. "Clay's on board with the promotion, and Uncle Arthur was super supportive."

"And your mom?" That was the part she'd been worried about.

"I'm going to go with 'begrudgingly accepting.'"

"Hey!" Devin grinned. "So basically wild enthusiasm?"

"Next best thing."

"Good." He leaned in and pressed another firm kiss to her lips. "Knew you could do it."

Curling a hand in the collar of his shirt, she kept him close for a second. "Thank you," she said quietly. "For believing in me."

They kissed again. He tucked a bit of hair behind her ear. "Always."

She let him go and settled back into her seat. "So, what's the plan?"

The nerves he'd felt earlier while thinking about this moment melted away. "You mind going for a drive?"

She scrunched up her brows at him. "Uh...okay?"

Once she was buckled in, he put the truck back into first and steered toward the road. While he drove, he asked her about her day, and he told her about his. They commiserated over how tough it was to get Arthur to delegate and rest. She spoke with pride about her juggling act taking over for him.

But she had good people with her. Sherry and Tania had been only too happy to start managing the supper service by themselves most nights. Volunteers had come out of the woodwork to lend a hand, because that was what people in Blue Cedar Falls did. They took care of one another.

As he glanced over at her, warmth grew in his chest.

He was so glad to call this place home.

He was so glad she was going to stay. Here. With him.

Clearing his throat, he forced himself to focus on the road. Before long, he turned off onto the country route leading out of town.

Zoe shifted beside him. "You're not taking me out into the middle of nowhere to act out some weird serial killer fantasy, are you?"

Devin laughed. "Is that really the first thing to pop into your mind?"

"I mean..." In his periphery, she waved a hand at their surroundings.

"Not much farther," he promised.

Five minutes outside town, he put on the blinker.

"Wait—isn't this...?"

Zoe held her tongue as they took the gravel road he'd been imagining driving down for the last three years. He came to a stop where the road ended.

It wasn't much. Just a small clearing in the wooded lot. He pulled the keys from the ignition and reached behind his seat for the camping lantern he stowed there. He turned it on and flicked his headlights off. Twilight settled over them, quiet and peaceful. Exactly the way he liked it.

He opened the door on his side. For a second, Zoe sat there, gazing out the front windshield.

"You coming?" he asked.

She looked at him. "This is Arthur's place, right? The old lot he snatched up in his real estate phase."

"None other."

"What are we doing here?"

"Just come on."

She followed him out, wary but smiling. Maybe she had a clue. They went to the center of the clearing. He breathed in the woodsy scent of the air. Tipped his head up at the stars just beginning to come out.

"I know you've been doing a lot of soul-searching lately," he told her. "I did some of that myself a while back."

"Yeah?"

"You know about my dad. I was...kind of directionless for a long time after I got out of his house. Just so glad to be on my own, I wasn't thinking about what I really wanted, you know?"

"Sure," she said slowly. "I can see that."

He held out his arm, and she came into his embrace.

The warmth of her against his side heated him all the way to his core. "Your uncle Arthur—he was a big part of helping me figure it out. I decided my goal was a place of my own. Not just a roof to live under that wasn't my old man's. A home."

His pulse sped up a tick, his mouth going dry. Getting nervous talking about this didn't make sense, but he couldn't seem to help it.

"Arthur promised me then and there that as soon as I could save up the money, he'd sell me this lot—at cost."

Zoe scrunched up her brow. "But he bought it twenty years ago. He must've paid, like, nothing for it."

Devin let out a quiet laugh. "It was a little more than nothing." A lot less than it was worth now, but on Devin's income, it was still a chunk of change.

A chunk of change that had taken him three whole years to save.

He was still a little shy, even with his promotion and his bonus. But that didn't matter.

"The other night, when I was keeping him company, he changed the deal."

"Yeah?"

Devin shrugged. "Apparently a heart attack gave him some new perspective. He doesn't want to make me wait anymore. He trusts me. Knows I'm good for it."

And he was. With the new promotion and the bonus he'd earned this afternoon, he'd be paying Arthur everything he owed in six months.

Pulling Zoe closer in against his side, he looked around. "He's signing it over to me next week."

"Devin. That's amazing."

It was. A kid like him who'd grown up with nothing,

living off what he could get at the local food bank. Cowering in a dark house with a dad who made him feel like dirt.

And now he was here.

He had the Leungs for his family. He had Zoe tucked beneath his arm.

He had this land.

His voice went hoarse. "This weekend, I was wondering if maybe you'd want to look at some building plans with me."

"Sure, I mean—"

"For when you move in here with me." He didn't want her mistaking him. He wanted to be clear. Looking down at her, he swallowed back his last remaining doubts. "I know it's soon, but I know what I want."

Her bright, beautiful gaze met his through the dimness. Her lips curled into a smile, and her eyes shone. "Devin..."

"Building a house. It'll take time. This isn't right now, but—"

"Yes," she said. She rose onto her toes and kissed him. "Of course, absolutely, yes."

He clutched her in his arms as tightly as he dared, returning the kiss with all the wonder in his heart. "I love you," he managed to get out.

"I love you, too." She pressed her mouth to his once more before pulling back. "There's just one tiny thing you're wrong about."

"What's that?" He was having a hard time concentrating. She felt so good pressed against him.

But then she grinned. "The soul-searching. The figuring out what I want with my life."

"Oh?"

"I'm done with that." Her smile widened, and he felt it in the center of his chest. "I'm exactly where I want to be."

And just like that, so was he.

Here. In this home that they would build.

Together.

About the Author

Jeannie Chin writes contemporary small-town romances. She draws on her experiences as a biracial Asian and Caucasian American to craft heartfelt stories that speak to a uniquely American experience.

She is a former high school science teacher, wife to a geeky engineer, and mom to an extremely talkative kindergartener. Her hobbies include crafting, reading, and hiking.

You can learn more at:

JeannieChin.com
Twitter @JeannieCWrites
Facebook.com/JeannieCWrites
Instagram @JeannieCWrites

Can't get enough of that small-town charm?
Forever has you covered with these heartwarming
contemporary romances!

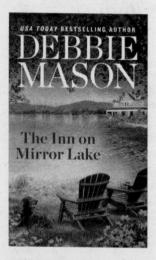

THE INN ON MIRROR LAKE
by Debbie Mason

Elliana MacLeod has come home to whip the Mirror Lake Inn into tip-top shape so her mother won't sell the beloved family business. And now that Highland Falls is vying to be named the Most Romantic Small Town in America, she can't refuse any offer of help—even if it's from the gorgeous law enforcement officer next door. But Nathan Black has made it abundantly clear they're friends, and nothing more. Little do they know the town matchmakers are out to prove them wrong.

FALLING FOR YOU
by Barb Curtis

Faith Rotolo is shocked to inherit a historic mansion in quaint Sapphire Springs. But her new home needs some major fixing up. Too bad the handsome local contractor, Rob Milan, is spoiling her daydreams with the harsh realities of the project...and his grouchy personality. But as they work together, their spirited clashes wind up sparking a powerful attraction. As work nears completion, will she and Rob realize that they deserve a fresh start too?

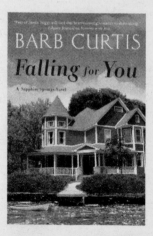

Find more great reads on Instagram with @ReadForeverPub

THE AMISH FARMER'S PROPOSAL
by Barbara Cameron

When Amish dairy farmer Abe Stoltzfus tumbles from his roof, he's lucky his longtime friend Lavinia Fisher is there to help. He secretly hoped to propose to her, but now, with his injuries, his dairy farm in danger, and his harvest at stake, Abe worries he'll only be a burden. But as he heals with Lavinia's gentle support and unflagging optimism, the two grow even closer. Will she be able to convince him that real love doesn't need perfect timing?

AUNT IVY'S COTTAGE
by Kristin Harper

When Zoey returns to Dune Island, she's shocked to find her elderly Aunt Ivy being pushed into a nursing home by a cousin. As the family clashes, Zoey meets Nick, the local lighthouse keeper with ocean-blue eyes and a warm laugh. With Nick as her ally, Zoey is determined to keep Aunt Ivy free. But when they discover a secret that threatens to upend Ivy's life, will they still be able to ensure her final years are filled with happiness...and maybe find love with each other along the way?

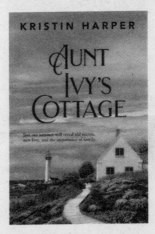

THE HOUSE ON SUNSHINE CORNER
by Phoebe Mills

Abby Engel has a great life. She's the owner of Sunshine Corner, the daycare she runs with her girl-friends; she has the most adoring grandmother (aka the Baby Whis-perer); and she lives in a hidden gem of a town. All that's missing is love. Then her ex returns home to win back the one woman he's never been able to forget. But after breaking her heart years ago, can Carter convince Abby that he's her happy-ever-after?

TO ALL THE DOGS I'VE LOVED BEFORE
by Lizzie Shane

The last person librarian Elinor Rodriguez wants to see at her door is her first love, town sheriff Levi Jackson, but her mischievous rescue dog has other ideas. Without fail, Dory slips from the house whenever Elinor's back is turned—and it's up to Levi to bring her back. The qui-etly intense lawman broke Elinor's heart years ago, and she's deter-mined to move on, no matter how much she misses him. But will this four-legged friend prove that a sec-ond chance is in store? Includes a bonus story by Hope Ramsay!

COMING HOME TO SEASHELL HARBOR
by Miranda Liasson

After a *very* public breakup, Hadley Wells is returning home to get back on her feet. But Seashell Harbor has trouble of its own. An injury forced her ex-boyfriend Tony Cammareri into early retirement, and the former NFL pro is making waves with a splashy new restaurant. They're on opposing sides of a decision over the town's future, but as their rivalry intensifies, they must decide what's worth fighting for—and what it truly means to be happy. Includes a bonus story by Jeannie Chin!

SUMMER BY THE SEA
by Jenny Hale

Faith can never forget the summer she found her first love—or how her younger sister, Casey, stole the man of her dreams. They've been estranged ever since. But at the request of their grandmother, Faith agrees to spend the summer with Casey at the beach where their feud began. While Faith is ready to forget—if not forgive—old hurts, she's *not* ready for her unexpected chemistry with their neighbor, Jake Buchanan. But for a truly unforgettable summer, she'll need to open her heart.

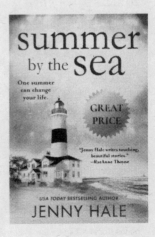